To Paul

with best wishes

Robert Brown

The

Pigeon Run

Robert Breustedt

Published by Silver Quill Publishing 2021

www.robertbreustedtbooks.com

ISBN: **978-1-912513-36-9**

UK spelling observed
Typeset in Georgia

Silver Quill Publishing

https://www.silverquillpublishing.com

For Evan

Be brave, be strong, be true, be kind.

**Dedicated to the memory
of
John Tyreman**

Whose knowledge of the pigeon world and, also, as an experienced police officer, was invaluable in the writing of The Pigeon Run.

Chapter 1

Day 1 – Friday

'Well butter me toast on both sides, smack me bare bum, and call me Mary!'

'Grandad! *Stop* it! Mum, *tell* him.' Ollie slammed his hands palm down on the table, causing his breakfast cereal to spill over the plate.

'Dad stop winding him up. You know he hates your silly nonsense, or I'll be calling you worse than Mary.'

Grandad sprang to his own defence, 'Eee lass, it's a bad job when a man can't pass comment about something in the papers without getting censored by his own family,' he replied with an embellished look of unimagined hurt.

'And you,' turning to Ollie, 'get a cloth and get that mess cleaned up.'

'Aye! Don't you go upsetting your mother,' Grandad winked conspiratorially to Ollie. 'But here, the paper's saying there's another bird of prey, a falcon, been found shot dead.'

Scrunching the lid firmly onto Ollie's lunch box, his mum turned to face them both. 'Another one. This *is* getting serious. That's the third or fourth this year. I hope whoever's doing it's caught soon.'

'Probably farmers,' Grandad said, nodding his head knowingly as he picked up his paper again.

'Mum, you could've let me come with you today. School holidays next week so we're not doing anything too important.'

'I've told you before, you can't come.'

'Oh Mum. Please. You could write me a note. Barry Finch's mum writes him notes tons of times just so's he can bunk off to help his dad at their shop.'

'Well, *I'm* not Barry Finch's mum. And Barry Finch and his parents will get a visit from school inspectors one day soon, and Mr Finch will face a big fine. Anyway, there'll be reporters and photographers at the safari park today and, I think, BBC cameras are going to be there too. A fine thing if you went in with a note on Monday and your teacher had seen you on the evening news today.'

'Awe, Mum. I could just say it was educational, that I fancy bein' a vet when I leave school.'

His mum snorted, 'I don't think so. You have to train for anything from seven to ten years to be a vet. Can't see you wanting to do that. You wouldn't be allowed in anyway. Elf 'n' Safety would have a fit. I might take you in next week on my day off. You can see Kukooru then.'

Grandad got up to get himself a fresh cup of tea. 'Aye, 'twill be a tricky job getting a giraffe's tooth out. What'll you do? Build scaffolding round it?'

'No, Dad, we'll relax her then put a big sling under her belly and lower her gently to sleep on a bed of straw till the vet gets at the bad tooth.'

'Something you never think about really, a giraffe with toothache.'

'Oh! Talking about toothache, remember you've got a check-up at the dentist this afternoon, Ollie. Grandad will pick you up after school.'

'I can get a bus, Mum,' Ollie said hurriedly, 'No need to trouble Grandad.'

'No, Grandad will take you and bring you back home afterwards.'

Ollie sighed. Loudly.

'What's wrong now?' his mother asked, stuffing the packed lunch into his satchel.

'You know fine, Mum. Grandad drives so slow.' Ollie stretched the word *'slow'* as if it were elasticated and in agony.

2

'Eee lad, don't exaggerate. Anyhow, better be slow and get there safe, than fast and kill thyself. You save money on petrol too.' The last sentence said with a self-satisfied little smile.

Ollie pushed back his chair and, on rising, gave his granddad a pat on the shoulder. 'Grandad, it's an urban legend now, of how you stopped and offered old Mrs Dixon a lift to town when she was walking up Ricketron Crescent, and she told you, "no thanks, son." She was in a hurry.'

Grandad spluttered and snorted tea out through his nostrils.

Mum laughed. 'He's not far wrong, Dad. If everyone got the mileage you got from ten litres of petrol, the filling station manager's children would be wandering the High Street in rags begging for small change. Ollie, your granddad will pick you up. And when you get home get your room tidied. If the government could harness the smell in that room, they could waft it across the whole of the southeast here and there'd be no more illegal immigrants trying to get into the UK.'

Ollie sighed and harrumphed before giving out a plaintiff, 'Mum!'

'Just get it done, or you can forget having Josh here for the weekend.'

'Muuum!'

'Just do it. How's he doing anyway?'

'Not to good really. There's stuff going on at home, with his mum's boyfriend's causing a lot of grief. He's more concerned for Nicola though.

'Is he managing to keep up with his schoolwork? It'll get harder when you move up a year next term.'

'I think homework's probably the least of his troubles, and yes, I think he's finding it really hard at home right now. But please don't start grilling him. I just want him to enjoy this weekend away from it all.'

'Okay Ollie, but if he does need to talk to someone, he can talk to me. And your dad will be home in three or four weeks, so maybe he'll be able to help in some way. He likes Josh, and we know it must have been hard for him this past couple of years.'

Grandad rose from the table, brushing crumbs from his cardigan. 'Aye moving up a year next term, eh? Aye, new challenges.' Shaking his head, he sighed and, in a sonorous voice, went on, 'Life starts gettin' tougher now. Pressure builds. Homework grows. Your mind gets stretched and overstrained like the last pound note in a Scotch-man's sporran. Exams loom like unleashed monsters from a dark and scary place. Aye lad, you'll begin to find that life's filled with much more pain than it is with pleasure.'

'Gee thanks for that encouragement, Grandad. I'll try hard to make that my life's watchword.'

'Oh, pay no attention to your grandad, Ollie. Sometimes listening to him's like digging into a lucky dip – you never know what's going to come out next.'

'Yep, a load of rubbish just like a lucky bag.'

His mum stood, one hand on the counter's edge, gazing at her son, and smiled. 'How do you kids grow up so fast?' Ollie was now slightly taller than her, his fair hair thick and always tousled. He had his dad's bright blue eyes, and, she realised, he was going to be just as handsome. 'You mind out for those girls now,' she said putting on a serious face.

'Mum! Stop with it!' His face tinged with embarrassment. His phone bleeped and glancing at the screen he said, 'That's Josh. He's on his way. I gotta go.' Taking the stairs two at a time he dashed into his bedroom, picked up his blazer and was heading back out the door when he remembered the game that he'd promised Rav. Picking it up from the general detritus covering the bedroom floor, he flicked a piece of jam doughnut of the box cover then hurried back to the kitchen and picked up

4

his satchel just as the doorbell rang. On opening the door, Ollie noticed again the dark rings that seemed to have taken up permanent residence under Josh's eyes.

Josh smiled. 'You ready?'

'Yep.' Before closing the door behind him, Ollie shouted, 'Bye, Mum. See *you* after school, Grumpdad.' Then to Josh, 'Let's go.'

Heading down to school, Ollie sighed and said, 'My mum's in a seriously kick ass mood.'

'Yeah? Why?'

'She says she's not having me sitting about the house all summer playing video games until my brain cells rot and I develop haemorrhoids.'

Josh laughed. 'What you going to be doing then? Takin' your grandad for long walks?'

'She says if I don't get mobile, she'll take me to the Safari Park and get me shovelling elephants' pooh for the summer. Says we should be more adventurous. Then Grandad got his ten pence worth in with his ramblings about when he and his brothers were kids, how during the school holidays they were out with friends roaming the hills, the countryside and the coast all day making their own fun. Looking to have some adventures. Searching caves on the coast for smuggled contraband. Going to old ruins on ghost hunts. Making their own kites and all kinds of other stuff. Really exciting, eh?' Ollie rolled his eyes heavenwards. Both boys sniggered. 'Then he goes on,' Adopting his grandad's Yorkshire accent, Ollie said in a deep voice, 'Eee! When I were a lad livin' on a council estate in the early fifties, there were enough young-uns to re-enact the Sioux nations uprising, the battle of Little Bighorn and Custer's last stand.'

Josh looked perplexed. 'What?'

'American history.' Ollie shrugged and shook his head. 'Anyway, what adventures are we going to have in this

5

place? The only exciting thing we've seen was when Rav's dad set fire to his uncle's turban by mistake. Remember how he came screaming out the restaurant followed by Rav's big brother trying to empty a bucket of sand over him.'

Josh laughed at the memory, 'Yeah, so funny.'

'Yeah well, I think my mum's serious. Out into the fresh air. Imagine, a whole summer banned from my Xbox. Maybe we should just go visit the co-op funeral services.'

Josh looked puzzled.

'We might die of boredom!' Ollie explained.

Josh laughed then, on a more serious note, said, 'I'm not sure what's going to be happenin' this summer, Ollie, but things are getting bad at home.'

'Is it Eddie?'

'Yeah. It's gettin' so bad I'm thinkin' I might have to go to Social Services.'

'Wow! Josh, be careful. You could be opening a whole can of worms if you do.'

'I know, but he's a real nasty piece of work, and gettin' violent with it. I'm really worried about Nicola... and my Mum.'

Concern in his voice, Ollie said, 'Okay Josh, we'll talk about it later and if you think it might help you could talk to my mum, or to my grandad.'

'Well, maybe. I'll think about it.'

Ollie checked the time on his phone, 'We'd better get a move on. Remember we're gettin' a visit from the police at assembly.'

'Yeah, what's that about?' Josh frowned.

'I heard it's about drugs, something about county lines whatever that is.'

Josh feigned a frightened voice, 'Honest officer, all I've ever had is a few aspirin and some cough mixture.'

Chapter 2

The day was already getting warm, and Ollie, deciding it was too hot to wear his blazer, loosened his satchel, took both off and slung them over his shoulder. He would have to keep his tie on but was glad to be wearing a short-sleeved shirt.

'C'mon, Josh, get your blazer off. It's going to be a scorcher today.'

'Na, I'm okay.' Josh's answer was quick and sharp.

'C'mon, Josh, you'll melt.'

Josh sighed as he started to slip off his blazer. 'Yeah, you're probably right.'

'Long sleeves! Long sleeves!' Ollie's voice incredulous. 'It's summertime. Duh!'

Josh's eyes flashed as he snapped, 'I'm fine. Just leave it.'

'Well, you're staying with me this weekend, so you better not be honkin'.'

The boys, coming down from Ollie's house towards the centre of town, joined the converging flow of students heading towards the High School.

'Only three schooldays left till the hols. Six weeks away from this dump. Yeah!' Ollie's fist pumped the air as he executed some imaginary football moves.

'Okay for you guys, but I've got to help out at my dad's place this summer if I want any pocket money. Slave labour I call it,' came a doleful voice from behind.

The boys turned to acknowledge the voice. 'Hi, Rav. All summer? Wow! Sounds like slave labour.' Ollie commiserated.

Rav sighed as he joined them. 'Yeah well, at least I might be able to save enough money to go to court and buy my way out the harsh regime of parental slavery,' he said with a sniff and a flick of the head.

'You're such a drama queen, Rav.' Ollie laughed, 'Lucky you anyway. I've got to get out in the fresh air and have "adventures" like they used to do in the olden days.'

'Neither of you getting summer jobs then?'

'I think most employers are reluctant to employ under sixteen-year old's now,' Ollie responded. 'Something to do with government legislation. My mum says she's gonna try to get me some hours at the safari park cafe, but I've not to hold my breath.'

Josh, adjusting the straps of his backpack, added, 'Yeah, and I need to be gettin' more hours at the takeaway. I've got a dance competition coming up and an audition for a ballet school, so every penny counts.'

'A star is born.' Rav beamed, 'Well, about to be born.'

'Yeah, but prat face,' referring to his mum's current boyfriend, 'keeps callin' me Josh-ophina.'

'Josh-ophina?' both friends queried.

'Yeah. Josh-ophina the ballerina. Thinks he's so clever. Says I should get a real job. Says he can get me some work in the summer, but I'd have to get my hands dirty. Get dirt under my fingernails. Make me a real man. Says the family needs more income. Income! I've no idea what he's putting in, but don't think it would buy a packet of Hobnobs.'

'Sounds a nice guy,' commented Rav.

'He's a pock-faced toad.' Josh spat with some vehemence. 'Only twice as ugly.'

'Well!' Rav stopped walking for a moment, 'Would it be fair to say there are some unresolved issues in this relationship?'

Josh stopped, turned and snarled, 'Take a hike, Rav.'

'Ouch!'

'Oh hey,' Rav gripped Ollie's arm, 'Your dad likes a good joke. He'll like this one. Why do Swedish warships have bar codes on the sides?'

'Dunno,' said Ollie.

'So that when they return to port, they can... Scandinavian,' he hooted as his own joke.

Ollie groaned, but then smiled, 'Yeah, right, Rav. Whatever!'

'When's he due home?' Josh asked.

'Another three weeks or so I think.'

'What is it he does again?' Rav asked.

'Well right now he's workin' in Germany on a short-term contract as a...' Ollie had to think for a moment, 'Yeah, it's got something to do with space stuff. He said was to do with what's called...' He paused a moment, 'an in-orbit system operations of low orbit Earth observation satellites. Don't ask! And don't quote me.'

Rav looked impressed. 'He must be clever.'

'Yep, but it means he's away from home for a bit, but at least when he gets home, he's got four weeks holiday.'

Nearing the school gates Ollie let out a groan as he saw Hannah Katakwa crossing the road and making a bee line for the boys. Her soft afro hair, dyed pink at the tips, spilling out to the ends of her skinny shoulders making a perfect frame for the rich honey colouring of her skin. When she looked at him directly, her dark-eyed, steady gaze tied knots in Ollie's stomach, knots that did a good job of tying his tongue too. Cocking her head to one side, arms folded, with her gaze scanning the group she said, 'Hey you, guys, what's up?' Then, 'You need to stop tryin' to avoid me,' she said poking Ollie in the chest. 'What you all doin' for the holidays?'

'Havin' adventures, supposedly. Well, these guys anyway. I've gotta work at my dad's place,' Rav answered for them.

'Great! If I can convince Ollie I'm the girl of his dreams, that destiny has brought us together, then he might bring me to your dad's restaurant on our first date. Mates' rates of course.' She looked at Rav for affirmation. Then moving closer to Ollie, whose face was now as red as any baboon's bum at the safari park, Hannah squared her shoulders and said, 'Man up Ollie. I'm only kiddin'.' Then a pause, 'You hope!' She winked, making Ollie squirm like a worm about to be impaled on an angler's hook.

Josh and Rav went into hoots of laughter at his discomfort. In truth, they all liked Hannah. She was smart and sassy, slightly small for her age, but what she lacked in height she made up for in tenacity. She could be really feisty when standing her ground on issues that mattered to her. She had made a name for herself on the school hockey team and had won a few medals for swimming. Her real talent though was on the track where she could run like a gazelle being chased by a coalition of cheetahs. Nobody in her year group could pass her.

Academically she was bright too, but she didn't seem to have many friends. Jealousy at her capabilities occasioned veiled taunts about her mixed-race heritage. But students who knew her, knew better than to have a go at her. Or if they did, it was at their own peril. Nobody was going to whisper 'jungle bunny', or anything like it, near her twice. Girl or boy! As they entered the school building, Hannah said, 'Listen, guys, seriously. If you're not gonna be stuck at home playin' your computer games stuff, or workin' like Rav, I'd like to hang out sometime. I really hate all the girlie stuff.' She screwed her face.

'Well...' Ollie glanced at Josh and Rav looking for support. 'We're not too sure what we're gonna be doing, and you might not like whatever it is anyway. We might even try doin' girly stuff ourselves.' He looked towards Josh and Rav for affirmation.

'Na, I doubt that, the three of you are too ugly. Listen, we're goin' a holiday late August but until then you could let me hang with you sometimes.' And, putting on a fierce expression added, 'Or I'll bash your brains out!'

The boys laughed and Rav said, 'You know what? We actually believe you, Hannah.'

'Ollie, le'me see your phone.' she demanded.

'Why? What for?' Ollie's defensive response.

'Just for two secs. Now would be good.'

Ollie, to the delight of Josh and Rav, grudgingly passed over his phone. She asked for his password. He hesitated. 'Ollie!' she snapped. Ollie gave her the password. She pressed some buttons, then handed his phone back. 'I've added myself to your contacts. Now you need to include me in your cosy little group. And of course, you can find me on all the relevant social media platforms. I'll expect to hear from you before the end of term. Right?' Head cocked and eyebrows raised, her full-on stare demanding an answer.

'Wow,' Josh taunted, 'you're mince, Ollie boy.'

'Right, Ollie?' she asked again, hands on hips and with a tight-lipped expression.

'Yeah, yeah. Right. But I've told you, Josh and Rav have both got part-time jobs and I'm not gonna hang out with you on my own.'

'Oh Ollie! Here was me thinkin' I was the girl of your dreams,' she fluttered her eyelashes then added, 'But don't worry, I can bring Julie along, and you can just hang with us girls.'

Ollie blushed again, while Josh and Rav went into fists of laughter at his discomfiture. 'Ha ha ha, she's got you tagged now. Can I be best man at the wedding?' Rav asked, 'And we could *maybe* do mates' rates at my dad's place for a slap-up wedding feast.'

Hannah gave Rav a shove, 'There's no man good enough to put a ring on my finger.'

'Thank goodness for that!' Ollie said.

Hannah looked at her phone, 'Hey, we better get a move on. Remember we were told we're to be in an assembly this morning. Something about the police wanting to talk to us.'

'We know! We think it's gonna be about drugs.'

'There's a surprise. And I heard they're going to the upper school classes individually during morning lessons.'

'Mmm. Sounds serious.' Rav now wearing a frown on his usually cheerful face. The Assembly bell rang and, as Hannah turned to go, she adjusted the shoulder straps of her bag, winked at Ollie and said, 'Later, boys.'

Chapter 3

At end of classes, Rav and Josh waited with Ollie until his grandad appeared. Stopping on double yellow lines opposite, he tooted at Ollie who'd already seen him. Sticking his head out the driver's window he shouted, 'Ollie, Ollie I'm here.'

Ollie groaned; certain the whole school now knew that his grandad was picking him up. 'See you guys. Josh, remember, after your detention, Mum says you've to be there for tea at six o'clock. Okay?'

'Sure. See you then. Enjoy the dentist.'

Ollie climbed into the passenger seat, trying to make himself small in grandad's ancient Nissan.

'Thy's not ashamed of thy grandad's car, are 'ee laddie?'

'Grandad!'

'OK. OK. Let's get you to the dentist. Have you got on clean underwear?'

'Clean underwear! Why would I have to have on clean underwear for the dentist? Anyway, you know I shower every morning.'

'Ah, well now, just as well.' Grandad nodded knowingly as he moved slowly into the traffic flow. 'I don't want to worry you, but things can sometimes go wrong. The dentist might decide he needs to give you an anaesthetic, then when you're under he makes a blunder – oh – poetry! Blunder, under!' Grandad chuckled, pleased with his poetic gift. 'Anyway, it involves blood and panic and ambulances and blue lights and emergencies. A phone call to your mother, and you know what she's going to want to know first?'

'*What?*'

'Has he got on clean underwear?'

Ollie, in spite of himself, had to laugh. 'You know, Grandad, you're right, but I'm just goin' for my six-monthly check-up.'

Grandad drew up outside the dental practice. 'I'll be round the corner in the supermarket car park when you're done.'

Half an hour later Ollie climbed back into the car and said, 'All done. Everything's okay.'

Grandad left the car park, but instead of turning right, the way they should be going, he turned left heading for the ring road.

'Grandad! This is the long way home.'

'I know, but I want to check something out.'

'See! I would have been quicker gettin' a bus.' Ollie moaned.

'You're not in a hurry, are you?'

'No, but Josh is coming for tea tonight so I don't want... what's that song on your old Beatles album? Oh yeah. I don't want to go on a magical mystery tour. I've my room to clean too.'

'Patience laddie, patience.' Grandad turned up the volume on radio four. Ollie sighed.

Turning off at the town outskirts, Ollie asked where they were going now?

'Remember that article I read in the paper this morning about another dead bird of prey? Well, I had a thought to myself. Up by Dalton's Mount, a couple of miles beyond a riding school, there's a guy keeps and races pigeons. Now, they say that hawks and falcons take pleasure in killing pigeons. They don't even kill 'em to eat 'em, they kill 'em for sport. So, I has a thought to myself, what if it's *this* guy, and not farmers who are killing off the birds of prey so as to protect his pigeons?'

Ollie was thoughtful for a couple of minutes before replying, 'Yeah. You could be right, Grandad. Maybe Josh can tell you something. His mum's boyfriend helps out there now and again. Does some driving for them.'

'Is that right? I'll maybe ask him tonight.' As they approached a pelican crossing, three older boys who Ollie recognised from his school were hanging about on the pavement. Initially, looking as though they had no intention of crossing, they suddenly dashed onto the intersection, causing Grandad to break sharply and give vent to some colourful language. The three of them started giving V signs and one fingered salutes.

'Stuff you, ya old coffin dodger!' One of them shouted as they high fived their way off the crossing.

Grandad was raging and for getting out the car to chase them. Car horns tooted impatiently behind them.

'Grandad, you'll have to move. They're not worth wasting your time on anyway.'

'You know them, Ollie?'

'Yeah, they're a couple of years above me. Jez Freeman, Scot Pinkman and Raffid Hakeem. They think they're big men and they're always gettin' into trouble. They're bullies too, always picking on those they think are weaker than them.'

'Bullies. I'll bully them if I get a hold of them.' Grandad growled at them and at the world in general.

'They know you can't touch them, Grandad. That's why they behave the way they do. If the police ever got involved, they would just get a slap on the wrist and told not to be naughty boys.'

Grandad muttered under his breath. Coming to the turnoff for Dalton's Mount, on the skyline off to the left Ollie saw the mixed woodland, beyond which he knew lay the town reservoir. To the right, a number of horses grazed contentedly in the fields attached to a riding school. Continuing up the road the surrounding land became more of a rocky wasteland sporting clumps of gorse, hawthorn and wild shrubs. To the left, near the top of the road, several impoverished looking single storey cottages and smallholdings were clumped together in a tight crescent as though conspiring to keep secrets. Three of the cottages looked abandoned. Outside one of the others, two unkempt looking men sat on a scarred old bench whilst a young girl, looking in her mid-teens and dressed in ripped jeans and a grubby green T shirt with long mustardy sleeves, leaned against a windowsill, a large dog of uncertain pedigree at her feet. They all scowled as Grandad drove passed, and, as he slowed down, the girl moved quickly into the house, the dog close on her heels.

'I don't think that can be the community welcoming committee,' Grandad muttered, his powers of perception obviously honed to the nth degree. About a mile up the road stood an old telephone box, minus the phone, with few windows still intact. Next to it, a derelict-looking small hall with its windows boarded up behind new looking metal bars. On its wall, a noticeboard riddled with wood-rot, whose sole purpose seemed to be to display its deteriorating state of faded green paint. In contrast, as well as a yale lock, two newish looking solid bolts and padlocks kept the door firmly in place. When Ollie pointed that out, Grandad muttered, 'Probably to keep out druggies.'

A mile or so up the road, and to the right, a wide driveway led to an old two storey stone-built house, probably quite imposing in its day but now showing signs of decay. Slightly below the house, and to the right of the drive, stood a large solid looking wooden structure, not unlike the old cavalry forts seen in movies of the American west. At intervals, rods extended up from its sides, each one with a CD attached which flapped and flashed in the breeze. At two of the corners seen from the road, stood realistically lifelike carved and painted wooden owls. On the side of the wall of the house were mounted a group of four CCTV cameras, two trained on the outside and the others in towards where the birds were kept. On a ridge behind the house was the beginning of an area of deciduous woodland.

Grandad, already slowed to a crawl, now came to a stop. 'Aye, I could be right,' he said, 'I would have thought you'd be asking for trouble breeding pigeons next to fairly dense woods. Maybe these owls are there to frighten of birds of prey. I think I once heard that raptors were frightened of owls for some reason,' he said, nodding in the direction of the wooden construction. 'He must have a fair few birds in there. And,' he went on, 'they've mounted cameras to frighten off any human intruders. Hmm. Must be a bit of money tied up in them birds.'

'So, what's with the CDs, Grandad?'

'Maybe the pigeons like to dance!' Grandad laughed at his insightfulness. 'Aye, that could be it right enough. There was a daft dance that women used to do at weddings an' that. Maybe they still do. The birdie dance. Daft looking eejits. And they aye looked that serious when they were doin' it too.' Grandad was shaking his head and smiling at the recollection. 'Maybe that's it then. Them birds 'll be entertaining themselves with the birdie dance.'

'Yeah. You'll be right, Grandad.' Ollie's sardonic response coupled with a nod. From their position, looking beyond the house, the ground appeared to plateau to a fair-sized parking area. An old blue transit van stood at one corner next to purpose-built trailer and an older looking lorry, with green side covers both bearing the words: "Pigeons in Transit" in bold gold letters. Standing closer to the house was a late model silver Range Rover.

'You don't see too many pigeon carriers like them I would think.' Grandad commented. 'Oh oh!' he said starting to put the car in gear. 'We're being watched. Someone's got binoculars on us from inside yon house.'

Ollie looked up and could see there was someone

standing in the doorway, binoculars on Grandad's car. 'Why's he checking us out, Grandad? What's his problem?'

'Well, I think some racing pigeons are worth a lot of money, both in race winnings and in stud fees. He's probably just being careful. But I think I'll see if I can have a pint with Ernie Broadbend tonight. He keeps a few racing pigeons. Might be able to tell us something.'

As they moved off Ollie sighed, 'Grandad you're outside the thirty-mph limit now. The speed of sound is seven hundred and sixty-seven miles an hour, so you don't have to worry about breaking *that*. The speed limit here's sixty, so I guess we don't have to worry about you breaking that either.' He sighed again.

'You're not in a hurry, are you?'

'Josh is coming to stay tonight and I need to sort my room out.'

'Plenty time, lad. Plenty time.' Grandad began to hum. Tunelessly.

Ollie sighed again. 'Grandad. Is there a special pump at filling stations reserved only for you pensioners?'

'What do you mean?'

Well, everyone else runs on petrol, diesel or electric power, but it seems some of you pensioners must fill your tanks with snail juice!'

'Hey, how would you like to walk home?'

Ollie sighed, 'Don't tempt me, Grandad. I'd probably get home before you.'

Chapter 4

Josh walked home with a heavy heart. Home had become hell. School not much better. He was still smarting from the mocking laughter in second class this morning. Maths would send anyone to sleep. Boring. But added to that, as the dark shadows under his eyes would attest, the underlying cause was that he hadn't been sleeping well recently because of his home situation. The booming voice from right beside his desk had roared, 'Josh Meadows.' Josh sat bolt upright trying to gather his thoughts. The voice continued, 'Dreaming is for in your bed at night. After lights out. Snoring if you must, but not to be indulged in my classroom at ten thirty-five in the morning. Report for detention after school.'

Prat!

In detention he was asked to explain why he fell asleep during class. He told the teacher he'd just been tired, that he hadn't intended nodding off. Questions had been asked about his home life, to which he had given evasive answers. Mr Donaldson, taking detention today, wasn't so easily fobbed off and persisted in asking ever more probing questions. Josh became annoyed and uncomfortable. But he had learned the hard way to keep things to himself. Glancing at the wall clock, and seeing the time, he asked if he might be released from detention.

He wasn't going to be telling anyone about what was going on at home. Not because he didn't want to, but to do so might only make matters worse. It was like being caught in a trap with, as far as he could tell, no easy way out. He walked slowly, still in two minds whether or not to cancel the weekend at Ollie's. With a sigh he thought he'd wait and see how things were when he got home.

Home! A two bedroomed flat above a Chinese takeaway. Bliss! He was pretty sure his clothes must stink of the cooking smells that permeated up into the flat. Turning into his street he wondered what he'd be confronted with when he got home. Going up the stairs he could hear the sound of a kids' programme blaring out. It was like his little sister, Nicola, played it loud to drown out all the bad noises in her young life.

Home life was a shambles. Josh had lost his dad in a car crash six years ago. He still missed him. Nicola was just a baby so never really knew their dad. His mum, who till then thought the term, 'broken hearted' was a melodramatic exaggeration, came to know the awful reality. She did not handle it well. Nearly three years ago, she met and started going out with Eddie. Josh never understood why. Eddie was everything his dad was not.

The family used to live in a decent new-build three bedroomed semi on the edge of town close to Ollie's home. The conservatory led out to the well-tended and sheltered back garden. The attached garage used for everything except the car. They went on holidays. His dad took him swimming and to football, not that Josh was really interested in the game. When he was younger, if his friends wanted a kick about, he was usually the timekeeper — or a goal post! But they had been happy. Life had been normal. Nicola hadn't really known 'normal'. Well, maybe the way they lived was the norm for some people, but if you've known a better life this one was hard to take. This flat was a dump. His mum's live-in boyfriend was a low life, won't work psycho who was always on the make. He had a real nasty streak in him and a vicious temper. Josh wished he was older and stronger himself, but that day would come, unless of course Eddie was in prison. Something that seemed entirely feasible.

Josh threw his bag into his bedroom, then, taking a deep breath he opened the door to the living room. Nicola jumped up and gave him a big hug.

'Hi you, how's your day been?'

'Okay, Josh. Thanks for helping me with my homework. Mrs Hashmi gave me three gold stars.'

'Well done little squidger.'

'Josh!' In a loud voice, and stamping her foot, 'I'm not a squidger, whatever that is.'

'You're a squidger to me.' Josh laughed and started to tickle her.

'Josh! Josh! Ha, ha. Josh, get of me.' She squealed. When Josh released her, she said, 'Mum's having a lie down, she says she has a headache.' Her brow furrowed, 'She gets lots, doesn't she?'

'Yeah, I'll go stick my head round the door. Maybe you could turn the telly down a bit, by the way.'

Josh went back into the small hallway, stopping to listen at his mum's bedroom door. Nothing. He knocked gently. Nothing. He pushed down on the handle and stuck his head round the door. The curtains were shut, and his mum was lying flat on her back, still in her dressing gown, arms outstretched and one leg hanging over the bed. The reason he had fallen asleep in class this morning was because his mum, and Eddie, had had some people in till very late last night. Loud voices, laughter and noisy arguments went on till the small hours. At times he'd just be drifting off and the volume would be cranked up again jerking him back to wakefulness. Thank goodness Nicola slept through it.

'Mum,' he said quietly, 'Mum, you awake?' A slight grunt from his mother's bed then nothing. Josh sighed and shook his head. His eyes filled with tears as he bit into his bottom lip. What a mess. Life for them just seemed to be on a downward spiral with no indication as to the extent of the depths to which it might ultimately sink. But Josh was determined he was going to protect his young sister. Social

Services had been sniffing around but his mum had been prepared and had, so far, allayed any misgivings they might have had.

Wiping his eyes, Josh went back into the living room and, trying to sound upbeat, asked Nicola if she was hungry. Giving the affirmative, Josh said he'd see what there was for eating. Checking the fridge and a couple of cupboards he shook his head. Not much by the looks of things. 'Beans on toast?' he shouted.

'Yes please. And brown sauce.'

'Okay, if we've got any.'

Nicola came into the kitchen. 'Are you not having something, Josh?'

'No. I told you I'm spending the weekend at Ollie's?'

Nicola's face fell. 'I'll be on my own, then,' her bottom lip trembled like a buttercup in a breeze.

'No. Mum 'll be here and Eddie 'll probably be away to France. Anyway, just think, you'll have our bedroom all to yourself.'

'But you know I feel safe when we're in the same room.'

'Nicola, you'll be safe. You don't have to be frightened of the dark.'

'I'm not frightened of the dark, Josh,' her eyes wide, her bottom lip trembling again. 'I'm frightened of the monsters.'

Josh sighed. There was only one monster they had to worry about, and he was all too real. Eddie.

In truth, Josh wasn't happy about sharing a bedroom with his young sister. He was a growing teenage boy and much as he loved and felt protective towards Nicola, he really didn't think it right to have her share his bedroom. But he tried to navigate the situation as best as possible. Ideally, he could have slept in the living room, but Eddie was prone to sit up late, with or without his mum, drinking and, Josh was sure, doing one kind of illegal substance or other.

He would have tried to do something about it, but Eddie, one step ahead, had gotten hold of Josh one night and told him if he caused trouble some serious harm would come to his sister. Sometimes too, he would give Josh a supposedly playful punch on the arm, but much harder that a playful punch warranted, so that Josh sometimes wangled out of PE at school in case awkward questions were asked. Eddie also threatened that if ever he wasn't around, or if Josh caused trouble for him, he had friends who knew what to do to him. Josh was sure he meant it. There was a coldness, and constant air of menace about him, and Josh, for the life of him, couldn't understand what his mother saw in him. Moreover, he seemed to be a good few years younger than his mum, which again, seemed strange to Josh. He'd asked his mum about Eddie and their relationship once and she'd snapped at him to mind his own business.

Josh poured a glass of milk and found a couple of digestive biscuits to give Nicola. 'I'm just going to get changed, Squidger.'

'Josh!'

He laughed, 'Okay *Nicola!* I'm gonna get changed and put my stuff together. I'll be back Sunday, probably after teatime, but if you're worried, get hold of Mum's phone and call me. Anytime, okay?'

'Can I not come with you, Josh?' A pleading look on her face tugged at his heart.

'No kiddo. I'm taking my bike if I can get it out the shed. But I'll be back Sunday. Remember what I've told you now. Oh, and don't forget to take your inhaler.' Silence. 'Nicola!'

'Yes, I'll remember.'

'See you do, Squidger.'

Josh put together a change of clothes, deodorant and

toothbrush. He collected some money he had secreted away in his bedroom. His mum had stopped giving him pocket money a couple of years ago. Fortunately, he made a few pounds working a couple of nights a week in the carry out beneath the flat, and sometimes cleaning the owner and his wife's cars on a Saturday morning. He'd get Ollie's mum a bunch of flowers for having him stay over for the weekend.

He went back and knocked on his mum's bedroom door. Still no answer. Opening the door, he said, 'Mum. Mum! You need to get up.'

A groan from his mum. 'Why? What time is it? Where's Eddie?' her voice slurred.

'I've no idea where Eddie is, but I told you I was going to Ollie's for the weekend. You need get up and look after Nicola.'

'Oh yeah,' Her voice muffled.

'I've given her beans on toast, but she'll be hungry later. Mum, you really need to pull yourself together.'

'I will Josh, I will. Just don't hassle me,' she said, pulling herself into a sitting position, with both feet on the floor. Her hair was dishevelled, her dressing gown grubby, yesterday's make-up smudged across her face. Josh shook his head. He was frustrated and so sad at what she'd become since Eddie came on the scene.

'Right, I'm heading. See you Sunday night.'

'You not got a kiss for your mum?'

Josh hesitated then walked over and took her hand; she smelled of stale sweat and alcohol. 'Mum, please, please sort yourself out. You need to get rid of Eddie. He's not good for you.' He leaned in and gave her a peck on the forehead. 'Okay, bye. I'll see you.' Giving Nicola a hug, he grabbed his bag and headed to the shed to dig his bike out from underneath all the junk. Checking the chain and the brakes, he was satisfied it would do. Pushing out onto the road, he mounted up and headed to Ollie's. Such a relief to get a break.

Chapter 5

Grandad drew up in front of the house leaving the short driveway free for Ollie's mum's car. 'She should be home soon,' he said. 'You'd better get in and get your room tidied before she does her inspection.'

Ollie sighed the kind of sigh that protrudes your lips. But Grandad was right. The deal was that Josh could stay the weekend if his room was properly cleaned. But what did his mum think Josh was going to do? Check his sock drawer? Run his finger along the furniture looking for dust? Look for cobwebs round the window frame? Fluff balls under the bed? Josh's whole house was a tip for goodness' sake, not that that argument held much water with Ollie's mum.

Hoover, duster, can of polish, can of air spray, bin liner, that'll do it, Ollie thought as he struggled up the stairs trying not to drop the cans. Grandad followed with the camp bed brought in from the garage. 'Good job Josh is a bit of a skinny stick.' he said as he angled it into the bedroom. 'Hope he sleeps okay.'

'I'm sure he will, Grandad. If he stops talking long enough that is.'

'Aye lad. You're the one to talk. Mr "Why use a sentence when a paragraph will do?"'

'Well guess who I take that from Mr "Why use a paragraph when a chapter will do". No actually, Mr "Why use a chapter when Encyclopaedia Britannica would hit the spot?"'

Grandad chortled. 'Eee lad, maybe there's many a true word said in jest right enough.'

'Right, Grandad, let me get on.' Ollie gently shoved Grandad towards the door. 'Mum's gonna be home soon.'

With Grandad gone, Ollie knuckled down to the task.

While he was working, he tried to think how he should broach the subject that had been seriously concerning him. Josh really wasn't his usual self and hadn't been for a while now. Ollie suspected his home situation had a lot to do with it. He knew Josh worried about his little sister, who suffered quite badly from asthma, and that stressful situations could set of an attack. She'd had to be admitted to hospital twice over the past couple of years because of the severity of attacks, and the current home situation was definitely causing some problems. Josh had said Social Services were starting to sniff about. But now, more importantly, Ollie wanted to check what Josh had said about his mum's partner. He had forgotten now, but was sure Josh had once hinted about there something suspicious about his involvement with that pigeon place. In fact, maybe they should bike out there tomorrow and see what they could see. He would have a word with Rav tonight and ask him to come too.

He heard his mum's car turn into the drive just as he finished hoovering. Gathering all the cleaning stuff together he headed back down the stairs reaching the bottom as his mum came through the front door. 'Hi Mum. Good day? How did Kukooru get on?'

'She was good. A bit edgy at first but once the vet had her tranquillised, we were able to lower her onto the built-up straw bed. The BBC were there so you'll be able to see it all on the news tonight.' Reaching into her jacket pocket she brought out a small white package and handed it to Ollie, 'Here you go. A souvenir.'

Ollie smiled and guessed what it might be, and he was right. Wrapped in a tissue, one of Kukooru's molars. 'It's okay, you can touch it, I had it cleaned before I brought it home. And you can just see a slight crack across the top of the tooth, that's been the problem.'

Ollie examined the tooth. He had expected an animal

the size of a giraffe to have huge teeth and big roots but this one was quite flat. Underneath he could see and feel the four small roots, one on each corner, as sharp as a needle at their tips.

'Hey, Grandad,' he shouted making his way to the sitting room, 'You'll be alright now if you need a dental implant. Look.' he said holding the tooth out for Grandad to inspect. 'And it's all spiky underneath, kinda like you, Grandad.'

'Aye very funny my bonny lad. At least I've still got most of my own teeth.'

'Shame about your marbles though!' Ollie laughed as he headed to the kitchen where his mum was rattling about with pots and pans.

'Did you get the sleeping bag looked out?' she asked.

'Yes, Mum.'

'And is your room properly clean and tidy? I'll check it out before Josh comes.'

'Yeeeees, Mum. It's only Josh for goodness' sake. What's for tea?'

'Macaroni cheese, you said Josh likes that. Why else would I be grating cheese?'

'Yeah, that's cool. But Mum,' Ollie hesitated, 'please don't go asking him about his home situation 'cause I think that would upset him a bit.'

Ollie's Mum stopped grating the cheese, wiped her hands on a wet cloth and turned to face Ollie. 'Listen Ollie, if you think Josh's problems at home are serious, or in any way threatening, please talk to me after the weekend, or even before if you have to. I know at your ages you think you can deal with things yourselves. But you can't always. Sometimes you have to get grown-up help. Okay?'

'Yeah, Mum, I will.'

'Promise?'

'Yeah, okay,' Ollie avoided eye contact. His phone

bleeped. He glanced at the message. 'Josh's here,' he announced.

'Why does he always send you an alert when he's already here? And anyway, I thought he was bringing his bike.'

'Oh, he'll have stopped round the corner to message me. He'll be here by the time I open the door.'

'Mr Impatient, is he?'

'It's just a thing with him Mum. Likes preparing for the next move before he makes it. Don't ask me why but maybe something to do with his dance classes, you know, being ready for the next move.'

Mum laughed, 'Will he want an alert two minutes before tea's ready?'

'No, a shout will be fine.' Ollie opened the front door to find Josh standing with a gym bag in one hand and a small bunch of flowers in the other. 'Oh, I didn't know you cared!' Ollie laughed, one hand covering his heart.

'Not for you, stupid. For your mum.'

'Creep!'

Josh ignored him and, pushing passed, headed for the kitchen, 'Thanks for having me, Mrs Saunders, I'll try to make sure Ollie behaves this weekend'.

'Oh Josh, that's very kind of you, you really didn't have to bother. But it's much appreciated.' Mum gave Josh a little hug. 'And I would appreciate if you can keep Ollie in line and don't allow him to entice you to stay up all night playing on his Xbox, or yacking.' She said looking at Ollie, one eyebrow raised in a warning sign.

'That could be a bit of a big ask, Mrs Saunders, but I'll try.' Josh nodded, a mock serious expression on his face.

'Right, tea will be ready in ten minutes. Take your stuff upstairs, Josh, and the pair of you wash your hands before we eat.'

'Mum! We're not children!' Ollie snapped.

'No. You're teenage boys which is marginally worse. Ten minutes!'

'Put the kitchen telly on, Mum. Got to catch Kukooru on the news. C'mon Josh we'll take your stuff up to my room. Leave your bike out front just now till Rav comes.'

'Excuse me! You'll see your *mother* on the news too, Ollie!' Her indignant cry following the boys up the stairs.

'Oh yeah great. Get your autograph later, Mum.' A look passed from Ollie to Josh. The boys laughed and tried to shoulder each other out the way going into the bedroom. Ollie pointed out Josh's bed to him.

'I have stayed here before, you know!' Josh's sarcastic response.

'How could I forget your snoring?'

Josh threw his bag onto the camp bed and himself after it. Looking round Ollie's room, he said, 'I've always really liked your house. It always feels,' he hesitated searching for the right words, 'homely... comfortable... no, I know – welcoming.'

'Really?' Ollie had never given it much thought, but then, he supposed Josh was right, particularly in light of his current home life. When he thought about it, Ollie realised that he really liked his home too. Built as a farmhouse, the kitchen and hall floors retained the original flag stones. A wood burning stove had been fitted into the cavernous stone fireplace in the kitchen with two comfortable old leather armchairs placed on either side. A favourite place for Grandad, and Dad when at home, to read their newspaper. Most meals were eaten at the large table in the centre of the kitchen. The house was spacious with generous-sized rooms. All the internal doors were made of pine, as were the stairs, handrails and skirting boards; the wood emitting a not unpleasant scent peculiar to aged wood which, that Ollie thought had a great deal to do with the homely feel to the building. All the external walls were

30

thick enough to keep the warmth in in the winter and out in the summer. It was a comfortable house. Not a show house, but a house for living in. A house that when you entered was a home in every sense of the word.

'Yeah, Josh, but your situation's going to change. You're not gonna be livin' in that flat forever. 'Specially when you become famous.'

'I sure hope so. But I worry about Nicola if I get accepted to ballet school in London in a couple of years. '

'A lot of stuff can happen in a couple of years, Josh.'

'Yeah, that's what worries me.'

'Well, London's not far away.'

'I guess.'

'Ollie! Josh! Tea's nearly ready.'

'Well let's just try 'n have a good time this weekend. Tomorrow's another day.' Ollie encouraged as the boys made their way downstairs.

Chapter 6

'Ignore Grandad, Josh. He's just a wind up,' Ollie said as he and Josh settled at the table.

'Eee lad, that's right, just thee write me off!'

'Grandad!' Ollie's voice sharp.

Grandad sighed and exaggeratedly let his shoulders slump. 'See Josh, when you get to my age, you're not of that much interest to anybody except the local muggers. You're just seen as a useless old fart.'

'Dad! Language!' The rebuke fired in Grandad's direction accompanied by a sharp look from Ollie's Mum.

'Eee lass, the lads are old enough to know what a fart is, surely.'

Enjoying the exchange, the boys looked at each other with huge grins on their faces, then Ollie chipped in, 'Course we know what a fart is, Grandad. It's something old, smelly and senile, usually on the pension, and pollutes the air 'cause it's an old windbag.' Grandad scowled and Ollie's Mum had to laugh.

'Well, you set yourself up for that one, Dad.'

'No respect,' he muttered. 'When I were a lad...' Ollie started humming a doleful tune and playing an invisible violin. 'You know, Jenny,' addressing Ollie's Mum, 'it would be easier to knit a cobweb than to get any respect from youngsters nowadays.'

'Well, you do tend to set yourself up for it, Dad. Right! I'm just going to lift. Josh, do you like tomato?'

'Yeah, thanks Mrs Saunders.'

Ollie's Mum busied herself plating the mac cheese, 'Oh Ollie, put some squash and glasses out please. I forgot.'

Ollie, with a sigh as he gathered glasses, jug and juice muttered, 'I have to do *everything* in this place.'

'Eee lad. If thy'd been...'

'GRANDAD! Mum! Tell him.'

'What? A man can't have an opinion? A man can't reflect on bygone times? Is there a law?' Grandad winked at Josh. 'Bet *you* wish you had a grandad like me?'

'Yeah, I do, Mr Caldwell.'

Ollie shot him a look, 'Don't encourage him, Josh. He's such a wind up. You know, when I turned thirteen, he said he would let me into a secret, but I mustn't let on to my mum, dad, or anyone else.'

Grandad, guessing what was coming, grinned, looking pretty pleased with himself.

Ollie went on. 'He said that when every kid reaches thirteen, official teenagers, the government send to your parents or guardians, a special and secret book. A book with warnings to never let it fall into teenage hands. They give advice on best ways to keep the book in a secure place. The book's called, "Five Thousand Ways to Make A Teenager's Life Miserable". They send it special delivery in a plain brown paper parcel and has to be signed for by the nominated parent or guardian. Then secreted away in the prepared secure location.'

Josh listened with some amusement, 'Yeah, right.'

'But there's more. He then said that Mum had got the very latest updated version, "Ten Thousand Ways to Make a Teenager's Life Miserable." Throwing his mother a look, and raising his voice, he said, 'Though I'm actually beginning to think he might have been telling the truth.'

'Yep, and I'm just up to three hundred and seventy-two. I'd better get a move on. I've only got a few years left.' She smirked and gave Josh a wink.

Grandad beamed, 'I was only trying to be helpful. Trying to prepare you. That's why teenage years are so miserable. Their parents all get one, then they have to send it back to the government when the kid turns twenty.'

'Grandad, you're just impossible. What a load of

absolute tosh!'

'Oh really.' Grandad leered. 'How do you think I learned how to annoy you so much? It didn't come naturally you know. But I think that's been quite successful.' Then went on, 'Oh Josh, while I remember, Ollie was saying yon boyfriend, is it, of your mum's, sometimes helps out at that pigeon place up Dalton's Mount.'

A wary look crossed Josh's face, 'He does sometimes, amongst other things. I think he helps with the cleaning sometimes and does a bit of driving. Takes birds out and releases them for exercise various distances from the loft. Then he always does an overnight to France on a Saturday to let the birds off somewhere down the French coast.'

'Aye, that pigeon place seems quite a set up.'

'It is. Eddie says he's got way more than seven hundred birds there. But, apart from his own birds, people give him their pigeons to be part of the breeding set up. His birds are specially bred for racing. Feeds 'em a special diet and uses the best of them in the breeding programme. When he's happy with their performance he sells them on, but he keeps the best of them himself. Eddie says he's bred some real champions and gets good money for them or from squabs from a good line.'

'Squabs?' Grandad looked mystified.

'Baby pigeons.' Josh said.

'Who'd have thought it. Mind you, he's got the loft built like Fort Knox. Solid. CCTV cameras and all.'

'Yeah, but don't be fooled, they're dummies.' Josh said.

Surprised, Grandad nearly choked, 'Really?'

'Yeah, one time I overheard Eddie tellin' his drinking buddies the guy has had all this money spent on vehicles, equipment and loft development, but skips on the cameras. He thinks the sight of them would be a big enough deterrent.'

34

'Ollie come and take these plates to the table,' his mum said, nodding in the direction of the steaming dishes. She joined them and said, 'Right boys, eat up. What are you up to tonight?'

'Well, Rav's, woops! Mum! That's Kukooru *and* you on telly.' They all looked at the screen attached to the wall as Ollie jumped up to turn up the volume, 'Hey Mum! You're a star!' His phone pinged. Glancing at the screen he saw it was Hannah on Snapchat. A big grin on her face and a message reading, 'See you later.' His face turned red. Fortunately his mum was focussing on the television.

'What a sight I am. Look at my hair. Oh, see how gently they were able to lay her down. She was so good, a bit unsteady when she was getting to her feet again, but at least her mouth will feel better now.' The clip ended. 'You were saying, Ollie?'

'Yeah. Rav's coming round about seven, unless his dad wants him to work tonight. Then we're goin' out for a while. Probably down to the beach, then along by the marina. Nothing too exciting. We'll get a coke and maybe some chips there.'

'You'll have just had your tea!'

'Well, we'll be hungry with running about playing football.' His mother shook her head with the kind of incomprehension familiar to mothers of teenage boys.

'Well, don't be doing anything dangerous or stupid.'

'Mum! We're not children! And you just said this morning you didn't want me sitting playing on my computer all summer.'

'Eee, when I were a lad...'

'Dad!'

'Grandad!'

'Mr Caldwell!' Josh joined in laughing.

Grandad scowled and rose from the table muttering something about lack of respect, and that they must all be a dab hand at the sewing 'cause they've been stitching him up for years. Then turning at the door said, 'I tell this, my lad, if your granny was still alive, she'd be birlin' in her grave at the lack of respect for your old grandad.' Laughter followed him along the hall.

Ollie's mum busied herself at the sink as the boys helped clear the table, then turning from the sink, a dripping dish still in her hand, she said, 'By the way boys, what did the police want to talk about at this morning's assembly? Was it about road safety or what?'

Ollie and Josh shared a look. 'No, not exactly mum. Something a bit more serious if what they were saying is true.'

'Oh.' She moved from the sink, wiping her hands on a towel as she took a seat at the table. 'Do tell.'

The boys joined her, Josh nodding towards Ollie as a prompt for him to begin.

'Well, they're asking us to be extra vigilant during the holidays because they're concerned about the possibility of the town becoming awash with illegal drugs.'

'Awash!' A startled look crossed Mum's face. 'What do they mean awash?'

'There's this thing goin' on from London druggie dealers. What was it again Josh?'

'County lines or country lines or something.'

A puzzled look on Ollie's mum's face. 'County lines! What's that?'

'Lines that are set up using untraceable mobile phones from what we were told this mornin'. Because drug dealing in London has more or less reached saturation point, dealers from there are setting up lines of drug supplies into counties and towns outside London. New markets for them, and they're seemingly quite ruthless.'

Ollie's mum looked shocked. 'Really! That's dreadful. Here in our town too?'

'We don't know yet, that's why the police came to school, to warn us to be on the lookout, particularly for teenagers, or maybe even younger kids who don't quite fit in and are behaving suspiciously.'

'Are they saying this is happening in our town now?'

'It could be, I guess. The London dealers seemingly place someone into an area, forcing people who're druggies, or maybe some who are socially inadequate, to put them up. They often use teenage runaways from kid's homes and set them up in one of these homes. Sometimes they use kids as young as eight, can you imagine?' Ollie looked troubled. 'But they said the peak age of running away is fifteen and these kids are often very vulnerable.'

Ollie's mum looked horrified, 'I know there's a real problem with drugs these days, but you never like to think it's on your own doorstep. And not using kids for goodness sake.'

'Seems the police are really concerned and asked us if we see anything suspicious to phone a special drug line number.'

'My goodness, I didn't realise things were as bad as that. Just you boys be careful and don't get involved in anything.' A frown cutting deeply into her brow she sat in silence for a moment or two. Then noticing Ollie's hands at rest on the table changed tack. 'Ollie Saunders. You get those nails cut tonight. You could mine coal in them. Disgusting!'

Rising from the table, Ollie sighed, 'Yeah, Mum, right. C'mon Josh, I need to get my football if we're goin' to the beach.'

Josh nodded sagely, 'Thanks, Mrs Saunders. Don't worry I'll look after him.'

Ollie gave a snort of derision.

Chapter 7

'What time did Rav say he'd be here?' Josh asked as they went up to the bedroom to get some money.

'About seven, if his dad doesn't want him to work.'

Ollie pushed the bedroom door open and threw himself on his bed just as his phone pinged. It was Hannah again. Checking the message, he groaned. 'Oh no, it's from Hannah, saying, "missing u already." With a blowing kisses emoji. Yech!'

'Ha, ha. You're doomed Ollie.' Josh laughed as he moved to the window. Placing his hands flat on the sill, he arched his back as if for his head to touch his right leg stretched out behind him, now curling up with practised suppleness, then lifting his left foot so as to stand on his toes.

'Wow, Josh, how do you manage that?' Ollie was impressed and jumping off the bed thought he would try for himself. 'Shove over.' He pushed Josh out the way, laying his own hands on the windowsill.

Josh laughed. 'You'll never do it.'

'Oh no! What can be hard about it? Just watch me.' Ollie stretched his right leg behind him.

'Yeah, but now bend it. High! The toes on your right foot, first pointed to the ceiling, then curling up towards your head. Your left foot needs to be further forward to balance properly. Then move not just your head, but your whole body curling back towards your right foot. And put you're left foot into point.'

'Point?'

'On your toes.'

Ollie had moved his hands off the windowsill to stabilise himself a bit better by gripping the edges, only to discover that he lacked the physical dexterity to get the appropriate bend to his back, or his right leg extended into the necessary curve, and in trying to balance and move his left foot to point, tottered and losing his grip on the windowsill, crashed noisily onto Josh's make-shift bed. 'Ouch, my leg. Ouch, my back.'

'Ollie!' His mum shouting up the stairs. 'What on earth's going on?'

'Oh, it's okay, Mum, I was just cutting my nails and lumps of coal were falling out.' Ollie winked at Josh.

'Are you both okay?'

'We're fine, Mum, just a little trip.' Then to Josh, 'Wow, Joshie boy, I don't know how you do it.'

'Practising helps,' Josh replied with a wry smile. 'A *lot* of practising.'

'You're really serious about this, aren't you?'

'Ever since I first saw the old Billy Elliot movie, now watched about a hundred times. I just knew that's what I wanted to do. It was the end bit really, when he was performing a major part as an adult and made the spectacular entrance onto the stage. That was it! Then I found sites on You Tube showing young people training in ballet, a good number of boys too. And I definitely knew that's what I want, even though part of me knows I may never make it. Lot of competition out there and standards are really high.'

'I guess it's quite unusual, not like science or technology, or business or sports. I mean some would say it's a bit... girly.' Ollie screwed up his nose.

Josh smiled looking unperturbed. 'Listen, any male' ballet dancer's body is incredibly supple, and if I fail at ballet, I can always take up kick boxing. Strong legs, supple body, inner core strength and power.' He laughed as he flexed both arms and moved clenched fists up under his chin, at the same time twisting sideways, making a T shape with his body to lash out with his right foot at his imagined

39

foe, then, twirled round three hundred and sixty degrees to come back into his starting position, before giving a sweeping bow.

'Wow, yeah, that's impressive. I guess you really could. Wouldn't that be something? I can just see the headlines, "Leading male ballet dancer kicks the crap out of heckling wrestlers". But Josh, you must have known what some people's reaction would be to you doing ballet.'

'Well at first I did feel a bit daft when I managed to find that school of dance in town and there was only one other boy there. But Danielle was glad to have me to give the girls another male to practice with. She teaches modern dance too, but majors on ballet. She's really encouraged me and now she's managed to get me an audition with the International School of Ballet and Modern Dance in London. I'm not sure about it, but she thinks I stand a chance of getting on to their student sponsorship and bursary programme 'cause there's no way I could get it financed myself. And she's been really great training me in *savate* too.'

'Yeah. Your secret weapon. Who's ever heard of it?'

Josh shrugged, 'Probably more awareness in France where it originated. It's incredible how well its' moves fit in with ballet. But of course, Danielle's French, and savate was first developed for close quarter fighting on board ships, then adopted by Parisian "gentlemen" to protect young ladies as they escorted them on the streets of Paris. Most people haven't heard about but it's really effective. Have a look online. You Tube's got some examples.'

'But you'd be moving to London. That sucks! When would you move if you get a place?'

'Not till I'm sixteen. I want it so much but I need to try and get things sorted out at home before then. And get some school qualifications.' His face clouded over. 'Or I may not go.' He moved back to the window, gazing out. 'I wish we still lived here.' There was a catch in Josh's voice, 'Especially for Nicola's sake.'

'Yeah, I know. I wish you did too. How old were we when you moved in?'

'Four, I think. We were one of the first families to move in, though of course Nicola wasn't born till a few years later. I remember my Dad saying your Dad objected to a new housing estate being built on what had been farmland.'

'Kinda spoiled our view out the back I guess was his objection.'

'We didn't half get up to some tricks though.' Josh looked over to Ollie, a wistful smile on his face.

Ollie laughed, 'Remember the time you got covered in tar halfway up your legs?'

'I can still feel my mum wielding that scrubbing brush as though I'd caught some kind of plague-like disease. Pain! And remember when we got caught up on the bare beams for the first floor when the ladder slipped.'

'I think that was the first time I was grounded, physically and metaphorically.' Ollie laughed. 'Anyway, we'd better get changed if we're goin' down the beach. I'll put on an old pair of trainers.'

Josh looked embarrassed. 'I've just got the one pair with me.'

Ollie felt for Josh realising that it may actually be the *only* trainers he had and was saddened to think how much Josh's life had changed from what it had been. The doorbell rang as Ollie was lacing his trainers. 'That'll be Rav, my Mum will let him in. Let's go.'

Leaving his room, Ollie looked over the banister to shout 'hi' to Rav, only to see Hannah standing in front of him, looking up and grinning from ear to ear. 'Hi, Ollie. Rav said I could tag along with you guys tonight.'

Josh gave him a dig from behind, 'Aha, you're in it now, Ollie.' He smirked.

'Shut *up* you!' he hissed as he pushed Josh into first place to descend the stairs. This was the first time he'd seen Hannah out of school uniform. She was dressed casually in denim shorts, a rust-coloured T-shirt and denim trainers. The loose afro hair style framed her face highlighting her pert prettiness. But it was her dark eyes Ollie really noticed. They made you forget any other part of her face. They were beautiful, flashing an inner fire that looked upon the world with a fearless confidence. A smile played about her lips as she held Ollie in her gaze. Unable to hold Hannah's stare, his face red, and feeling tongue-tied, Ollie managed to splutter, 'Hi Hannah. Josh will be so happy to see you. He was just saying earlier how much he liked you.'

Hannah ignored him and turned to address his mum hovering in the background, 'Nice to meet you, Mrs Saunders. I hope you don't mind me hangin' out with the boys?'

Highly amused, she responded, 'I'm sure I don't but I'm not sure about that lot.' She nodded in the direction of the boys.

'Oh, don't mind them. They're definitely needing a girl's perspective on life. And physical protection.' Looking Ollie's mum up and down, she added, 'Pity you're not a few kilos heavier, Mrs Saunders.'

A bemused smile crossed Ollie's mum's face, 'Oh *really*?'

'Yeah, then you could have a choice of these three's big girls' blouses to wear!'

The indignant boys started shoving Hannah about, protesting the slur against their masculinity.

The strange female voice in the house roused Grandad to abandon his programme to come and investigate. He eyed Hannah through narrowed lids, then smiled. 'Well, well, well, Ollie got a girlfriend, then? He's kept that pretty quiet.'

42

'Come through to the kitchen,' Ollie's mum beckoned.

As they made their way through, Hannah slipped her arm through Grandad's telling him that, yes, his grandson had a girlfriend, then looking back at Ollie and winking, said, 'He just doesn't know it yet.'

'Aye lass, I like thee fine. You're a feisty one you are.' Then, 'Now Ollie, don't you let this one slip through thy fingers, she seems a good catch to me.'

'Grrrrran*dad*!' Ollie's normally fair complexion turned scarlet, what a nightmare. 'Ignore him, Hannah. He's already on the last loop of the roller coaster. There's some funeral directors out there just waiting for it to stop to see him off on his way to the great fairground in the sky.'

'Pay him no mind, lass. He hasn't learned to appreciate when someone special comes along.'

Josh and Rav hooted with laughter, 'Can I be best man?' Rav asked, receiving a swift kick on the shins for his trouble.

'Never mind them, Hannah.' Ollie's mum said as they assembled in the kitchen, 'Come and sit down and tell us a bit about yourself.'

Ollie howled, 'There's nothing to tell Mum. She's just a pest who's causin' me a lot of grief right now.' Laughter from Josh and Rav. 'Quit it you two, you're just makin' it worse.'

Hannah tutted, 'Pay no attention to them, Mrs Saunders. You'll know that boys lag a bit behind us girls in reaching maturity. I'll try to help Ollie grow up a bit.' Ollie spluttered in the background.

Laughing, his mum said, 'Please do. Any help would be appreciated.'

'Mum!' Ollie's peeved tone set Rav and Josh into peals of laughter again. He determined it was time to take control of the situation. 'Right! Let's get going.'

'Where to?' Rav's face was quizzical.

'We're thinkin' about down the beach for a kick about, then along to the marina to chill.'

'Mmm, well okay.' Rav's response somewhat lacking in enthusiasm, 'But I don't want to get my trainers messed up. And I've got clean jeans on.'

'Rav! You're so OCD. Chill for goodness sake.'

'Could we not just stay here and play on the Xbox?' Rav's voice pleading.

'This is to be an all computer and video games *free zone* from now until the end of the holidays.' Glancing in his mum's direction and clicking his heals together, 'By order of the Obersturmbannführermutter.'

A look of astonishment crossed Grandad's face, 'Obersturmbannführermutter! You doing World War Two in history now then?'

'No, Grandad. Video games.' Then to the others, 'So come on let's get a shift on. D'you really want to come with us, Hannah?'

'Well to be honest, it might be more interesting staying here with your Mum – and your grandad. I bet he's got lots of interesting things to share.'

If Grandad were a cat, he'd be purring louder than he snored. 'I'd like that fine lass, but I've to meet a friend down the pub tonight.' Glancing victoriously towards Ollie, he added. 'But I'll be happy to see you again if you're Ollie's girlfriend, or not.'

'Grandad! Don't encourage her. She already thinks she's somethin'. Why don't you just get back to watching the telly? What's the rivetin' programme tonight? Another of those antique programmes? One day we'll probably see you on one.'

'You might that,' Grandad protecting his dignity.

'Yeah, but as one of the antiques for sale.'

Sniffing, Grandad responded, 'Well I'd be worth a lot of money then, wouldn't I? Probably be a bidding frenzy.'

'Grandad, they'd probably get change from a pound.'
Sniggers from the direction of Rav and Josh.

'Eee Sheila lass, what're you going to do with him? No respect.'

Ollie's mum laughed, 'I've told you before Dad, you set yourself up for it.'

Hannah, grinning, said, 'Don't you worry Mr... Caldwell, is it? I'll get him sorted out for you.'

'Good luck with that then.' Ollie's mum was amused by the whole discourse, 'Right you better get moving. You got your phone, and money for the marina?'

'YES, Mum.' Ollie let out an exaggerated sigh. 'You two,' to Rav and Hannah, 'stick your bikes in the garage till we get back. We'll just walk to the beach.'

'But what time are Rav and Hannah supposed to get home?' Ollie's mum questioned. 'You better be back here by nine thirty at the latest.'

Ollie just raised his eyebrows and tutted, 'C'mon you guys. Let's get going.'

'Bye, Mrs Saunders.' Hannah beamed at Ollie's mum. 'Bye, Grandad. Hope to see you again,' giving a sparkling smile and wrinkling her nose at him.

Ollie and Josh were heading through to the garage when they heard Grandad's reply, 'You're welcome here any time, Hannah. A real pleasure to meet you. Bye for now, bonnie lass.'

Hannah stuck her tongue out at Ollie as she headed out through the garage to park her bike. Ollie, his face red, his emotions confused, grabbed a football, ushered them out then swung the door down as they headed for the beach. And trouble.

45

Chapter 8

Ollie was not joining the conversation the others were having about the upcoming holidays as they headed to the beach. His mind was in a turmoil about Hannah's forthrightness. He hoped she was just winding him up – but then – maybe a part of him hoped she wasn't. He knew for sure he was going to get ribbed mercilessly from Grandad and goodness knows what his mum would be thinking. Hannah came alongside him, 'Hey Ollie, you don't really mind me taggin' along, do you?'

'Do we have a choice?' Ollie's voice flat.

'Now, Ollie, don't be mean.' Jumping in front of him and walking backwards she continued, 'I did tell you I didn't want to be doin' all that girlie stuff, *and,* I actually think you guys are cool.' She leaned her head to one side, winked and said, 'Well nearly anyway. But hey – I can work on you all.'

'Oh, bog off Hannah! We're quite happy the way we are. And did you *have* to say all that stuff at the house? You've no idea the misery I'm going to have to put up with.'

Moving to his side, she slipped her arm through his. He flinched. 'Chill, Ollie. It was just a laugh. I think your Grandad's really cute, by the way.' She laughed unaffectedly.

'You don't have to live with him.'

'At least you've still got a grandad, Ollie. I wish I did.'

'Not one like mine!' Ollie snorted. 'He's such a pain in the bum.'

'You're exaggerating.'

'Oh really! On my thirteenth birthday, I came home from school to a big cardboard sign hangin' from my bedroom window saying, 'Happy Birthday Ollie – 13 today'.

'Well, that's nice. What's wrong with that?'

'Because he added under that, 'Teenager! Free to good home.' Then he crossed out 'good' and underneath in big letters 'ANY'.'

'Did he get any offers then?' she laughed.

'Obviously not. I'm still there.' They laughed together.

Hannah let go his arm and started to skip towards Josh and Rav. She looked back momentarily with a cheeky grin on her face, 'I wouldn't want them to think I had any favourites.'

Ollie started to relax a bit. Maybe Hannah wasn't so bad. She certainly had personality and a sense of fun. She *might*, just *might* be okay to have around. He'd have to ask the guys what they thought, though. He stopped for a moment, the sky was still cloudless, the sun's warmth little diminished from earlier in the day. The promise of a good summer, he hoped. He caught up with the others as they reached the sand dunes and followed well-worn paths to the beach.

Rav stopped suddenly, causing Hannah to bump into him. 'Yech! Sand! Sand everywhere.' He stood shaking sand from his right foot, 'Could we not have beaches without sand? Could we not just have gone straight to the marina? My trainers are full of sand.'

'Can't kick a ball about at the marina, stupid,' Ollie grouched.

'Why do we even have to kick a ball about anyway? We could've gone up to your room and hung out listening to Spotify or something. Or had a game of chess.'

'Rav, stop whinging,' Ollie said with a raised voice, 'or we'll bury you up to your neck in sand and use your head as one of the goal posts.' Then, 'Hey look.' indicating to a firm area of sand further down the beach, 'That looks like a good place, Josh, go 'n' grab a couple of stones for goal posts.'

The beach was nearly deserted apart from a game of

what looked like five aside football going on in the distance. As was usual at this time of day, a few people were walking their dogs. A couple of families, looking like they had been making a day of it on the lower parts of the dunes were starting to pack up. As the foursome headed down to the flat sand, Ollie grabbed Rav's wrist and held him back a bit. 'Rav, why on earth did you bring *her* along?' nodding in Hannah's direction. 'She could just become a pain!'

'I had no choice, Ollie. She was lurking at the top of my road and when I rode past her. She caught up with me and insisted she was coming along with us.' Rav shrugged his shoulders, his palms held out in an upwards position. 'She said we needed an outward-looking female perspective in our miserably narrow male-centred and bourgeois lives.' He shrugged again. 'Also, some backbone!'

Ollie sighed, rolled his eyes and said, 'Suddenly summer's not looking quite so bright.'

The boys selected the place they thought best for the kick about. 'Right,' Ollie said, 'let's get started. Penalties for a warmup. Okay?' He placed two stones to form goal posts. 'Hannah, you go first in goals. The other three will take six shots at goal each and the two with the most goals over all have a six-shot play-off.'

'Hey! That's a lot of work for the goalie,' An indignant Hannah complained.

'See guys,' Ollie nodding his head, 'this is what you get when you let a girl play.' Then to Hannah, 'Maybe you should have stayed home and washed your hair or played with your dollies or something. This is maybe exactly why we don't include girls. We'll *all* have to take a turn in goal.'

With her hands firmly on her hips, and an indignant look on her face, Hannah's retort came fast and spirited, 'Hey, I could outplay you guys anytime, and I would still be playing on when you were all wimpin' 'bout gettin' home to mummy for your hot milk and bedtime story. Let's play –

48

wussies!'

'So much aggression Hannah!' Ollie laughed as he led Rav and Josh away from the goals, 'Right Hannah, let's see what you're made of. You're first, then Rav, then you, Josh, and I'll go last.' Then as an afterthought, 'Oh, I think I've put the goal posts to close Josh, we need to widen them out a bit.'

Hannah scowled, 'Do your worst. But it won't be enough.'

Ollie laid another stone to mark the kick-off point.

'Hey, take it back a bit, that's too close. Give the goalie a chance to see the ball coming.' Hannah objected.

Ollie moved the stone back and called Josh and Rav into a huddle, 'Now listen guys, we know she's fit, and we know she's determined, but we don't want her to make a fool of us, so make sure you get the ball past her or she'll crow about it for the rest of our time at school. Our honour's at stake here.' The other two nodded in agreement. 'Right, Rav, go to it.'

Rav grabbed the ball and laid it to the left of the marker then walked back a few paces, stopped, turned and started to run at the ball. He was just getting there when he stumbled, did a little dance to regain his balance, and overshot the ball. Groans and disgruntled 'Rav's!' from behind, and Hannah splitting her sides with laughter in front. 'Killer shot that,' she jeered.

'Sorry guys.' Rav apologised looking shame faced. Things didn't get much better with the next five goes. Due to both his ineptitude, and Hannah's athleticism, he only managed to score once. Now in goal himself things deteriorated even further. Hannah scored five goals, Josh four and Ollie demolished him with six, his last kick sending the ball way past Rav.

Frustratingly slow, Rav was being careful as he went after the ball. More like tiptoeing quickly than running, his arms held out at shoulder height and flapping like an agitated hen who discovered she'd sat on an ice cube instead of an egg. Rav hated to get dirty so was particular to sidestep whatever he thought might mess up his trainers. Josh had once commented that Rav always looked as if he'd left home going through a human car wash, washed, scrubbed, polished and ironed, his specs sitting neatly on his nose, his hair immaculately groomed — and able to return home in the evening looking as though he had remained untouched by the dust, dirt and grime of everyday life.

'Come on Rav.' Ollie shouted in exasperation. Reaching the ball Rav picked it up and dusted off damp sand then, tucking the ball under one arm, brushed the sand from his hands with a look of such distaste it might have been pig's vomit instead of sand. 'Rav, for goodness sake get a move on.' Ollie raged.

'Patience, Ollie. Patience. As my great uncle Rashbude Abershantan always says, "Tomorrow is a new day. And tomorrow the sun will always shine, the birds will always sing, and the kangaroos will continue to jump for joy."'

'There are no kangaroos in India.' Hannah pointed out.

With a superior look on his face Rav turned to her, 'My great uncle has a world view, anyway, there are kangaroos at the Balta Rashinda Safari Park outside Delhi.'

The other three had to smile at this exchange. 'Is that even a real name anyway, Rashbude Abershantan?' Josh asked.

'It's very much a family name. My ancestors were famed noble warriors and explorers.'

Josh smiled, 'Oh, maybe that's how he saw a kangaroo. Here's another.' Feet together, he jumped on the spot three times then went into three forward flips, hands hardly touching the ground, landing firmly on the third flip, then immediately going into three backflips making great

50

clearances on both forward and backwards movements. He then stood bouncing on the spot, a pleased grin on his face.

'Wow!' Hannah applauded, 'So good kangaroo boy.'

Just then Ollie's eyes picked up on three new figures swaggering from the dunes onto the beach. Ollie hoped they wouldn't recognise the four of them and just go wherever they were going. But they stopped, Raffid Hakeem nodding in their direction, then they started heading over to where their game was. 'Trouble's comin' guys.' Ollie said quietly. Hannah, Rav and Josh looked behind them, 'Trouble! I don't see any trouble comin'.' Hannah said following Ollie's gaze. Rav slipped in behind Josh and Hannah, 'Whatever happens, just remember I'm right behind you. Or maybe we should just make a run for it.'

'I'm not running from anyone.' Defiance in Ollie's voice.

They stood their ground preparing for the worst. No strangers to local police and school inspectors, the approaching trio seen earlier by Ollie at the pedestrian crossing, had an unenviable reputation for bullying and vandalism. Ollie put himself out front of his friends squaring up to Jez Freeman, the unelected leader of the group.

'What's your problem?'

'You are twat face, you, and your nerdy friends.'

'Why? We're not bothering you.'

'You're breathin', aintchu? And you were with that decrepit excuse for a corpse this afternoon. Gonna have a go with me, was he?' He sniggered, 'Listen ya dweeb, the very fact you and your nancy-boy mates exist is enough to bother us. Ain't that right boys?' to his two companions. 'And now you've started playin' with girlies too.' He sneered and spat onto the sand.

Hannah stepped forward bristling defiance, 'You want

51

to start playin' with me knuckle head? You're not big enough, fast enough, tough enough but worst of all, you're just plain ugly.'

His face, inflamed with anger, Jez started towards Hannah just as Ollie stepped in front of him. With a snarl Jez shoved him in the chest causing him to stagger back a couple of times before regaining his balance and launching himself at the aggressor. Hannah joined in grabbing a handful of Jez's hair and kicking him in the shins. Full scale war was about to break out when Scot Pinkman glanced behind him then stopped, and shouted, 'Hold it, hold it, she's here, guys.' The other two distracted, turned to see the figure of the person referred to walking along the bottom of the dunes.

Turning back, Jez spat at the ground, 'We're not finished with you lot. Better watch your backs,' he threatened as they turned and made their way back towards to the dunes.

Ollie looking at the direction they were headed, recognised the T shirt the girl was wearing. Green with long, mustard-coloured sleeves.

Chapter 9

'I know that girl.' The other three following Ollie's gaze to the figure standing waiting as Jez, Raffid and Scot headed in her direction. 'I saw her this afternoon up Dalton's Mount.'

'But you don't actually *know* her?' Rav queried, a quizzical expression on his face.

'No. No, I mean I *saw* her outside some cottages on Dalton's Mount.'

Josh joined the questioning, 'Dalton's Mount! What were you doin' up there? Thought you were goin' to the dentist.'

'For some reason my grandad wanted to take a detour that way to get home. The long cut! He was havin' a nosey at the pigeon place. Don't ask.'

'Well, why's she meeting up with that lot down here? How did she fall in with them?' Hannah demanded.

With a look of exasperation Ollie snapped, 'How would I know? Am I the All Knowing One?'

'No. That would be God you're talking about. And since you're not, why don't we go check it out?' she challenged.

'Go check it out! Just go and demand to know what they're up to? That the plan then Hannah?'

Annoyed, Hannah said, 'Don't be a complete prat Ollie, of course not! But it looks like they're goin' to be goin' into the dunes, so what are they up to in there?'

'Don't ask, Hannah. We might not want to know.' Rav answered quickly, reluctant to become involved.

Hannah, doing the hands on her hips thing again said, 'Wow, you lot have got a serious case of woosievitus! Man up for goodness sake. Whatever they're up to, it's not going to be on the top of the dunes. They're goin' to go in there to be hidden from view, which means they've got *something* to hide.' She looked each one in the eye in turn. 'And... we want to know what it is. *Don't we?*'

'Good luck then, Hannah.' The measured response from ultra-cautious Rav.

'Oh, for goodness sake. Ollie! You and me can get up close to the top of the dunes and scout around to see where they are, and what they're up to, hopefully without them seein' us.'

'Okay, you're right Hannah,' Ollie acknowledged his agreement, 'But we're goin' to have to be careful. Josh, you and Rav grab the ball and start headin' to the marina and we'll catch up asap.'

'You sure, Ollie?' Josh asked, concern in his voice.

'Yeah, it'll be okay,' then, with an exaggerated upwards roll of his eyes added, 'I've got Hannah to look after me.'

The four started walking towards the dunes, and as they got closer Josh and Rav veered away heading for the marina. Getting closer to the dunes Hannah stopped and grabbed at Ollie's T shirt, 'Hug me Ollie,' she demanded.

With a look of shocked surprise Ollie spluttered, 'What! Why? Get lost you.'

'Don't be so stupid. It's so you can be lookin' over my shoulder and see what's goin' on.'

Seeing the sense in her demands Ollie took her into his arms.

'Tighter, Ollie. Look as though you mean it.'

Ollie squeezed her more tightly.

She giggled, 'Oh Ollie, you're quite a squeeze.'

'Shut up you.' Ollie's face reddening while he watched carefully as Jez and his mates grouped in an earnest conversation with the girl. Raffid was gesticulating about something and the girl was responding by shaking her head. He then moved closer to her shouting, though from a distance Ollie couldn't make out what it was about. Then Scot Pinkman grabbed Raffid's arm and drew him away in an effort to calm him down. The girl said something and nodded her head towards the dunes. The three huddled in conversation, then nodded to her before following her.

Ollie let go of Hannah saying, 'They're moving into the dunes.'

'Quick, let's get up there and see what's goin' on.' Hannah turned and started sprinting towards the dunes.

Ollie, following, had cause to remember Hannah's reputation in athletic prowess as she widened the gap between them. Stopping behind her at the dunes Ollie speaking in a low voice said, 'Okay, we're goin' to have to be careful. I don't think they'll have gone too far in. Let's go this way,' pointing to a pathway through the dunes other than the one Jez and his gang had taken. 'Quick.' Ollie urged as they scrambled up the path hoping to get beyond where T shirt girl was leading the boys.

'Quick' was not the best description to use for trying to make haste in sand dunes, especially as they had to climb having to grab hold of patches of rough grass, at the same time trying not to let their feet slip away. Hannah, the lighter and more agile made better progress than Ollie and, on nearing the top of the dunes, waved him to keep quiet. Carefully raising her head above the crest of the dune she turned nodding her head in the negative and started back down, 'Nothin' doin'. Let's get further along.'

When they began to ascend the third dune, as they neared the top, they could hear voices on the other side. 'It's them.' Ollie warned, recognised Jez Freeman's raised voice. 'Careful,' his voice now a whisper as they sought some kind of camouflage to enable them to look over. Half a metre to their left some weedy looking seaside plants intermingled with clumps of long grass seemed to offer some kind of cover. They skittered across the sand and settled behind the meagre cover.

Jez Freeman, Raffid Hakeem and Scot Pinkman were

standing in a loose circle with the girl, who, now that they were close, could see only looked about fourteen of fifteen. Their age. Her naturally curly blonde hair looked unkempt and dirty, likewise the green and mustard top and ragged jeans. Though it looked like the boys were trying to intimidate her, she remained unbowed. Even from their sheltered position Ollie and Hannah perceived a hardness of features in one so young.

Jez Freeman stepped closer to the girl, 'Listen bitch, you're askin' twice as much as the first couple of times, so you can just take a hike, we ain't no mugs, we'll find someone else.'

Hannah, always the perfectionist, tutted quietly and whispered, 'A double negative,' to Ollie, who looked at her as though she'd just announced she was the Queen of Sheba in a tutu.

The girl held her ground unflinchingly, 'That's the way it is guys. And you *won't* find someone else because my friends are gonna make sure there is no competition. We're gonna be the one stop shop for your needs. And you *are* gonna need.' She stood tight lipped her gaze never wavering. 'You want the stuff or not? Get a move on. I've a customer base to build in this dump.'

Ollie and Hannah were astounded at her brazenness. The three boys were, as Rav used to say, a legend in their own lunchtime, renowned in school for bullying and often suspended for bad mouthing teachers. They were, all three, at least a head taller than the girl, but she stood square-on, defiant and confident.

'Just a minute,' Jez said, taking the other two by the arm and moving them out her earshot. All Ollie and Hannah could hear was indistinct murmurings as they made their decision. 'Right, okay.' Jez said as the three joined her again, 'But we've got a proposition.'

'A proposition,' she mimicked.

'Yeah. You're actin' pretty tough, but then you don't really know who you're dealing with.'

She looked at Jez with disdain, 'Neither do you. And believe me, you don't want to get on the wrong side of those guys.'

'No, what I'm sayin' is, most of the kids at school are shit scared of us. We could help you drum up some business, then make sure we're on top of things at school. Be enforcers like.'

The girl looked thoughtful. 'I'll get back to you on that one, but first, you want the stuff or not?'

'Yeah, right, you gonna' bring the price down after my proposition?'

'Not for me to say. You want it or not? 'cause if not, you're wastin' my time and I'm outa here.'

Jez turned to the other two holding his hand out. They both dug into their pockets bringing notes out. Jez took them, added his and handed it to her. She went into the back pocket of her jeans and handed over three small packages wrapped in something like cling-film, one to each of them. They snatched the packages furtively and stuck them in their jeans' pockets.

Just then Hannah's phone rang.

A look of panic momentarily crossed both Hannah and Ollie's faces as she dug the phone out from her back pocket and switched it off. At the same time, they simultaneously rolled onto their backs, skittered down the dune, their legs and arms working like pistons, the angry and frustrated shouts of their three antagonists adding propulsion to their efforts.

'Don't let them get away,' Jez's angry voice spurring the other two on in their attempts to climb the dune. Curses rose from behind the sand dune as progress for the trio was frustrating. A case of the harder they tried, the less advancement they made.

Having reached a path, and a slightly firmer footing, Ollie pushed Hannah in front of himself, urging her forward. 'Up to the road,' he gasped. 'We'll outrun them if we can get there.' Glancing behind he was relieved there was no sign of Jez and the others yet.

'We could try to hide.' Hannah gasped, frantically weaving her way up the uneven path.

'Not enough time. Keep going.' A breathless Ollie knew there were going to be repercussions from what they'd witnessed. The police visit to school had only reinforced what they had already heard about drug dealing on the grapevine. High schools thrived on gossip, the more extreme the more satisfying.

Hannah yelped as her left ankle twisted beneath her. She turned to Ollie, pain etched on her face, that then turned into a look of panic, 'Ollie! Behind you.'

Ollie looked behind to see a snarling Scot Pinkman gaining on them. He moved quickly to Hannah's side throwing her left arm over his shoulder and his right arm round her waist. He urged her on, already conscious that their efforts were probably not enough to escape their adversary. Their restricted progress was a major handicap, so he removed Hannah's arm from his shoulder urging her to keep going while he tried to divert Pinkman. Giving her a gentle push forward he turned to face the approaching bully. Quickly scanning the surrounding dunes for a possible way of escape, he noticed the dune to his right was covered with a good bit of scrub. Good handholds.

'Come on then, monkey brain, let's see how fit you are.' He gibed, noticing his adversary was already beginning to flag. He then started to scramble up the dune, grabbing at the scrubby plants and grasses, praying that they'd take his weight.

He was about two thirds of the way up when Scot Pinkman, breathing heavily and mouthing oaths, started the ascent behind him. Ollie put more effort into his climb; scrambling and grabbing at whatever could stabilise himself, even if some had a nasty sting. The top of the dune, now less than half a metre away when, with a determined, but wheezing effort, Pinkman manage to grab hold of Ollie's right ankle. Panicking, Ollie lashed out with his left foot trying to loosen Pinkman's grip, only to be met with grunts, oaths and threats of terrible violence. The kick had made Pinkman tighten his grip, but in Ollie's attempts to break free his trainer came off in Pinkman's grip. He managed to twist round so that he was on his back. Pinkman was now using two hands, one over the other, trying to either pull Ollie down, or to clamber up towards him, whichever so as to inflict some serious pain. Ollie pulled back his left leg, bending it at the knee and with a grunt, straight legged it into Pinkman's face with as much power as he could manage. The grip on his right leg loosened as Pinkman fell back, blood gushing from his nose and his mouth. Quick as flash Ollie slid down to retrieve his trainer. Pinkman scrambled onto his hands and knees promising untold suffering to Ollie, if not now, certainly in the future. He started to rise unsteadily, using the bottom of his T shirt to try to stem the blood from his mouth. Ollie hopped about on one leg to pull on his trainer and, having done so, scooped up two hands full of sand and flung them in Pinkman's face. Pinkman screamed, staggering about, blinded and spluttering, cursing as the sand mixed with the blood in his mouth, greatly increasing his agony. Ollie, his heart pounding, his mouth dry, took off up the path, knowing that he had now made a real enemy, or more probably, three *real* enemies.

On reaching the road, Ollie stopped momentarily to catch his breath and to consider his options. He knew they had opened a hornet's nest and that now summer might not pan out the way they'd been planning. But he was relieved to see that Hannah must have made good progress hobbling to the marina. He heard the angry voices of Jez and Raffid who, now having caught up with Scot, were berating him for letting Hannah and Ollie get away. Hearing them acted as a spur to Ollie, so whilst they were caught up arguing, with a sigh of relief, he started jogging towards the marina.

Chapter 10

Keeping an eye out behind him, Ollie was relieved the three antagonists hadn't bothered chasing him. 'But why should they?' he thought. 'They know they can get me at school. And there's still two days left till we break up.' Slowing his pace as he neared the marina, he guessed Hannah's twisted ankle wasn't too serious so that she'd been able to make it here safely. He slowed to a brisk walk, taking in the scene before him.

He approached the marina coming past the exclusive private yacht club, highlighting its exclusivity by being surrounded with high metal railed fencing and tall metal locked gates, no riff-raff allowed in there then. He had always loved this place, the smells, the clinking of the mastheads on the tethered yachts as they lay secured in their designated dock. The sound of water gently lapping against their hulls. The sight of the big powerful cabin cruisers, the toys of the wealthy.

Moving past some restaurants, he crossed over the metal walkway covering the first of two sets of huge gates that would open to let the boats in or out of the marina.

The whole area had been redeveloped from being dirty docks for industrial use, to become a social hangout. A place of coffee shops, bars, restaurants and music venues. On a warm night such as it was, the place was busy. Lots of people strolling or leaning against the safety rails, some pointing out things of interest, or to a particular boat. People sitting round tables outside bars relaxing with coffee, a meal, a cold beer or chilled wine and a lot of laughter. Parents with children licking big ice cream cones. Posers cruising slowly in flash cars blaring loud music. Girls looking for boys, boys looking for girls. And Ollie was glad to be here.

His phone beeped, a message, from Hannah, 'u k? X'. The kiss jumped out at him like a slavering creature of unknown intent. Why was the kiss 'X' in upper case? Okay, he thought, maybe it was intentional. Was she just teasing him, or was it something she always put on her messages? He sent a reply, 'Yep.' No kiss. Then he called Josh, 'Hi, is Hannah with you?'

'Yeah, Rav and me hung about at the marina's sea gates till she came.' Then with a note of concern, 'How're you? Did they follow you?'

'Nah, I managed to get away. I'm at the marina now. Where are you?'

'We're at the Captain's Bridge, at the back.'

'Okay, be there in a mo.' Though Ollie knew the place, the Captain's Bridge would be hard to miss with a big neon sign of a ships steering wheel on its roof proclaiming its presence. It was a place they would sometimes meet up. The owner always had funky music going on in the background and was happy for younger teenagers to hang out in the earlier evenings so long as they did not get riotous. The back of the building was raised to resemble a ship's bridge and had huge picture windows looking out to sea. Set near the window was a genuine old ships wheel on a raised block of wood for children to stand on to pretend they were steering a ship. When Ollie entered the bridge area, Hannah stood up at one of the tables in front of the windows gesticulating for him to join them.

Josh and Rav were sitting on one side of the table, Hannah sitting opposite. Ollie slid in beside her. Rav was quick to ask what had happened, how he'd got away.

Hannah, a concerned look on her face, and putting a hand on his arm asked if he was okay. Ollie said he was fine but went on to tell them about what had happened with Scot Pinkman.

'You did what to him?' A shocked Rav blurted, 'Man...

you're dead meat.'

'Well, I'm not gonna be his, or their, favourite buddy of the month that's for sure. But it's all I could do. I'm just lucky the other two were slow in catchin' up.'

'Oh Ollie!' Hannah squeezed his arm.

Josh, speaking in a low voice, and looking directly at Ollie, joined the conversation 'I guess that's war then.'

'Looks like it, Josh, but hey, we'll worry about that later. Hannah, how's your ankle?'

'Yeah, it's good, eased up when I got to the road.'

'Good. I'm gonna get a shake. Anyone want anything?'

'Nah, we're good.' The other three were more anxious to talk about the drug deal in the dunes. Hannah had already told them about the exchange Ollie and she had witnessed. After which, Rav had been emphatic that he was not getting caught up in any of that stuff.

Ollie returned with his drink and slid in beside Hannah again. 'You know what we witnessed there, Hannah?'

'Yep. A drug deal for sure.'

'I'm not getting involved.' Rav reaffirmed quickly, looking decidedly uncomfortable.

'Yeah, you've said Rav.' A note of sarcasm in Josh's voice.

Ollie continued, 'I don't think there could be any doubt that's what it was. Definitely drugs, and these guys are not happy we saw them buying, and with Ollie giving Pinkman a kickin', you know they're gonna be comin' after us.'

'Shouldn't we report it to the police, anonymously of course, and just leave it to them?' Rav looked at Ollie hopefully.

Ollie thought for a moment, 'We could, but they'd have gotten rid of the stuff by the time the police got to them. More worrying is that they've offered to start dealing at school and to control the supply. And... she only looks about fourteen or fifteen, sixteen at most, told you I saw her this afternoon skulking about up Dalton's Mount. She shot out of sight when my grandad slowed down a bit to have a nosey.'

'I think we should tell the police.' Rav chipped in again. 'She's like what the police spoke about this morning.'

'Not at the moment, Rav, we've nothing solid to give them. But that girl — boy she's a hard-nosed piece of work — wouldn't want to cross her.'

Hannah joined in the conversation, 'Listen, Ollie, Jez and his guys aren't *that* much bigger than us. Ollie, you'll be as tall as Raffid Hakeem and you do play rugby. They may think Josh is soft because he's doin' ballet. Sorry Josh, you know what I mean. But you're probably fitter and stronger than these three put together, and Rav...' her voice trailed off then picked up again, 'Well Rav's got a techy know how look, and you never know when that might come in handy.'

'That's true,' Rav agreed. 'But I still don't want to get involved.'

Ollie leaned over the table and gripped his wrist, 'It's okay, Rav, we'll look after you.'

'I still don't like it.'

'But there's me too, Rav,' Hannah assured him, 'No one better mess with me 'cause I can kick ass when I have to.'

'Oh yeah, what *actually* happened in the dunes then superwomen? Leaving Ollie to stand alone. Run into some kryptonite, did you?' Rav's sarcastic response.

Hannah shot him a look fit to frazzle an iceberg. Instantly and completely. 'Have you never heard the saying, "discretion is the better part of valour"?'

'Do you maybe spell that, c...o...w...e...r...d...i...c...e?'

'Well, you'd obviously know more about cowardice than me, but not how to spell it. 'It's "A" not "E".'

'Okay you two, cool it,' Ollie cut in.

Rav scowled and came back with all kinds of excuses to

64

have them avoid interfering in things that, in his opinion, were best left alone.

'Enough Rav!' Ollie cut in, 'That's all just bum fluff and snot balls and you know it.'

Hannah burst out laughing, 'Bum fluff and snot balls?' she shrieked. 'What?'

Ollie and Josh were nodding and smiling, 'Just a couple of irritating little things it's necessary to get rid of sometimes. Rav's becoming a pain. He's putting up all kinds of stupid suggestions we don't even need to consider. Like I said, all bum fluff and snot balls.'

'Yuck! That's disgusting,' Hannah said, a look of distaste on her face then, turning to Rav, she said, 'But they're right Rav. We have to figure out what to do.'

'Going to the police might be a good place to start.' Rav remained unmoved.

'One thing's for sure.' Josh took a deep breath before continuing, 'This could get serious, maybe even dangerous, maybe we should go to the police.' Then as an afterthought, 'Or even tell our parents. Well, *your* parents anyway.'

Ollie shook his head, 'No Josh, if we told them about this stuff, stuff we don't really know enough about yet, they'd probably insist on grounding us to keep us safe.'

Rav, alarmed at the prospect, added, 'Mine sure would.'

Glancing at the clock on the wall, Ollie suggested they make a move as Hannah and Rav had to get back to his place to pick up their bikes. 'We'll take the back way just in case Jez and crew are hangin' about in the centre of town.'

Before leaving the marina, they headed over to look at the boats, leaning over safety rails to take in the scene. With the sun setting, the whole vista was bathed in a warm pink glow, and, with a pale moon already rising, Hannah nudged Ollie's arm, 'Romantic ain't it?' she smiled demurely.

Ollie made some gruff, non-committal noises before

suggesting they got a move on. Setting out to take the longer route back to his home, Ollie admitted it was a bit of a bummer, but that they were going to need some time to work out what they were going to do about what they'd seen, reluctantly conceding that the police might be the best solution. Maybe he should have a word with Grandad.

They passed through some of the quieter residential streets of the old town. Turning off the main street, they climbed a fairly steep cobbled alley that would take them back onto the road they'd taken from the beach earlier. Reaching the main road Ollie made a point of walking with Josh, leaving Hannah and Rav following a little behind. The road descended gently, an old stone-built wall on their left hiding the remains of a now defunct boat building yard. When the sound of raised voices came up to them, Josh stopped suddenly. Ollie looked at him questioningly.

In a low and urgent voice, Josh said, 'That's Eddie! I'm pretty sure it's him.' More heated exchanges went on, the other voice that of a female. Pointing to a tree on the other side the wall a couple of metres away, Josh asked Ollie to help him up so that he could use the foliage as cover so as to see what was happening. Tucking the football against the wall, Ollie cupped his hands with fingers entwined. Josh put his left foot in the makeshift stirrup and was lifted up to see over the wall. What he saw made him gasp.

'What?' Ollie's voice low and urgent.

'It's the girl on the beach!' Josh whispered, 'Eddie's got a tight grip on her shoulder and she's fighting and hissing like a cornered cat. They're havin' a real set to.'

'I can hear that, but what's she got to do with Eddie?'

'Dunno... but wait... he's saying somethin' about bein' on his patch.'

She raised her voice in a scornful response, 'Your patch! Maybe yesterday, but now it's mine.' She spat.

Eddie grabbed her hair, and pulling her head back with

such violence, she cried out, 'Yours? Yours you little bitch? You'll be needin' patched by the time I'm finished with you. You think I don't know about slipping brats like you into new territories? If you county liners think you're goin' to take over here, you're goin' to be disappointed. You tell your handlers to stay outa this place, and you, on your bike or I'll really sort you.' He gave her face a resounding slap.

'You're a dead man, a dead man who's goin' to get fed to the fishes,' she spat at him.

'Yeah right. You got some of your girlie friends helpin' you?'

'Nothin' girlie about the people I'm workin' for, you prat.'

Eddie let go, only for the girl to launch herself at him, punching, scratching and kicking like a thing possessed.

Hannah and Rav had stopped and stood silently beside Ollie, curiosity etched into their faces. 'What's happenin'?' Hannah questioned.

Ollie shushed her, 'Just wait.'

Josh, already shocked at what was going on, was even more so when Eddie, grabbing the front of the girl's T shirt tightly in his fist, shoved her with such force against the wall, she cried out in pain. Dragging her away from the wall again he gave her a resounding back handed slap to the side of her face causing her to stagger a couple of steps backwards before crumpling to the ground, blood pouring from her nose. He then moved close to her, and Josh had to stop himself from shouting out, as Eddie drove a series of kicks into the girl's side, causing her to howl in pain. Josh was horrified. This was the man his mother had living with her, the man who shared the same house as his little sister. Shaken, he indicated to Ollie he was coming down.

Ollie could see Josh was upset and was quick to voice his concern, demanding to know what was going on.

'Things are way worse than I realised,' Josh said, a look

of shock and bewilderment on his face. 'Maybe we *should* phone the police.'

'No, not yet Josh. If she is what we think she is, she's not goin' to co-operate with the cops, and the police showing an interest would probably make things worse for her.'

Visibly agitated, Rav once again said they should get the police involved.

'No! Not just now,' Ollie insisted. 'We have to be careful, that guy's Josh's mum's partner.'

'Really?' Hannah exclaimed.

'Yeah. C'mon, let's get out of here before he knows that we know what he's up to.' Josh said as he started off down the road. With a mixture of apprehension and tension written all over his face he continued, 'But we don't really know *what* he's up to yet. I suspected Eddie was involved in drugs and what I just heard confirms it, but how, and has it got anything to do with the Dalton's Mount set-up? He does drive over to France with pigeons for them. He calls it the pigeon run. And what did he mean about "his patch"?'

'Well, we'll make it our business to find out. C'mon, let's move.' Ollie urged again, passing the ball to Rav for safe keeping. All four of them began to walk quickly. Ollie was deeply concerned for Josh and what he'd just seen, and angry at the naked brutality Josh had described to the others. He doubted things were going to end well. The question was — for whom?

Chapter 11

Josh was quiet as they made their way back to Ollie's house, his stomach in knots, still in shock by what he had just seen. The other three tried to commiserate and give some encouragement but Josh was not really taking it in. His mind in a turmoil, his first instinct was to grab his stuff and go home to protect Nicola and his mum but realised there would be questions about why he had come home so soon, and anyway, because of her growing dependence on Eddie, he could not be sure if his mum would still blindly support him. Questions would be asked that might be difficult to answer. Also, having seen Eddie's violence he did not want that unleashed on his family, but for sure he knew he needed to find a way to get Eddie away from them.

On nearing his home Ollie warned them to say nothing about what had happened on the dunes, and especially, nothing about the violence behind the boatyard wall. 'We'd just be opening a can of worms that we definitely don't want squirming about making life awkward and restricting our freedoms.'

Hannah, wanting to offer Josh some support, moved up beside him and slipped her arm through his, 'Hey, Josh. You know we're here for you.'

Ollie was surprised to feel a twinge of... what? Jealousy? 'Yeah, Josh already knows that, Hannah, and you hardly know him anyway,' surprising himself by how peevish he sounded.

'Oh,' Rav joined in sniggering, 'Is that the green-eyed monster then?'

'Shut up, Rav.'

'Now, now boys, no fighting. We've got enough to deal with, and we *all* need to be helping, Josh. Right?'

'I've always been there for him, Hannah, and that's not

goin' to change now.' Taking out his front door key, Ollie reminded them again to say nothing and just act normal. 'Hi, we're home,' he shouted as he opened the door ushering the others through first, 'Just head for the kitchen and we can go through and get your bikes. Rav, pass me the ball.'

Ollie's mum appeared from the sitting room, 'You're back quick. Everything alright?'

'Of course, Mum, but Hannah and Rav have got to bike home before it gets too dark.'

'You want a bite to eat first?'

Hannah quickly pulled her phone from her back pocket, glancing at the time she nodded, 'That would be great, Mrs Saunders, if it's no trouble.'

'No trouble at all, let's get into the kitchen,' she said, ushering them along the hallway.

The age of the building with small windows and thick walls meant, though the kitchen was cosy, later in the day daylight struggled to brighten the room. Putting the light on, Ollie's mum's inquiry if anyone fancied some French toast was met with unanimous approval. As she started preparing, she asked what they'd been up to. A swift glance passed between the four as Ollie answered, 'Just a kick about at the beach, then a wander to the marina. Nothin' much really.'

Josh, unsurprisingly, was looking dejected and fretful so Hannah jumped up and said, 'C'mon, Josh, teach me how to become a ballerina.'

Josh looked startled, 'In five minutes!'

'No, you idiot, just give me some basic moves. You never know, I might be good at it and join your ballet class,'

'There's not enough room in here.' Ollie cut in sharply.

'No, it's okay, Ollie. Mrs Saunders, do you mind if I move the table up a bit and shift Grandad's chair?' Josh asked, relieved to be doing something to take his mind of the evening's events.

Ollie's mum laughed, 'As long as you don't break anything.' And as an afterthought, 'Or damage Hannah.'

'Damage Hannah?' Rav laughed, 'I don't think there's much fear of that, Mrs Saunders. Be better to warn Hannah not to damage Josh – or the kitchen!'

Josh went to the heavy table calling on Ollie to give a hand then moved Grandad's old worn leather armchair to make some room at the bottom of the kitchen. 'Right, Hannah, shoes off and come and stand here. Don't worry Mrs S, there's not going to be any leaping, jumping or pirouettes, I'm just goin' to show Hannah the first five basic positions.'

Hannah moved to stand in front of Josh, 'Right, Hannah, first position in ballet is a position of the feet where a dancer's standing with their heels together and toes facing out equally to either side.' Hannah giggled as she complied with the instructions, 'No, a bit further, ninety degrees from your torso. Keeping your legs straight.' Moving to kneel in front of her he made minor adjustments to her stance, then standing back he said, 'Feet and legs need to be equally turned out.' He demonstrated. 'Now – hold your arms out in front of you as though you're holding a beach ball into your stomach with your fingertips towards each other without actually touching.' He ran his hands down her arms moving them into the correct position, stepping back he nodded, 'Perfect.'

Hannah smiled looking pleased with herself. Ollie glowered.

'Now,' Josh went on, 'the second position's quite similar to first, but with your feet about hip distance apart. And what I said for the first position's true for the second, remember? Where you want to have your feet and legs equally turned out.' Hannah adjusted her posture, 'No, bring your legs closer. It's important not to have your

71

second position too wide that it's not useful, or too narrow that it looks closer to a first position. Shoulders back, Hannah, neck stretched with your chin up.' Hannah was looking quite pleased with herself.

'Nice, Hannah,' Rav encouraged her.

Ollie, though having limited knowledge about ballet sensed that Hannah might actually have something. There was a fluidity and grace. She was such an enigma; tough and feisty, gentle and empathetic, asking Josh to show her ballet moves, taking his mind, however briefly, of the things they'd seen and done tonight.

'Okay,' Josh said taking hold of Hannah's arms, 'the second position of the arms in ballet's kinda like the second position with the feet. It looks very much like first, but is open.' Josh demonstrated then moved Hannah's arms from the first position to open them at the elbows, only moving them slightly back a couple inches. Moving away from her he said, 'Now Hannah, keep the same shape of the entire arm, so that your elbows are higher than your hands with your hands ever so slightly tilted upwards.'

'Like this, Josh?'

'Yep! The key to a great second position is to remember to keep your hands below your elbows and not open them too wide. A proper second position's placed just slightly in front of your body.' Josh made some slight adjustments, 'For a nice looking second position of the arms Hannah, you'll also want to try to keep them slightly rounded; not quite as rounded as first, but still rounded so you're making a slightly curved shape.' Josh stood back scrutinising Hannah's stance and, nodding his head, said, 'You know I think you could make a ballerina girl.'

'Yes, but not tonight,' Ollie's mum said laying plates on the table, 'Who wants tea or coffee or juice? The toast's nearly ready, clean hands everyone.'

Ollie groaned. 'The bathrooms just out the hall first left

Hannah, lights a cord just as you go in.'

'S' okay, I'm good. Hey Josh, you'll have to give me more lessons, I could get interested. Somethin' I never thought of doin'.'

'Well, you'd be super fit, and super strong. Unlike what some people may think, ballet ain't for wimps.' Josh raised himself on to his toes and went into a neat pirouette.

'Show off!' Hannah laughed.

'Right, I'll leave you to it.' Ollie's mum said, then glancing at the wall clock added, 'Ollie, remember the time for Rav and Hannah. They've to bike home and it's going to be dark soon.'

'Yes, Mum,' Strong emphasis on the 'yes', 'they won't be long.'

Settling round the table they sat looking at one another for a couple of minutes before Ollie said, 'Well, this has sure been some night.' The others nodded in agreement, 'Where do we go from here?'

'The police,' Rav jumped in quickly.

'Yeah, Rav, you're probably right, but...' he hesitated, 'but there are implications we need to think about for Josh and his family.'

Rav shook his head, 'There's implications for us too.'

Hannah reached out and put her hand on top of Josh's, 'Rav — we've got to help Josh, how would you feel if it was you and your family?' then as an afterthought, 'What words of wisdom would great uncle Rashbude Abershantan share with us, d'you think?'

Without hesitation Rav came back with, 'Go to the police. Immediately!'

Ollie turned to him, 'Rav, maybe we will have to go to the police, but not right now, so give it a rest. And please do *not* go and blab about what's happened tonight to anybody. And that means anybody!' Turning to Hannah, he he asked her to also keep things to herself.

'For sure,' she affirmed, and with a determined look said, 'But Josh, Ollie's right, and we *are* going to help you. If we have to go to the police then we'll have to, but let's dig about and see if we can get something more before we do.'

Josh was thankful for the support but was also concerned that he might end up getting his friends into trouble, or even worse, into danger, 'Thanks guys, Ollie 'n me 'll talk things through and see what we can come up with. In a way I agree with Rav, maybe we should go to the police, but what would we say? We don't have anything tangible we can give 'em. So, I certainly want to do a bit more digging before I'd go to them, but more, my biggest concern's for my little sister.'

Hannah patted Josh's hand again, 'Well I'm with you, Josh.'

'You *know* I'm gonna back you, Josh.' Ollie said, 'And Rav, we really are gonna need you, and maybe your big bro too, he's a real techy, isn't he?'

'Yeah, but don't mention the word geek near him, he has noble ideals. He prefers to be thought of as someone of high intellect with an ability to use science and technology to further the good of mankind. At a price!'

The noise of a car door being slammed outside drew their attention, 'Must be Grandad, but he's back early.' Ollie said, 'Taxi's must be cheaper at this time of night.' They heard the front door open, then Grandad called out, 'I'm home.'

'Yes, we heard, Grandad.'

'I guess we should be going, Hannah.' Rav started to rise.

'Just a minute, Rav,' Grandad said as he came into the kitchen, 'Your brother's into science stuff, isn't he?'

A questioning furrow on Rav's brow, and a tentative reply, 'Yes. Why?'

'Well, I just heard of the most amazing new product

74

scientists have invented.' Grandad stood a with befuddled look dawning on his face, 'Oh, but can a liquid be called a scientific invention?'

'More like a discovery probably,' Rav ventured, 'We know that oil and water don't mix. But a French inventor, Bruno Berge, I think he was called, well he invented the liquid lens that combines these liquids in a closed cylinder shaped into an optical lens.'

They all looked at Rav in amazement. 'What?' he demanded, 'I'm just interested in that kinda stuff.'

Ollie said, 'Must run in the family then. Grandad, what was this invention you were talkin' about?'

'Well this American scientist has invented, or produced, this liquid that can melt anything! Absolutely anything!'

Josh looking particularly impressed said, 'Wow that's amazing.'

'Aye. But there's only one problem... they can't find anything to put it in.' He burst into laughter at the look on their faces.

'Yeah, right, Grandad. I should know better by now,' Ollie shook his head, then addressed the others, 'Right guys, Hannah and Rav you better make tracks. Josh 'n me will talk through some stuff tonight and give you a call tomorrow. Okay?'

They both said that was fine.

'Eee, lass, are you going so soon?' A forlorn look on Grandad's face.

'Yes, but don't worry, Grandad, I'll see you again soon.' Hannah smiled a sweet smile. 'And Josh, you need to give me more ballet lessons, think I might enjoy that.'

Ollie took them through to the garage and helped them out with their bikes. 'See you then.'

'Yep. C'mon, Hannah, let's go.' Rav sounded tetchy as he rode out onto the road.

Hannah, leaned in towards Ollie and planted a kiss on his cheek then mounted her bike, 'Bye, Ollie.' A coy smile on her face. 'Don't be jealous, I'm just trying to help Josh.'

Ollie was speechless, sure his face must be scarlet as he turned back into the garage pulling the overhead door closed behind him. He touched the spot Hannah had kissed. His cheek burned.

Chapter 12

Ollie stood in the garage for a few minutes, his mind in turmoil trying to compute the day's events. Violence, revelations, threats, drugs and, on top of all that, the uncertainty of knowing if Hannah was just toying with him or if she was being serious. And if she was, how should he respond? If at all! Things were going way too fast.

Taking a deep breath, he opened the door into the kitchen. His mother, washing up the supper dishes, turned to look at him. 'Everything okay?'

'Yeah, fine mum.'

'What kept you?' A mischievous look on her face.

'What d'you mean? Nothing kept me.' Ollie blustered, conscious that Josh and grandad seemed to be taking a keen and amused interest in the proceedings.

'Oh! Is that you blushing now?' Grandad not missing a trick.

'No! It's just a stupid question that's all.'

'Mmm... it did seem to take a while for Hannah to leave.' His mum toying with him like a cat with a mouse whose fate was almost certain.

'No, she left right away. I was just trying to figure out some stuff for a few minutes,' then quickly added, 'before Grandad starts messin' with my head.'

'Figure out some stuff! What stuff have you got to figure out?'

'It's nothing, Mum. Just stuff.' And quickly trying to change the subject inquired of his grandad what he'd found out from Ernie Broadbend about the Dalton's Mount pigeon loft man.

Grandad rose from his armchair and, taking a seat at the table, beckoned the boys to join him. 'You can join us too, Sheila, you might find it interesting.'

'No, I'm just going to bed, I've got an early start in the morning, the animals can't feed themselves. I'll see how Kukooru's doing, and we need to be getting organised for the new young elephant's arrival next week. Poor thing, I think it'll find the south coast of England winters a lot cooler than the Chobe National Park in Botswana. And I hope Motty doesn't try to bully her, she's getting old, arthritic and crochety and might not take kindly to new young company. So, it's a busy time, not helped with school holidays coming up. It's been bad enough since the Scottish schools got their holidays, but it really starts taking off now. We might even get extra visitors with Kukooru being on the news.'

'Aye, I've no doubt they'll be putting the prices up then.' The curmudgeonly comment from Grandad.

'Right, I'm going up. And boys,' putting the "I'm being serious" face on, 'don't lie awake all night yapping, or playing on computers.' Getting no affirmation, she demanded, 'You hear me?'

Ollie's phone beeped, the audience of three giving him unremitting attention as he pulled it from his pocket. Looking at it he blushed — Hannah! Who else? He opened the message, a request to know what was happening tomorrow.

'Well!' His mum stood, arms folded, head cocked to one side, a smile playing around her mouth, 'Who might be contacting you at this time of night Oliver?'

'Hannah.'

'Oh, this *is* getting serious. Is she inviting you for tea to meet her dad?'

'Mum, give it a rest.'

'Okay, but remember what I said, no blathering till the wee hours. I've to get up for work tomorrow.'

Ollie sighed and rolled his eyes, 'Right Mum. Gotcha. Goodnight.'

78

'Right Dad, you heard me. Don't you keep them up blathering either.'

'Me?' Grandad put on his offended look then winked at the boys.

'Yes, you. Right, goodnight.'

'So, Grandad, what did you find out?'

'A lot more than I thought I would. It seems that the guy at Dalton's Mount, Ronnie Macintosh is his name, a big Glaswegian, is pretty big in racing pigeon circles. He's had lots of successes and made a lot of money out it.'

'Outa racing pigeons?' Ollie sounding sceptical, asked, 'What kinda money's in pigeon racing?'

'Well now laddie, would a million dollars impress you?'

'A million dollars? A million! Where? America?'

'South Africa. Every year South Africa hosts the Million Dollar Race. What did Ernie call it again?' Grandad sat staring into the distance and stroking his chin. 'Yeah... it's The Sun City Million Dollar Race, and Ernie says over four thousand birds from twenty-three countries compete for a share of the one point three-million-dollar pot.'

'One-point-three million dollars!' Ollie was shocked. 'In pigeon racing!'

A low whistle from Josh, 'Wow! Unbelievable.'

'Yes. There's other big money races, but that's the biggest by far. There's the, what was it again? Aye, the Iron Eagle race in China with a five-hundred-thousand-dollar pot. The Chinese are seemingly right into racing and prepared to spend big bucks. And Ernie was saying good birds can change hands for into hundreds of thousands of pounds. In fact, seemingly in 2013, a Belgian racing pigeon was sold to a Chinese businessman for 310,000 Euros, that's £260,000. But since then, one was sold for over a million pounds. That's *pounds* not dollars!'

An incredulous Ollie responded, 'No way, Grandad. A million pounds for a bird! That's crazy.'

'Yep. And McIntosh has had some big wins *and* has seemingly got some big money prize birds, *and*, has set up a lucrative breeding programme, selling some of his birds for thousands of pounds, so it beats me why he uses fake cameras. Oh, and Ollie, Ernie says the CDs are a good way of frightening of hawks and other raptors, because they hate the reflected light when they move in the wind. And for some reason birds of prey *are* frightened of owls, that's why he's got them two carved ones perched on the corners.'

Ollie nodded, 'So, how many pigeons has he got then?'

'Something like over eight hundred Ernie guesses. But they're not all his own. Other pigeon owners stable them there for training and one loft racing.'

'One loft racing, what's that?' Josh asked.

'Seemingly, if the loft has a good reputation, it can be advantageous for smaller fanciers and breeders to be a part of it.'

A look of surprise crossed Ollie's face, 'Surely he must get help looking after them. How can he look after that many birds on his own?'

'Ernie says he seemingly spent thousands of pounds on an electronic system that relies on grated floors so the pigeon waste falls through onto a conveyor belt system, then all he has to do is press a button that runs a cleaning cycle which brings the belt upside down below and drops it into waste boxes. He's also put in a system where feeding's automated through large, what they call, bean hoppers and the birds' water is delivered via an automated hose system. Very impressive Ernie says. Word is he's got a wealthy backer or syndicate who put a lot of money into his loft. But McIntosh is well thought of in pigeon circles and helps set up breeding programmes through the local and national pigeon racing federations. He's got some champion birds and has won significant prize money. There's a lot of competition too. Ernie says huge transporters go over to

80

France, from Portsmouth to Caen with Britany Ferries every week. They take thousands of birds over for racing from Falaise, Alencon and lots of other approved race points, some using big purpose-built transporters that can carry up to twenty thousand birds.'

Ollie's jaw dropped, 'Twenty thousand! Bit bigger than the one we saw this afternoon then.'

'McIntosh gets involved in the big races but has to use the big transporters. Ernie says the carrier we saw this afternoon will probably hold a few hundred birds, that's the one he uses for himself especially for the weekly runs with birds from his own loft.'

'What Eddie calls his pigeon run.' Josh said.

Ollie turned to him, 'And you didn't know any of this Josh? You've never mentioned it.'

'Come on, Ollie, you know I have as little to do with Eddie as possible. I don't have little chats with him. We don't ask each other how our days been. He's my mum's boyfriend,' a note of disdain in the word "boyfriend", 'and he helps out up there, but he never says much about it. He does a bit of driving so's to release the birds for exercise and thankfully, he goes over to France every week. Stays away overnight.'

'But why would he go to France himself, or rather send your mum's fella, every week? Why France?' Grandad asked.

'Something to do with avoiding birds of prey. McIntosh's pigeons are let off near the French coast, fly up into the channel and land here, pretty close to our coast. Raptors seemingly don't hunt over the sea. But best of all for me, it gets Eddie out our house one night a week.'

'Is he employed there, or does he just volunteer to help out?' Grandad's face a question mark.

'Look, Mr Caldwell, I don't really talk to him that much if I can help it, but I think he helps out when needed and he

81

gets paid for it, okay?'

'But he obviously doesn't help clean the lofts or help the feeding, that kind of thing.'

'I don't really know. Mainly driving, I think, but other jobs as well. There's lots of shorter trips inland just to exercise the birds and to train the young ones in homing. It's not a full-time job though.'

'Well, I could be right, then. I took Ollie up Dalton's Mount after school today. The paper this morning was reporting the death of another bird of prey, a falcon that had been found after having been shot. Now... who would have more to worry about predatory falcons than someone with prize winning pigeons, *and* breeders set to make a fortune.'

'By Jove, Holmes, you could be right,' Ollie mocked.

Grandad chortled, 'I think maybe I should be getting a few wee birdies. We could clear that bit ground at the remains of the old barn and build a loft there.'

'Yeah right, Grandad, you do that. Josh, time for bed before my mum starts shouting downstairs.'

'Josh, laddie,' Grandad stopped them before they could leave the kitchen, 'that Eddie, your Mum's fella, is he causing you problems?' Before Josh could answer he went on. 'It's just the way you talk about him, or don't want to talk about him. I know things have been difficult for your mum, and sister too, and I'd hate to think he was making things worse for you all.'

Josh was discomposed, not wanting to show any emotion, 'No, things are good thanks Mr Caldwell, I'm just a bit tired, and worried about my training with a couple of auditions coming up, and I just know Ollie 'll snore all night.'

'Okay then boys, up you go. I'll just check my post office savings book and see if I've got enough to start investing in pigeons.' Then continued, a glint in his eyes.

'For racing.'

'Okay Grandad, just don't *crow* about it.' Josh and Ollie hi-fived, 'Night, Grandad.'

Entering the bedroom Josh flung himself on Ollie's bed, it being more comfortable than the camp bed. 'Wow, what a day. What a pazooza of a day.'

'You can say that again.'

'Boy, what a pazooza of a day!'

Ollie laughed and shoved Josh's legs off the bed to get some room. 'Yeah, whatever that means.' Then with a more serious expression. 'Tonight's not goin' to go away Josh.' He remained quiet for a minute or two, his brow creased, deep in thought.

'What d'you mean?' Josh now sitting upright on the bed.

'Well, just think, we stumbled on Jez Freeman and his lot doin' a drug deal *and* offering to deal and be enforcers at school. And *they* know that *we* know. Well, they know me and Hannah know. Then there's the kick in the teeth I gave Scot Pinkman. There's no way he's gonna forget about *that*. He's gonna be wanting to use me as a punchbag for sure. Then you see Eddie Swinton givin' that weird girl a kicking 'cause, he says, she's moving in on his "patch". So now you know for sure he's dealing drugs, and that he seriously is a nasty piece of work. Not exactly what we'd normally be expecting at the start of the holidays, is it?'

Josh expelled a low breath and with a sombre expression on his face agreed, 'I'm really angry... and worried Ollie, I knew he was a bad sod, and I nearly didn't come this weekend 'cause Nicola was upset about me being away. But tonight confirms it! My mum's living with *and* become dependent on a drug dealer. 'As well as him bein' a violent thug.' A silence hung in the air for a minute or two, Ollie not being sure how to best commiserate with his friend.

Josh broke in again, 'But there's one positive.'

A baffled look on his face Ollie replied, 'A positive! What?'

'Just that Eddie Simpson doesn't know that I know. Yet! So, I need to use that to my advantage.'

'Josh! To *our* advantage. You're not alone. You know I'll try to help. My dad's not going to be home for a few weeks yet, he'd know what to do. Maybe we need to talk to my mum, or to Grandad.'

'No, we need to see if we can get something more definite on him. We'll have a think about it and I think the pigeon place could hold some answers. So, it looks like there sure could be trouble ahead. And... the three Muskrateers are gonna make life difficult. And there's no avoiding them.'

'Three Muskrateers! Muskrateers! What?'

'Ollie. Ollie, Ollie, just think on natural history. You've heard of muskrats, right?'

'Yeah.'

'Tell me what you know?'

'Well, as I remember, they're North American rodents that get their name because of their musky smell and rat-like appearance. And they can be quite destructive.' A look of awareness and a wide grin crossed Ollie's face, 'Yeah Josh, good one, "The three Muskrateers"! An accurate description. And you're right, they're gonna be trouble. D'you think we need to tell the head, or even our form teacher? You know what the police were tellin' us about at assembly this morning.'

'I think we need to think about it. But first we'll keep an eye out to see if we can see if they start trying to deal drugs at school. I'm not sure that girl tonight will still be around after Eddie's beating.'

Ollie nodded, 'Yeah, you could be right. So what we gonna do tomorrow? Maybe we need to meet with both

Hannah and Rav in the mornin' and include them 'cause they're involved now, whether they like it or not. Oh, I forgot Hannah's message.' He stood up to read the message. He sighed.

'What? What's up?'

'It's Hannah wondering what we're *all* doin' tomorrow. Get the 'all'. Pushy, isn't she?'

Josh sat up, brushing his hair back, 'Listen, Ollie, you don't need to worry, she's not really interested in *you.*'

'Good! And I never said she was.' His quick retort.

'No. You see what you have to understand is how the female mind works – doesn't work like us guys; they play these kinds of games to confuse the issue. You see it's really *me* she's interested in, and, 'cause I'm so devastatingly good looking she doesn't want to appear too keen in case she scares me off and I reject her.'

Ollie snorted in derision. 'Yeah, right.'

'Uh huh! She's tryin' to make *me* jealous by flirting with *you.*'

'Oh, that'll be why she kissed me when no one was looking then I suppose.'

'Get outa *here*! She never did... Did she? She never did, you *liar*!' Josh threw a pillow at Ollie.

'She did, I'm tellin' you. Just as she was leaving. Leaned over as she was getting her bike and kissed me on the cheek.'

'You sure she didn't just lose her balance and fall into you, her mouth accidentally brushing your cheek.'

Ollie shrugged and flopped onto the floor, leaning his back against the wall. 'Think what you like, Joshie, but she's askin' bout tomorrow, what we gonna tell her? Do we want her hangin' around?'

'Well, what's the plan for tomorrow?'

'I think we should get Hannah and Rav to come here. Or I guess we could meet at the marina again. Think here would probably be better though.' Ollie took out his phone to message them, 'What time d'you think?' He questioned Josh. 'Ten, eleven?'

'Let's say ten thirty then.'

Ollie sent the message. Almost immediately Hannah responded with a 'cool c u then XX'

Ollie groaned.

A bedroom door down the corridor opened. 'Get to sleep you two.'

'Yes, Mum. It's not me, it's Josh bummin' about how much Hannah fancies him.'

'Get to sleep!' Her bedroom door slammed shut.

The boys started getting ready for bed when Ollie caught sight of a large ugly purple and yellow bruise at the top of Josh's left arm. He gasped, 'Josh,' moving closer to take a look. 'What happened? How did you get this?'

Josh, looking uncomfortable, shrugged and moved away saying, 'It's nothin'. Just leave it.'

'Doesn't look like nothing to me, Josh. Is that why you insisted on keeping your blazer on and why you wore a long-sleeved shirt to school today?'

'Just leave it, Ollie. I can handle it.'

As he began to turn away, Ollie was sure he could see tears welling up in Josh's eyes, 'Josh, Josh, c'mon, what's the problem. You know you can tell me.'

Josh sat back down on Ollie's bed, wiping tears from his eyes, 'It's just all getting too much Ollie. He's a pig. I could kill him, and I'm so, so worried about Nicola.'

Ollie could see anguish in his eyes as Josh fought to keep back the tears, 'Josh, maybe you need to talk to my mum and to Grandad, they'd try to help you, you know they would.'

'You heard it for sure tonight, Ollie. The guy's involved in dealing drugs.'

Ollie put an arm round his friends' shoulder, 'Listen,

there's defo something goin' on, and if we can find out what, and get some proof, you could see him not only out your home, but tucked up in jail well out your way and the way of your family. And get your mum help.'

Josh lifted his head, a look of hope in his eyes, 'You think so?'

'I really think so. We better get some sleep, gi'me my bed back, and oh, maybe we don't want to give too much away to Rav and Hannah. Just play it cool, okay?'

'Yeah.' Josh climbed into the camp bed. 'We'll worry about it in the morning. Night!'

'Night!'

Chapter 13

Nicola was wakened by the clamour of raised voices, followed by the sound of her mother crying. She pulled the bedclothes more tightly around herself and, lying on her side, curled into a ball as though trying to shrink into herself. Through eyes that were tight shut, tears squeezed out to trickle onto her pillow. Occasionally her hand would appear from under the covers to rub tearful snot from her nose.

Her home, once a happy place, a place of fun and laughter, had become joyless, a place of fear and sadness. There were too many nights like this, nights of anxiety and apprehension. Nights when Eddie had some of his friends in, which meant nights of loud talking, even shouting, and sometimes violence. Nights when she longed for the return of happier times. Nights she wished her mum's "boyfriend", Eddie, would disappear forever. But it was worse tonight because Josh was not here. He rarely stayed away from home and when he was here, she always felt protected. What was it Josh said to her to do if she was ever frightened? She was to be brave. But it was hard to be brave when Josh was not here to be strong for her and help her to be brave. And what would she do if Josh really did move to London in a couple of years?

She heard the living room door open as Eddie headed to the bathroom. With the living room door still open she could hear her mum sobbing gently, interspersed with great shuddering intakes of breath. She wanted to run through and try to comfort her, but Josh had warned her to stay out the way if she ever heard loud noises and shouting. Screwing up her fists under the blankets she muttered through clenched teeth, 'I hate you!' I hate you!' 'I hate you!'

She pulled a pillow over her head to try to blank out the noises. Josh had tried to tell her about something called mindfulness about learning not to be overwhelmed by things going on round about us. But she didn't really get it. How could she ignore the all-too-real noises that caused her to shrivel up inside?

She heard Eddie come out the bathroom and as he went into the sitting room, she heard her mum say in a slurred voice, 'You're an evil pig. I'm going to my bed and you just leave me alone.'

'Or what bitch?' his reply.

'Just leave me alone.'

Nicola heard the bedroom door slam then a few minutes later the sound of loud music from the sitting room. Even so, she felt herself giving into tiredness. She fluffed her pillow and, even with the loudness of the music, she felt herself starting to drift off. She was jolted back to wakefulness by the sound of her bedroom door opening. Afraid to open her eyes fully she could tell it was Eddie by his smell. He always reeked of tobacco smoke and stale sweat and other scents she could not identify. Terrified, she froze, but still managed to open her eyelids very slightly. A streetlight too close to the bedroom window effortlessly penetrated the thin fabric of the curtains allowing her to clearly see he was standing looking down at her, a strange expression on his face.

'Go away! Go away!' the silent scream of her fears. What was he doing? Why was he looking like that? He crouched down, resting his elbows on his knees, and she could smell alcohol on his breath. He was breathing heavily. She held her own breath until she thought she would burst. Her heart was thumping so hard that surely he could hear it. Though he squatted beside her bed for only a few minutes, it felt like an eternity to Nicola. Then he rose again and left the room, closing the door quietly behind him. Nicola gave a great sigh of relief and pulled the bedclothes more tightly around herself. She would ask Josh not to leave her alone again. No – she would beg Josh to never leave her again. Ever!

Chapter 14

Day 2 – Saturday

Ollie and Josh were startled into wakefulness by a clattering and banging sound outside the bedroom door. Ollie, bleary eyed and still half asleep, stumbled to the door and, on opening it, was met with the site of Grandad in his old, checked dressing gown, rapping on a pot lid with a wooden spoon, a gleeful expression on his face. 'Oh, sorry! Did a wake thee, lad?'

'Grandad! You're *such* a pain in the *bum!*' Ollie slammed the door shut again.

Grandad's voice, a bit cushioned through the door, 'It's ten-to-nine, your mum says you're not to laze about all morning.' The lid started its wild cacophony again, 'I'll put some breakfast on for you, so get up now.'

Josh groaned and pulled the sleeping bag over his head, 'You go. I'll catch you later. And by the way, you *were* snoring last night. That's why I'm so tired this mornin'.'

'Rubbish. You better get up and do your morning exercise routine. I'll tell Grandad to hold breakfast till you're down.'

Josh burrowed down in the sleeping bag again.

Ollie, grabbing one side of the rails round the camp bed, tipped Josh onto the floor. 'Get up, you.'

Josh's head appeared through the top of the sleeping bag, 'Zit head! I didn't sleep too well on this thing. And your snoring didn't help. Now you're gettin' me up at the crack of dawn.' He promptly disappeared back inside the sleeping bag.

'Well Josh, if Hannah, who really fancies *you*, is comin' at ten thirty, you'll need time to try prettify yourself. A hopeless endeavour I would think, though a shower might help.'

A muffled, 'Jealous pig!' from inside the sleeping bag.

Ollie aimed a kick in the general direction of Josh's backside, 'Get up, you!' he repeated before making a quick exit to the bathroom.

The smell of bacon wafted up the stairs and, as Ollie neared the foot, he was met with the noise of Grandad's tuneless but relentlessly cheerful singing, mixed with the clamorous sound of plates and cutlery being carelessly distributed round the table. On entering the kitchen, Grandad's twenty-four-hour news channel was, as usual, chuntering out repeat news, sometimes interspersed with long-winded analysis by self-important looking pundits.

'Ah, Ollie me lad, does Josh like a cooked breakfast or is he watching his weight for the dancing stuff?'

'He's a growing lad, Grandad, sure he could manage a cooked breakfast, but could you wait till he comes down. He's got to do his stretches first.'

'Really! Ballet is hard work then? Always looked kind of easy to me.'

Ollie shook his head, 'Well, Josh says they reckon top male ballet dancers are more fit than professional footballers, or even some Olympic athletes. And, also, they're very strong. The men have to strengthen their back, shoulder and arm muscles *and* leg muscles for all the lifting they've got to do. Josh is no wimp.'

'Never suggested he was, son, but is he alright, Ollie? I didn't like to say last night but he was looking a bit... I don't know. Like... not his usual self.'

Ollie knew it was not the time to share last night's events, especially about Eddie Swinton's violence and the drug dealing. 'He's okay, Grandad, just a bit worried about Nicola bein' alone in the house with their mother's boyfriend. He's a mean piece of work.'

'Why doesn't she just dump him then?'

'Bit more complicated than that, Grandad.'

Grandad shook his head, 'It's such a shame. They were such a nice family, and Josh must be like a brother to you, you've been pals for so long.'

'Yeah, I guess.' Then, with a smile. 'Yep, we even have crackin' barneys sometimes, just like real brothers.'

'And it's always his fault, Grandad Caldwell.' Josh cut in as he entered the kitchen.

Grandad laughing now, shook his head, 'Aye – just like real brothers right enough. The one blaming the other. Right get yourselves sat down boys. Josh, do you like your eggs sunny side up?'

'Yeah, great thanks, Mr C.'

'That was quick.' Ollie remarked glancing at the kitchen clock.

'Yep. Taking it a bit easier this weekend.'

The boys settled at the table and, after serving them, Grandad settled into his armchair, daily paper in hand, 'So what you lads up to today?'

Ollie and Josh shared a look, before Ollie said they weren't really sure, but that Hannah and Rav were coming at half-ten, so they'd decide then.

'Hannah comin' back again, then? That's nice. Where have you been hiding that lass, Ollie? A right cracker she is.'

'Don't get excited, Grandad, it's seemingly Josh she's after. Of course, that is according to Josh and some weird psychological flibberty-flabber he was givin' out last night.'

Josh smirked.

'And he's welcome to her. I'd rather have a dose of your haemorrhoids, Grandad, than kiss Hannah. They'd probably be marginally less painful.'

Grandad winced.

Ollie rose from the table, and after gathering up the breakfast dishes to put in the dishwasher, turned to Josh,

'Right you, we better get a move on. You always take ages in the shower; thought we might have had time for a quick game of Battlefield before Hannah and Rav come, but we're not gonna have time now, and I need a shower too, so don't faff about.'

Josh made a face at Grandad, winked, and barked out. 'Yes sir! Right sir! Certainly, sir!'

Grandad rose from his chair. 'I better go and get cleaned up myself if we're expecting company.'

'Grandad! Nobody's comin' to see you, and we'll be going out when they arrive, so don't trouble yourself.'

Looking somewhat crestfallen Grandad informed them that the forecast was for rain this morning, but clearing this afternoon, 'Maybe your friends 'll cancel this morning.'

Ollie glanced out the window, the weather certainly looked overcast, but so far, no rain. 'No, I don't think so.' Ollie knew they had too much to talk about. About stuff with the possibility of frightening consequences.

Ollie had just finished getting dressed when Grandad shouted up the stairs, 'That's your friends here boys. Shake a leg.'

'Wonder if Hannah will be wanting more ballet lessons today then.' Josh gave an exaggerated sigh. 'What it is to be talented.'

'Shut up you, you're such a ponce.'

'Oh! Be still his jealous heart.' Josh laughed mockingly.

Hannah and Rav had taken seats at the kitchen table by the time Josh and Ollie came down.

'We've not dragged you out of bed, have we?' Rav, looking as immaculate as ever, loaded the question with sarcasm.

'No, we've been up for hours. Just ask Josh.'

Grandad gave an Oscar deserving performance in coughing and spluttering.

Hannah laughed.

Grandad gave a loud sigh, 'Eee, thy knows.'

'Grandad! Stop with it.'

Grandad ignored him. 'As I was going to say, when I opened the door, I thought I must have died.'

Ollie, a look of puzzlement on his face said, 'You must have died? What *are* you talkin' about?'

'Well, there were a knock on the door, and when I opened it, there she were... an angel, obviously come to take me to heaven.'

'Oh Grandad, you're so sweet.' Hannah beamed in response.

'And you're so perceptive, my dear,' Grandad's face wreathed in smiles. 'But I'll just take my paper through to the living room and leave you all in peace.'

Ollie stood to close the kitchen door behind him. 'Did it seem like rain when you guys came? Grandad says the forecasts not good for this morning.'

Rav glanced out the window. 'It's possible, why, what's the plan this morning?'

'Well, I think we need to talk about last night, and what we should do about it, if anything.'

Without hesitation Rav quickly replied, 'We should go to the police.'

Ollie sighed and sat quietly for a moment, a thoughtful expression on his face then, taking a deep breath, he responded to Rav's suggestion. 'Rav, you know, you're probably right, but – let's think for a minute. The three Muskrateers, as Josh calls them, haven't actually done anything yet.'

'They bought illegal drugs and offered their services for dealing at school, we should go to the police.'

'Rav,' Ollie was carefully choosing his words, 'it was only Hannah and me who saw them, but the police aren't just going to take our word for it, they'd need to have more evidence than that.'

Rav persisted, 'Well at least it'd put them on the police radar.'

'Yeah, okay, but they're probably just tadpoles in a pond of sharks. The girl is a bigger fish. She's obviously got people behind her if what she was threatening Freeman's lot with is true. The real bad guy so far is Eddie Swinton, and in what Josh *saw*, and we all *heard* last night, he spoke about his 'patch', so it would seem he's already got something established in the area. But quite what we've yet to find out, and, from what the druggy girls said, she's got some serious muscle behind her.'

Hannah, a perplexed look on her face interrupted, 'But hold on a minute,' she glanced towards Josh, hesitated a moment, then said, 'Josh, Eddie doesn't exactly come across as Mr Big. I mean, he shacks up with your mum livin' in a small flat above a Chinese takeaway. Does he even have a car?'

'Yeah, but you're right. He's got a beat-up old Citroen. Not sure if it's even taxed or MOT'd.

Hannah nodded, 'Well he's probably just a minor player too, so who supplies him? Who's *behind* him? Who's *he* workin' for?'

The four friends were silent for a moment or two, then Josh broke the silence, 'I could be wrong, but there's one possibility I can think of. Maybe. But I don't think he'd need to be dealing drugs from what I've heard of his set up, and the money he must make breeding champions.' He hesitated. They all looked at him expectantly, 'I think it *could be* the pigeon guy up Dalton's Mount.'

Ollie, looking doubtful said, 'Na, surely not, from what Grandad was saying last night he's got a pretty sweet operation. Must make him a comfortable enough living.'

Hannah argued that they still couldn't be sure. 'And what about the girl Eddie beat up last night? She's obviously not operating on her own. Ollie an' me heard her threaten Freeman and his gang with some heavy action if they screwed with her.'

'It would be fine if these heavies wanted to sort Eddie out. I'd help them.' Josh added.

'So, what we gonna do?' Ollie challenged. 'Probably not much... except... we could sniff around and try to find somethin' more definite we could take to the police.'

Hannah nodded. 'Sounds an idea, but we'd have to be careful. You think we should maybe bike up there later?'

Ollie looked at the kitchen wall clock. 'Well, it's half-eleven now, anyone fancy heading into town first?'

The other three agreed, so Ollie shouted through to let Grandad know they were leaving, also adding that since the rain hadn't come, they'd head downtown and get a burger before heading out to the country for a while.

Grandad appeared at the kitchen door clutching his paper, specs balanced halfway down his nose, 'But you've had a big breakfast, you can't still be hungry.'

'Well, we won't be goin' straight to Burger King, we'll be checking out the mall first, see what's what in the gaming shop 'n' stuff.'

'Pah! Silly games. Your mum's right to ban you from sitting about in the house all summer playin' on that Xbox, and it's these violent killing games that can lead to a higher tolerance to real violence — and to scrambled egg brains.'

'Yeah, right, Grandad, you can climb down from your tree of self-righteousness now. We'll look for that new game, "Bumping off Grandads".'

'Hannah,' Grandad spluttered. 'Do you see the kind of people you're gettin' mixed up with? Just you be careful, my lass.'

Ollie ushered his friends out the door. 'See you later, Grandad.'

'And don't forget your helmet, laddie.' The words

97

followed Ollie out the room.

Outside Rav was asking Josh what happens if they run into Jez Freeman and his mates. 'They never saw you or me Rav, only Ollie and Hannah. Mind you they might consider it guilt by association, even though it was Ollie who kicked Scot Pinkman in the mouth.'

'Yeah, they're not gonna forget that in a hurry,' a visibly uneasy Rav responded.

Hannah chipped in, 'And remember, Eddie Swinton doesn't know Josh saw what he did to that girl last night.' And, annoyed by Rav's negativity and lack of backbone went on, 'For goodness sake, man-up Rav. And anyway, I've already said that the four of us together could probably take them on.'

'Not me, I'm a pacifist.'

Annoyed, Hannah reached for her bike helmet, 'Well don't worry Rav, we'll fight your battles for you. Are we going guys?' She pulled her helmet on, 'Woops! Just a minute,' she said heading for the kitchen. They heard her calling down the hall, 'We're off, Grandad. See you later.'

As she came back out the door, Ollie shook his head, 'Creep.' And pulling his helmet on added, 'You can adopt him if you want, but you'll have to take him to live with your family.'

'What? And lose my excuse for visiting you, Ollie?' A wicked smile on her face. 'Let's go, guys.'

Chapter 15

Having secured their bikes to the metal bars at the bike park, with helmets in hand, they headed into the shopping mall. Being an easy train journey from London, the mall was not a particularly sought-after destination for people in need of some serious retail therapy. Nowadays it only offered a limited shopping experience with some outlets closed, and not looking likely to be occupied any time soon. But the boys weren't too interested in most of what was on offer anyway, as long as the games store was there and, especially for Rav, some of the trendier clothes stores, and of course the fast-food outlets.

The mall also adjoined a cinema complex outside of which were a Burger King, a Mexican restaurant, a Pizza Place, a couple of coffee shops, a newsagent and, on a Saturday, a fruit and vegetable stall all within the same pedestrian area. On a narrow street just beyond the mall pedestrian area was a comic store carrying a large variety of new and not so new publications, mostly American imports, along with related gizmos and geeky stuff. A place in which the boys could forget the meaning of time as they knew it.

'Why don't we do the comic store first then grab something to eat?' Ollie suggested and turning to Hannah added, 'We usually spend the morning in there.'

Josh and Rav readily agreed, but Hannah looked heavenwards emitting an exaggerated sigh.

'Hannah! If you want to hang with us then this is what we do, okay? We're not lookin' at perfumeries, or girls' clothes shops, or lookin' at *any* girlie stuff *whatsoever*. Right?'

Hannah sighed again, screwed up her eyes and, tight lipped, replied, 'One day, Ollie. One day.'

'What does that mean?' and deepening his voice added, *'One day, Ollie.'*

Hannah answered with a haughty, 'Nothing!' Then turning to Josh said, 'Oh well, you might get a nice comic for your little sister, Josh.'

Josh gave a derisory laugh. 'Don't think so, Hannah, it's not that kinda comic shop. It's big boy stuff. Sci-fi stuff and weird stuff and Super Man and The Lone Ranger and horror and more, but not for little girls. Anyway, guys, let's go.' He led the way past the cinema complex, through the pedestrian area and the hunger inducing aromas from the food outlets as they headed towards the comic store.

Hannah did not move. Instead, attracting Ollie's attention with a beckoning gesture, she asked if he thought Josh was okay.

'What d'you mean?'

'It's just that... he sometimes seems quite distant, and he goes really quiet, like he's looking into himself to find an answer to an elusive something.'

'He's got a lot of stuff goin' on in his life right now.' Ollie glanced towards Josh and Rav checking they were out of earshot. 'There's things goin' on at home that... well let's just say his home life is a mess... more than a mess really. Things have gone way downhill since he lost his dad. His mum ended up having to sell their home a few years ago, and about two years ago took up with that Eddie he *saw*, and we *heard,* beating up that girl last night.'

'Wow!' she gasped. 'Really?'

'Yep. And he worries about his little sister 'cause she's frightened of Eddie's quick temper. Little Nicola's seen their Mum become dependent on him, and on the drugs, though she might not be aware that drugs are the root of her mum's problems.' Ollie hesitated. 'No. I guess it's Eddie that's the real problem. There's never really enough food in the house, so Josh uses some of his pay to buy extra biscuits and crisps he keeps hidden in the bedroom for Nicola. And he's not happy that at his age he's got to share a bedroom with her. But mostly — he just fears for the future. That's about all.'

'Bummer! Poor Josh,' Hannah looked into the middle distance, chewing on her lower lip. 'Can his mum not get help? Don't Social Services get involved?'

'She's become too dependent on Eddie. And I suspect, frightened of him too. In fact, Josh nearly didn't come this weekend because he was frightened to leave Nicola — and I know he's still edgy about it.'

'But you're a good friend to him. And Rav is — and of course... me.' She held Ollie's gaze as though looking for affirmation.

Ollie smiled. She really was irrepressible, just bludgeoning her way into their lives then burrowing her way down into what they were as a group. But — Ollie thought — she *is* kinda cool. And she's feisty for a girl. And okay, she *is* kinda hot. And she did have real personality. And when she was hugging him on the beach, she did smell kinda nice. And warm. His face went red thinking about these things. What was happening to him? A little flustered, he responded gruffly, 'Yeah, well we've known each other so long, he's like a brother to me.'

'Is there no way out for him?'

'I guess his dancing. He's really good and that's already been recognised, so he's hopefully goin' to win a bursary if he impresses at his auditions this summer. But, if he gets it, he's going to have to leave home and board in London, so he's really worried about leaving Nicola, and of course, he's concerned about his mum.'

'So really, it's that Eddie who's the real problem.'

'Yep, him and his mum's drug dependency. But until Eddie's out the picture, think things will only get worse.'

Josh's head reappeared from the comic store, 'Hey,

you coming?' he shouted.

'Yeah. Come on, let's go.' Ollie placed his hand in the small of Hannah's back to steer her toward the shop. She turned her head and smiled sweetly at Ollie who promptly gave her back a push and growled. 'Let's move it, Hannah.'

'Yes, Ollie,' she giggled.

When they entered the store Rav was busy checking out a range of fantasy books while Josh was checking out some American super-hero comics. Not unusually for a Saturday morning, the store was busy with people excusing themselves and squeezing through tight spaces to a place they could occupy for a while as they vetted the comics. Behind the counter were two hairy men in T shirts decorated with artwork promoting heavy metal bands. Their muscly arms filled with tattoos, their faces with metal face jewellery, in addition, one had long black hair with purple stripes, the other had dyed bright red hair with an electric green flash running through it. Both were over two metres tall, and neither would see twenty-one again.

'Wouldn't want to meet them on a dark night in a back alley,' Hannah whispered to Ollie, compressing herself into as little space as possible as she squeezed her way towards Josh. 'See anything you like?'

'Still looking.'

'Mmm,' was Hannah's non-committal contribution to that conversation. The crush was too much for her to endure, so she tapped on Josh's shoulder. 'See you guys outside.' Navigating all obstacles to reach the door, she breathed a sigh of relief to be out in the fresh air. She leaned her back against the shop window, her left knee bent with her foot flat against the glass. She checked the time on her phone, wondering how long the boys would be in the store. Looking up, she scanned the pedestrian area, now filling up with people eating carry-out sandwiches and pastries. There was, as usual, on a Saturday, a good number of teenagers hanging about. Some sitting on walls, some standing in groups, three boys perched on the dried-up fountain. Some moving in and out the mall. Then she saw something causing her to screw up her eyes; the girl from last night, limping from the mall, one arm in a sling. As she came fully into the open Hannah saw her face was bruised and her bottom lip swollen with a crust of dried blood formed on top. She still wore the same long-sleeved T shirt and, and it seemed to Hannah, even from a distance, it was spotted with the dark stains of dried blood. The left-hand sleeve of the T shirt seemed to be hanging by a thread. Hannah was shocked. This was Eddie's work. No wonder Ollie was worried for Josh.

The girl made her way over to a group of girls, some sitting on a bench with others gathered round them, all seeming to be talking and laughing at the same time. Though noticing her approach, the group deliberately ignored her. The druggy girl tried to talk to them but was met with a wall of silence and disdainful looks before being told in a very unladylike way to "go away". She shook her head and moved towards another group to be met by the same reaction. She looked around then, quickening her pace, headed towards a small, but boisterous, group of teenage boys busy trying to look cool and making loud comments about any passing girls.

They seemed more receptive to the girl's approach. She started talking and, after five minutes or so, a couple of the boys looked around furtively before moving closer to her. One of them took his mobile phone from his pocket, his thumbs quickly moving as he added something, then, looking to the girl and reading back whatever he had added. She nodded, they pumped fists, and she walked away. The boys became animated, laughing and joking as they talked about what had just taken place.

Hannah had a fair idea about what had been going on.

There had been warnings in yesterday morning's school assembly. It was probably a phone number being given to these boys for them to contact her for drugs. Hannah could not believe it; in broad daylight in an open area with lots of people around, but then she thought, actually, no drugs had been bought, but from what she understood, the phone number would be all it took to get them delivered to a pre-arranged location.

'Boo!'

She jumped, hand over her heart. 'Aargh! You guys! I'm gonna belt you one,' she said as she turned to face them, then landed a solid punch to Ollie's shoulder.

'Ouch! Not so hard, Hannah.' Rav and Ollie laughed. 'Lost in a daydream were you, Hannah?' Ollie asked putting on a mock caring face.

'Not a daydream, some real serious stuff going on. We need to talk.'

'Okay, Hannah. What say a burger, guys?'

They all agreed and headed for Burger King, Rav showing Ollie a couple of comics he had bought.

'You get anything?' Hannah asked Josh.

'Nah. Couldn't afford 'em.'

Hannah felt a twinge of pity and, now knowing a little of Josh's home situation, was angry at herself for being so insensitive. 'Yeah, sorry Josh, I should have thought.'

'It's okay, Hannah, it's not your fault. Anyway, when I'm the lead male in a famous ballet, and acknowledged as the new Rudolf Nureyev...'

'Rudolf who?' Hannah cut in, a querulous expression on her face.

'Nureyev.'

Hannah laughed, 'I've heard of Rudolph the red nosed reindeer, but I've never heard of...' her nose twitched, 'Rudolf Nureyev.' A question mark in her voice.

Josh sighed and shook his head, 'He's acknowledged

as being probably the greatest male ballet dancer of all time. In fact, he influenced the acceptance of crossover from ballet to modern dance. He was the man responsible for raising the bar for male ballet dancers. He's my hero. You can catch some of his stuff on YouTube. He's the man.'

Slipping her arm through Josh's, she smiled and said, 'You're so modest, Joshie. Not!' Laughing, she tightened her grip on his arm and added, 'But you'll have to dance for us so we can see for ourselves.'

'I'll get you complimentary tickets when that day comes.'

'No, now! Then when you're famous, I can say I knew you before you were. And I can say you danced just for me.' With a twinkle in her eye she added, 'Won't that sound romantic?'

'Hannah!' Josh snorted, then shaking his head started to laugh, 'C'mon, let's go you.'

They entered the Burger King and joined Rav and Ollie at the end of a queue. Ollie turned to see them approaching arm in arm. 'Uh huh – you two an item then?' sounding a little peeved, which he instantly regretted.

'Don't worry, Ollie, you'll get an invite to the wedding.' Josh laughed.

'Won't come, can't dance.' An extremely noticeable tinge of petulance in Ollie's voice.

'Oh, I'm sure I could teach you a few basic steps.'

When it came to ordering, Josh ordered a small bag of fries and a carton of milk. 'Hey, I'll get you a burger, Josh.' Ollie offered.

'Nah. I'm good.' Josh's replied, 'Anyway, Hannah, go and grab that table in the alcove before it gets taken. Have you got the right money, and I'll bring yours across? Oh, and here take this,' he added handing Hannah his helmet.

'Mine too.' Ollie handed her his.

'And mine.' Rav added.

'Clutching all four helmets, Hannah snorted, 'What am I? Your hand maiden!'

'Yeah, now *leg* it.' Ollie laughed.

'Just wait you lot, you don't know who you're messin' with.' She snorted, moving off to claim a table.

When their order was fulfilled, the boys joined Hannah. Hannah asked Rav to let her see the comics he'd bought.

'But no touching with greasy fingers.' Rav instructed as he flipped through some pages to show them.

Hannah cut in, 'Guys, I need to tell you somethin' serious.'

They stopped looking at the comics to focus on her. She looked round about, then signalled for them to move their heads closer together she said, 'While you were all in the comic store, that girl who got beat up last night turned up and looked like she was touting for business amongst the school kids. And she didn't seem to care that there were adults and families with young children goin' about. She approached some girls, but thankfully they just ignored her. But I guess some others wouldn't.'

The three boys looked concerned. 'Is she still around?' Ollie questioned.

'No. She took off after it looked like she'd given her phone number to some boys.'

'Children?' Rav questioned.

'No, they looked like year elevens. I've seen them about the school.'

Ollie asked how the girl looked after last night's beating.

'Pretty bad. She looks real messed up and was walking with a limp. Her face was bruised and cut, and she was wearing a rough kind of sling, but that's only the things I could *see*. Eddie's given her a real beating. She might have broken or fractured ribs, even have internal injuries. But I don't think she'll have been to see a doctor.'

The boys exhaled in unison, their faces reflecting concern. 'Listen,' Ollie continued the conversation, 'To be honest I don't care too much about her, or her fate, but without being moralistic, I *am* concerned with the dangers of kids our age getting caught up in drugs. Big temptation to experiment and be cool for some.'

'We definitely need to go to the police.' Rav's response.

Ollie looked into the middle distance, drumming his fingers on the table. The others waited for him to say something.

'I think we need to try to figure out some stuff first.' He fell silent before continuing. 'Don't forget, whatever happens could have terrible consequences for Josh's family. Eddie Swinton's an evil sod. But he's small time, maybe if we could find out who *his* supplier is, we'd have more to go to the police with.'

Hannah, looking concerned added, 'Ollie, I'm not sure we should be getting involved in this. It could be dangerous. Maybe Rav's right.'

'I am,' Rav confirmed defiantly.

Ollie knew what Rav and Hannah were saying probably was true but suggested they take time to think things through before doing anything definite.

'Has anyone got change for a pound?' Hannah looked at the boys hopefully.

'What do you need change for?' Ollie asked.

'Never mind nosey,' her response.

Josh dug into his pocket, pulled out a handful of change and put it on the table.

'What's them?' Ollie's curiosity aroused by a couple of small metal canisters amongst Josh's change, both with little round clips on the side and with small, hinged lids.

'Nothin' much. Eddie sometimes drops them out his pockets at home. He says they're for putting lead pellets into, then they get clipped round pigeons' legs.' Seeing their bafflement, he continued. 'It's to strengthen the pigeons as part of their training to help make them have more stamina, and to make them able to race faster − and if necessary, to have the strength to fly longer.'

'Wow, a serious business then,' Ollie said picking up one of the containers to examine it. 'Who'd have thought,' and, handing it back to Josh, started to rise, and suggested they maybe take a run out to Dalton's Mount for a nosey.

Rav looked concerned. 'Why? You're crazy! We might get into all kinds of trouble. Especially from the police if the guy sees us nosing about. He might think we're up to no good, maybe trying to harm his pigeons.'

'We're just going to try and see what's going on, Rav. Might be nothing.' Then raising his eyebrows added. 'But then again... who knows? I'll have to go back and borrow my granddad's binoculars. Come on, let's get moving. Hannah, you okay for this afternoon?'

'Yep. I'll just phone home and let my mum know I'll be back late afternoon. But you'll have to give me a minute, got to go to the loo.'

Ollie started to rise, 'Okay. We'll see you outside.'

Chapter 16

Eddie Swinton was still angry thinking about last night. His conscience untroubled. That bitch deserved the kicking she got, who did she think she was trying to muscle in on his territory? Sure, he knew she had to be part of something bigger, but the trouble with these London pushers was they thought they could just move into towns like this, set up these county lines using young kids like her, and take out any competition.

That's what they used. Young homeless kids, runaways who had slipped through the net and were happy to have a sense of belonging to something. Happy to make some money for themselves, regardless of the misery they could be inflicting on others. He had heard their suppliers were always ready to provide muscle, if necessary, but violence could also be administered to them if there was any suspicion of being ripped off, or of setting up dealing for themselves. It was only later last night he remembered where he had seen her before, hanging out with the hippy commune not too far from McIntosh's lofts.

Eddie thought – he hoped – that was merely a coincidence. He knew he was, for the moment, a small cog in a bigger wheel, in which he understood his place, whilst waiting for bigger things. But for now, being part of it made him feel a somebody, somebody to be feared, even respected by the easily impressionable in the community.

He sometimes carried a knife himself and owned a brass knuckleduster that was just a little too awkward to carry about unless he knew he was going to use it. But more, he knew that McIntosh had a Glock automatic and some ammo stashed at the bottom of the feed bins in a waterproof package. Something the police missed on a recent visit, as well as the rifle.

There was concern about birds of prey being found shot in the area, so two months ago, the police had been in with a search warrant looking for a rifle. They reasoned that someone like Ronnie McIntosh had enough of an incentive to kill raptors, that any breeder and racer of prize birds might have a lot to lose financially, so he was in the frame. However, McIntosh assured them that he most often sent his birds over the channel so that the major part of their homing run was over water, with much less danger of being lost to birds of prey. After a cursory check, and failing to find anything suspicious, and being impressed with the set up and satisfied with McIntosh's assurances, the officers left, apologising for their intrusion.

But Eddie also had another problem. When he first took up with Miranda Meadows, the fact she had a couple of sprogs did not bother him too much at first. Now they were becoming a nuisance. The girl was just a little sniveller, always ready to burst into tears. But he kind of liked the way she cringed away from him and the sense of power that gave him. But the boy, 'the poof', well, Eddie reasoned, he must be since he was training to be one of them ballet dancers. He acknowledged that the kid was looking fit – and getting muscly, and that he had a panther like way of moving, lithe and ready to pounce, with eyes filled with undisguised hatred every time he looked at Eddie. He was very protective over his sister and was starting to face up to him more, so Eddie thought it was time to be teaching the kid who was the main man here.

And Miranda, well since he introduced her to some illicit substances, she had become unpredictable. One minute, upbeat and happy, the next, weeping and moaning and begging for more stuff. She was also starting to lose her looks, and that was what first attracted him to her. The flat was tired and far from clean, so he determined that when he got some real deals going for himself, he was out of there. The sooner the better. But today he was going up to Dalton's Mount to see about next week. Today's trip had been cancelled, however, he reckoned he would be heading for France with the birds next Saturday but needed to know for sure. Ronnie McIntosh gave him a good bit of work and until he could get himself established properly, he still needed to be doing the runs – and for the opportunities this gave him. Right now, if he was not going to France four or five times a month, what else would he be doing? But he had plans.

Chapter 17

The four, on arriving at Ollie's, dropped their bikes on the front drive and walked round to the back of the house. There, Ollie's Grandad was leaning on a garden fork and gazing at a tin can at his feet. Looking up he smiled at them, 'You know, I'll swear there's enough slugs and snails in this garden,' pointing to the tin at his feet, 'that I'd only need a puppy dog's tail and I could make a small boy!'

'You're not gonna replace me that easily, Grandad.' Ollie laughed.

'Mmm... now there's a good idea lad. A boy that's not cheeky and always knocking a rise out his old grandad. A lad as 'ill show respect and bring me a cup of tea in bed now and again. Worth a thought, right enough.'

'C'mon now, Grandad, you could never replace Ollie. He's so sweet.' Hannah wrinkled her nose and smiled.

Ollie blushed.

'Sweet! Huh! I've had sweeter early season rhubarb!'

Sidling up to Grandad and slipping her arm through his, Hannah said, 'But would it be as cute and as good-looking Ollie?'

Ollie blushed again, and muttered through clenched teeth, 'Shut *up*, Hannah.'

Rav and Josh burst out laughing.

'Cute *and* good looking! Ollie?' Grandad spluttered, 'Dear, dear lass, you're needin' to get thyself a pair o' specs.'

In exasperation, Ollie snapped, 'Grandad! Don't start.'

'Eee lad, don't thee get thyself all worked up now. You'll be showin' thy lass thy true colours.'

'She's not *my* lass.'

'So you say, lad.' Grandad winked at Hannah who was grinning at the exchange. He put his arm round her shoulder and started leading her away from the boys, 'But since you're here, lass, let me show you to my roses. When they see *true* beauty, they might well hang their heads in shame.'

'Ooh Grandad, you know how to charm a girl.'

Ollie groaned loudly. Rav and Josh delighting in his embarrassment started to chant an old primary school chant, 'Ollie and Hannah up a tree, gonna get married and never break free.'

'Very funny! Right guys, let's get into the house.' Ollie turned to lead the way into the kitchen then stopped, and looking over his shoulder and thinking the better of his previous advice added, 'Oh, by the way, Grandad, can we borrow your binoculars?'

'Binoculars! Why do you want my binoculars?'

Josh jumped in, 'We want to do a bit bird watching this afternoon, Mr Caldwell, we've got a wildlife project to be working on for next term. We're supposed to do some research over the holidays.'

Grandad doing his stroking of the chin, narrowing his eyes thing indicating a measure of doubt at the veracity of that statement, retorted, 'Really? You're going to spend the afternoon birdwatching?'

'Grandad, I swear, we really *do* want to go bird watching this afternoon.' Ollie, aware Grandad was playing games with them, added. 'We'll look after them, promise.'

Grandad looked skywards, 'I think there's rain coming in.'

'Well, we'll be sure to keep your binocs dry. C'mon into the kitchen guys and I'll go get them.'

Back inside the house, Hannah, Josh and Rav waited in the kitchen till Ollie returned with a pair of binoculars in their own leather case.

Rav showing particular interest, asked to see them. On taking them from the case he exclaimed, 'Wow! Top shelf.'

'Top shelf! What's that mean?' Hannah said looking at

113

the case.

'They're a quality brand. Some of their stuff's even been sent into orbit on the International Space Station. Your grandad sure knows a thing or two about optics, Ollie.'

'Guess we'd better take good care of them then.' Ollie took the binoculars back from Rav, locking them into their case. 'Right guys, take a pew for a minute till we figure out what we're gonna do, and how we're gonna do it.'

Then, balancing on the rear legs of his chair, hands locked behind his head, Josh asked, 'You got a plan then, Ollie?'

'Well, we want to get to a place where we can see what there is to see behind these high fences at the pigeon lofts − see what's goin' on. In particular, see if we can find anything that might help us to incriminate Eddie. So... I have an idea. Don't know if it will work though.' He hesitated.

Intrigued, Hannah asked, 'C'mon Ollie? Don't keep us in suspense.'

Ollie leaned forwards, stretching his arms onto the table, 'Well, we need to scout about the place without anyone getting suspicious, right?'

They all agreed, but *how* was the question.

'Okay... so... here's my thoughts. We get up there, and, within sight of McIntosh's house, one of us fakes having a puncture.' His suggestion was greeted with questioning faces. 'And... whoever has the puncture takes their time to repair it. Meanwhile, one... or two of us take a walk up behind the lofts with the binoculars to see if we can get a good look to see what's going on over the fencing.'

'But wouldn't that make them suspicious? Why would we go up there?' Josh asked.

'Could just be exploring.' Ollie suggested, 'Or, like we told Grandad, just doin' some bird watching.'

Shaking his head, Rav said, 'Nah, I don't think they'd

114

fall for that.'

'Think Rav's right,' Josh agreed.

Hannah drummed her fingers on the table as though helping her to think, 'I know how that could work.'

They all looked at her. 'How?' Ollie queried.

'Well,' Hannah said, 'It could work if... say... say Ollie n' me went up behind the lofts holding hands, like we're an item and just taking a few minutes to ourselves while you guys are fixing the puncture.' She turned to Ollie, a challenging look in her eyes.

'Why me?' a look of alarm on Ollie's face.

Josh laughingly asked, 'Not frightened of girls are you, Oliver?'

'Don't be stupid.' Ollie snapped.

Hannah looking slightly deflated asked, 'Is it because I've just pushed myself onto you guys this weekend, Ollie?' She hung her bottom lip out in an exaggerated fashion.

Ollie's tongue tied tighter than a wet granny knot stuttered, 'No! But... but it's a bit unexpected... and...'

'And?'

They all looked at him waiting for what came next. Josh and Rav smirking. Ollie, now looking as startled as a frog who had landed in the mouth of a hungry pike instead of on a lily pad, hesitatingly replied, 'Well okay, and I think you're kinda... okay... maybe.'

Hannah jumped up from the table and threw her arms around him, 'I knew you liked me.'

'Gerrof, you.' Ollie squirmed, burrowing down into the seat.

'Now, now, now. What's going on here, then?' Grandad asked as he entered the kitchen. 'That you getting' some attention at last, Hannah?'

'Well, I think Ollie's beginning to appreciate my talents a little.'

'Be a fool if he didn't, lass.' Grandad smirked.

115

'Grandad!' Ollie snapped and pushed his chair back, 'Why don't you dig a big hole and bury yourself? But thanks for the binoculars, we'll look after them.'

Before Ollie could rise, Grandad said, 'The *answer* to your question is... because I want all the trimmings, fancy coffin, Rolls Royce hearse, lots of flowers and stuff, and for you to be weeping and wailing, clinging to my coffin racked with guilt for the way you treated your old grandad.'

'Grandad you ask for it.'

Grandad spluttered loudly, 'Ask for it? I ask for it? Me, a harmless old age pensioner?'

'Harmless! So what about that deadly disease you told me the doctor had diagnosed you with two weeks ago?'

Grandad lowering himself into his armchair, chortled to himself.

'What was it again Grandad, this *dreadful* disease?'

'I only told you what the doctor told me,' he replied with a look of feigned innocence, 'He told me I've got early onset onychorrhexis.'

A look of shock crossed the faces of Josh, Hannah and Rav. Hannah blurted, 'Oh Grandad, that sounds awful. Will you be okay? Is it painful? Is it *hereditary*?'

Ollie snorted, 'I think he'll be *perfectly* okay Hannah, that whatever it's called again, means vertical ridges rising on the backs of your fingernails. Something that comes with *old age* quite *naturally*.'

Grandad looked towards Hannah, and with a shrug, and a huge grin on his face said, 'It worked though lass, I was getting treated with kid gloves till his mother told him what it was. I would have milked it for years. So, where are you going to be bird watching this afternoon?'

'Goin' up past Dalton's Mount and the reservoir, there's good light woodland a couple of miles beyond.'

'Oh! You're sure?' A narrow-eyed look of suspicion on Grandad's face.

'Yes Grandad, don't worry we won't be stopping at the pigeon place. Probably even sail past it without even noticing.'

'So, tell me, one pair of binoculars among four, how's that going to work?'

'Oh, we'll all get five or ten minutes at a time.'

'This is kind of sudden, is it not? This new interest in bird watching.'

'Grandad, it's Hannah who's into it, and she wants to show us how fascinating it can be.'

Hannah, initially taken aback gulped, 'Yes, it really is, Grandad. They might really get into it.'

Grandad still did not look convinced, 'I see, but I would have thought you'd have had a camera in case you spot some rare wee birdie worth photographing.'

'Phones have perfectly good cameras, Grandad.' Ollie countered.

'And notebooks. I thought budding ornithologists carried notebooks.'

'We have notebook facilities on our phones, Grandad.'

'Mmm – well, be careful. And stay away from that pigeon place.'

Ollie, glancing at the kitchen clock, got to his feet, 'C'mon guys, let's go.'

As they were getting organised Hannah asked Josh if he was really determined to be a ballerina. Josh laughed, 'No Hannah, that's what female ballet dancers are called, us males are called, *danseurs,* but ultimately I'd like to become a *danseur noble,* that's the principal male in a *corps de ballet.*'

'Hey, I never knew all that,' Rav commented.

'Neither did I. And I'll ask you more later, Josh,' Hannah added.

Josh smiled. 'Learn something every day, eh? And yes, Hannah, I am determined, and if you're interested, sometime over the holidays I might present you with a '*pas seul*' Danielle's been having me work on it for my auditions.

'A what? A parcel!'

'No Hannah, it's a ballet dance for one. A '*pas seul*'.'

Ollie finding himself become irritated by the exchange and, sounding surly, ordered them to get their helmets on and get on the road as he mounted his bike and started to lead them towards Dalton's Mount.

As they headed out, Ollie remembered they would be passing the place he had seen the drug pushing County Line girl scuttling into one of the cottages. He wondered if they would see her this afternoon. Of course, she hadn't seen Hannah and himself hiding up in the dunes, so she wouldn't recognise them if they did see her. Thinking about what they had witnessed last night, Ollie felt a twinge of anxiety as he realised they still had two days of school left before the summer break, so they were bound to encounter one or all of the three Muskrateers. In fact, they'd probably be hunted down by them. 'Oh well,' he thought, 'I'll worry about them on Monday.'

Rav, concerned about getting dirty, had volunteered for Josh to be the one with the puncture. He also got an assurance from Josh that if, for any reason, they were challenged, he would claim some kind of association with Eddie, hoping that would give them immunity from suspicion.

Turning off the main road onto Dalton's Mount, Ollie signalled them to stop opposite the riding stables. 'What's up?' Josh asked as he dismounted his bike, leaned it against a stone wall, grabbed his water bottle and plonked himself down on the grass verge. Rav and Hannah joined him while Ollie stood astride his bike.

'Right guys, we know what we're doing, right?'

They all answered in the affirmative. 'Just take your time mending the puncture Josh, Hannah and me 'll head sup the right side of the lofts to the high ground behind where there are some trees. There's scrub and bushes before there that could give us some cover, but we'll see what we can figure will work best when we get up there. And Hannah, I don't think we'll be doing any hand holding, specially climbing up though bushes and rocky scrubland, it's fairly steep.'

'Huh, you'll probably be begging for me to give you a hand to get up to the top.'

Ollie laughed, 'Okay guys, let's go.'

'Give us a few minutes Ollie, I'm sweating.' Josh wiped his brow with the back of his arm to emphasise the point.

'Oh, by the way, I saw the druggy girl up here yesterday afternoon when Grandad was havin' a nosey, but if we see her just ignore her.'

Chapter 18

They cycled past the crescent of cottages where Ollie had seen the girl yesterday, but no sign of her today. They passed the boarded-up hall and on to McIntosh's place. As they drew near, Ollie looked over his shoulder, 'You ready, Josh?'

'Yeah, go for it.'

As they came opposite the driveway to McIntosh's properties, Josh pulled up, calling the others to stop as he dismounted to crouch down before his front wheel. The others gathered round as though supporting him. Rav nodded towards a large silver car parked outside the house.

Ollie gave a low whistle, 'That's some machine.'

'Yeah. It looks like an Audi 6.3 quattro 500 Tiptronic. Costs just under a hundred grand new,' Rav informed them.

The other three looked at him askance. Hannah asked, 'How do you know that, Rav?'

'Oh, my uncle Devansh has one.'

'Plenty money in your family then, Rav,' Hannah said, giving him a gentle nudge.

Ollie quickly scanned the area of the house and the loft. He could see McIntosh and the car owner move into what he supposed was the sitting room.

'What height d'you reckon that fencing is?' He queried as he and Hannah dismounted, laying their bikes on the grassy verge.

Rav sized up the fence, 'Couple of metres at least, probably more,' he estimated.

'Okay Hannah, you could be right, let's pretend we're an item then,' Ollie held his hand out to her and, giving a coy look, she clasped it.

'Ooh Ollie, you're so masterful,' she giggled.

'Shut up, you. And come on, let's get up there. Here you carry the binoculars.'

Josh started to work the tyre off the wheel while Hannah and Ollie made their way up the side of the pigeon loft. The climb was more awkward than they anticipated as there was a lot of loose pieces of rock and grit. Nearing the top, they had to grab handfuls of scrub or bushes to get some leverage. Ollie warned Hannah to avoid the thorn bushes but at one stage, losing her balance and trying to avoid grabbing a bush, she tipped forward, and putting her hands out to break her fall, stumbled, landing heavily on her right knee. 'Bummer!' she wailed clutching her grazed and bleeding knee. Ollie came down to help her, 'You okay?'

'Yeah. You got a hanky?'

Ollie rummaged about in his pockets, drawing out a couple of grubby looking paper tissues he proffered them to her, 'All I got. Sorry. Here, let me help you.' He knelt down beside her trying to brush away bits of grit sticking to the graze in her knee and her hands. 'Be brave.'

Dabbing the heels of her hands she said, 'I'm fine. C'mon, let's get up there.'

On reaching more level ground first, Ollie stretched out to take hold of her hand and help her to the top. They stood for a minute brushing themselves down. Hannah passed him the binoculars. Then realising they still could not yet get a good look into the loft, Hannah suggested they moved up to the trees where they might be able to see better. When they reached the trees, they turned to check, 'Mmm... still not great,' Ollie sounded disappointed, 'Because it's built on a hill, the back section's higher than the rest. Good for protecting the birds I suppose... or hiding secrets maybe.'

Ollie was so busy focussing on the loft he didn't see the man coming out from the back of the house and putting his hand over his eyes to shield them from the sun as he looked up towards them. Hannah grabbed his left shoulder and swung him round to face her.

'Hey!'

Now she pulled at the front of his T shirt drawing him to herself, 'Quick, put your arms around me, we're being watched.'

Ollie looked down towards the rear of the house, where another man had joined the first. They were both looking towards Hannah and Ollie. 'Ollie, you need to kiss me, or at least pretend to.'

'What!' A look of panic on Ollie's face. 'Kiss you?'

'Just do it Ollie,' she said, putting a hand behind his head and pulling him to her lips. Ollie's eyes were wide open, his lips clamped shut, his face scarlet. Her lips started to move gently. He froze. He knew that nowadays most kids his age had probably engaged in snogging sessions, but he'd never really kissed a girl before. Manoeuvring his head slightly, lips still firmly together, he was able to look down towards the men who, thankfully drawing the wrong conclusion of the purpose of their climb, turned back into the house.

Breaking away from Hannah, Ollie said, 'Well that's been a waste of time. But I guess we managed to fool them. Good thinking, Hannah.'

'Yeah,' came Hannah's dry reply, 'a real waste of time!'

'But hey, Hannah, this is becoming a bit of a habit, grabbing me and hugging me and now... trying to get me to kiss you.'

'Would that be so difficult, Ollie?'

Ollie chose to ignore the question. Looking around he spotted a tree that looked climbable, 'Hey, look, I think I could get up that tree. I think from there I'd get a better view and I'll be able to take some photos.'

Hannah never commented and stood, arms crossed and nursing a frosty expression.

'You'd need to give me a foot up, Hannah. Think you could manage?'

'Are you kidding me? If I set my mind to it, I could probably throw you over it. Wimp!' She moved over to the tree, locked her finger together and adopted a semi-crouch position. Swinging the binocular case behind him, Ollie put his left foot into her cupped hands and, resting his hands on the tree, lifted his right foot off the ground a little.

'Just testing. I need to get up a bit to grab that first branch.' Stretching up, his fingers were touching the branch but not enough yet to take a hold. 'Okay Hannah, just need a little lift.' A slight grunt as she obliged. Ollie pulled himself onto the branch and checked the view. He would need to get up a bit higher to get a fuller picture. With a bit of effort, he managed to reach a branch strong enough to hold him with a perfect view into the loft. From this viewpoint he could appreciate that this was no ordinary pigeon loft. Definitely had money invested in it. Built in a perfect square probably about twenty-five metres each length. On each side, assuming the one he could not see from this angle was the same, rows of wooden structures, all with slanting roofs, built to house the pigeons. Each one standing on concrete blocks raising them about forty centimetres from the ground. Interconnected casing running underneath the lofts probably had something to do with the automated cleaning and feeding system. In a corner stood a solid looking rectangular wooden structure with a flat roof, opaque windows and a couple of heavy-duty padlocks on the door. Maybe a food store or a place to keep all the paraphernalia connected with breeding and racing pigeons.

Pigeons cooed and flapped about inside the lofts. The whole place looked immaculate. The door into the loft area was on the side closest to the house. Ollie let a low whistle escape then, lowering the binoculars, dug into his pocket, took out his phone and took a few photos of the set-up. The back door of the house opened again. He held his breath, hoping McIntosh would not see him through the foliage. Hannah had slipped behind the tree. McIntosh stood scanning the tree line for a couple of minutes before going back into the house. Probably time to move, Ollie thought. Carefully placing one foot on a branch below, he started the descent. He had to hold onto a branch, turn his body slightly and let his foot connect with a lower branch. He gave it a couple of pushes to test its support factor. Fine. Placing both feet down more firmly, he lowered his weight letting go of the branch above. When he reached for a lower handhold, there was a crack as the branch beneath him broke. Startled pigeons fluttered and flapped about in the loft as Ollie tumbled to the ground, the side of his T shirt being ripped in the process. Winded and wounded, two heavy scratch marks on his back, one bleeding, Hannah rushed to help him. She put one arm under his shoulder as he started to rise. She spotted the back door of the house open again, so she pushed him back flat on the ground. She lay down alongside him, 'Shh. Someone's come out again.'

'Ow! Am I bleeding? Is anything broken?'

'Shh!'

McIntosh stood scanning the area around the lofts before moving to the door in the fencing. He placed his hand on the door and pushed, it remained locked. He looked up to the tree line again and stood for fully five minutes then, seeing nothing, he made his way back into the house.

'Ollie, are you okay? Nothing broken?' Hannah asked quietly.

He winced as he rested on one elbow, raising his other arm to check the damage to his side. His T shirt was probably beyond repair, but at least he had stopped bleeding. His face broke into a broad grin, 'Look at us, your

124

knees and hands and my side, plus I'm pretty sure I'm bruised too. I don't know what my mum's goin' to make of it. Could get grounded at the start of the holiday... but at least Grandad's binoculars are undamaged.

Hannah rose slowly to her feet, her eyes on the back door of the house. Holding out a hand to help Ollie, she said, 'The guys should have the tyre sorted now. We better get down there and get away before McIntosh spots us in this state.'

'Just a minute.' Ollie phoned Josh and asked if he and Rav could move back this way, pushing his and Hannah's bikes till they were out of site of the house.

When they approached the road, Rav and Josh were standing holding two bikes each, relieved to see the pair return. Noticing Hannah's scraped knee and Ollie's ripped and bloodied T shirt, they asked if they'd been in a fight.

'Nearly. Ollie and me had a fall out.'

'Really! What about?' Rav asked a look of surprise on his face.

'Oh, nothin' really, 'cept that he's an emotional retard.' She scowled at Ollie who merely laughed then ignored her.

'Yeah, only *my* fall out *was* out a tree. Hence the bleeding wounds. Good job I didn't break anything.'

'Just Hannah's heart by the looks of things.' Rav commented.

At which Ollie grabbed him round the neck, bent him near waist height and knuckled the top of his head. Protesting volubly, Rav stamped hard on Ollie's foot, so securing his release.

'Oh my side! Oh my side! Oh my foot! Oh my foot!' wailed Ollie.

'Serves you right.' Hannah gloated at his discomfiture.

'Right! Enough! Did you see anything?' Josh asked as he passed Ollie his bike.

'Not at first, fence was too high. I know he's got the CDs

and the model owls there to ward off raptors, but does the fencing have to be quite so high because of them? I mean they could swoop into the area without climbing fences or opening gates.'

'Maybe. But his birds *are* supposed to be quite valuable,' Rav answered.

'And I think I've got a pretty good idea why that might be.' Ollie said as he mounted his bike. 'C'mon, let's get out of here.'

Rav and Hannah said they'd just head home instead of going back to Ollie's, 'Send Grandad my love though.' Hannah said as she kicked down on her pedals, a cheeky grin on her face.

'You want to meet up tomorrow?' Ollie asked.

She stopped, 'Oh, we're friends again, are we? Well, I have church in the morning and evening.'

'Really Hannah. Religious family then?'

'A Christian family. Baptists.' She smiled sweetly.

'Oh. Okay, so are you not allowed out on Sundays?'

'Yeah, but we've got family coming in the afternoon and I want to see my cousins.'

Josh joined the conversation, 'Shame, Hannah. I'm goin' down to the dance studio tomorrow afternoon to do a run through of a couple of the routines I'm gonna use for the October auditions. Thought you might like to come and watch.'

'Oh!' Hannah hesitated, chewing on her lower lip before asking where the studio was.

'Edgerston Court just off Monkfortune Avenue and behind the petrol station. Nelsons the printers are on the corner.'

'What time 'll you be there?' Hannah began to look interested.

'Danielle's gonna be there to open up at two.'

'Who's Danielle?'

126

'She runs the studio, and because she's preparing me for my auditions, she opens up for me to rehearse on my own on a Sunday afternoon.'

'What time?'

'Two o'clock.'

'Maybe. I'll see. And try and keep out the way of the Muskrateers.'

'I'll worry about them on Monday,' he shrugged. 'How about you, Rav?'

'I'm working in the restaurant tonight, and tomorrow I'm going up to London with my parents. Got to visit some relations. Dad says we'll maybe catch a movie while we're there.'

Looking towards Ollie, Hannah asked, 'Yeah. You gonna be there then?'

'Of course, I'm his best critic.'

Josh snorted.

'Okay. Take care, Ollie.' She smiled.

'You too.'

'See, I knew you cared.'

'Shut up!'

She pulled away from them, Rav following closely behind.

Chapter 19

Cycling two abreast, Ollie and Josh passed the old, abandoned hall. Ollie jammed on his breaks. 'Whoa!' his call bringing Josh to a halt, his rear wheel skidding as he hit some grit.

'What? What's wrong?'

'Back up a bit,' Ollie said turning his bike the way they'd just come. They got off their bikes and pushed them back to the hall. Reaching the building, Ollie looked around then leaned his bike against the wall. 'Look, notice anything?'

At first, Josh was wondering what Ollie was referring to. Then he saw what it was. Fairly obviously, one padlock was missing. The other, though at first glance appearing to be locked, on closer inspection revealed that it was made to look that way while, in fact, the lock wasn't properly secured.

The boys looked around then Ollie suggested they should maybe have a quick look inside. Josh was not so sure but Ollie pointed out that there couldn't be anyone there because they wouldn't be able to open the door from inside.

Josh, being cautious responded, 'But there could be. They've maybe been put in there as a prisoner and can't escape. Who knows what's in there?'

Ollie looked around again and said, 'You're not chicken, are you?'

'No, but I'll keep watch here. I'll hold the bikes ready for a quick getaway.' They turned the bikes around and Josh mounted his, holding Ollie's parallel to his own. 'Be careful Ollie, he cautioned looking over his shoulder to check the coast was clear.

Ollie removed the padlock and opened the door slowly.

There was no light from within, but with the door open he could see a table at the back of the hall. Running his hand down the wall to his left, he connected with a light switch. Expecting a single bulb to come, on he was startled to hear the clicketing noise of strip lighting firing up. Three of them. Now there were no hidden corners, no shadows. Two strip lights ran along the ceiling the length of the hall and one was placed halfway up the wall above a large wooden table. The table was covered in thick clear heavy-duty polythene as was the floor around the table. Apart from the table there was not much else to see, but Ollie's attention was drawn to the boarded-up windows. As on the outside, all six had iron bars welded into iron struts fitted as frames around the old brickwork. The metalwork looked new. There was a strong vinegary smell combined with something Ollie could not quite put his finger on. He was perplexed. From outside, the hall looked abandoned with boarded-up windows and the probability of weeds growing on the inside. But the place was clean. No rubbish. No dirt. The old toilet off from the main hall was clean with a plastic bottle of bleach and other cleaning materials on a shelf. What on earth was going on here and why had the padlock not been secured? Josh called to him, saying they shouldn't hang around. Ollie stopped just inside the door, scanning the room one more time. He was just turning to leave when he caught sight of something down by the skirting board. He moved quickly to check. Yes. A little canister just like the one Josh had pulled from his pocket at the burger place. He picked it up and pocketed it. Time to go.

Ollie came out shaking his head, and, closing the door he replaced the padlock the way it had been found. He told Josh there was nothing going on there that he could identify, but that there must be *something* going on. That there were polythene sheets covering the table and the surrounding floor. They looked at each other, puzzlement on their faces.

'Let's go,' Ollie said as he mounted his bike. Ten minutes later, as they slowed on approaching the main road, he burst out, 'Aargh! Bummer! We'll have to go back. I never switched the lights off.'

'Oh man, what a *dufas*!' Josh's angry response. 'How could you not think to put the lights out?'

'Because you were hassling me! You wait here. I'll just go back myself.'

'I'm not hangin' about here. I'll come with you.'

'Please yourself.' Ollie's curt response, angry at himself for being so stupid.

As they turned the corner before the hall Ollie let out a groan, in the distance they could see parked outside the old hall was the silver Range Rover they had seen beside McIntosh's house.

'Can't go up there, then.' Ollie said as they drew to a halt. 'We better get out of here in case he sees us and puts two and two together.'

Josh agreed but tried to reassure Ollie. 'Listen, he might think that he'd left the lights on himself. It looks like he'd shot back to his place for his visitor coming and he'd forgotten. Easy to forget the lights if he was coming back. He hadn't even secured the place.'

'Yeah, you could be right. Let's go.' They turned to face the way they had come and set off at speed.

Slowing down as they neared the main road, Ollie said, 'Well I guess when we get home, we're gonna have a, stuff hitting the fan, situation.'

'Yep. Can't see you slipping that ripped T shirt past your mum lady.'

'Never mind the T shirt — what about my side! I guess she'll reason that my cuts and bruises will heal, but the good T shirt's for the bin.'

'Could've been worse. Could've been the other way

round. But you did look a bit shaken when you came back. And you're lookin' more shaken now!'

'No wonder, what if I'd still been in the hall when McIntosh came back? But before that at the loft, if I was looking shaken, it wasn't 'cause I fell.'

'Oh! What then?'

'Hannah was tryin' to get me to kiss her.'

'Wow! What d'ya mean trying? Did you? Was there tongue action?'

'Well... maybe... not really... I don't think.'

'Ollie! Was there, or not?'

'Well, when the two guys came out the back door to check on us, she grabbed me into a hug, tellin' me to put my lips on hers.'

'Woo! Did ya?'

'Yeah... but just like, no movement at first but then she started to try 'n' kiss properly... and her lips felt so soft – her tongue was probing a bit, but I kept my mouth tight shut.'

An incredulous Josh blurted, 'Ollie! What's wrong with you? She's so cute. Man, I'd kiss her without too much encouragement. Tongues and all!' He laughed.

'Yeah well... it just wasn't the right time... or place... I guess.'

'But you do fancy her, don't you?'

Ollie was grateful that they were moving into more heavy traffic so avoided an answer as he pulled in front of Josh to be safe. They rode in silence for a bit, till they turned off onto a minor road. Ollie let Josh draw alongside again and said, 'There is somethin' goin' on at those pigeon lofts – I mean that car – a hundred grand! Whoever owns that has to be pretty loaded. But what's he doin' there?'

'Maybe McIntosh is training young birds for him. Maybe whoever it belongs to has put the money in for the state-of-the-art set up. Maybe they're in some kinda

131

partnership.'

'Mmm...'

They cycled on in silence again until Josh, a smile flickering at the corners of his mouth said, 'I got a feelin' you and Hannah's gonna be an item before the end of the holidays.'

Ollie smiled without replying and they cycled the rest of the way to his place in silence. His mum's car was parked in the driveway and Grandad was sitting in the garden doing a crossword in his newspaper. He glowered over the top and shouted hello. Putting their bikes into the garage they headed for the kitchen. Ollie's mum was sitting at the kitchen table speaking to his dad on Zoom, and, on seeing the state of him, with a panicked expression crossing her face demanded, 'What on earth's happened? Are you alright? Look at your T shirt. It's ruined. Is that blood?'

'I'm fine mum, I just fell out a tree.'

'Fell out a *tree*! What on earth were you doing up a tree?'

'Bird watching.'

'Bird watching!' Then turning back to his dad, incredulity in her voice, 'Did you hear that? He fell out a tree! Here, you talk to him while I get some TCP and hot water.'

Ollie plonked himself in front of the laptop. 'Hi, Dad, how you doin'?'

'Hi, Ollie. I'm doing fine but never mind me, what you been up to? Your mother's having a fit.'

'Well you heard, Dad, I fell out a tree. No big deal, just a few scrapes. When you comin' home?'

'About three weeks now.'

Ollie let out a low laugh, 'Hey, Dad, maybe one of your satellites picked up on my downward orbit.'

'Yeah, I'll check later.'

His mum, looking over his shoulder cut in saying,

'Right, Peter, I'll get him sorted out then call you back.' Then pulling him to the kitchen sink and the basin filled with hot water and TCP she fussed about checking him for cuts, bruises and broken bones.

'Mum! I'm not a child.' Ollie squirmed away from her.

Taking a step back she said, 'Up a tree! Up a tree! It's the birds who are supposed to be up trees, I thought people bird watched from the ground. Even from hides. But up a tree? Really?'

'Don't worry, I don't think I'll do it again, Mum. At least the tree wasn't hurt.'

She moved closer to him again, her nose twitching like a rabbit scenting a piece of fresh lettuce, 'What's that smell?'.

'What smell?' Ollie had to think fast, 'Oh, that'll be when I fell out the tree. Don't know what I landed on but it wasn't anything sweet smelling as I recall.'

She gave him one of her "I think you could be pulling my chain here" looks.

Grandad had entered the kitchen, taken the scene in, and immediately questioned what had happened to his binoculars.

'Your *binoculars*! Never mind your binoculars, what about your grandson?' Ollie's mum demanded. 'He could have broken his neck. Or an arm, or a leg.'

Grandad snorted, 'Sheila, he's a lad. Lads have been falling out of trees for millennia, but what about my binoculars?'

'They're fine, Grandad. Not a scratch.' Ollie was quick to reassure him.

'Unlike you then,' his mother grouched, 'And that T shirt is for the bin.' She pulled out her first aide box to put a large Elastoplast on one of the cuts.' At least I don't think you need stitches. It's more like nasty scrapes.'

Zoom rang again. Ollie's mum returned to the table

and reconnected to his dad and, in answer to a question, said, 'No, okay, I think. No broken bones.' Then turning back to Ollie, 'Your Dad asking if you're concussed. Did you bang your head when you fell?'

'No, I don't think so.'

'You don't think so?'

'Mum — will you stop being a parrot!'

Throwing him a look of disapproval, she said, 'Your dad wants to talk to you.'

Ollie moved swiftly to plonk himself in front of the screen, 'Hi Dad, don't worry. I'm fine,' he assured him. They spent about ten minutes talking until it became obvious his mum was becoming impatient to talk to his dad again. 'Okay, Dad. Mum's agitated, but I'm really looking forward to our holiday. Take care.' Giving the seat back to his mum he laughed, 'Here you are Mrs Pushy, aren't you the one who keeps tellin' me patience is a virtue?'

Josh had been standing quietly while the drama took place. Ollie looked at him and laughed, 'Nobody's asked how you are, Josh.'

'Well, I didn't fall out a tree, did I?' Josh's dry response.

Grandad stood looking at the pair of them without speaking. It became a bit unnerving to the boys, as though he were computing the input of information and the wheels were still whirring, searching for something that remained just out of reach. Then stroking his chin, eyes narrowing he said, 'So... you've been bird watching, eh?' Nodding his head gently as if to say he understood, then, 'So, did you see any *kind* of bird in particular?'

Silence.

'Maybe a wee robin red breast. Oh, wrong time of the year. You wouldn't be watching the seagulls now, would you? No... of course not, not up the Dalton's Mount way. More like the marina for them. So... wrens maybe? Mmm... wee wrens.' A quizzical look directed at the boys who remained silent, their faces expressionless. 'Blackbirds? Yes, maybe blackbirds – or swallows. Swallows?' His eyebrows raised as though signalling that was a bright suggestion worthy of answer. None came. He stood silent, just looking at the boys, his lips pursed, then, 'No, I don't think swallows. Certainly not vultures, I would think. Not in this neck of the woods. No not vultures.' Followed by a silent stare.

The boys knew perfectly well what was coming. 'So, if I was bird watching up Dalton's Mount way, from up a tree mind you, I wonder — might I have, inadvertently of course, been able to look *down* and in doing so be doing a wee bit *pigeon* watching? Would that be a bird worth watching? Interesting would you think?'

By now Ollie's Mum had come off Zoom and was standing listening to Grandad, 'Well Ollie?'

'Mum! For goodness sake. What is this? The Spanish Inquisition? We were just bird watching. Hannah was keen to teach us some stuff, so she wanted to show *us* some birds worth looking out for.' His face a little flushed.

'Birds worth looking out for, aye,' Grandad paused, 'Maybe something like the albatross from the tale of the Ancient Mariner. That would be something worth seeing.' He bent forward leaning his hands flat on the kitchen table and, looking up at the boys, added, 'Now listen, I don't want any of you going near those pigeon lofts, Ollie. I think there could be something going on there. Ernie phoned earlier to say he'd been speaking to Trevor Blackford, who, Ernie says, is Secretary of the Southeast England Pigeon Racing Federation, and he too seems to think there could be something dodgy going on there. He says that Ronnie McIntosh takes little to do socially with the Federation and only seems to use it for his own ends and accreditation. Oh, and rents them his bigger carrier when needed.'

'Okay, Grandad. Got it. What's for tea, Mum?'

'Just doing fish and chips tonight. That okay for you, Josh?'

'Great! Thanks, Mrs Saunders.'

Ollie's phone beeped and, drawing it from his pocket, he saw it was a 'snapchat' message from Hannah. He blushed and opened it to see a picture of her beaming smile along with a message, 'Missing you already! How's the wounds? XXX'. His blush intensified.

Josh, noticing his embarrassment, smiled and, with a superior look on his face, inquired of Ollie if that was his girlfriend.

'Really, his girlfriend? Who *is* this girlfriend then?' Ollies Mum demanded.

'Oh, I think you'll have to ask Ollie that, Mrs Saunders.'

'Ollie! What girlfriend?'

'I don't have a girlfriend, Mum. Just ignore Josh. He's just a trouble-maker.' Then turning to Josh, 'You're a dead man. Creep!'

Now Grandad got involved, 'A girlfriend, eh? I hope it's the wee lass Hannah. Bonny wee thing she is. Even with her purply hair. Good choice, Ollie.'

'Grandad! I do *not* have a girlfriend.'

Josh's snort progressed to an exaggerated laugh. '*Well...* if you say so, Ollie.'

'Josh – I'm gonna batter *your* bones for you, you stoolie!'

'Right you lot, get out my kitchen and give me peace, I'll give you a shout when tea's ready.'

'C'mon, Josh, let's go to my room. It's designated a grandad-free zone by the United Nations Security Council. We'll get some peace up there.'

Upstairs, Josh moved to the bedroom window and, leaning his hands on the sill, his back towards Ollie, said, 'It's been good to be here, Ollie. You're really lucky to have good parents. Even a good grandad. And a good home.'

'Well, you know you're always welcome here, Josh. You're practically one of the family anyway.'

'And I really appreciate it, but I hate being away from Nicola. She's so unhappy, and she's so frightened of Eddie. I could kill him.' There was silence for a couple of minutes, then he added, 'We've virtually lost our mum, you know. Her, as well as our Dad. What I'd give to get our old life back.' Ollie detected a catch in Josh's voice. 'But then that was so long ago.'

Ollie sat on his bed and leaned back to be supported by the wall, 'Listen Josh, we've been best mates forever, you're as close, maybe even closer than any brother I might have had. I know things are tough just now, and I know your whole life's taken over with concern for Nicola...'

'Not just Nicola,' Josh cut in. 'I don't know what's goin' to happen to my mum. She's wrecked and she needs to get that leach out her life and get herself cleaned up. 'Cause that's not gonna happen as long as he's around.' Turning to look at Ollie, his face a picture of sadness, he added, 'I just don't know what to do.'

Ollie rose from the bed moving to put an arm round Josh's shoulder. 'Josh, listen, it's his very badness that you can use to get rid of him.'

'No! He's said if I make trouble, he'll see to it that Nicola will suffer.'

'Listen. We know he's got some kind of link to the Dalton's Mount pigeon place. You said he can be driving trailer loads of birds over the Channel a few times a month. Why?'

'To release them somewhere in Brittany I think.'

'Why? Why go to the bother of going through the tunnel and releasing them in France?'

'Seemingly because a lot of McIntosh's birds are so valuable, it's safer to have them fly over expanses of water than countryside.'

Ollie looked puzzled.

'No hawks or peregrines out over the channel.' Josh informed him. 'They don't like water.'

Ollie nodded slowly, 'Well I guess that makes sense. But listen, Josh, I'm gonna help you see what we can get on him. If there *is* something there, and I'm sure there could be, he might face prison for long enough for your mum to get the help she needs, and for you, your mum and Nicola to move to somewhere he can't find you. Deal?'

'Deal.' Josh smiled.

Ollie was relieved to see him smile but reminded Josh that there was something more immediate they we're gonna have to deal with – the three Muskrateers. And that was not a situation that was going to disappear like a morning mist.'

'What d'you think they'll do? Or try to do, anyway?'

'Quite simple really. They're gonna want to inflict pain and spill some blood and possibly break a bone or two. But then again, they may just want to make up and be friends... Not!' he snorted. 'We've only got two days of school left before the holidays and I don't think they'll try anything there. But anyway, it's me they're after. You'll be okay.'

'Hannah seems to think we could take them on. Without Rav of course.'

'She might be right. You're really fit, me too. And when you think about it, none of that three do sports. They smoke and we know they're doin' drugs. I know they're older than us, but not much, and I'm sure not gonna run away from them this time.'

Josh nodded in agreement. 'You've got a point. But there's still three of them and only two of us.'

'Look stop worrying. C'mon, let's go get fed and we can talk about it later.'

Remembering, Ollie rose from his bed and pulled the little canister from his pocket. 'Is this a match for the one you showed us?'

Josh took it from him and pulled the one he still had in his pocket out to compare them, 'The same!' A look passed between them. 'Interesting.' he said.

'Anyway, stop worrying.' Ollie encouraged, 'C'mon, let's go get fed and we can talk about it later.'

Josh said, 'Great. What we gonna do tonight?'

'Xbox?'

'Yeah, great. I can give you a tanking.'

'You wish!'

Chapter 20

Day 3 — Sunday

'Are you two never getting out your beds? It's nearly eleven o'clock.' Ollie pulled the duvet down from over his head to see his mother's head sticking round the door. 'What time were you playing that Xbox thing till last night?'

'Oh, not late. Josh didn't like getting smashed.'

Josh's head appeared from the sleeping bag, and raising himself on one elbow, sneered, 'Hey! Who smashed who? I think I won, Mrs Saunders. It's pitiful how your son can't face the reality that he's just one of life's losers.' A pillow hurtled across the room to bounce of his head.

'Right, boys, I'll put on some breakfast. Be down within the next ten minutes.'

'But I need a shower, Mum.'

'Well, you can get one after breakfast, what's your hurry this morning?'

'No hurry, Mrs S, he's just coming to see me practice a routine, but not till this afternoon.'

'Hannah joining you, is she?' his mum inquired, a little smile playing around her lips.

Ollie felt himself blush — again. 'No, she's got church 'n family stuff on today.'

'Right. Ten minutes.' Her head disappearing behind the closing door.

'Pair of lazy beggars, aren't you!'

'Good morning to you too, Grandad. Grab a seat, Josh.'

Ollie's mum stood, pan in hand, just looking as the boys settled themselves at the table, 'You two are really shooting up, it seems like only yesterday you were coming in from the garden, covered in dirt looking for juice and biscuits.' She sighed, 'Right, do you like your eggs poached

140

or fried, Josh?'

'Poached, please, Mrs S.'

'How are your wounds, Ollie?'

'Well, kept me awake a bit last night, but gonna be fine.'

Grandad joined them at the table.

'You not had your breakfast yet, Grandad? Waiting for us, were you?'

'Waiting for you? I had my breakfast at seven o'clock. Like most right-minded people. What time of day is this to get up?'

'Grandad, it's a well-known scientific fact that teenage boys need a lot more sleep than other age groups. We're growing and using megatons of energy.'

A smile on Grandad's face. 'Aye, well in your two's cases it certainly can't be for beauty sleep, because if it is, it's not working. The only energy you use is sitting on your backside staring at a computer screen or doing whatever it is you do with your phone. Not using enough energy to light a torch bulb.'

Looking towards Josh, Ollie said, 'Excuse him, Josh, he's very, very old and for him it's like he's landed here from some distant planet of cave dwellers and hasn't quite come to grips with how us superior homo sapiens exist in such an advanced civilisation. Neither, it seems, is he aware of the amount of energy expended in ballet or rugby.'

'Don't cheek your grandad, Ollie. Right, let me put these plates down. Anyone want a cup of tea?'

'Yes thanks, Mrs S.'

Giving Ollie a look, she said, 'That's what I like about Josh. He's always so polite.'

'Thank you, Mrs S, and yes, Ollie, don't cheek your grandad. I wish Nicola and I had one like him.' Then turning to Grandad, added, 'So glad you came to live here to help out Grandad. Ollie certainly needs a firm hand.'

141

Ollie snorted, 'Creep! It's not me that needs a firm hand, it's him, the wind-up king. Did I ever tell you how when I was younger, he told me he used to work for the government? Very hush hush he said. Couldn't say too much, official secrets and all that. Said that before that he'd been an officer in the SAS. The SAS mind you. Grandad!'

Josh, looking uncertain, said, 'So he wasn't then?'

'Oh yes. Turns out 'my hero' was in the SAS, but something more like the Softies And Scaredy-cat's, a secret organisation something like the masons. They'd supposedly meet once a month in the only place they could rent cheap, a crypt in an old church.'

Josh sat looking bemused, 'Now you are winding me up.'

'As if! They only ever had one meeting though.' Ollie smirked, 'When they were sharing about the things that had scared them the previous month, they got so scared they had to get a police escort to see them out the building and the meetings were disbanded... permanently!' Ollie sat back in fits of laughter at Grandad. 'Oh, but there's more. He then told me when he came out the SAS, the government approached him to become a double 'O' special agent, licensed to kill. Said a lot of the James Bond thing is based on *his* life in the service.'

Josh looked at Grandad, who was wearing a mask of studied innocence, then turning to Ollie said, 'James Bond? And you believed him?'

'Oh yes, because he had another trick up his sleeve. He told me when he was retired from being a special agent, he had to hand back the Walther PPK but was allowed to keep his "strap to ankle", what did you call it again, Grandad — sub compact automatic pistol — for future protection, just in case anyone from his past caught up with him.'

Josh screwed up his face signalling disbelief. 'And you *believed* that?'

'Oh yes, because he showed me it. In fact, he still has it somewhere, don't you, Grandad?'

'Might have,' came the tight-lipped response.

'Oh, he's got it all right. Looks like a real small automatic pistol, but it turns out it's a starting pistol he bought at a flea market.'

Grandad shrugged and with a smile, rose to leave the table, 'Well it was a good story while it lasted.' He winked at Josh who was shaking his head in amusement.

'You're somethin' else, Grandad!' Josh laughed, then clearing his dishes, asked Ollie's mum if he could help with the washing up but she pointed to the dishwasher, asking them to wait ten minutes to shower till she got hot water.

'Come on you, let's go.' Ollie nodded towards the door. 'Showers.'

The boys had been late last night, not only playing games, but talking about the pigeon loft set up. The size of the loft, the state-of-the-art trailer and truck used to transport the birds and the fact that McIntosh entrusted Eddie to take the birds to France. Josh thought they should contact the police, or at least tell Ollie's mum. Ollie had argued that they didn't want police up investigating stuff near the pigeon lofts just yet. He wanted to find a way they could connect what Eddie had said to the girl he beat up about "his patch" and his involvement with the loft. Was McIntosh dealing in drugs and supplying Eddie? But then, surely not. Surely, he wouldn't want to jeopardise his already lucrative business.

The ideas went back and forward and the more they spoke about things the more convinced they were that they were on to something. And that something might just get Eddie out Josh's family's life which, was his main concern.

After showering, Ollie said, 'You want rid of, Josh. So let's see if we can get something to pin on him.'

Josh chewed on his bottom lip for a moment before

sharing his thoughts. 'We saw what he did to the druggie girl. He's not for messin' with, Ollie. And anyway, don't think she'd want police sniffing about anywhere either since she's hardly little miss innocent. But okay, we'll think about it. Anyway, we'd better get a move on before your mum starts shouting.'

'Better get some clothes on first. Time you got to be at the studio this afternoon?' Ollie said hopping about on one leg as he tried to line the other one up to slide into his jeans.

'About two. Danielle's gonna open up for me.'

'Just for you?'

'Only 'cause she thinks I've a real future in ballet.'

'Oh — Mr Modesty. I'm comin' to watch a star in the making.'

'Okay, but I'll be going straight home afterwards. Need to get back for Nicola.' Josh slipped on a T shirt and pair of shorts. 'I'll get a shower this afternoon.'

'Minger!'

After they had dressed, they folded up the camp bed and Josh packed his few things in his holdall. 'Well, it's been good to stay here for a couple of days,' he said, zipping the top of his bag.

'You know you can stay anytime, Josh. Get out that hellhole you call home. But we've *really* got to get Eddie out you guys' lives.'

Josh lowered himself to the floor, sitting cross-legged, and drumming his fingers against his lower legs. 'I think the only way is if he gets done for involvement in any illegal drug stuff, or maybe for assault, but I don't know how we go about that. Whatever we do, I have to see Nicola's kept safe and my mum gets help to get out the mess she's in.'

'I'm sure there'll be agencies that can help, Josh.'

'Well, maybe, but they might want to separate us, and I wouldn't want that to happen.' Pulling his phone from his pocket to check the time, he said, 'Quarter to one. We better

144

be ready to leave about twenty-past. D'you mind if I run through some warmup exercises before we go.'

Ollie asked if he had enough room before heading downstairs. Now he was alone, his Mum asked how he was feeling, lifting his T shirt and tut-tutting about the bruises.

'I'm fine, Mum. I'm more concerned about Josh's bruises.'

A look of puzzlement on his mum's face, 'He never said. How did he get bruises? Did he fall out a tree too?'

'No, Mum, it's the bruising inside I'm worried about. He's beating himself up about his home situation.'

'Poor Josh. Is there nothing can be done? Can he not speak to Social Services?' She hesitated, 'Or even the police? It's such a shame, his mother used to be really nice, always dressed nicely, seemed a really warm person.'

'Those days are long gone, Mum.'

'Well... it maybe doesn't help that much, but he should know there's always a place here for him, and, if necessary, we could squeeze Nicola in for a while too.'

'Thanks, Mum. I'll tell him, but I somehow don't think he'd just walk out on his mother. For all she's become, he still loves her and just wants to see her get back to her pre-Eddie-and-drugs days. But from what we've seen, I don't think you'll ever have to worry about Josh 'n' me doin' drugs.'

'Glad to hear it, Ollie. It is a worry nowadays. Us parents know how many temptations and pitfalls are out there now.'

It was on the tip of Ollie's tongue to say something about Friday nights escapades, and about the druggie girl on Saturday, but he knew his mum would have a fit. Probably literally. And he'd possibly even be grounded for his own safety. Better to let it lie. Before Josh's mum took up with Eddie, they'd heard stuff about drugs and addicts and associated crime but seeing his friend and his family being torn apart made it personal. And made Ollie angry and determined to help Josh get Eddie out the picture, whatever that took.

Chapter 21

Coming back down to the kitchen, Josh thanked Ollie's mum for having him to stay for the weekend. 'It's been good. My home from home.'

She smiled, 'You know you're welcome here anytime, Josh. So, what are you two up today?'

'We're just goin' up to hone our skills on Warcraft,' Ollie answered. 'Then Josh's got a practice session this afternoon and I'm going along for a while to see how he's doing. We'll grab a sandwich or somethin' before we go.'

'Well, I'm due at the Safari Park at twelve and won't be back till after seven. Are you staying for tea, Josh? Ollie's grandad's a good cook.'

'I'd love to, Mrs S, but I really need to get home. See how Nicola's doing. She wasn't too happy about me being away for the weekend.'

'What a shame. I hope things get better at home for you, Josh. And for Nicola. And your mum.'

'Oh, I hope to see that they do,' Josh answered softly.

Ollie rose from the table. 'Right, come on. I'm gonna blow you away. Right, Mum, have a good day. Hope Kukooru's feeling better now.'

As the boys headed upstairs, Ollie's mum's voice followed them. 'Did you have any homework for tomorrow Ollie?'

'Nope, just two days till we break up,' he shouted, shutting his bedroom door firmly behind him.

When the boys got to the studio, Danielle was running through some music tracks, searching for the ones Josh needed for his rehearsal. She looked like she was, or had been, a dancer herself. Probably late thirties to mid-forties, slim and wearing a dark blue leotard and woollen leg warmers, her feet bare. Her slightly greying auburn hair was swept up and pinned to the top of her head. When she turned to the boys, seeing Ollie, she frowned, 'Hi, Josh, you brought an audience today?'

'Critic more like. His name's Ollie but I've told him he's to sit quietly in a corner. I'll bring through a chair from the storeroom.'

Danielle, arms folded, her body leaning slightly to the right, looked Ollie up and down. 'Mmm... Not bad. Bit of work we could maybe do something with him, Josh.'

Ollie spluttered and was quick to dissuade her from that idea, 'No, definitely not me, sorry.'

Danielle just looked at him, a smile hovering around her mouth. 'Really, you're not one of those boys who think ballet's for sissies are you?' The hint of a French accent in her speech.

'No! Definitely not. Just not for me. Not my thing.' His face now red with embarrassment. He took in the surroundings, the studio had a sprung wooden floor, one wall completely mirrored with a barre running its length. The other three walls were bare. Speakers were mounted in the four corners, and three high arched windows allowed sunlight to flood the room. The floor space was devoid of any kind of furnishings leaving Ollie wondering where he could place a chair.

The double doors to the studio swung open and Hannah stood, body half in and half out of the room. 'Hi guys, mind if we join you?'

'Oh, you want to dance too?' Danielle asked, her hands on her hips, her head cocked to one side.

Hannah stepped fully into the studio dragging another girl after her. 'No sorry, we've come to watch Josh, if that's okay? He did invite us.' Josh nodded in affirmation. 'My cousin,' she said addressing the boys. The girl looked about Hannah's age, wore her hair in dreadlocks and had the same skin tone as Hannah. 'Her names Joanna, Jo for

148

short.' Then nodding in Ollie's direction, said, 'This is Ollie,' then towards Josh, 'and that's Josh.'

'Oh! So, this is the Ollie?'

Ollie blushed – again. And he was mad at himself. This was a new thing and he felt like a twerp every time it happened.

Danielle looked questioningly at Josh who was quick to reassure her, 'I'll bring through three chairs, they won't get in the way honest.'

'I hope not. Right! Go and get ready. But bring through the chairs first.'

'Actually, we don't mind sitting on the floor if that's okay.' Ollie suggested.

'Right but keep your feet tucked well in.' Danielle ordered, not looking too happy about the arrangements.

The three moved to an area where they could sit in a corner that, hopefully, wouldn't impinge on Josh's space. They stopped momentarily to see themselves in front of the mirrored wall. Ollie caught his breath; Hannah was wearing a light grey crop top, blue cut-away jeans, trainers and her usual air of confidence. And something he'd noticed before: she smelled so good! And it wasn't perfume, it was pure Hannah. She looked at Ollie and smiled. His heart flipped and he blushed. Again! She reached out her hand and with a demure smile, touched his cheek gently, winked, then, taking Jo's hand, went and sat in the corner, where he joined them. When they were seated, Hannah asked how his side was.

'Scraped, bruised and scarred. Think I might have a couple of cracked ribs, but I guess I'll survive.'

Hannah put her hand over her heart and, fluttering her eyes at him, said, 'Oh, I know how that feels Ollie, to be scraped and bruised and scarred,' only to burst out laughing at the look of consternation on his face.

Danielle clapped her hands together and chivvied

Josh, 'Right young man, go get changed then come and do some warm-ups and we'll get started on your pieces. You're nearly there with them.' She smiled encouragingly.

After he left, Jo leaned over to Ollie and in a low voice asked, 'He doesn't wear those men's ballet outfits I've seen on the telly, like women's tights, does he?'

'Don't think so, not today.'

As though to confirm Ollie's words, Josh came back into the studio wearing a loose blue T shirt, blue shorts over grey footless tights and, like Danielle, woollen leg warmers. There was a subtle difference in the way he walked. Now in bare feet, it was as though he hadn't just changed his clothes, but somehow, his whole persona. The littlest movement seemed to take on a smooth fluidity, his steps as light as angels dancing on clouds. Ollie and the girls were transfixed. Josh smiled at them and made his way to the barre as Danielle put some music on. He spent some time warming up and stretching, Danielle making the occasional adjustment to his stance, 'Right,' she said, 'remember, tight bum, long neck, straight back and elongation of the limbs, and... in all things... *graceful*.' Then, slapping her outer thighs lightly as though to emphasise what she was saying. 'You, my darling, are to be an irrepressible bubbling stream dancing over and round immovable obstacles with the sole intent of reaching a mighty ocean. That ocean for you, Josh, is the beautiful world of international ballet. You are to rise up as on wings of eagles and soar into a glorious golden sunlight, not my darling, to spend your life grubbing about down here with the turkeys. You have such potential.' She clapped her hands again, 'Right take your position.'

'Some mixing of metaphors there,' Hannah whispered.

Josh turned away from the barre giving his friends a cheeky wink as he walked to one end of the studio, 'I think you might be better sitting along that back wall.' Danielle waved her hand in its direction. 'Sit in a row as an audience

150

would, the rest of the room is a stage for our danseur.'

Josh moved to the other end of the studio and took up a central position. Danielle came and stood facing him, running her hands over his shoulders, 'Loose now, loosen them, rotating your head at the same time.'

Josh moved his shoulders about, letting his arms and hands shake freely. He then did a bit of extreme leg stretching.

'Right.' Turning to the three friends Danielle said, 'What you're about to see first is Josh's presentation piece in ballet. He has to perform a five-minute piece, and a five-minute modern dance piece for his auditions later this year. The modern dance piece does incorporate ballet but is not ballet in its purest form and, unusually, includes aspects of *savate*. It's an interesting piece Josh has been working on.' Facing Josh again, this time resting her hands on his shoulders, she said, 'Now remember what I told you about Cecchetti's teaching methods — that you should *always* demonstrate ease and a *softness* in your dancing. What else did he say?'

'We've not to let our presentation seem as though it's hard work, that it would rob the beauty of the presentation if any of the effort of the dance were to be seen in our performance.'

'Good. So, are you ready?

'Yep.'

'Oh, and the *entrechat* is one area I want to focus on today, and also the *pas de brise*. You need to be more graceful with the legs. I know it's not easy at this stage, but it's important. So, we'll run through your routine then we'll start focusing on what needs improvement, alright my darling?'

'Yep.'

Turning to Ollie, Hannah and Joanna, she explained that *entrechat* is a ballet leap with alternate legs crossing

151

and, importantly, coming down gracefully, and the *pas de brise* is where Josh will leap from one leg, with legs beating together before landing *gracefully*. Smiling and focusing on the girls, she added, 'Perhaps we'll make you all into fans. Maybe even dancers! Josh has been working really hard on this and I'm sure he'll do well in the auditions.' And turning back to face Josh, said, 'Right Josh, take your position,' then moved over to play the chosen track.

Josh shook his body, moving his head from side to side then stood, legs together his feet meeting at the heels forming a ninety-degree angle. Looking straight ahead, his chin slightly tilted, and, as he had taught Hannah, his arms somewhat lower than his shoulders and forming a wide but graceful arc as though he were hugging someone without familiarity. As the music started Josh began to move. It was as though the music gave him wings. His initial steps light and urgent, as though his feet were reluctant to be in contact with the floor. His movements flowing into each other as easily as the irrepressible bubbling stream of which Danielle had spoken. He extended the scope of the dance using the whole floor to dazzle his audience. His body now become a finely tuned instrument anticipating the next note and ready to reach out to meld into it. To interpret crochets and quavers, minims and semibreves into a visible manifestation of music in human form, so that at times it seemed as though he were so light that he was more in the air than on the ground.

Ollie, Hannah and Jo were left gasping in awe. His *entrechat* seemed pretty impressive as he launched into the air, but on landing, Danielle clapped her hands loudly, 'No. No! Not good! Not Good!' Clutching her hands to her heart she shouted, 'Stop, stop, you're trying to kill me, *mon cher!*'

Josh stood before her, a look of confusion on his face, 'Not good then?'

'Not good! It was like a circus elephant trying to look

elegant jumping over a barrel. No, no, no my darling. Practice, practice, practice. Do you want to give me a bad name at your audition? Do you want to ruin my reputation and break my heart?'

Ollie and the girls thought she was being harsh. They had been stunned by the dexterity of Josh's movements and the smooth transitions performed whilst using the whole of the floor. Pirouettes, jumps, at times balancing on one leg whilst the other was raised at his side at a ninety-degree angle, the knee bent to bring the flat of the foot to rest against the inner thigh of the straight leg. Other moves where he balanced on one leg, his body parallel to the floor, then launching into the air, one leg reaching forward the other straight back, both making a near one-hundred-and-eighty-degree angle to his torso. Which, when commented on later, Josh informed them was ballet's classic *élévation*. When he danced, every move was so fluid, so light of foot leaving Ollie, Hannah and Joanna gasping at the beauty of his interpretation, though he later confessed it was mostly Danielle's interpretation. That's why she took it personally if she didn't think he was putting enough effort in.

When the music and his dancing came to a close, the three spectators sprang to their feet, applauding loudly accompanied by, 'Wow!' and 'Amazing!' and 'Encore!'.

Josh gave a sweeping bow, held his hand out to Danielle and said, 'My mentor without whom... I'd be as nothing,' and bowed this time, to her.

Danielle tutted but looked pleased nonetheless, 'You may have impressed your audience, Josh, but there are some areas that still need worked on so don't get carried away. The people for whom auditioning will not be so blinkered nor as kind as your friends.'

Josh turning to Ollie, Hannah and Joanna, asked if they wanted to stay, that it might get a bit boring for them as he would be made to repeat and re-run till Danielle was happy. If ever!

'We don't mind, Josh,' Hannah looked at Ollie and Jo, 'Do we?' They readily agreed. Danielle looked at Hannah as though she were sizing her up for a purpose, then asked Josh if he had been doing his weight training. He said he had as much as was possible considering his domestic situation.

'Right then, Josh, and you Ollie, go and bring through a couple of the big mats from the storeroom. Make it three and your friends can help you.'

When they were brought into the studio, Danielle formed an island in the middle of the floor with them. Then getting Josh to stand in the centre, she asked Hannah if she would mind lending a hand, to which she agreed. 'Now here's what I want you to do. I need Josh to place his hands on your waist or upper pelvis if that's better.'

Josh stood frowning then said, 'Yes. And?'

'I want to see how effective your weight training has been. Hannah looks really light, so with her permission, you're going to attempt the overhead lift. Now remember, you're to put the weight onto your right leg bent at the knee, the left leg set straight back to perfect your balance and hold her above your head for sixty seconds, okay?'

'Yeah fine, I think I can do it.'

'You better do flippin' more than 'think' you can, Josh.' Hannah chided.

'Don't worry, Hannah, Ollie's here to rush to your rescue with the kiss of life, but anyway, I promise I won't drop you.'

Danielle now addressed a nervous looking Hannah. '*Bien, ma chère.* In this lift, you stand with your *back* towards Josh and he is going to lift you above and partly behind his head. At the completion of the move, your body will be above his head and you will be facing the ceiling. Then I will help you to arch backwards with your legs

154

hanging in front of his chest and your arms stretched out straight above you. Are you okay about that? You don't have to if you don't want to. But you must trust him.'

Though looking a little nervous Hannah agreed after being assured the mats provided a well-cushioned landing.

With her back towards him, Josh placed his hands on Hannah's hips and, with Danielle' guidance, he lifted her into position. Holding her above his head, he never wavered holding the position for the sixty seconds till Danielle told him to take ten steps forward *gracefully* and *slowly* before lowering Hannah to the floor. He did as he was asked, gently lowering her down the front of his body with Danielle helping her to come down safely with her back towards Josh before he stepped back from her. Danielle clapped, 'Well done, Josh. I think you stand a good chance of getting into the National Ballet School. But no resting on your laurels. Still lots of work to do. And thank you Hannah, you sure I could not interest you in ballet my darling?'

Hannah shook her head.

Turning back to Josh, Danielle said, 'Right, next I want to see your male *pirouette,* and *la grande pirouette à la seconde,* followed by the series of turns on one foot, the free leg raised to ninety degrees in front of the body. Okay?'

Ollie checked the time and said they would leave Josh to his practice. Hannah asked if he wanted to join them for a coke at the marina. Ollie asked Josh how long he was going to be.

Josh looked enquiringly at Danielle who told him it that would depend on the progress he was making. That he would have to run through his whole routine at least a couple of more times. Kinks to iron out. Moves to perfect and, if time allowed, maybe spend thirty minutes concentrating purely on his *savate*.

'Looks like it could be some time, so I'll just head

home. I need to get back for Nicola anyway.'

'Okay, we'll probs be at the Captain's Bridge but I don't think I'll hang around too long.'

Hannah scowled at him, which made him laugh, earning him a side of the fist thump on the shoulder. 'Ollie! Am I hard work or something? If you don't like me, just say so.'

'Hey! Stop harassing me. I like you fine but you've just come on kinda heavy this weekend.'

'Kinda heavy? Kinda heavy! Ollie Saunders, you should think yourself lucky that I show you any interest in you at all, but if you're too immature, or I'm too much for you, just let me know and I'll move on.' She did the folded arms thing again, eyebrows fiercely knitted.

Ollie laughed at her indignation, 'Okay, Hannah, but there's two conditions if this is goin' anywhere.'

Her brow wrinkled into a frown, 'What?'

'Stop *hitting* me and... do *not* encourage my Grandad and his nonsense.'

'Oh, Ollie, you ask too much. He's such a sweetie.'

'Just don't, okay?'

'I'll try.' She smiled, 'Let's go then.'

Ollie turned to Josh to say goodbye, 'Give me a call after you're home to see how Nicola's doing.' Then he headed for the marina the girls walking on either side of him, 'I guess people are going to think I'm a babe magnet,' he smirked.

Hannah hit him on the arm again. Jo hit him on the other.

Chapter 22

Since the showers had a notice saying that for technical reasons hot water was not available, Josh used a hand towel to dry his face, hair and upper torso after the hard work-out Danielle had coached him through. She was such a perfectionist, but that was good because he didn't ever want to be just mediocre. His body, though tired, felt energised, supple and strong and he was becoming quietly confident about the upcoming auditions. But now he needed to get home. He hoped Eddie would be out. In fact, he hoped Eddie would just drop dead. That would solve a lot of problems.

After thanking Danielle and arranging the next session, he headed home. The closer he got to the flat, the heavier both his heart and his feet felt. Climbing the stairs to his home he was overcome by a great sadness which, by the top step, was turning to a simmering anger. Anger at his dad for getting killed when he and Nicola were so young. Nicola not even remembering her dad now. Angry at his Mum for ever getting in tow with Eddie and for all she'd become. Angry that he and Nicola no longer had the mother she used to be. But all that anger was magnified into a fierce and raging hatred when it came to Eddie.

A deep sigh escaped him as he put his key in the lock and, on opening the door, was met by Nicola running towards him and bursting into tears as she threw her arms around his waist, 'Oh Josh, Josh, I'm so glad you're back. Josh, don't ever leave me again. Please, Josh, please!' Great sobs racking her young body. He dropped his bag and crouched down beside her drawing her to himself and kissing her forehead. 'Hey, what's wrong Squidger? I've only been away a couple of nights.'

His mother appeared at the sitting room door. At least

it looked like she'd made some kind of effort to tidy herself up today.

'Oh! You're home. Will you tell your sister to stop snivelling like a spoilt brat?'

Nicola clung more tightly to Josh.

'Hi Mum, how's your weekend been then?' sarcasm in his voice as he emphasised, 'your weekend'.

'Would have been a lot better without her whinging and moping,' she spat.

Josh got to his feet, pulling Nicola in by his side, 'Mum, what on earth's become of you? How have you got into this mess?'

'What mess?' Then realisation hit her, causing her to go into her drama queen mode, 'You don't understand how hard it's been for me since your dad died. I know you don't like Eddie, but at least he's looking after me.' She ran the back of her hand under her nose and sniffed.

'Mum! He's not good for you. He's not good for us. You need to get yourself sorted out.'

She leaned her head against the door frame, tears filling her eyes, 'I can't, Josh, I can't. I need him.'

'No, you don't, Mum, you most definitely don't. He's killing you with his drugs.'

At this, Nicola's sobs turning into a wail. Josh held her more tightly and shook his head. 'Welcome home, Josh,' he muttered under his breath. 'I take it he's not home, then?'

'He got back from France early but he's gone out again, says he's got some people to see.'

Josh sighed, 'Why not put the kettle on, Mum? I'll bring my washing through in a minute, come on, Nicola, you can help me.' He led Nicola into their bedroom.

Josh threw his bag on the floor, and sitting on his bed, drew Nicola into a reassuring embrace. At first, she clung to him tightly, her head burrowed under his chin, her young body quivering as tiny sobs refused to be quieted.

158

'Hey, I told you I'd only be gone a couple of nights. What's all the tears for? I'm back now.'

She clung to him more tightly, 'Don't leave me again, Josh, please don't leave me here alone.'

'Did something happen Nicola? Did you see something bad? Did you hear something bad?'

She lifted her head from his chest, and, her eyes red-rimmed with tears, appealed to him, 'You have to take me away from here, Josh.'

Josh pulled her into himself again and, stroking the back of her head to comfort her, sought to reassure her. 'Hey, I'm home now. I'll see nothing bad happens to you.'

'I'm frightened, Josh. I'm really frightened.' Her voice muffled as she still clung to him.

Putting his hands on her shoulders he moved her back slightly to see her face, 'Is it Eddie? Has he done something to you?' His anger rising, his attention fully focussed on what she would say next.

Her head dropped, her shoulders drooped, her arms hung loosely by her sides and a tear dripped from her chin. In a muffled voice she whispered, 'Yes.'

An icy chill ran through Josh as he placed his fingers under her chin, and raising her head again said, 'Tell me, Nicola, what happened?'

Never having seen her big brother with such a look on his face, she became frightened again. His eyes were narrowed, his mouth clamped tightly, his body taught.

'Josh, now *you're* making me frightened,' she whimpered.

Drawing her back into himself and resting his chin on the top of her head he sought to reassure her. 'Hey you, don't worry. I'll make sure nothing bad happens to you but you need to tell me what happened this weekend,' He gave her a little squeeze to calm her. 'Would you like a drink of juice or something?'

159

'No,' came the muffled reply.

Josh raised her head gently and, grabbing a tissue to wipe her nose, said, 'Tell me, Nicola. I'll keep you safe. Promise.' Then putting his hands under her shoulders, he lifted her onto the bed beside him, put his arm around her, and cosied her into his side.

Looking up at Josh with tear-filled eyes, she said, 'He came into our room,' then burst into tears again.

Josh's whole body tensed, his voice harsh when he asked, 'When?'

Nicola shrank back as though frightened she was going to get into trouble and, in a timorous voice answered, 'Friday. It was Friday night. He was away to France yesterday'.

'What did he do, Nicola? What happened?' Sensing his young sister's fear and confusion, he added, 'Listen, if I'm looking angry it's not at you, you know that. It's about him. But you need to tell me what he did.'

Nicola was nervously pinching at her jeans as though that helped her put her thoughts together. 'He was down beside my bed.'

'Where was Mum?'

'I heard them arguing. That's what woke me. Then Mum went into her bedroom and slammed the door shut. I didn't like that... then... that's when he came in. I think it was very late.'

'So, he crouched down beside your bed. Did he think you were sleeping?'

'Yes. I kept my eyes tight shut and I could hardly breathe. I wanted to shout for Mum but I didn't think she'd hear me.' Her bottom lip started to tremble. 'I could smell his breath. It was horrible, all beery. He just kept looking at me, and Josh,' She hesitated then started to cry again, 'I wet myself.' She sniffled through the tears.

Josh gathered her into his arms again, assuring her he

160

would sort her bed and pyjamas out. He sat stroking her back till she cried herself out, then kissing her forehead again, said, 'Trust me, Nicola, I'm going to get him out the house, out our lives and we're gonna get our Mum back, okay?'

'How, Josh?'

'I'm not sure yet, Squidgle, but I will, I *promise*.'

The bedroom door swung open and his Mum stuck her head into the room. Seeing Nicola's tear-stained face she demanded to know what was going on.

Josh stood up and, taking advantage of being a couple of inches taller than her, drew himself up to his full height, disgust and fury etched across his face. 'I'll tell you what's wrong. That 'boyfriend' of yours came into this room on Friday night when you were passed out in your bed and crouched beside Nicola's bed just looking at her. She was terrified.'

A look of confusion crossed his mother's face then, defensively, 'What are you trying to say you dirty minded pig? He would just be checking she was okay. That she was asleep.'

'I've told you Mum, you need to get rid of him, 'cause if you don't, I will.'

'Oh, Mr Big Man now, are you?' she sneered.

Josh shook his head. 'What's happened to you? Have you lost all self-respect? Has he got you so hooked on stuff that you just don't care anymore? Just look at yourself. Look at the state of your clothes. And when did you last wash your hair?'

She stood glaring at him for a couple of minutes, the atmosphere in the room so strained Josh was waiting to see what, or who, was going to yield. But turning on her heel she snapped, 'Your tea's ready.'

Josh gave Nicola's face a wipe with a tissue then led her through to the kitchen. Two plates of spam, spaghetti

161

hoops and oven chips lay on the table.'

'You not eating?' Josh questioned his mother.

'Not hungry. And see you wash your plates when you're finished.' She was already lighting a cigarette as she moved through to the living room.

Nicola played with her food protesting that she wasn't hungry, but Josh encouraged her to eat at least half of what was on her plate. 'Well only another two days of school, Nicola. You looking forward to being on holiday?'

Josh's heart went out to her as she answered 'No,' with a weight of anguish and despair in that one little word. After tea, he changed her sheets and put them, her pyjamas and his own stuff from the weekend into the washing machine and told her to get showered and he'd come help her wash her hair when she was ready. After she was showered and into fresh pyjamas, he got a couple of board games out he knew she enjoyed playing and, having cleared the kitchen table set one up. His phone beeped. From Ollie. 'U OK?' He shook his head, smiled and replied, 'Yeah fine.'

A minute later, 'U sure?'

'Yeah, fine, honest.' No need to have Ollie and his family worrying about him, he thought. He'd tell him tomorrow. Nicola and he played the two board games, Josh letting her win, then played a couple of games of snap and of slap jack. Josh was pleased to see the tension falling away from her. Their mother came through a couple of times to get a can of beer from the fridge, completely ignoring them in the process. Eventually Josh got Nicola through to bed with the promise he'd tell her a "made up in your head" story, which he was happy to do. After which he tucked her in, as he did, she wrapped her arms around his neck and said, 'I'm glad you're home, Josh. Promise not to leave me again.'

A heaviness filled his heart as he knew, if everything worked out, he could be leaving home in a couple of years, or less. Hopefully, by then, Eddie would have disappeared and their mother be sorted out. Still, he assured Nicola he would never leave her, then went and joined his Mum in the living room, prepared to watch whatever rubbish she was tuned into. As he took a seat on the couch, he had a sense of being utterly trapped and knew with a certainty, something would have to change. Monumentally.

His mum had been drinking steadily all evening, then at nine she announced she was going to bed and to tell Eddie to go down to the Chinese if he wanted fed. Josh wasn't sure if he would still be up when Eddie got home, or if he'd want to be, aware of the anger still simmering deep inside. Wishing he had an iPad he watched till the end of the Sunday night drama on the BBC then went through to the kitchen to make a cup of tea. He heard the front door open then being banged shut with little regard that Nicola would be sleeping. 'Selfish pig' Josh muttered. Eddie went to the toilet before coming into the living room and dumping his holdall on the couch.

'Where is she?' he demanded, an aggressive scowl on his face.

'Bed. Just where I'm going.'

'Bed! The cow can't be tired? She does bog all, all day.'

Josh felt something inside snap, his whole body tensed. Eddie was older and probably stronger than him but, by the sound his slurred speech, had either had a good few drink or on the wacky-backy, or both. Moving swiftly, he took up a position immediately in front of Eddie, who stepped back, momentarily surprised by the suddenness and boldness of Josh's movements. He swore at Josh and, putting the flat of his hand on his chest, gave him a shove, causing him to stumble against an armchair.

Eddie sneered at him, 'Think you're the big man, do you? Well you're not — and you never will be, you poofy nancy boy. Away and dance with the girlies, or boys more

163

like. Get to wear a frilly tutu do ya?'

'You stay away from my sister.'

'Your sister! Your sister! Away an' chase yourself, you little ponce.'

Josh knew this was a dangerous man. There was no pity him, no compassion, only a repressed kind of hatred because, so Josh thought, he was frustrated that he wasn't as big time as he wanted to be and was probably aware Josh held him in contempt for being the person he truly was. A low life nobody.

Eddie pushed passed Josh, on his way to the fridge. Coming back into the sitting room with a can of beer, he threw himself on the couch and started to roll a cigarette. Looking up at Josh he said in an icy tone, 'You better not give me any trouble,' he paused, 'cause if you do... I'll see your legs get so badly broken you'll *never* dance again. You hear me? Never!'

Josh believed him but knew that would never happen. He knew he could have countered Eddie's strength when pushed earlier but instinctively had held back for fear of upsetting Nicola. He felt a surge of confidence. He may be young, but he was gaining in strength and agility. The day was coming when he would be able to take Eddie on. Soon. But not just yet. Tomorrow had its own troubles to deal with first.

Chapter 23

On returning home, Ollie was surprised to find Grandad's friend Ernie Broadbend sitting at the kitchen table with him, the two of them deep in conversation.

'Aha! Talk of the devil and he's sure to pop up in a cloud of sulphurous smoke,' Grandad said as he leaned back on his chair.

Ollie placed his arm round Grandad's shoulder and said, 'There now, Grandad, think yourself lucky, 'cause if I *were* the devil, you'd be feelin' my trident, heated in the eternal fires of hell, prodding your backside to help you on your way to join me.'

Shaking his head, Grandad turned back to his friend, 'See, kids today, Ernie, no respect for their elders.'

Ollie patted him on the head, then looking around as though expecting her to appear, he asked grandad if his mum was home yet.

'No, she told you she'll not be home till after seven tonight. We'll eat then. Now then Ollie, you'd better sit down. I think you'll be interested in what Ernie has to say.'

Ollie joined them at the table, 'Hi, Mr Broadbend. You the pigeon expert then?'

'Hardly an expert, for me pigeons are just a hobby.'

'What's the goss then?'

Ernie's face a mask of incomprehension till Grandad informed him Ollie meant 'gossip' before commenting about the falling standards of education today.

'Blah, de blah, blah.' Ollie brushed the criticism aside then, speaking to Grandad's friend, said he'd been amazed about the things he had told his grandad about racing pigeons and especially the big money pots involved. He asked if he could shed any light on what was going on with the pigeon man at Dalton's Mount. 'Is he making big money

165

then? That why there's so much security?'

His head nodding gently, Ernie began, 'Aye, your grandad and I have just been talking about that. By all accounts his loft is up there among the best.'

'Aye. So's his transporters. Have you seen 'em, Ernie?' Grandad asked.

'Not up close, but I heard he had them shipped over from the States apparently. The truck especially is in a class of its own – state of the art and must have cost a packet. Supposed to have a great ventilation systems and water supplies for the birds in transit, these things are important, especially for long journeys. I believe they also have a centre walkway with about a two-meter headroom. He rents it out to different associations. But mind you, the trailer's an expensive piece of kit too.'

'I just don't get it,' Ollie interrupted. 'I thought racing pigeons were for people up north with cloth caps, braces and rolled up sleeves. Not a sport like horse racing or somethin'.'

Eddie laughed at Ollie's suggestion. 'People like me, you mean? Well, I suppose it has changed a bit. Some say that the sport has become all about the money, that 'the little guy' has no chance at competing. Well at least not at some of the bigger races.'

'Yeah, Grandad was tellin' me about the big money involved nowadays and that McIntosh has had some top-class winners.

Ernie nodded, 'He certainly has, and when you have a consistent winner, not only is the bird valuable for its racing ability. If you get a really good racing pigeon with the kind of exceptional strength that allows it to race in all weather conditions, the income from breeding can be mind-blowing too. McIntosh seemingly has one or two birds that have never lost a single race, and I tell you that's really something. Prize birds, now worth a fortune I'd

166

think. The sport's really changing nowadays. Some reckon that stories about big prize pots actually helps it get more recognition. As I said, others think that the good old days of pigeon racing are simply gone, now replaced with those who have the biggest cheque books.'

'So how do your birds do?' Ollie questioned.

Ernie gave a little laugh. 'Well I don't think any Chinese billionaires will be beating a path to my loft. For me it's just a hobby, just a bit of fun, gets me out the house.'

'Yeah, Grandad was tellin' me about the Chinese billionaires. I'm thinkin' I should just give up school, get myself a few pigeons.'

'Not just the Chinese, but wealthy buyers will travel far and wide and pay huge sums for champions and top breeders. A few years ago, a Chinese businessman bought a Dutch pigeon for three hundred and twenty-eight thousand dollars, which set a world record for the most valuable pigeon ever sold. And some American breeders make in excess of two hundred thousand dollars a year racing and selling pigeons.'

Ollie, disbelief in his voice asked, 'Wow! So... McIntosh's pigeon loft is a reputable business then?'

'Yes... I would say so. The size and the cost of his loft would be well beyond the reach of your average pigeon fancier, and I mean seriously beyond reach. There's a rumour going about that someone has sunk a lot of money into the loft, that's how McIntosh has managed to accomplish so much.'

That explained a lot, Ollie thought, 'How many birds will he have then?'

'Oh, they're not all his. He operates a "one loft" system where owners consign their birds to the loft at about five weeks old, then McIntosh is responsible for both training and racing the birds and gets a percentage of any winnings as well as charging them for their upkeep. He also has his own breeding programme and consistently breeds winners. From what I've heard, he keeps about two hundred high quality breeders separate from the rest of the loft. But there's certainly a few hundred, maybe even up to eight hundred birds there.'

'Wow!' Ollie was shaking his head. 'So, can I ask you, do you think he'd ever get involved in drugs in then?'

'Be stupid if he did, he's got a good and respected set-up there. Why would you ask that?'

'My friend Josh, his mum's partner does some work for him, goes over to France just about every week with the trailer. He said it's because it's safer for the birds to fly over water to avoid raptors.'

'Yes, he's right, but also there's a lot less danger of them hitting pylons or wires and stuff. But it seems a lot of effort to go to.'

'Not if some of the birds are worth what you say they are, Ernie.' Grandad added, 'Are they insured against loss.'

Ernie gave a wry smile, 'No, I'm afraid not. You can insure the loft but not the birds. Though in my case, say my loft got wrecked in a high wind, because it's in my back garden, I could probably claim on my house insurance. But McIntosh couldn't with his set-up.'

'You could be right then, Grandad. McIntosh would have every reason to shoot birds of prey.'

'Well, the thing is,' Ernie added, 'I heard the police searched his house and the out-houses just in case it was him shooting the birds, but they didn't find anything.'

Grandad thought for a minute, 'What about the loft? Did they search that?'

'Again, just a general look round. Maybe they thought that McIntosh wouldn't risk his birds being upset, so he wouldn't use the loft itself for anything dodgy. Plus, the pigeons would be upset and disturbed by plod messing about. But who knows?'

Ollie's phone beeped. Hannah! The message read, 'SYS' along with a smiley face emoji with two hearts in place of eyes. He smiled and put his phone away again.

'But there is one thing,' Ernie continued, 'I've heard he gets a visit every Saturday afternoon from someone who drives an expensive car. Think he could be the money behind the loft?'

'Could be Grandad. The car's an Audi something or other. A top of the range model, Rav says.'

Grandad jumped in, 'And how would Rav know about that then?'

'We cycled past it when we were out bird watching yesterday.' Ollie hoped his face wasn't as red as it felt.

Grandad stared at him.

'Rav seemed to think it was about a ninety-odd-thousand-pound car,' Ollie said.

'Ninety odd thousand pounds! Who's got that kind of money to spend on a car?' Grandad blurted.

'A very rich one, I'd think,' Ernie answered, 'Or a very bad one. Maybe both.'

As Ollie rose from the table, Ernie suggested that Ollie and his friends should not hang about up Dalton's Mount and added, 'That McIntosh isn't someone you want to mess with I'd think.'

'Yeah, we'll stay well clear,' Ollie said just as his phone rang. He saw Josh's name and excused himself to take the call. Going out to the garden he opened the connection, 'What's up? How was Nicola?'

In answer, Josh spat, 'I could kill him.'

'Eddie? What's he done now?'

'He went into Nicola's room on Friday night when my mum went to bed the worse for wear.'

'What? Never!' Ollie was apprehensive about asking, but knew he had to, 'What for?' Then, his voice quietening, added, 'He never touched her, did he?'

'Thankfully not, but she was terrified and really, *really* upset when I got home. She couldn't stop crying and just clung to me. She's begging me never to leave her alone with him.'

Ollie started pacing round the garden, 'Does your mum know? What's she saying.'

'Nothin'. She's in denial. She's become so dependent on him she's always gonna take his side, no matter *what I* say to her.'

Shaking his head Ollie said, 'Listen Josh, you're maybe gonna have to get Social Services involved. This is not good.'

'No! Never! You know what would happen. They'd probably split us up, get us foster homes, and Nicola really needs me, Ollie.' There was a low groan, then he went on, 'What am I goin' to do? If I get a place in London, she'd still only be eight. I can't leave her.'

Ollie could sense the despair in his friend's voice, 'Is he there now?'

'No, he's out — but I tell you, I'm gonna kill him!'

'Calm down, Josh, and don't do anything stupid. Listen, we know he's involved in dealing and we can maybe find a way of gettin' something on him that could get him nicked... and hopefully put away for a long time. Even an anonymous phone call to the police.'

'Well something's got to happen sometime soon.'

'Okay, Josh, it's coming up to the holidays so we'll see what we can come up with. By the way, I've just been talkin' to Grandad's old mate Ernie and he's told us quite a bit about Dalton's Mount. He thinks it could be a bit shady.'

'Really?'

'Yep, I'll tell you later. However, right now I've got a more immediate problem. I'm going to have to deal with Jez Freeman and his lot tomorrow, or at least in the next couple of days.'

'They won't do anything in school, surely.'

'You know what, Josh? I say "bring it on". I'm not frightened of them and I think I could hold my own with one of them at least.'

'Yeah, but that's the problem. You're gonna have all three come after you.'

Ollie gave a little laugh, 'I can outrun them easy. Oh, by the way, I just got a message from Hannah.'

'Oh, love and kisses, was it?'

'Nearly, I guess. SYS and an emoji with love hearts in place of eyes. Yech!'

'SYS. Mmm! See you soon. Were there kisses after it?'

'Shudup you! You're just jealous 'cause I'm *such* a babe magnet. By the way, her and her cousin were really impressed with your rehearsal today. Think Jo really liked you too.'

'Get lost, you!'

'Listen, we're going to have time on our hands soon and we're going on holiday for a couple of weeks when my dad gets back, but that's about three weeks away. So, I think maybe I should tell my mum about yours and Nicola's situation. What d'you think?'

'No! Not yet. Let's see what we can figure out first. I've got to look after Nicola. She's got no one else and she depends on me so much that I can't let her down.'

'Yeah, I understand. You calling in for me tomorrow morning?'

'Yep, see you then.'

Ollie felt for Josh. So much had gone wrong for his family this past few years, and yet he, Ollie, had so much better a life and he wanted to share some of that with Josh. He had reluctantly agreed not to say anything to his mum or to Grandad, though he suspected they already had a fair idea things were not good in Josh's home life. But whatever, he was going to be there for Josh no matter what the cost. No matter what the danger.

Chapter 24

Day 4 – Monday

His mother's voice from below demanding he get up dragged him from sleep. 'Coming, don't nag!' Ollie turned onto his back, stretching his arms out in front of him before turning back on his side, drawing his knees up, and pulling the duvet over his head. 'Just five minutes,' he promised himself. But he surfaced to full wakefulness when he remembered today could be the day of reckoning with the Muskrateers.

'Oliver James Saunders! Get out your bed, now! You're not on holiday yet'

Ollie groaned, threw the duvet back and lowered his feet to the floor. Running his fingers through his hair, he looked around for his dressing gown. Finding it on the floor at the end of his bed he dragged it towards him, put it on, then headed downstairs.

'Mornin'!' he mumbled.

Grandad shook his head, 'Aye, a vision of loveliness wafted in on a breeze from paradise right enough. If yon Hannah could see you now, she would run a mile. Hmph, a marathon more like.'

'So Mum, have you had a response from the geriatric unit yet? I think it would be a kindness to get him in there. They could give him the care he so obviously needs.' He stuck his tongue out at Grandad.

'Ollie! You need to show your grandad a bit more respect.'

'Tell *him* then, Mum. He started it.'

Exasperation in her voice, she responded, 'It's the two of you. You're as bad as each other. Just wait till your dad gets home.'

'Well Mum, it's all Grandad's fault, he's the eldest, so I must have inherited that gene from him. It's his fault.' He smirked towards Grandad.

'Ee Sheila, it's a shame we're not allowed to smack 'em anymore. When I were a lad...'

'Blah-de-blah-de-blah! Heard it all before, Grandad. Time to sing another song.'

'For goodness sake you two. *Enough!* Ollie, eat some fruit and I'll do some toast.' His mum fussed about making toast and putting packed lunches together for herself and for Ollie.

'By the way, Grandad, it was interesting to talk to your friend yesterday. He seems to know quite a bit about pigeons. I never would have guessed the money involved. Kinda makes you realise why McIntosh would be so edgy.'

'Yes, and mind what I've told you. You stay away from there.'

Ollie gulped down his breakfast and headed up for a shower with his mother's voice following him upstairs. 'And get a move on. You don't want to be late just because you're breaking up for the holidays this week.'

He shook his head without responding but muttered, 'Mothers' under his breath.

When Ollie, reeking of deodorant, came back down to the kitchen, Grandad was asking his mum how many camels they had at the Safari Park.

'Nine, why?'

'Well, Sheila lass, you always want to pack so much stuff when you go on holidays, you'd probably be better off with a camel train than an aeroplane.' As usual, he beamed at his wit.

'See Mum, it's him. He can't help himself. That's who I get it from.'

'Will the two of you just *stop it!* And Dad, Ollie's right, you just encourage him.'

Grandad reacted by dressing his face with an air of bewildered innocence, 'Me?'

Ollie's phone beeped, 'Josh,' he said heading to the door. His heart dropped when he saw his friend. An air of utter despondency emanated from Josh, his stooping shoulders carrying the weight of the world, dark rings under bloodshot eyes. 'What's wrong Josh? You look freekin' awful.'

'Oliver!' His mother's voice sharp and condemnatory at the same time.

'It's not swearing, Mum.'

'It sounds like swearing to me, young man. Enough!'

Ollie made a face as though to dismiss the reprimand. 'Come in, I'm nearly ready. Just goin' up to get my shoes. Go on through.'

When Ollie's mum saw him, she was shocked, 'Are you alright Josh? Come and sit till Ollie's ready.'

'Aye lad, did you not sleep last night?' Grandad joined the conversation.

Josh's sigh was big enough to raise his shoulders. 'It's just... just stuff at home.'

'Is it your mum? Is Nicola alright?' Ollie's mum questioned.

'Things are getting a bit... difficult,' he said, 'but it'll get sorted soon.'

Ollie's mum took the seat next to Josh, wringing the dish cloth in her hands. 'Do you want to talk about it, Josh?'

'Not really,' a solitary tear escaping from his eye.

She put her hands out and, gripping his shoulder, said, 'Josh, you're practically part of our family, you know. You're the brother Ollie never had. But listen, I just want to say this, and I mean it. If things are bad at home, you can come here for a while and share Ollie's room. Nicola can come too; we have a spare room.'

'No!' Ollie came into the room, 'Mum you can't do this!

175

He's got sweaty feet. Two nights have been enough.' Then to Josh, 'Right, you, let's get going or we'll be getting detention last days of term.'

Josh rose and, nodding to Ollie's mum, said, 'Thanks anyway, Mrs Saunders. We'll see what happens. But Ollie's feet stink worse. And he talks in his sleep, 'Oh Hannah babee, babee, babee, kissy, kissy, kissy, babee. I loves you, sweety bum.'

Ollie shot back, 'Shut up you! Anyway, *nobody* farts quite like you. Sheet rippers they are.'

'Ollie! That's not a word we use in this house.'

'Mum. You're so middle class and bourgeois. Honestly! We've already had this conversation. Everybody farts!'

'Ollie! People pass wind. That's the polite expression. Not that things like that need to be spoken about at all in good company.'

'Well, they sounded like farts to me,' he laughed at the indignant expression on his mum's face, 'And it sure smelled like 'em. Every one of 'em. You'll have to sew up the sheets now. C'mon, Josh, let's go.'

'I didn't have to tell my Mum about your home stuff, your face did the telling,' Ollie said as they headed for school.

'Yeah, I suppose. Sorry.'

'What you sorry for? We're mates, aren't we? And my mum means it.'

Josh told Ollie about last night, especially sharing his deep concerns for his young sister.

Ollie stopped, and alarmed by what he had just heard responded, 'You don't think he's a paedo, do you?'

'I don't know, but now, for Nicola's sake I might have to bring in Social Services and I really don't want to have to do that. But you've got other things to worry about today.'

'Yeah, I know. I haven't forgotten.'

'I'm in your corner Ollie. I won't leave you to deal with

three of them on your own.'

'Nothing might happen. They'll probably dog off these last couple of days, or they might have forgotten.'

'Doubt that, but I'm not scared of them.'

'Me neither.'

Nearing school, Hannah caught up with them. '*Really, really* impressed with you yesterday, Josh. So cool. Oh, and Jo likes you too.' She smiled a cheeky smile, 'Mornin' Ollie. You miss me?'

'Seems like I don't get a chance to,' Ollie answered drily. 'Ouch! Hannah, will you stop *hitting* me?'

'Well don't be mean. I was goin' to help you with these three scum bags.'

'Don't think we'll need girlie help, thanks.'

She looked miffed. 'Rav gonna help then?'

'I don't think Rav would wade in. He might get blood on his shirt.'

As they drew close to the school, they saw Rav hovering around the gates, a worried look on his face.

'Hi Rav, good day yesterday?'

'Yes, thanks, but listen. Raffid Hakeem cornered me before he went in, said you were going to get a doing.'

Ollie looked to Josh, 'They've not forgotten, then. Not letting bygones be bygones.'

'But listen guys, I've brought you a secret weapon.' Rav said as he started rummaging about in his satchel then drew out three small black bags, the type used for picking up dog pooh, each with cardboard bag-tie securing the top. 'Now,' he said passing one each to Ollie and Josh, 'Inside these bags is a mixture of curry powder, ground red chilli peppers, ordinary pepper and a few other legal but nasty bits and pieces my brother recommended to help temporarily incapacitate these three knuckleheads. Just slide them in your pocket and be ready to use them. But be extra careful to avoid blow-back into your own face.'

Ollie and Josh took a bag each, both thankful for Rav's forward thinking, 'It's not illegal to use it, is it?' Josh asked.

'I wouldn't think so. Anyway, you can reserve them as your nuclear deterrent and only use them if you're heading for a serious kicking.'

'Yeah, thanks then, Rav. Good thinking.' Ollie nodded in approval. 'You ready to use the other one, then?'

Looking slightly embarrassed, Rav coughed and said, 'Unfortunately I can't. Today just happens to be the ancient Hindu day of the peace god, Lord Viashmangutta. A day celebrating and practising non-violence.' He paused for a moment, consternation on his face, before adding, 'In fact — it lasts all week.'

'Really? I don't remember you mentioning this before,' Ollie said looking doubtful. 'In fact, I don't remember that name when we were looking at Hinduism in RE. I thought it was the Lord Vishnu who was the deity of peace. Lord Viashmargotto... really?'

'Viashmangutta,' Rav corrected.

'Well, whoever. I don't remember him.'

'Maybe that's because I've not actually faced a threat of violence before during this festival.' He paused, then indicating towards Hannah, 'But I thought maybe Hannah would want one of the spice bags since it was her and Ollie they chased of the beach.'

Shaking her head, Hannah reached out for the third bag and said, 'Thanks, Rav. Very thoughtful,' her words leaning towards sarcasm.

They headed to the school's front entrance discussing whether, or not, the Muskrateers would try anything in school. The consensus being that that was unlikely. Ollie said Josh always came his way anyway, and that they could both run fast.

As they entered the school reception area, Raffid Hakeem and Scot Pinkman moved from the wall they'd been leaning against and came towards them.

The four friends stopped, and Ollie moved forward to face his antagonists. The two stopped directly in front of him, and Scot Pinkman, his face bruised and with a cut running along his top lip, moved close to Ollie and spat, 'You are so dead. You and your pissy girlfriend. If you think my face is bad, you ain't seen nothin' yet.'

Ollie's dad had taught him from a young age to never back down from bullies and he sure wasn't going to start now, 'Tell you what Pinkman, why don't you make like a Christmas turkey – go get yourself stuffed.'

Josh and Hannah burst out laughing. Rav, looking fretful, only managed a sickly smile.

Pinkman let out a roar and made to grab at Ollie when Raffid Hakeem pulled him back, hissing, 'Not here you fool. Not here. We'll deal with him later.' And sneering at Ollie's friends added, 'And them too for good measure.'

Ollie's blood was boiling and before he could stop himself, he blurted out, 'Why wait? You name a place and I'll meet you tonight. Let's get this sorted.'

Pinkman turned to Hakeem, 'What you think?'

'Yeah, let's do it. Back at the dunes we were at on Friday night.'

'Fine, I'll see you there,' Ollie toughed it.

Pinkman sneered, 'Better tell your mummy to start makin' funeral arrangements, 'cause you're a dead man. Be there at seven.'

'For sure.' Ollie turned back to his friends who were all looking concerned.

'Are you insane?' Rav demanded, 'He'll kick seven bells out of you.'

'Aha, but I've got my secret weapon, remember!' Ollie sounded more confident than he felt.

'Yeah, but there's three of them and you won't be able to spread the pepper mix over all of them.'

Hannah grabbed Ollie's arm and, holding onto it as they walked down the corridor to the assembly hall, said, 'I'll be there Ollie. You're not facing them alone.'

'Me too,' Josh added.

Though sounding a little reluctant, Rav said he would try to turn up too even though he couldn't get involved.

'Hey! They're beaten already.' Ollie sounded pleased. "One for all, and all for one". Let's do it. But Hannah, we don't need your help. Thanks all the same but this is just about us guys.'

'Oh – if you say so, Ollie,' Hannah tilted her head to the side, and coyly fluttering her eye lashes, said, 'You're so masterful.' Then burst out laughing as she walked away.

Chapter 25

Ollie came into the kitchen, dressed in black shorts, an orange T shirt, zebra patterned trainers, and on his phone. His mum looked at him and shook her head before reminding him this was still a school night, inquiring if he didn't have any homework.

'Okay, see ya!' Pocketing his phone, he answered, 'Mum, there's only one day of school left. I don't know why they didn't just finish on Friday. We're not really doing much anyway.'

'Mmm... So, what are you getting up tonight?'

'Just hangin'. You know, the usual stuff.'

'No Ollie, I don't know the "usual stuff". And what does "just hanging" mean? Are you hanging paintings on a wall? Do you intend hanging someone from a noose? Are you hanging Rav's mum's washing out? No – I'm afraid I don't know what "just hanging" means.'

'Mum! We're just goin' down the beach again.' At least that much is true, he thought. 'Probably having a kick about, if Rav remembers to bring a ball.'

'Will Hannah be there?' A cheeky smile on her face.

Looking defensive Ollie shrugged, and said, 'Dunno! Maybe. She does her own thing. Does what she wants. She's actually a pain in the bum. And I wish you'd stop askin' about her anyway.'

'Mmm...'

'Mum! Will you stop you with the "Mms!" Where's Grandad? Thought he'd be in the garden.'

'No, think he's through glued to one of his antiques programmes.'

Ollie shook his head, 'This what happens when people get old then? Come rain or shine, they've got to settle down at the same time every day to follow their antiques programmes, their gardening programmes, their quiz shows and, not forgetting of course, "The News"'.

'I'll let you know when I get there. But listen to me, don't you be coming in late tonight, you've still got school to go to tomorrow. And I don't believe that they'll just have you all navel gazing or watching cartoons on smart boards all day. And if they do, I'll want to know the reason why.'

'Mum!' Then remembering he had forgotten his curry bomb, said, 'I'm going to get some money 'case we go for a coke or somethin'.'

'You'll need money for your holidays, remember.'

'Yes, Mum, that's what generous grandads are for.' As he climbed the stairs he shouted, 'Hi Grandad,' stopping for a second to stick his head over the banister. Instead of a reply, he could hear the television, though its sound was being drowned by the noise of loud snoring. Ollie shook his head. Probably best to let sleeping grandads lie.

He retrieved his satchel from the bedroom floor and dug Rav's 'bomb' from the bottom, flattening it as much as possible before pocketing it so as to avoid his mother's unwanted interrogation.

His phone beeped, 'On my way — bts.'

'Be there soon', probably meant Josh was ten steps from the front door. Sure enough, the bell rang.

'Ollie, the door,' his mum shouted up the stairs.

'Coming, just gotta go to the loo. Tell him I'll be there in a minute.' On exiting the bathroom, he heard Josh talking to his mum, and was halfway down the stairs when the doorbell rang again. His mother threw him a quizzical look as she went to answer it.

'Oh, hi Hannah! I wasn't expecting to see you tonight.'

'Hi, Mrs Saunders. Yeah, me 'n' the lads need to get a game on. Ollie you ready? Oh, hiya Joshie!'

'Is that Hannah?' came Grandad's voice from the sitting room.

182

'Oh, oh! Now you've aroused the curse of Methuselah's tomb.' Ollie made a face.

Hannah bounced into the hallway, 'Hi, Grandad. I hear ya! Yeah, Mrs S.' She stopped for a moment, a mischievous grin appearing on her face, 'I'm afraid these boys need the kind of sharpening and training only I, as an accomplished and all-round athlete can give. They definitely need to make improvements. They're a bit kinda wimpy.'

Grandad's head appeared round the sitting room door, 'Hello my dear. Always nice to see you again,' his face wreathed in smiles.

Ollie made an impression of sticking his fingers down his throat to induce sickness before addressing Hannah, 'Hannah! For goodness sake, I keep tellin' you, don't encourage him. He's turning creepy.'

'Hi, Grandad, great to see you. And you too, Mrs Saunders.' She smiled at them both, then, looking to Ollie, said, 'Okay if I leave my bike here then?' the tone of her voice inferring permission was already granted.

'No, you can't come tonight.'

A shocked look on Hannah's face, 'What d'you mean I can't come?'

'We told you earlier, Hannah, this is a guys' only night.'

His mum cut in, 'Don't be horrible, Ollie. What can you possibly be doing that Hannah can't be with you?'

Ollie groaned and looking uncomfortable knowing she definitely would not want to hear the truth, answered, 'Look, we just want a guys' night, okay? She's just being pushy 'n' awkward. We *did* tell her.'

Hannah, with a defiant air about her, told Ollie's mum not to worry. If they didn't want her company that was their loss. She sniffed and said goodbye to Grandad and to Ollie's mum, snapping, 'See you,' towards Ollie and Josh as she left.

This unleashed a whole torrent of grief from his elders.

'Ollie, I'm disappointed with you. You could have let Hannah be with you,' Grandad griped.

Ollie sighed.

'What's come over you? That was very cruel,' his mum added.

'For goodness sake, can't I decide who I hang with and when I hang with them? It's my life. My friends. C'mon, Josh, we need to go. Rav 'll be waiting.' Then snapped, 'Bye,' to his mum and Grandad as he ushered Josh out the door and followed, slamming the door behind him.

They were only a few metres down the road when Ollie's phone beeped. Taking it from his pocket, he snorted after reading the message. 'Oh well, Rav's really sorry but he can't make it tonight, he's got to help in the kitchen.' He shook his head, 'Well there's a surprise.'

'You want to cancel?' Josh asked.

'No, I wouldn't give them the satisfaction of thinkin' we'd chickened out. And talkin' about chickening out, I think our Rav seems to need a bone transplant.'

'Eh?'

'Yep, transplant a backbone to replace the chicken bone. But I'm glad Hannah's not with us. Things could get hairy.' As they headed towards the beach, the boys were aware the odds were stacked against them. Ollie's mouth felt dry, his shoulders tense, his senses were heightened. However, in his and Josh's favour their opponents might be older but Ollie guessed, remembering Josh's brilliant routine yesterday, they couldn't be fitter or stronger than he and Josh. Scot Pinkman and Raffid Hakeem were heavier and a good half-a-head taller than either of them. Jez Freeman was about their size and definitely on the pudgy side. But Josh and Ollie had speed, agility and strength which Ollie hoped would be enough to counteract their adversaries' height and weight advantage as long as they did not get into close quarter grappling. But if push

184

came to shove, he and Josh could probably outrun them and, they also had their secret weapons.

'You bring your curry and pepper powder bomb?' he asked Josh.

Josh patted his right pocket, 'Yep, locked and loaded.'

Ollie stopped suddenly, 'Hey Josh, you really okay about this? It could end up bad. Not good for launching your new life if you get broken bones at this stage.'

'Well, I'm not leaving you to face them alone. You're such a wimp.' Ollie gave him a shove and they both laughed nervously. When they reached the beach, they had to figure out where exactly Ollie and Hannah had exited last time.

'Here.' Ollie pointed to a sandy path leading through the dunes, 'Pretty sure this is it.'

'Okay, let's go.' Josh encouraged. They looked at each other, each trying to not show any signs of apprehension. Ollie started to lead the way down towards the beach. 'It's over there.' Ollie pointed to the big dune on their left.

'You sure?'

'Yep, that's it okay, but we'll get in from the beach.'

Finding the opening where they'd seen the druggie girl do the deal with the Muskrateers, they entered warily, not knowing if they were first there or not.

Ollie asked Josh if he was okay. 'After all it was only me 'n' Hannah they saw.'

'Ollie! I'm in your corner okay!'

Ollie checked the time. 'Only quarter to seven, fifteen minutes if they're on time.' He and Josh paced about, their inner tension building.

'Maybe they'll chicken out,' Josh said as he went into a shadow boxing, kick boxing routine.

'Nah, I don't think so. They've got their big "hard men" reputation to protect.' When Ollie checked his phone again it was seven. He loosened his shoulders and moved his head from side to side and shook his legs one at a time.

185

Another ten minutes passed, and they were still alone. After twenty minutes the boys were as tense as coiled springs. Was this a ploy to set them on edge?

Ollie went to look along the beach. Still no sign of the Muskrateers. 'Think they're trying to get us uptight with waiting. Or... they've chickened out!'

Then the shout of a familiar voice behind them. They turned and Ollie groaned.

Hannah stood at the top of the dune with her hands on her hips and a smug look on her face, 'So... you think you can handle things without me, do you?' She scowled down at them.

Ollie and Josh burst out laughing, some of their tension evaporating. 'I guess these guys are in for more trouble than they bargained for,' replied Ollie, shaking his head. 'We could get a real doing, you know. These guys are not gonna stick to the Marquess of Queensberry's rules.'

Hannah, a puzzled look on her face, said, 'Eh?'

'Rules for boxing fair, Hannah,' Josh told her.

'Ha! If you guys don't know it yet, girls can be the dirtiest fighters on the planet.'

'Yeah, we believe you.' Ollie laughed, 'But we really don't want you getting hurt.'

She snorted, 'You mean I don't want to see you guys gettin' hurt!'

Ollie thought for a moment, then said hopefully, 'They should be here by now. Maybe they've chickened out.'

Josh looked unconvinced but Hannah seemed unperturbed. She slid down the dune to stand with them. 'Rav not here then?'

Ollie's hollow laugh was followed by, 'Does it look like it Hannah?'

'Well, he might turn up yet.'

'Wouldn't bank on it.' Ollie worked his shoulders, rolling his head, and shifting from foot to foot. Josh joined him, the tension spring tightening.

Ollie stopped. 'You look surprisingly relaxed, Miss Katakwa.' He fixed her with a look of suspicion.

'Well, I got you boys to look after me, haven't I?' She smiled sweetly.

Ollie and Josh glanced at one another. 'What you up to, Hannah?' Ollie demanded. 'There's something goin' on here.'

Hannah had a look of wide-eyed innocence on her face. 'Up to? Up to! I'm just here to help you, and if you get beaten to a pulp, I'm here to bind up your wounds while we wait on an ambulance.'

'Hannah! This isn't a joke. There could be a lot of pain here tonight.'

Hannah checked her fingernails and smiled.

Ollie frowned, and shaking his head, demanded to know what her game was.

'Time is it?' was her response.

Josh pulled his phone from his pocket. 'Seven twenty-five.' And glancing round, added, 'Where *are* they?'

'Maybe they forgot which path it was. I'll have a look and see if there's any sign of them,' Ollie said, starting to move out towards the beach. Returning a few minutes later, and shaking his head, 'No sign.'

'Maybe they've chickened out,' Hannah said with an unconcerned air about her.

'Hannah! What's goin' on?' Ollie's voice sharp. 'I mean it. You're up to somethin' and we want to know what it is.'

Hannah began to laugh.

'Hannah!' Both boys exploded with exasperation.

Looking pleased with herself, Hannah plonked herself down at the base of the sand dune, forearms resting on her knees, 'Okay guys, confession time.' She smiled at them. 'After this morning's threats, I made a point of finding them at break time and suggested it might not be to their

187

advantage to pursue this particular course of action. They then informed me I was going to "get a doing" too since I'd been there with Ollie. I said I sure was with you, but what they didn't know was that I filmed the little drug deal and offers of pushing the stuff at school. You should have seen their faces.' She smiled as she remembered, 'And – I added, in case they thought they'd mug me, grab my phone and destroy it, that it was, of course, loaded onto my PC and to the Cloud.'

'Yeah? Wow! Hannah, I could hug you.' Ollie grinned from ear to ear, all the tension flooding from his body.

'Oh! Is that what it takes?' her quick retort.

Ollie moved to where she was sitting, held out his hand and helped her to her feet. Putting his arms around her he lifted her off her feet twirling her around and, as he was putting her down, he kissed the tip of her nose.

She gasped, her eyes wide with surprise, then buried her face in the space between his neck and his shoulder. Then lifting her head, she whispered, 'See, I knew you cared.' Ollie, still with his arms around her, looked into her eyes, smiled, and said, 'Maybe I do.' Squeezing her tightly he kissed her forehead. They hugged again, only to be reminded of the presence of Josh by the sounds of exaggerated groaning, retching and coughing.

Hannah and Ollie turned to look at him. Hannah sighed, 'You know the problem with your friend, Ollie? He's not got a romantic bone in his body.'

'Oh, save me!' Josh wailed before bursting into laughter. 'C'mon, let's get out of here before I really puke. Let's head for the marina. By the way, where's your bike, Hannah?'

'Round the back of Ollie's house.'

Both boys looked surprised.

'Do you think I'm goin' to take orders from you guys? You never heard of girl power? Well, I've got it in spades. I do what I do and no guy's gonna tell me otherwise.' Her head raised in a mock disdainful manner.

Josh burst out laughing, 'Good luck there then, Ollie.'

Ollie just laughed. 'Okay if we go to the marina then, Hannah?'

'Yeah, you're learnin'.' Hannah's retort as she swept past them leading the way to the marina.

Chapter 26

Back at The Captain's Bridge they were fortunate to get an empty table looking towards the sea. Ollie slid along the bench-seat to be next to the window. Josh went to join him, but Hannah elbowed him out the way and moved in beside Ollie.

'You don't have to squeeze me out the window, Hannah.' Ollie laughed, pushing her gently.

'But you're my hero, Ollie.' She batted her eyelids and smiled sweetly at him then poked him in the ribs with her elbow.

'Ouch! Hannah! Stop it.' Ollie glanced around before saying, 'Right, here's what I think, now we've got the Muskrateers on hold, we need to concentrate on getting into that loft and hopefully finding something that will show Eddie's involvement in criminal activities.'

'Oh well, I guess we should manage that by the end of the week then.' Hannah's dry response.

'Hannah, we just have to get something on them. We think there's probably a rifle hidden somewhere in that loft, and we could maybe find it.'

'You're crazy. Where you gonna look? Under pigeons' wings? And what's Eddie going to have to do with a gun? And anyway, even if there was one there, he'd surely have wiped any prints, so he could deny all knowledge.'

'Well, someone's been killing birds of prey round about here and, with the value of some of his pigeons, McIntosh would be the prime suspect. And... if Eddie *is* involved in something with McIntosh, whatever it is, we wouldn't be surprised if it's Eddie who's doing the shooting. Don't think killing birds would trouble his conscience too much. And if the rifle's hidden, would he bother to wipe his prints off?'

Josh looked thoughtfully at Ollie without commenting.

Hannah snorted and, with unconcealed sarcasm in her voice, asked, 'What you goin' to do then, Ollie? March up to McIntosh's front door and demand he lets us turn the loft upside down?'

Ollie's phone rang. On answering, it was Rav with a hesitant inquiry, 'Hi, you okay?'

'No, Rav, Josh an' me are in hospital and Hannah's just come in with grapes, flowers and in tears.'

A gasp from Rav, 'No. Really? I'm so sorry. No. Really? I wish I'd been there to help. You hurt bad?'

'Na, we're fine. We're at the marina.'

'Really? Cool. Well, we had some cancellations so it seems they don't need me now. You goin' to be there long? I could come and join you.'

'Yeah, we're not long here. We're at the Captains Bridge. We're at a window seat. See ya!'

'Rav,' he said to the other two.

Hannah frowned, 'Yeah? Thought he had to work.'

'Seems there were cancellations, so he's coming down.'

Josh checked the time on his phone, 'Well he's maybe got some ideas, 'specially if it involves techy stuff?'

'Can't imagine what they might be, but okay, we'll wait till he comes.' Ollie said.

Fifteen minutes later Rav, mopping sweat on his brow, joined them. 'Hi guys, don't usually get many cancellations but I'm not complaining.' Then looking at Josh and Ollie intently, he went on, 'So what happened with Freeman's lot?'

Ollie winked towards Josh as he answered, 'Well, the three of them came, two in from the beach, one from the top of the dunes. Freeman was clutchin' a knuckle duster and Hakeem was carryin' a big stick.'

Rav gulped, his eyes like saucers.

'Yep,' Josh went on, 'then Pinkman came over the dunes carrying an axe.'

'No! Never!' Rav gasped. 'Did you run for it?' Are you okay? Have you told the police?'

'Run! Us? Never.' Ollie spoke confidently, 'Josh went into his ballet-come-*savate* routine. His *entrechat* was superb, though Danielle would have been disappointed that after having executed it so beautifully he only managed to finish in a crouching position. But that was because he'd knocked Freeman of his feet and virtually out cold. At the same time, Hakeem went for me with his stick, Hannah managed to trip him and he just happened to stumbled onto my fist which was already on an upward trajectory. Meanwhile Pinkman came raging down from the dunes to get me off Hakeem, but Josh got in his way. Pinkman went wild waving the axe about and Josh gave him a demonstration of some of his *savate* moves, ending up smashing his heel into Pinkman's groin area. Boy did he howl and, unfortunately, as he bent double, he happened to bang into Josh's knee. A lot of blood. Job done.'

Rav was still wide eyed. 'Oh! They're really going to come after you now.'

Hannah sat, arms folded and shaking her head. 'No, they won't Rav, I took care of things.'

'You! What did you do?'

Josh and Ollie burst out laughing, 'Ha, your face Rav!' When they finally stopped laughing, they told Hannah to tell him the truth.

Before she did, Rav shook his head, and scowling at Josh and Ollie, said, 'You're a pair of wind up's.'

'Yeah, and you were well and truly wound up. But Hannah's right, she did take care of things. Tell him Hannah.'

When she did, Rav looked truly delighted, 'Well done, Hannah. So they won't be bothering us again.'

'Not for a while I wouldn't think,' she answered. 'And the thing is, it's not just about tonight, because I wouldn't expect any more trouble from them in future for the fear of us sharing the clip on some social media sites, or directly to the police.'

Rav looked impressed. 'Way to go Hannah.'

Hannah smiled modestly.

'Yeah, our hero.' Ollie smiled at her, 'But okay, I think we're all agreed there's stuff goin' on at McIntosh's place that shouldn't be going on.' Ollie looked from face to face.

The other three looked at each other, each waiting to see who was going to speak first. Then Josh said, 'Well, we now know for sure that Eddie's involved in dealing drugs, but who's supplying him?'

Ollie nodded, 'Yep, and what about the guy who turns up on a Saturday? I think he could he be involved.'

Hannah frowning said, 'Maybe McIntosh looks after some birds for him. With a car like that he'd be able to pay big money for champion birds, wouldn't he?'

Shaking his head to express doubt, Ollie said, 'Maybe there's something more to that loft than we realised.'

'What?' Rav asked.

Ollie hesitated before answering, 'Josh, remember on Saturday morning at the burger place you pulled a couple of little canisters out your pocket?'

Josh nodded.

'And then when we got into the hall, I found another one on the floor. You said Eddie had told you McIntosh put lead pellets in them and clipped them to pigeons' legs to build their stamina for distance racing.'

Josh nodded, wondering where this was going.

'What if it wasn't lead pellets? What if it was something else?'

A bemused looking Rav broke in, 'Well, what else would you put in them for goodness sake? D'you think the birds would be carrying a little packed lunch with them in case they get peckish?'

Hannah laughed. 'Peckish, that's good Rav, peckish pigeons packing pots of packed lunches. Keep them going during the race maybe.'

Rav's question hung in the air for a moment, till Ollie said, 'Drugs maybe?'

The other three looked shocked. 'Pigeons! Smuggling drugs!' Hannah exclaimed, a look of disbelief on her face. 'Get outa here Ollie! How much would that be worth? Not much I wouldn't think, and... an awful lot of effort for a small return.'

'I guess,' Ollie concurred, 'But then if he's sending the birds over by the hundreds, that would mount up, surely.'

'But what a fiddle-faddle.' Josh was doubtful. 'But mind you, when you think about it, if that is what's going on... the birds are doing a run from France four or five times a month. Could mount up I suppose.'

Shaking his head, Rav said, 'Just don't see it.'

Hannah said she thought they were clutching at straws and, if Josh wanted Eddie out his family's life, he should speak to Social Services and tell them they'd heard Eddie say to the girl he beat up about "his patch", so he was obviously dealing and supplying in town.

The discussion was going back and forward when Rav said, 'Listen, if you seriously want to do what you're suggesting, there's a way you could maybe find out what's going on, but it's risky.'

He got the immediate attention of the others, though Josh sounded sceptical, 'Really, Rav? How?'

'It's risky,' Rav repeated, 'But I can't think how else we can do it.'

Ollie, looking uncertain asked, 'What you gonna tell us, Rav, we need to bug McIntosh's house?'

'Yep.'

'Yeah, right! So how we gonna do that then? You got friends in MI5?' Ollie questioned.

'No, you forget I've got a techie geek for brother.'

'Yeah, right, but I can't see what he'd be able to do.'

'He told me something once that could maybe work. All you need is a mobile phone, in this case a burner.'

'Isn't that what we heard these county line druggy people use?' Josh asked.

'Exactly, they get a prepaid phone to use temporarily and then they get rid of it, in other words, 'burn' it. Usually a cheap pay-as-you-go you can buy at a market, or you can buy online or in a supermarket. There's even an app called "Burner" now.'

Ollie shaking his head asked, 'But how would that be any use to us?'

'Well... my brothers got two or three old phones kicking about but there's one major problem.' Rav hesitated. The others looked at him quizzically. 'Somebody would have to get the phone into the house and into the room they meet in. Remember they moved into the sitting room when we went up there on Saturday, so that's maybe where they go to talk.'

A perplexed Josh then wanted to know how it would work.

'Well, the phone needs to have an earpiece and a microphone on the cable. You plug in the hands-free and you can now set the phone to answer automatically, but of course and most importantly you've got to set the ringing volume to zero.'

The others said they needed to be convinced.

'Easy-peasy, I'll get one of my brother's phones. I'm pretty sure he's got one with the cable with the extension earpiece kickin' about. I'll have to have a rummage when he's out. Then we set up a trial run. We could set it up in your bedroom, Ollie.'

Hannah gave a little laugh, 'Oh Rav, wish you'd done that over the weekend, we could have slipped it into Ollie's room, heard what that pair were plotting and scheming.'

'Might have been bored, Hannah. We weren't talking about you.' Ollie lifted his arm swiftly to block the flurry of blows she rained on him. His laughter just increased the level of the assault.

'Ollie Saunders, you're such a pig!'

'Oink, oink.' Then he started to tickle her sides, causing her to squeal, drawing the unwanted attention of the staff. Saying, 'Behave yourself, Hannah,' brought one final blow.

'Children, children, enough!' Josh admonished, 'So, Rav, if we test it and we're confident it would work at McIntosh's, we still have the problem of getting it into the room, *and* quickly finding a suitable place to hide it. Not gonna happen I wouldn't think.'

Rav did not respond immediately. They waited quietly until his brain cogs slipped into gear and he said, 'I might have a way to get him out the house and get one of us in. But it's risky,' he hesitated, 'We want the phone to be in the house for the shortest possible time but there's this life hack I discovered.' He hesitated while they others waited in silence. 'We would need to get hold of a quantity of table tennis balls.'

'To throw at the pigeons?' Hannah asked doubtfully. 'Or to throw at the house windows?'

'No... to get McIntosh out the house. But we'd need to trial this before we actually did it properly. What you do is pack a load of the balls cut into pieces into a polythene bag, tie it at the top and insert a fuse that'll ignite the balls. You get a real blast of black smoke, but... the smoke doesn't last too long, so we might have to work out how we can have three or four bags set of consecutively to prolong the smoke. We could test the smoke thing a few days before, then set them off outside the loft on Thursday or Friday and be ready to activate the phone on Saturday. We're gonna need to have him stay *out* the house as long as possible. So, we let them off behind the furthest away point of the loft from his house and he's got to come out and investigate. But it's risky, the longer the phone's in there, the more chance of it being discovered.'

Ollie was nodding and looking thoughtful, 'You might be on to something there Rav. But it would be risky. And what if McIntosh was out the back at the other side of the house or something and doesn't see the smoke, it would just be a waste of time.'

Looking thoughtful, Josh said, 'But... if one of us knocked on his door to alert him about the smoke, he'd probably leave the house door open when he went to see what was going on, and we could shoot into the house and plant the phone in the sitting room.'

Ollie was nodding in agreement, 'Yeah, that's a possibility, Josh, but how do we get it out again?' There was silence for a couple of minutes as they considered.

'Aha!' Josh broke in. 'Ollie, your grandad's pistol.'

Hannah was shocked, 'Grandad's got a gun, Ollie?'

'Yep, but it's just a starting pistol.'

'Does he have blanks for it?' Josh asked.

'Yeah, I think so. Keeps them in a small tin in his sock drawer – six-millimetre blanks along with the pistol.'

Hannah leaned forward on the table and, turning to look up at Ollie, said, 'Only six? But I guess that'll be enough.'

'That's the calibre, Hannah. I should think he's got a good few dozen the last time I saw 'em. They certainly make a bang. A real loud crack. Good thinkin' Josh. As McIntosh started back to the house, even if we let a few off up in the tree line, that would probably keep him out a while longer. Might even come chasing you.'

Josh nodded, 'Yeah, and we would get away faster than he could chase us. But instead of heading down the road, we head for the track round the reservoir. There's a lot of trees and bushes there to give us cover. One of us could guard our bikes down there and have 'em ready so's we can make a faster get away.'

The staff were starting to give the impression they had outstayed their welcome. Ollie gave Hannah a shove and started to rise. 'I guess we need to move guys. Rav, can you look into the phone thing? That'd be useful. We agreed then, we get something on Eddie, and the sooner the better?'

They all agreed. As they left the building Hannah said to Ollie, 'I need to come with you.'

'But I'm headin' home, Hannah.'

'I know, and that's where I left my bike.'

'I know what this is all about Hannah.'

She turned on an air of wide-eyed innocence. 'Oh!'

'Yep, you just want to see my grandad again.'

'Mmm... yeah, of course. You know me so well. And just think, one day he might actually be my grandad-in-law!' she laughed. Ollie groaned, a look of mock despair on his face as they said their goodbyes to Josh and Rav.

Chapter 27

As they left the marina and after separating from Josh and Rav, Hannah tentatively reached to take Ollie's hand. He glanced at her, then responded with a gentle squeeze. She skipped a couple of steps ahead, and, still holding his hand, turned and looked at him, a huge grin on her face. He smiled at her. Encouraged, she drew alongside him again and, putting her other hand on his upper arm, briefly rested her head on his shoulder.

'How you for time?' she asked, 'We could go back by the town. I'll buy you a coke.'

'You sure know how to treat a guy. Would there be an ice-cream included with that?'

She gave him a shoulder shove, 'Ollie Saunders, you're so demanding!'

He laughed, 'Maybe just a coke, Hannah, but I'll get them.'

'No, I'll get them. I said first.'

'Hannah, it's my treat. Okay?'

'Oh, our first argument.'

Ollie laughed, 'Hardly our first. I seem to remember a few.'

Hannah pursed her lips then burst into a smile, 'Yeah! But the first one since...' She hesitated.

'Since when, Hannah?'

'Since...' she frowned as she sought the right words, 'since we last had one. Right? So, let's go get a coke. We'll go to Batavia's and sit in, and I'm defo paying. You need to remember I'm independent, not *man*-dependant.' The look on her face intended to discourage disagreement.

Ollie laughed but shrugged in agreement, 'Okay! You're buying, your choice.'

Arriving at the cafe, Hannah ordered a couple of cokes,

and they took seats facing each other at a vacant outside table. Ollie remained silent, for once unsure of how to proceed following recent developments. Things were moving too fast. He'd never had a girlfriend. Oh, he had had girl 'friends', but not like this, now, with Hannah. She had just thrust herself into their company but, he had to admit, she was cool and a lot of fun. She was fearless too, and a bit of a looker. He really liked her.

As if reading his mind, Hannah fixed Ollie with a penetrating gaze, 'You do like me Ollie, don't you?'

'Wouldn't be sitting here if I didn't.'

'Hmm... I wonder if you'll be as cute as your grandad when you're older.'

'You might not think he was so cute if you lived with him.'

Hannah slid her hand across the table and took hold of the fingers of Ollie's free hand. He closed his thumb over the back of hers. Then he took hold of her other hand. Hannah looked unusually coy whilst Ollie, normally outgoing and confident, was hesitant, unsure of where this was going. They sat in silence, just gazing at one another. Hannah sometimes glancing demurely away from his gaze, then looking straight into his eyes again and smiling. When she did, he was sure his heart literally skipped a beat. Ollie thought it was as though he had never truly looked at her before. She really *was* pretty, with her natural, soft, afro coloured a sort of pink mixed in with her natural colour so that the pink wasn't overpowering. Her eyes dark brown, her nose pert with a cute upturn, her teeth sparkling white and a smile that could lighten the darkest days. He loved her honey gold skin tone. And she *always* smelled *so* good. Reaching out he tentatively placed his hand upon her cheek. Her skin was as smooth as velvet. Hannah covered his hand with her own, tilted her head and smiled a beautiful smile. His heart flipped, his face flushed and his tongue tied tighter than a boy scout's reef knot.

'Did you never notice me, Ollie? Were you not surprised that we kept bumping into each other at school? Could you not see I had a thing for you?'

Ollie hesitated before answering, his face reddening, 'Yeah, yeah. I kinda did notice you, but...'

'But what, Ollie?'

'But I thought you were just winding me up.'

Hannah shook her head gently, a smile playing around her lips, 'Ollie, Ollie, Ollie! You ever see me showing the same interest in anyone else?'

'I dunno... No, maybe not. But, to be honest, I did notice you and I thought... think... you're hot, and... I thought maybe you were maybe a bit out my league.' he hesitated, '*And...* I thought you were a bit pushy.' He smiled. 'Are a bit pushy!'

'Yeah, I probably am on both points, but still...' She realised Ollie's interest had shifted.

He had caught sight of the girl from Dalton's Mount approaching on the other side of the street. 'Don't look behind you, but the druggie girl's over the road.'

The girl was limping slightly. Ollie could see her face was still pretty bruised and that above her left eye, was a fresh red scar. She had dumped the green and yellow top though and was now wearing what looked like a pair of skinny designer jeans along with an expensive-looking, plum-coloured, cropped leather jacket on top of a white T shirt. The proceeds of crime, Ollie thought.

'Really?' Despite the warning, Hannah began to turn.

'Hannah!' Ollie's voice low and urgent.

'Right. Right, okay.' With a look of defiance in her eyes, 'Bitchin' wardrobe though!'

'She's stopped – now she's standing up against the war memorial. She's all cut and bruised.'

The girl kept scanning the street, obviously agitated.

201

She took out a phone, made a call whilst keeping glancing up and down the road, then crossed over to the side Ollie and Hannah were at and backed into a shop doorway.

'What's happenin'?' Hannah urged.

'Not sure, but I think we'll find out soon.'

Sure enough, in under five minutes three teenage girls, arms interlinked and giggling, came down the street and stopped at the war memorial. They looked around and spotted druggie girl coming out the shop doorway and heading towards them. The girls became more serious as the druggie girl reached them. She glanced around then ushered them to the back of the war memorial, reappearing only minutes later stuffing something into the pocket of her jeans. The three girls came out from round the other side of the memorial looking about nervously before scuttling away in the opposite direction. The druggie girl crossed over to the shop doorway again.

'What's happening'?' Hannah whispered.

'Not sure. Think that was a drug deal goin' down with some girls, but druggy girl's back over this side of the street again. Looks like she's on her phone again. We should maybe buy another coke or somethin' 'cause now we're finished we can't keep sittin' here.'

'Don't think they're too bothered but go get one if you want. I'm okay.'

Ollie went back into the cafe and was queuing at the counter when Hannah rushed in and grabbed the top of his arm, 'Come quick, come on. You need to see this.'

When they got outside, he saw immediately why Hannah had come for him. The druggie girl was leaning into the open window of the front passenger side of a pimped matt black BMW. The car boasted lowered suspension and was fitted with aggressive looking front and rear spoilers. The wheels were also finished in matt black, the windows were of impenetrable dark glass, making it impossible to know how many people were inside the vehicle.

Ollie let out a low whistle, 'There's cars and there's cars, and that there's a car!'

Hannah remained unimpressed, 'Yeah, but what's she up to with them? Think we need to be hugging up again?'

'No, it's okay Hannah. I can see what's goin' on without bein' too obvious.' An arm, every centimetre covered in tattoos, appeared from the car window and, reaching out, whoever it belonged to ran their thumb along the ridge of the scar on the girl's face. She backed off slightly then stuck her head back inside the car. The back door opened and the girl moved to get into the car. When she reappeared, she was holding a package which she furtively tucked inside her jacket, glancing around at the same time.

Hannah had turned to glance the car now turned back to Ollie 'Guess what's goin' on there then, Ollie? Get their reg number.'

Ollie told her to stand quickly and get herself into a position where he would have the car in shot. 'Okay, do a couple of moves like you're a model on a shoot.' He took three photos then said, 'That's great Hannah. Okay, sit down again.' Then glancing at the time on his phone, he said, 'In fact, we need to make a move.'

As they stood to go Hannah suggested maybe best thing to do was to call the police. 'After all that's what they asked us to do at assembly.'

'Yeah, but we want to be sure Eddie's in the frame too. The guys in that car are goin' to want to know where she got these cuts and bruises.'

'I understand that, Ollie, but there's far bigger issues goin' on here.'

'Well let's see if we can catch all the fish in the same net. We might find nothing at the loft. But then again, we might. Even if it's only pinning the killing of raptors on them.'

They held hands as they headed back to Ollie's home. He liked how it felt. 'I think if we meet up at lunch time tomorrow, we can set a quick timetable. We're goin' to have to do a run through with the smoke screen stuff.'

'Has Rav done it before?'

'Don't think so, but anyway, I'd still want to do a run through, so we all know what to expect.'

'What about the starting pistol?'

'I should be able to sneak that out okay. Grandad won't miss it for a day or two.' Ollie hesitated a second, 'That's a thought though, we'll need to give that a trial run too to make sure it's loud enough for McIntosh to hear.'

'Yeah, you're right.' Hannah slowed down a little. 'Ollie, I hope we're doing the right thing. We could get into a serious amount of trouble.'

'Hannah, the only reason we're doing this is for Josh, but you don't have to be involved. Nobody would think bad of you.'

'Okay, but let's see how effective Rav's smoke screen's gonna be.'

As they neared Ollie's home, he slipped his hand away from Hannah, 'Don't want to give Grandad any more ammunition than he needs.'

Ollie's mum raised an eyebrow as he and Hannah came into the kitchen, 'Oh! Just the two of you tonight?'

'No, Mum, we've been with Rav and Josh but Hannah had to come here for her bike.'

'It's getting a bit late. Are your parents happy for you to be out this late, Hannah?'

'Yeah, they're fine. Term's finishing. Schools a waste of time now really.'

Grandad came into the kitchen, all smiles.

'You won the lottery or something then, Grandad?' Though Ollie rightly surmised the reason for his chipper appearance.

'Hello, my dear, how nice to see you again.'

'And to see you too, Grandad,' Hannah all sweet smiles.

Ollie gave a grunt, 'I'm here too you know.'

Grandad looked at him still smiling, 'Aye, I knows lad. I could smell thee comin' from half a street away. Did thee put on clean socks an' pants this mornin'?'

Ollie, his face turning red, glared at him. When Hannah laughed, Ollie told her not to encourage him.

'Right, Hannah. You'd better get on your bike. I'll see you out.'

Laughing, Hannah said, 'Okay, just rush me away from Grandad. Jealousy's a terrible thing.' Then to Grandad, 'See you soon, Grandad – but parting is such sweet sorrow!'

'By gum, the lass knows her Shakespeare. Don't be too long in coming back now, Hannah. You're always welcome.'

Even Ollie's mum was getting fed up with it now, 'Dad, just leave the pair of them alone.'

'Oh well, a man knows when he's not wanted,' he sniffed, turning to go out the door.

'C'mon, Hannah.' Ollie ushered her out through the garage. She moved her bike from the wall, her hands on the handlebars.

'You gonna open the door for me, Ollie?' Her head was cocked to one side with a look of confidence inferring she knew she was becoming someone special to him.

Ollie passed her to go and open the side door of the garage. He was flustered, all tangled up inside. She drew alongside him, the bike between them, and stood making the kind of eye contact hinting maybe the next move should be his. He stepped as close to her as the bike allowed, slid his arms around her waist... and kissed her. Then he kissed her again. A lingering kiss, no lessons needed.

Hannah pecked him on the cheek. 'I have to go!'

Ollie reluctantly released her then helped her get her bike out the garage. He gripped her hand again and gave her another brief kiss. 'I really gotta go, Ollie. See you tomorrow.'

He waved goodbye and went back into the kitchen. Of course, Grandad had something to say. 'Did the lass have a puncture then? She was a long time going away.'

'Well, Grandad, I don't want you to get big-headed but she found it difficult to leave the nearness of you. You're such a babe magnate.'

'Ee well, I already knows that, my lad. When I were younger...'

'Dad! Enough!' Ollie's mum said, tired of his ramblings.

Grandad left the room muttering under his breathe, 'It's a bad job when an old man's not allowed to reminisce about the old days.'

'Right, Mum. I'm just goin' up, and no, I don't have any homework.'

'You've still got school in the morning.'

'Yeah, but a waste of time. They should have just finished on Friday.' In his room he checked to see if he could get some action on online. He was only playing about twenty minutes when he gave up. He could not stop thinking about Hannah There was something going on in his heart he had never known before. And he liked it.

Chapter 28

Day 5 – Tuesday

'Last day! Then freedom.' Ollie enthused as he came into the kitchen. So happy was he, that as he passed Grandad, he leaned over and planted a kiss on the top of his bald head. 'Mornin', Grumpdad. Mornin', Mum.'

'My, my, my, methinks love must be in the air, Sheila. Who is this lad light of heart and full of joy? Did you swap our Ollie for 'im?'

Moving over to his mum who was peering into the fridge and muttering beneath her breath and as she rose, he slipped his arms round her waist, 'Mornin', Mum – again!'

One eyebrow raised questioningly, she too commented on his light heartedness.

'I'll just go and call the police, Sheila. Seems we've got an imposter here. Probably heard about my pension and he's working a con but it's failed because the *real* Ollie's a grumpy wee bugger.'

'Dad!'

'Grandad! Bad word! Bad word!' Ollie hooted with laughter.

'Don't encourage him, Ollie. You better get a move on. You're not on holiday yet.'

'Yeah, Mum. Oh, by the way, any chance of getting me an ostrich egg before the holidays?'

'I thought you still had one.'

'Yeah, I did, but Josh sat on it.'

'He sat on it? How did he manage that? More of your nonsense I suppose.'

'Yeah, well he didn't mean to. He just didn't see it. It's okay, it had been emptied.'

Tutting, his mum said she'd see what she could do. 'Right. Breakfast. Shower and teeth brushed and get a move on.' Ollie moved to give her another hug but she shrugged him off. 'Get off. For goodness sake what on earth's the matter with you?'

'Think you might have to our ask Hannah 'bout that, Sheila.' Grandad smirked.

Ollie grabbed a bowl of cereal and some fresh orange juice, gulped them down and gave his mum a kiss on the cheek. 'Case you're away,' he said, and hurried upstairs to get ready for school. He was gathering his stuff together when his phone pinged. Josh, he thought. It was Hannah.

'Can't wait to see you xxx.'

'Not surprised! xxx'

'Ollie Saunders! You're such a big head. xxx'

He responded with a winking emoji, then had a quick shower, brushed his teeth, sprayed on a can of deodorant, dressed, grabbed his bag and was heading downstairs when he got Josh's usual alert of his approach. The doorbell rang as he reached the bottom step. He opened the door, telling Josh to come in till he said his goodbyes. Then, as they headed down the road, Ollie was quick to talk about everything he and Hannah seen the previous night.

'That car...' Josh hesitated.

'The beamer?'

'Yeah, pimped, black you said, and darkened windows?'

'Yep, a real mean machine, with I think, mean people in it.'

Josh stopped walking, a look of consternation on his face, 'When I came out this morning, if it was the same one, it was parked down the road a bit from our flat.'

'Why would it be there? Getting an early carry-out maybe?'

'Well, you said they were connecting with the druggie

208

girl, giving her some kind of package.'

'Yep.'

'This is the girl Eddie beat up and told to get off his patch?'

'Yeah,' a look of comprehension birthing on Ollie's face, 'Wow! D'you think they're after him?'

'What d'you think?'

'Wow, yeah. Josh, you maybe better tell the police, you and Nicola could get hurt.'

'No, I think they'd just be after Eddie, if they even are.'

'Josh, these kinds of people are not normal, I mean I don't want to stress you but they could even torch your flat to send out a message to anyone else thinkin' of muscling in on their operation.'

Josh came to a stop, shocked, 'You think? Yeah, you could be right, maybe time to speak to the police.'

'Only thing is, we don't have any actual proof of anything. Okay the police might catch Eddie with a stash of drugs, but they might not. They could put him under surveillance, but I don't think these guys in the beamer are goin' to be playin' a game of patience with him.' Checking his phone, Ollie started to move again. 'We need to go or we'll be late.'

As they neared the school gates, they saw Rav and Hannah talking animatedly. 'Hey, what's up, what's all the excitement?' Ollie asked, letting the back of his hand brush against Hannah's. She hooked her pinkie round his.

'Tell them, Rav. So cool,' she said.

'Yeah, right. I spoke to Samar last night, told him we wanted to make a smoke bomb, or smoke bombs. 'Course he wanted to know why, so I told him your grandad had a wasps' nest in his shed and we want to smoke it out, so he told me where we might get a load of table tennis balls cheap.

'How much?' Hannah questioned.

'Not as much as I first thought. Did a search online. Think we'll maybe need a couple of hundred, so there was a pack of a hundred and forty-four for twenty-eight pounds.'

Taken aback, Ollie asked, 'How much?'

'Patience, patience,' Rav replied, with a superior look, 'We knew the balls we needed didn't have to be good quality, so then clever Samar calls our cousin Sajid in Southampton and he says he can get us a load of used but numbered old bingo balls for free.'

Ollie looked a bit more enthusiastic. 'Doesn't matter if they're numbered or not. Numbers won't be recognisable in ashes, but how're they gonna get them to you?'

'No problem. He's sending out a delivery run along the south coast tomorrow morning and he'll get the driver to drop a box of at Dad's restaurant. No charge!' Rav looked pleased with himself.

They all congratulated him then Ollie asked how it was all going to work. The school bell rang so Rav said he'd tell them later.

They met up in the canteen at lunch time, taking a table a little away from the main throng. 'Okay,' Rav glanced around him, 'I was thinking at first of how we could sustain smoke long enough for us to be able to alert McIntosh, 'cause we need to get him out the house and round the back of the loft.'

He went on to share how he had looked up stuff on the internet and found what he thought would be the best solution. 'It's gonna take a bit of work, and we'll need to do a trial run first.'

'How d'you mean, "a bit of work"?' Ollie asked.

'Well, we're going to need to cut all the balls into short strips.'

The other three looked baffled at this, 'Why?' Hannah asked.

'Look, just let me explain everything, then if you've any questions, fire away, okay?' They nodded in agreement and he went on to explain, 'We need to get hold of some tinfoil but that shouldn't be too difficult. Then we need to cut the balls into strips or bits.'

Hannah looked perplexed. 'How on earth can you cut table tennis balls into strips?'

'Hannah! I'm just gonna tell you. Patience! Okay, so you puncture a hole in the ball, you can get a tool that'll do that in any craft shop, or a dart if you've got one, then you widen it a bit so you can start getting scissors in, then cut round in one continuous movement, then you'll have a strip. Then you just cut the strips into two or three pieces. Easy.'

'Yes, but why?' Ollie asked.

'Because they burn better and give of more smoke. And the more strips we have, the longer the smoke will last.'

'Okay, and?'

'Well... then you spread a pile out on the sheet of tinfoil and make a parcel out of it, but you have to wrap it in about four layers and make sure it's all really tight. Then you poke a few small holes all over to spread the smoke, but you need to make one slightly bigger hole for the fuse.'

'Fuse! Where are we gonna get a dinkin' fuse?' Ollie demanded.

'Patience, patience. Samar can get us some potassium nitrate from a chemist, and if they ask why he wants it, he'll just say it's for an experiment for uni. We'll need some of those flat laces for trainers and we soak them in the compound, then when they're dry, we put them into the prepared hole, seal it, and off we go. And by the way, the fuse itself will make a lot of smoke. Win, win!' Rav finished, smiling broadly.

Josh looked sceptical. 'You think it'll work?'

'Well, I think we should have a trial run – or two. There

is one small problem. The smoke doesn't last that long, but it is impressive. We'd probably need to make three or four and space them 'cause we need to get McIntosh out the house and well away from the front door.'

'Sounds a bit risky, Rav.' Ollie said.

'There's no way that's gonna be easy, Ollie. And the only thing that concerns me is that the smoke's really toxic and we don't want to harm the pigeons, so we'd need to be a bit away from the loft yet try to make it appear close. That's why we've got some work to do.'

Ollie was nodding gently, a thoughtful expression on his face. 'Well done, Rav. It could work.'

Rav shrugged. 'Well has anyone else got any other suggestions?'

Hannah joined in. 'No, sounds good Rav, but we're gonna have to be careful. We've not had a lot of rain and the ground up at Dalton's Mount could be dry. We don't want to roast the pigeons,' she added.'

'Yeah, you're right Hannah.' Ollie said, 'So if we're all agreed the next question is, who takes the phone into the house?'

Hannah was first up, 'Me, I'll do it.'

'No, you won't, Hannah.' Ollie's voice was sharp.

'I think I should do it,' Josh cut in. 'Let's face it, I'm probably best equipped to get out of tight corners. Ballet's not just for dancing.' He grinned. 'But we'll need to leave it till a week on Friday and till we test run the smoke bombs.'

Ollie frowned, 'No, we can do it this Friday if Samar gets the stuff tomorrow. Then we can have one made, or two maybe, and try letting them of amongst the sand dunes at the beach on Thursday. People would probably think we were havin' a barbecue. Or maybe a barbecue gone wrong. But if it works, we can do it this Friday.'

Looking pleased with himself, Rav said, 'I'll make sure the phone battery is charged up, and that the hands-free

212

works okay.'

Hannah laughed. 'Let's do it then. We all agreed?'

The school bell rang and they had a round of high fives as they rose to go to their next classes. The last classes before the holidays.

Chapter 29

Day 6 – Wednesday

Having gathered all the essentials, they met at the marina at ten the next morning. Rav rocked up with a bulging backpack and his rugby kit bag, complaining that this was the school holidays and they should all want to lie in till at least eleven.

Hannah poked him on the shoulder. 'Stop whinging, Rav. We've not got a lot of time if we want to do this on Friday.'

Ollie helped Rav shed the backpack saying, 'Great thanks, Rav. Right, we're going to need to get this right on the day, and that' going to take a bit of practice. Did you get the stuff we needed?'

'Well, all *I* had to get. Balls, tinfoil, fuses. Was there something else?'

'No,' Hannah confirmed, then digging into a small bag worn across her body, drew out four pairs of scissors. She grimaced, 'Just hope my mum doesn't decide to take up sewing again today.'

'Great, Hannah! And I remembered the darts,' Ollie added. 'Where we gonna find a good spot for a run through?'

'Probably where you and Hannah saw the druggie girl deal goin' down with the Muskrateers,' Rav said. 'That was pretty secluded, wasn't it?'

Ollie did not look convinced, 'Yeah, but there's the path on the other side of the dunes that Hannah and me came off to shin up to see what was going on. So someone might want to get up to see what we're up to.'

'Yeah,' Rav shrugged. 'So what are we up to? A bunch of 'youfs' messin' about in the holidays. What's the harm?

We're not trying to set fire to anything. Just a little experiment. Part of a project for next term's science class.'

They agreed that Rav was right and that his suggestion was all the reason they would need if anyone did challenge them. Arriving at the dunes, it didn't take long to reach the spot where they wanted to test the smoke bombs.

Rav said, 'Only thing is, as I said last night, the smoke's a bit toxic so you really want to stay downwind and to be careful on Saturday, we don't want smoke blowing into the loft and upsetting the birds. They'd be gagging.'

'Yeah, you're right, Rav.' Ollie agreed, 'I was thinkin' that about the starting pistol too. Could really upset them.'

'Did you manage to get it yet? Josh asked.

'Yep! Got it with me.'

Rav's eyes widened, 'Wow, can we see?'

Ollie scanned the tops of the surrounding dunes then took it from his pocket. They all gasped.

'Doozer! It looks so real.' Rav was amazed. 'How come you've never mentioned it before?'

'Never came up.' Ollie's curt reply.

Impressed, Rav added, 'But it does look so real, doesn't it?'

Ollie agreed. The small black pistol cradled in his hand certainly looked the business. A snub-nosed black automatic about eleven and a half centimetres long, a safety-catch on the inside of the grip and a magazine clipped into the base of the handle.

Josh asked if he had managed to get the blanks.

'Practically full tin of a hundred. I've preloaded the gun. It holds eight blanks.'

'You mean it's loaded right now? Can we hear it?'

'Okay, but just one shot, don't want to bring in the cavalry.' He flicked off the safety catch. 'Ready?'

Hannah covered her ears but they all still flinched at the noise.

215

Josh said, 'Man, that'll scare the crap out the birds.'

'Never mind the birds! It did it for me.' Rav laughed. 'Such a noise, but I wouldn't go waving it about, 'cause though it's only a starting pistol you could still maybe get charged with causing fear and alarm. And I saw a flame come out.'

'Yeah, I know, but don't worry, it comes out this hole in the top of the gun not the barrel. You can't really see unless you look closely, but there's solid metal blocking the barrel, and of course there's no rifling and it could never be loaded with real bullets. But it could maybe fool some. It's certainly loud enough. And anyway, we're not trying to be threatening, just creating a distracting noise. So, after Saturday it'll just be gettin' put back unloaded in Grandad's sock drawer. And I doubt he'll miss any blanks we use.'

Rav delved into his backpack, and drawing out six flat laces, he waggled them about and said, 'Oh yeah, I steeped these babies in white spirit last night and they are gonna be smokin'!' Literally.' Then, reaching into the backpack again, he brought out a bag full of mixed colour table tennis balls and a box with a roll of tinfoil. They made themselves comfortable in the sand and concentrated on preparing for the test run.

Josh questioned Hannah and Ollie again about the car they had seen last night. When Hannah confirmed Ollie's description, he was certain it was the same car he had seen in his street.

There was a note of caution in Ollie's voice when he said, 'I think they must be looking for Eddie. The druggie girl's obviously working for them and they'll know about the beating Eddie gave her, and the warning about 'his' patch. So, could be that your Eddie's tweaked the tiger's tail and now he's gonna get his bum bit.'

With a hardness in his voice, Josh said, 'I hope they do. I'm in a hurry. I need to get my family back.'

Hannah stopped cutting up the balls and sat thinking for a minute or two, then said, 'Listen Josh, how would it be if Nicola came to stay at my home for a few days? My little sister's about the same age so she'd have someone to play with.'

'Sounds great, Hannah, but how's that work? I mean I can't see your mum and dad just having someone to stay that they don't even know. And they'd sure want to know the reason why.'

Hannah sat in silence for a couple of minutes chewing on her bottom lip, then she shared her thoughts, 'Okay, listen. Does Nicola really trust you, Josh?'

'Absolutely.'

'Right. I can tell my parents that your mum has to go into hospital tomorrow and you're frantic 'cause Eddie's away to France and that you've got a...' She racked her brains, then concluded, 'Yeah, you've got a big audition for a student sponsorship and bursary programme in London over the weekend and you've no other relations or friends you can call on at short notice.'

Josh looked doubtful, 'But why would they just take her in? They don't know me.'

'I've told them about your amazing talent, Josh. They'd believe me.'

Josh was silent for a minute or two, then said, 'Thanks Hannah, I really appreciate it, but I don't think it would be good for her to be with strangers. She'd be upset and shy, and, she might say too much about the home situation and Eddie.'

'Yeah, he's right Hannah,' Ollie said. 'Look, I'll have a word with my mum, Josh. You know she's already said you and Nicola could come and stay for a while.'

Josh let out a sigh. 'Well, I'll need to speak to my mum. I can't see her letting Nicola away on her own.'

'She wouldn't be alone, Josh. You'll be there too.'

Josh shook his head slowly, 'Look, just let me think things through. We need to get on with what we're doin' right now.'

They worked well together, though cutting up the table tennis balls was tedious. 'We're going to have to do a lot more than this for Friday,' Hannah said flexing her forefinger and thumb, now going stiff with the effort of cutting the plastic balls.

'And we'll have to hope it doesn't rain on Friday.' Ollie said, 'C'mon, Hannah, keep cutting.'

Rav finished cutting up the tinfoil for the test run, 'Okay, let's see if this is gonna work.' He parcelled the cut plastic strips in the centre of the triple laired tinfoil, prepared a hole into which he put the fuse then, taking one of the darts pierced a number of small holes in the foil. 'I might have to do two or three test runs because there won't be any second chances at the loft on Friday.'

'Did anyone bring matches?' Hannah inquired.

'Yep.' Rav reached into his backpack, brought out a box of matches, and rattled them with a triumphant air. 'Don't forget the basics is what my dad tells the restaurant staff.'

'Good principle, Rav.' Ollie said, 'Okay. Looks like we're ready for test number one and thankfully there's no wind today. Okay, you want to do the ignition?'

'Yep, but you need to stand well back cause we're surrounded by the dunes so the smoke's gonna be pretty dense. Ready?'

Rav had been right in his prediction. The thick smoke trapped as it was amongst the dunes, caught their throats and made their eyes water.

They were coughing and spluttering, and about to escape from the dunes, when the package stopped emitting smoke as quickly as it started. 'Wow, impressive,' Ollie said, 'but doesn't last very long and that could be a problem.'

'There is another method we could have used which I

218

think would give a longer burn, but I'd need to prepare it tonight and test it tomorrow.'

His curiosity aroused, Ollie asked Rav to explain.

'It involves sodium nitrate, highly-refined sugar and coloured wax crayons. It would give a longer burn time.'

'Why didn't you tell us before?' Hannah demanded.

'Hannah! It involves putting the sodium nitrate and the sugar into a pan and liquidising them, then putting in some wax crayons, allowing them to melt as you stir the whole thing into a paste and then when cool, spoon it into containers. Even empty toilet rolls would do. Insert a short fuse and off you go.'

With a nod of approval, Hannah said, 'Wow, you're so knowledgeable, professor.'

'Yeah, but I think I'd have had some tough parental questions to deal with because I don't think they'd believe I was working on an interesting new sauce recipe for the restaurant. And if they tried to sample it, they'd blow their bums off.'

'Good point, Rav,' Ollie laughed. 'We'll just go with table tennis balls. How many you think we'll need?'

'Well, the balls from Southampton should be home by the time I go back, so if this works now, I should be able to figure it out how many we'll need for Friday. Then I'll work away making the bombs and do another test run. I'll have to connect the bombs with the treated lace so that when the first one's burning it ignites the fuse for the next one and so on till the last one.'

Ollie was impressed. 'Sounds promising, Rav. Well done. What about your parents?'

'They'll be at the restaurant.'

Josh stood up brushing sand from his clothes. 'So, who's going to be the one to knock on McIntosh's door to warn him about the smoke?'

'I'll do it,' Hannah volunteered immediately.

219

Ollie told her he didn't think that was a good idea.

'Why?' she demanded. "Cause I'm a girl, is it?'

Exasperated, Ollie shot back, 'Hannah! We're all for equality, but we don't want you getting into trouble. And you have a pink afro! A bit of a giveaway in a police line-up.'

Hannah harrumphed, annoyed that Ollie was so obviously right, then muttered, 'I could wear a hat or a wig or something.' The boys laughed which just got her even more mad.

Ollie placed his hand gently on her shoulder, 'Hannah! Just forget it.'

Josh volunteered to do it and said there would be no arguing about it, that he was 'the man' and it was basically his problem, not theirs.

Ollie shook his head, 'Nah, Josh, I'll do it. We don't want you gettin' hurt right now. You've got too much at stake.'

'But!' Josh glowered defiantly.

'No, Josh, I mean it. Not sure how the timing would be for McIntosh to come out the house. And bear in mind, he might be working in the loft anyway,' Ollie said. 'I think we need a combination of the smoke and the starting pistol. When the smoke's disappearing, a few cracks from the pistol from up at the tree line would probably keep him out a bit longer. That could be your part, Josh. Then he sees the smoke, goes to check, you could get up to the trees and shout stuff at him and at the same time fire of another few blanks hoping he'll maybe try and come after you, 'cause we do need to keep him outside as long as possible That should give me that extra bit time to plant the phone. I'll give you some extra blanks in case you need them.

'Yeah, that could work.' Josh nodded his approval.

'Okay, that's the plan. We agreed?' When they agreed, Ollie went on, 'Then hopefully, on Sunday morning, when we get into the loft, all it'll take will be the pistol firing to bring him out again, then you guys will need to keep him distracted for a few minutes till I get the phone back.' On saying this, he asked if Rav had the hands-free with him.

'Yep, in the bag.'

'Okay, can we do a run through?'

'Yep. This phone was just one of a few Samar has. Don't ask! It's charged up okay. I've put a new sim card in and, when we get it back, I'll put the old one back in and destroy the temporary one. So, then it's just a matter of calling the new number and, hopefully, we'll be able to hear what they're up to. I've set it to answer automatically.'

Ollie tapped his chin with his forefinger as he was thinking through any pitfalls. 'But how long will the battery last? 'cause if it gets low, it'll start beeping and they'll know there's something going on.'

'Na, it's fine. When the phone connects it should still have two or three hours before the battery runs down. More time than we're gonna need.' Rav was already calling the burner from his own phone. As it rang, he said, 'Yep, that's it, 'cept it 'll be on silent. We're ready. Now, Ollie, if you're going in to plant it, you've got this much cable to play with. The phone needs to be well hidden, hopefully that shouldn't be difficult, but the cable needs to be placed in a way the microphone can pick up what they're saying and that needs to be hidden too. But listen, there might not be an obvious place to hide it, if not we're going to have to think of a plan B.'

Looking unconvinced, Hannah questioned if they were going to be ready for Friday.

Josh nodded, 'Yep, we'll be ready, but it's going to have to be either in the morning or at night 'cause I have to get to the studio in the afternoon. Danielle wants to up my practice sessions during the holidays.'

'Yeah, it's important for you,' Ollie encouraged Josh

221

before addressing Hannah. 'Eddie does stuff for McIntosh, including driving the birds to France, so... is that where he's getting the drugs *he's* dealing? And... is McIntosh involved in illegal drugs? Is the trailer being used to smuggle stuff in? We need to find out what's goin' on. That's why we're doin' it and, if we find something, we go straight to the cops. And the sooner we can do it, the safer Josh's family will be. Okay?'

A contrite Hannah muttered, 'Yeah, right. Get it. Killing two birds with one stone kinda thing.' She chewed her bottom lip for a moment, 'But you could end up getting charged with breaking and entering'

'Doubt it, Hannah. Not if we come up with the evidence we need. Okay, so we know what we're doing. Rav, we'll leave you to the smoke bombs, and don't forget the phone. If you're going to need a hand tomorrow for transport, then message me. Josh, you okay to come and scout out Dalton's Mount to see your best approach and look for escape routes?'

'Yep.'

Hannah looked on expectantly, arms crossed, head tilted and brow furrowed. 'And me?'

'Mmm... I think we need to leave our bikes down where we were supposedly bird watching. That way if they see us run away, we're heading away from town. Maybe throw them off our tracks,' Ollie said. 'Hannah, could you guard them for us and have them ready for a quick getaway?'

She scowled, 'Ollie Saunders, you're such a sexist pig! What's wrong with me bein' with you guys.'

'Pink hair maybe. But lookin' after the bikes is important, Hannah. Okay, we all agreed?'

They were — except a tight-lipped Hannah.

'Okay,' Ollie said, 'So Rav, you'll get the smoke bombs, fuses and phone organised. I'll get the starting pistol and we'll all make sure our bike tyres are okay, we don't want any punctures on the rough tracks. My mum's taking me to the safari park tomorrow to see Kukooru, so I'll be there all day, then we've got relations coming tomorrow night including two young girl cousins and my mum said I've to entertain them.' He made a face. 'So, I won't be around tomorrow.'

'Me neither.' Hannah said, 'My mum's taking me to London to get clothes for the holidays.'

Josh said he would take Nicola to the beach in the morning then try and entertain her for the day.

Rav was going to work on refining the smoke bombs and triple check the burner. They all agreed to meet at Ollie's on Friday morning.

Chapter 30

Day 8 – Friday

'Come on, Ollie, out your bed.' Grandad's voice grumbled up the stairs, intruding into his dreams. 'Thought you said your friends were coming here this morning.'

Ollie groaned, stretched and threw back the duvet. 'Okay, Grandad, keep your hair on.' He yawned, stretched, then tensed as, like a spectre of doom, today's plans, and the possibility of all that could go wrong, rose up before him. He tensed, an uncomfortable knot forming in his stomach. Now that this was the day of action, he hoped their resolve would hold. After all, they were all still kids. And more, they could get into serious trouble with the law and end up grounded for life. They were also putting themselves in the path of real danger. All these concerns had been suppressed in their determination to get Eddie out of Josh and his family's lives. But it could so easily end in disaster. He groaned. What was he leading them into?

He checked the time. 'Bummer!' Nine thirty-five and the guys were coming at ten. After a quick wash, he threw on yesterday's clothes and joined Grandad in the kitchen. 'Mornin'. Got to rush, Grandad.'

'Why? Is there a fire or something?'

'Nope. The guys will be here soon.' He grabbed a banana and gulped down a glass of milk. Through the kitchen window he saw Josh arrive. 'Gotta go. Josh is here.'

Grandad shook his head and sighed.

Josh dismounted and leaned his bike on the inside of the boundary wall. He turned to see Ollie come from the house, a slight milky moustache above his top lip and using both hands to try to smooth unruly bed hair.

'Mornin', Joshie. Saw you coming,' Ollie said, selecting

a spot on the wall to park himself. Josh joined him.

'How you feeling?' Ollie asked.

'A bit... tense... to be honest.' Then eyeing Ollie up and down, said, 'You sleep in them clothes, you minger?'

'Nope.' Ollie hesitated to ask, 'Any news on Eddie? You seen that car again?'

'No. But he never came home last night. Not seen him since Monday and my Mum's getting frantic. He's left all his stuff in the flat though, so I guess he must be comin' back.'

'Maybe we were right. Maybe the guys in the beamer have run him out of town.' Ollie hesitated before going on, 'Or worse!' They looked at each other in silence for a moment, the implication being that they would not need to get into the loft.

'What do you think?' Josh asked, 'If you're right, I'd certainly agree, but he's maybe just lying low for a few days. If this all blows up, I'm frightened Nicola could be put into care, but whatever, all this crap's got to stop, 'cause now I'm sure my mum's cold turkeying and I need to get her help.'

Ollie's heart went out to his friend, 'Wow Josh, that bad, is it?'

Josh let out a sigh and a shudder ran through his body. 'Yeah, it's bad. She's wrapped in three blankets and curled up on the couch. She's sweating, shaking and pukin' into a basin She's not sleeping and gets really irritable. I checked on Google. She's got classic signs of withdrawal from class A drugs. Nicola's terrified. No idea what's going on. I told her mum's got a bad dose of the flu and that she'll be better soon.'

'Josh — all three of you need to get out that house, or else you need to get *him* out.'

Josh shook his head slowly. 'My mum wouldn't leave. She's waiting for him to come back with another fix. She's terrified he's dumped her 'cause his phone's switched off.

And he doesn't usually do a pigeon run till Saturday.'

'Mmm... maybe he *is* hiding from the guys in the BMW. Anyway, I'm sure my mum will be okay about you and Nicola coming to our place. I'll tell her your mum has got a bad bout of flu and can't cope.'

'Well... if you think. Yeah, great. Thanks. But... you guys are going on holiday soon.'

'Yes, but not Grandad,' Ollie winked. 'Only thing is, do not sit on my new ostrich egg. I've not blown it yet, so you'd get covered in a load of yolk 'n' albumen 'n' stuff.'

'Another one! What for? You're not a kid anymore.'

Hannah drew up and, having heard the last part of Josh's comment, added, 'I sure hope not!' She wheeled her bike in behind the wall then, cocking her head to one side and with a cheeky grin, said, 'Unless you think I should park it in your garage, Ollie.'

He blushed. She was dressed in light tan jeans and a short black sleeveless top bearing her mid-riff. And smart trainers. A small gold cross rested at the base of her neck. All kinds of confusing feelings raged inside him leaving him momentarily speechless. He coughed loudly a couple of times before saying, 'No, we'll be leavin' soon as Rav gets here.'

Hannah smiled. 'Lost your comb?' she asked looking at his unruly mop.

He ignored her.

'Anyway, why would Josh think you were a kid?' she demanded.

'Because my mum brought me home an ostrich egg yesterday.'

Hannah looked blank. 'Really! Hungry, were you?'

Ollie slid of the wall and turned to face them. 'Sarcasm is the lowest form of wit my old grandad says, Hannah. Depending on what we hear tomorrow, if we get the phone in today, I might want to get into the loft to see what's there

226

– if anything. So, if I was caught, and I had the egg, I could plead my case and say I was going to put it in one of the lofts to confuse the owner. Just havin' a laugh. I think that would hold. The kind of daft things teenagers might do.'

A look of understanding crossing Josh and Hannah's faces, 'Ah!' Josh nodded, 'Yeah, I get it. Then if McIntosh catches you, you've a reason for being there, even though he still wouldn't be happy about it.'

'Yep.'

'Yeah, Ollie, great idea.' Hannah added. 'But... how would you get in there?'

'I've an idea I'll check today when we're up there. But we will find a way.' Movement caught his eye, 'Oh, here's our fire starter.'

Rav came to a stop, slipping a backpack from each shoulder, 'Don't know how many times I nearly crashed. Should have had one of you to help me.'

'You only had to ask, Rav,' Ollie said.

'Never thought, to be honest.' Throwing the backpacks over the wall he wheeled his bike in and parked beside the others.

Grandad appeared round the corner of the building. 'Aye, what you lot up to? You usually come into the house, so methinks there must be something underhand going on.' He raised his left eyebrow.

Hannah went over to him, hooked her arm in under his, scrunched into him and said, 'It's summertime, Grandad. Start of the holidays! We've got to make plans 'cause Ollie's mum said he was to get out into the fresh air like she did when you used to throw her out the house when she was a kid. See these backpacks, we're goin' on a treasure hunt looking for fossils 'n' stuff.'

'Aye, well... just behave yourselves,' he said as he disengaged from Hannah's arm and returned to the kitchen. The kitchen window opened. 'What about your lunch?'

'Eh. We're eh... we're goin' to Rav's dad's restaurant. He's going to let us sample some, erm... more unusual Indian dishes.'

Unconvinced, Grandad asked, 'Curried fossils maybe?'

'Grandad, I'd never let you be curried.'

'Pah!' The window slammed shut.

Hannah and Josh sat on the wall whilst Ollie and Rav settled cross-legged on the grass in front of them. Rav drew the two backpacks closer, 'I'm all ready to go. But...' He opened a flap on the front of one of the backpacks and drew out a couple of sheets of paper. 'I'd also thought maybe we'd need something if Ollie was caught in the loft tomorrow. I remembered a couple of years ago when my dad dragged us up to the Edinburgh Festival, we also took in some stately homes. Every thirteen-year old's idea of a great holiday! Anyway, at one place there were some old menus from centuries ago on display and I took photos of them.' He hesitated.

'And? What's so special about old menus?' Ollie sounded unimpressed.

Rav passed the two sheets to him, and, with an air of superiority said, 'Well, just check them out.'

Ollie took them and burst out laughing, 'Wow guys, two old recipes for pigeon dishes.' Then asked Rav if he wanted to cook up some of McIntosh's birds for Sunday lunch.

'Don't be stupid.' Rav snatched the sheets back, 'I was just thinkin' if we got into the loft and we had these printouts, and we were caught, again we could just say we were havin' a laugh and were gonna pin them to one of the lofts.'

'Actually, that's a great idea Rav.' Flicking the paper so he could read it to the others, he said, 'Listen to this. This is a French recipe from 1390. He then went on to list the ingredients. 'Four pigeons. Twelve cloves of whole garlic. Two teaspoons chopped thyme. Two teaspoons marjoram, whatever that is! Two teaspoons sage. Two teaspoons parsley. Half pint stock. Juice of half a lemon. Pinch of saffron. Half teaspoon of ground cinnamon. Half a pound of lard and a quarter teaspoon of ginger. Wow!'

'Maybe we should take a big bag with us and stuff four pigeons in it and take them and the recipe to your mum, Ollie. Sounds delicious.' Josh laughed.

'Mmm, don't think that would be a good idea somehow. I'd have to eat it. But actually, Rav, it is good to have this as well as the egg. The egg could get broken before we could get it in place anyway, so that's great. Remember some pins.'

'Right, what now, Ollie?' Hannah wanted to know.

'Good question, Hannah. Tomorrow, if we go ahead, I think you three need to take turns calling the hidden phone, 'cause one of our phones might run out depending how long we have to listen. But once we know McIntosh's visitors there, I'll record it on my phone.'

'Right.' Josh nodded in agreement.

Hannah lowered herself from the wall, 'Got to go to the loo,' she said heading to the kitchen door.

Ollie rose, 'So... how we all feeling about this?'

'Anxious. I mean we could be getting in way out our depth. And I really don't think Hannah should come.' Rav's expression conveyed the seriousness of his words. 'She's too recognisable with her pink hair.'

'I think it's more kinda purply,' Josh said.

'Yeah, she does kinda stand out a bit. And...' Rav trailed off.

'Rav! She's going to be looking after the bikes.'

A scream, followed by hoots of laughter came from the house, then Hannah shouting, 'Grandad!' She reappeared at the kitchen door, 'Come and see this, guys.' A huge smile

229

on her face. As they entered the kitchen, Grandad lowered his newspaper, an unmistakable twinkle in his eye. 'Something wrong?'

Hannah ushered them through to the toilet then stood back to let the three of them look in. They burst out laughing. 'Grandad!' Ollie exclaimed. The white lid of the toilet was closed. Lying side by side on top of the lid, were two white toilet rolls. Between the lid and the seat, a brown cardboard inner roll, flattened at one end, was stuck between the seat and lid. The whole impression was that of a cigar-smoking frog.

Ollie turned and headed back to the kitchen, 'Okay, Grandad, that's a good one.'

'I nearly had a heart attack.' Hannah laughed.

Ollie started to usher them from the kitchen. 'Right, Grandad, we're heading. Catch you later.'

'Better men than you have tried,' Grandad retorted.

'Surprised you still remember the Boer War Grandad.' Ollie said giving his grandad's shoulder a pat on the way past.

Looking over Ollie's shoulder, Hannah gave a little wave, 'Bye, Grandad.'

'You take care, lass, and don't let them lot lead you astray,' Grandad responded as he shuffled his newspaper.

'It's more the other way round, Grandad.' Ollie closed the door behind him.

Hannah hit him on the top of his arm. 'Enough, you.'

Chapter 31

'We ready then?' Ollie said as he picked up one of the backpacks and pulled his bike from the wall. They all agreed as they prepared to push their bikes out onto the road. As they mounted their bikes, the seriousness of their expressions now a contrast to their normally outward bravado.

'Okay, guys, here we go. Do or die!' Ollie rallied them.

They were unusually quiet as they headed out. Ollie thought, now they were doing what they resolved to do, the awareness of the seriousness of their objectives and the possible adverse consequences hung over them like a bucket of warm dog's dirt, or worse. And if everything went wrong, they would all be in it up to their necks! He fell in beside Josh while the road was still quiet, 'Hey, Josh, you really need to be careful this weekend. We don't want you getting broken bones before your big audition.'

'Ollie, if what we're doing this weekend gets Eddie out our lives forever, I'd happily never dance again.'

'I know, Josh. But we'll do it. We'll get your family life sorted, and you to become a world-famous dancer, okay?'

'Sure hope so,' Josh answered, not sounding quite so positive.

Weaving their way through heavier traffic in town, Ollie slowed and waved to the others to do likewise. 'Look,' he said nodding in the direction of the Mall, which, now school holidays were on, had a good number of teenagers milling about. And, on the fringes, the druggie girl hovering like a bird of prey seeking to spot and swoop on a target.

'Bitch!' Ollie spat venomously.

'Yeah, but there's nothing we can do right now,' Josh reasoned.

'Yes, there is.' Hannah's voice coming from behind,

'We could call the police anonymously and report her.'

'They could probably still track you through your number,' Rav said.

'Not if we use the phone we're goin' to plant,' Hannah went on. 'It's got a new SIM card in it.'

Ollie drew up by the kerb, dismounted, and pushed his bike over to a bench overlooking the Mall. The others followed and he said, 'I think we should. Hannah's right. They wouldn't be able to trace us because after tomorrow we can put Samar's phone back and destroy the SIM card we bought.'

Rav shrugged his shoulders and asked, 'So do we do the 101 number or just call 999? Or is it 102?'

Hannah answered, 'No, 102 is, I think, for non-emergency medical stuff. 101 is for calling the police about something serious but non-emergency, like if you come home and your house has been burgled but there's no one in there to threaten you. 999 is for emergency anything, police, fire, ambulance. To use it for the police I think it's supposed to be if you see a crime in progress.'

'Well, aren't we?' Ollie questioned nodding in the direction of the druggie girl.

'I think we could be,' Hannah said, glancing round to see where the girl was. 'But if we call the police and she's no drugs on her, it 'll just make her more wary in future.'

Ollie stood up. 'Good. Pass me that phone please, Rav. Even if she's nothing on her today she'll know the police now have her in their sights. Might make it less attractive to be here.'

Josh said, 'Yeah, but the people running her won't care. Look at her, she's just a kid herself probably not much older than us. If she goes, they'll just put someone else in her place.'

A determined look on her face, Hannah said, 'Well, tell you what. If they put someone else in, if we identify them too, we'll call the police again. Or... there's Crime Stoppers. In fact, they're anonymous and you might get a reward.'

A worried-looking Rav said, 'Sometimes you're better just leaving things alone, you know. If these guys who were in the BMW found out it was us, they'd probably come after us too.'

Ollie shook his head. 'No, don't think so, Rav. How would they know it was us?'

Rav sighed, then dialled 999. The call was answered almost immediately. He passed on the relevant information but switched the phone off before they could ask any personal information. For added security he removed the sim card. 'I hope they get her. And I hope if she needs help herself, she'll get it. We don't know anything about her or how she got involved in this.'

An irate Hannah jumped to her feet. 'Oh! Right, Rav! Never mind all the other kids lives she's messin' up.'

'Hannah, we don't know her circumstances. You're a Christian, is not forgiveness and compassion supposed to be the basis of your faith?'

Hannah stamped her foot, grabbed her bike and, mounting it, challenged, 'Yes, but not naivety. And... we're called to fight against evil. Well, are you lot just going to sit there all day?'

The boys laughed at her. 'Right,' Josh laughed, 'we're comin' vicar.'

She could not hide a smile. Once on their bikes they headed for Dalton's Mount, all four with differing measures of anxiety about the undertaking ahead. And the very possible dangers.

Having slowly passed by the druggie girl's meagre accommodation, they drew to a stop outside the old hall.

'Okay, from here we're going to have to push or carry our bikes up into the trees and get down past the back of McIntosh's place. Then when we get down the other side,

233

we leave Hannah to look after the bikes.'

'You mean to have their engines running?' Hannah's displeasure evident in her sarcastic tone.

Ollie crossed over to her and put his arm around her shoulders, 'Yes, Hannah, if we left the bikes unattended there's a fair chance they could be stolen. A rare gift for opportunists.'

'Oh Ollie, I'm impressed. You know some big words.'

'Like antidisestablishmentarianism you mean?'

She hit him on the shoulder. 'Hannah! Will you *stop* it.'

'Well, stop showing off. You probably don't even know what it means.'

Ollie groaned.

When they reached the point where they were leaving their bikes, Ollie questioned, 'Ready guys? Got everything? You did remember matches, Rav?'

'Yep.'

'Okay, who's carrying the bombs?'

'Both of us.' Rav nodded looking towards Josh.

'Okay, let's go. Bye, Hannah.' Ollie said giving Hannah a hug.

Josh and Rav gave her a quick hug too before the boys headed up to the pigeon loft. Hannah watched them totting the bags. Fretful for them, she knew the boys were going into a difficult, if not, downright dangerous situation.

Ollie drew to a stop as they neared the rear of the house, a frown creasing his brow.

'What if he's not in?'

'Perhaps we might have considered that earlier,' Rav answered drily, adding matter-of-factly, 'If he's not, we'll just have to come back again.'

Josh encouraged them. 'He'll be around, I'd think. His Range Rover's still here. He might be out in the loft anyway 'cause he'll have a lot of birds to get ready for France tomorrow.' Josh went on, 'And if he's in the loft, he probably won't have locked his house door. And you'll be coming in from his blind side, Ollie.'

Rav let out a sigh of exasperation. 'Look — whatever happens we'll deal with it! It doesn't have to be right now. We could come back tonight.'

Josh agreed, 'Yeah, you're right, Rav, as long as we can get the phone in before the Audi guy gets there.'

'Just a minute,' Ollie came back. 'I've got the pistol with me.' He dug into his pocket and drawing it out, handed it to Josh. 'There's eight blanks in it. You could let off three rounds up in the trees if he starts to head back to the house. Remember, *three* rounds.'

Josh examined the pistol, weighing it up in his hand. 'And this is the safety catch?' he asked fingering the button.

'Move it up so the red mark shows. And if you have to make a run for it, don't lose it,' Ollie warned. 'You two have to do everything you can to allow me the time I'm gonna need. It's a risk because if I'm too rushed, I might not hide the phone properly... or get the cable in the right position.'

Josh, looking concerned, said, 'You just need to get in and out as fast as you can.'

Ollie did not want to admit to his friends that his anxiety levels were so high his pants might get an unwanted gift. His neck and shoulders were tight with tension, his mouth was dry and the back of his head felt prickly with sweat. He moved his head from side to side, as he had seen boxers do preparing for a match to begin, and bounced gently on the balls of his feet a few times. 'I'm fine. Honest!'

Josh moved over to him and drew him into a big hug. 'Thanks Ollie. I really appreciate this and if we get Eddie out our lives, 'specially for Nicola's sake, I'll be indebted to you forever.'

'Yeah, I know, you just better make sure that when you're famous I get the best seats in the house. For free! Forever!'

Josh smiled. 'For sure.'

The tension that had been building between them lessened. Rav reminded them that, anyway, if they were caught and reported to the police, at their age they'd hopefully just get a slapped wrist.

Ollie straightened his back and squared his shoulders. 'Right, let's do it.'

Ollie scanned the properties lying beneath them. A few pigeons fluttered about on top of the loft, even on the roof of the house. Others seemed to be sunbathing. There were no other vehicles about apart from those belonging to McIntosh. 'Okay, his car's there, let's get the bombs out and check everything's okay.'

Rav was careful in removing the tinfoil packages from the backpacks. Laying them out he checked the fuse connections between the chain of four. 'Yep, they're good.' He pulled the single, larger one out and laid it beside them. 'I made this a bit bigger because this is the one I've got to set off first. I hope the timing works okay so's it's smokin' as McIntosh appears. So, Ollie, you have to have your finger on your send button to message when he starts to open the door. When I hear my phone ping, I'll set light to the single fuse, so hopefully, there'll be a real cloud of smoke when he comes round the corner. Then I'll start the chain smoking and head up to join Josh fast as I can. Hopefully, McIntosh won't see me.'

While they were talking, Ollie had been keeping watch on the loft. 'Oh, McIntosh has just gone into the loft. He's had to open two serious lookin' heavy duty padlocks.'

Josh's face screwed up, 'Bums! How long is he gonna be?'

Rav groaned, 'We'll just have to wait.'

They could see the top of McIntosh's head as he made his way slowly along the near side of the loft. He then moved to what they thought was the store of the loft, checked the door was locked, then moved to go into furthest away section of the loft. The boys could hear the birds' unsettled fluttering as he made his way slowly through the structure. He looked as if to be checking some kind of machinery in one corner. Satisfied, he left the loft and, after replacing the padlocks, he headed back to the house.

The boys looked at one another, tension rising. Ollie prepared them, 'Right, guys, this is about Josh and his family and if it works – goodbye Eddie, we hope. So let's do it.'

Josh and Rav made their way up through the trees and past the back of the house. Taking a moment to check everything was clear, they scrambled down to the loft, settling on a position furthest away from the house, and started to quickly arrange the packages.

Ollie crept down the slope, past the vehicles and stopped at the front corner of the house. His heart was thumping, his mouth was dry. With one hand in his pocket gripping his phone and fingering the send button, he moved to the door. A set of storm doors were pinned back with an opaque glass door fitted inside the porch. Ollie gulped and stepped in to knock sharply on the door, keeping it up till he saw a figure appear on the other side of the glass. He messaged Rav. As soon the door opened, without giving McIntosh a chance to say anything he stepped back outside gesticulating to the loft, and, trying to sound as convincing as possible, shouted 'Mr, your loft's on fire! Your loft's on fire.' He stepped outside the doorway frantically gesticulating to where there was now a cloud of billowing smoke.

A look of surprise morphing to panic crossed McIntosh's face as he rushed out, pushing Ollie aside and cursing when he saw the belching smoke. He could hear pigeons squawking and flapping about in the loft.

As soon as McIntosh got to the corner of the house, Ollie rushed inside. He could hear McIntosh roaring profanities. The door into the room on the right was open. Yes, the sitting room. His heart was racing as his eyes darted around the room. Where? Where? The room was fitted out with heavy old-fashioned furniture. On top of an old sideboard stood a number of impressive looking cups and trophies. The wall behind them was adorned with photographs of pigeons and some of McIntosh holding cups or rosettes. There were three overstuffed armchairs in the room, with an overstuffed couch placed in front of the window, all big cushions, frills and folds. He instinctively knew he would be able to push the phone down behind a cushion and out of sight. But the earpiece, where could it go?

His anxiety levels were rising already when he heard a couple of cracks from the pistol. He was running out of time. As he moved quickly to the couch, he glanced nervously out the window as he pulled the burner phone from his pocket. In his hurry, he dropped it, and as he bent to pick it up his foot accidently kicked it under the couch. Getting down on his knees, he fished about for it but on contact, managed to push it further back. Panic levels rising, he got to his feet and bent down to grip the bottom of the couch and managed to move it away from the wall. Changing the position of his hands, with a great heave, he lifted it high enough to enable him to use his foot to try and make contact with the phone. When he did, he kicked it out to the left then let the couch crash to the floor. He then stuffed the phone down the back of a cushion, running the wire with the earpiece along the inner side of the cushion. There was enough length in it to take it to the front of the cushion where Ollie tucked it into one of the pleated folds of material, the earpiece hanging hidden behind a pleat but not smothered by it. That would have to do. He wanted out of here as quickly as possible but, as he reached the sitting room door, a shadow passed the window. McIntosh!

Ollie shot from the room and, turning right, sprinted down the hall looking around for a way of escape. The hallway ended in a T junction, turning off at ninety degrees to the left and right, straight ahead a staircase. Turning to the left he saw there were two doors on either side and, at the end of the corridor, a door stood open that, by what he could see, was the kitchen. Surely there would be a back door. His heart jumped as the front door slammed shut, followed by the sound of footsteps marching down the hall. Ollie realised if the kitchen door were locked, he could be trapped. In a panic, he opened the door on the right. A cupboard, filled with coats, various kinds of footwear, a couple of walking sticks, a set of binoculars hanging from a hook. He quickly pushed his way in pulling the door closed behind him. His heart was pounding. It was dark inside. Claustrophobic. He held his breath as he heard McIntosh go into the kitchen followed by the sound of cupboard doors being slammed. His footsteps passed Ollie's hiding place and Ollie assumed he must have gone back into the sitting room. He heard him speaking, presumably on the phone, so he tentatively pushed open the cupboard door, listening for any sound of McIntosh heading back this way.

The man sounded angry. 'Bloody smoke bombs. S'pose they think it's a bloody laugh, but they'll be laughing on the other side of their faces if I get my hands on them.' Then silence as McIntosh listened to a response followed by, 'No. How would they know? Why would they suspect anything? Just a couple of stupid kids. Bloody delinquents! If they cause me any problems, they could find themselves on a trip to France, no passport needed.'

Silence again as he listened before going on, 'Nah, as far as Customs would be concerned it would just be my normal pigeon run, they'd be well hidden.'

Ollie needed to move, his heart was thumping, his legs like jelly but while he was trying to get more comfortable, he could hear McIntosh pacing about, still talking on the phone, and sounding as mad as a bear with a thorn up its bum. This was probably a good time to try to sneak out the back door. Ollie was stepping into the corridor when he tripped over one of the walking sticks, stumbled, and crashed into the opposite wall, the stick clattering to the floor adding to the noise. McIntosh's voice stopped and Ollie heard the sound of him heading in his direction.

The prospect of being caught energised Ollie to run down the hall and through the kitchen, only to find the back door locked. McIntosh was gaining fast. Panic stricken; Oliver noticed a key hanging on a nail to the left of the door. He reached out to grab it as McIntosh came storming into the room, roaring threats of extreme if not fatal violence. A large solid oak table stood in the centre of the room, and, using all his strength, Ollie drove it into McIntosh's legs. He bellowed with pain and rage. As he was pushing the table away, Ollie caught sight of a can of fly spray on a shelf to the left of the back door. He grabbed it and, in his hurry to remove the lid, it slipped out his fingers. McIntosh shoved the table again trying to trap Ollie against the door. Ollie dropped through the gap, grabbed the fly spray and skittered along the floor coming out at the side of the room closest to the hallway. McIntosh closed in on him, his face twisted with rage. Ollie brought the can up and sprayed him full in the face, keeping his finger on the depressed button. McIntosh staggered back, coughing, spluttering and cursing as he tried to clear his eyes. Ollie, on wings of fear, rushed into the hall and out the front door, slamming it shut behind him.

Josh and Rav had heard banging and shouting coming from behind the back door, followed by a cry of pain. Then, thankfully saw Ollie come rushing round the corner of the house, as though fleeing from the hounds of hell, before scrambling up to meet them in the trees.

They moved to meet him, reaching out to help him up. 'You okay? That you he's shoutin' about? What's all the banging?' Josh demanded.

'Let's move.' Ollie started down the track. Josh and Rav followed, all breaking into a jogging pace as they headed back to Hannah. Rav wanted to know if Ollie got the phone into position.

'Yeah... I think. But we'll know for sure tomorrow. McIntosh is spitting nails. Tell you all about it when we get Hannah. I take it the bombs worked okay?'

'Brilliant. Timed to perfection,' Rav replied looking pleased with himself.

Hannah had their bikes leaning against a couple of trees. She looked relieved when she saw them. 'You okay Ollie?'

Ollie grabbed his bike, 'Yeah. Tell you later. We need to go.'

Hannah mounted hers muttering something about just being the bike watcher as they headed back the longer route to town. Once there, before separating, they agreed to meet again tonight at the marina to finalise plans for tomorrow.

'Sure you want *me* there, Ollie?' Hannah's pointed question.

'Yeah, of course, Hannah. Wouldn't be the same without you.' He rolled his eyes towards the guys. Hannah retaliated with a thump on the top of his arm.

'Ouch! Ouch! Will you *stop* that, Hannah.'

'Only when you stop being a total pig.' She looked like she meant it.

'Okay, okay. Just stop.'

'Wimp.'

Ollie made a face at her. 'Okay, guys. We all set? Seven o'clock at the marina, yeah?'

Hannah took off shouting, 'See you there, teddy bear.'

Ollie shook his head as Josh and Rav made lip-smacking kissy-kissy noises.

Chapter 32

Arriving home, Ollie was surprised to see his mum's car parked in the driveway. Leaning his bike against the garage door, he checked his clothes for any marks that might elicit unwanted questions from the mistress of the inquisition. After brushing unwanted bits of dirt from his jeans, he ran his hand through his hair and muttered to himself, 'Clear to go.'

The kitchen was empty but hearing the telly in the sitting room he assumed at least Grandad was home. 'Hi Grandad! Where's Mum?' he shouted down the hall.

'Think she's going through your drawers, cupboards and wardrobe looking for teenage contraband.'

Ollie experienced a moment of panic as he mentally scanned his room, then relaxed assuring himself there was nothing incriminating. He hoped! He heard his mum's footsteps coming down the stairs.

'Oliver Saunders, where have you been?' She came into the sitting room clutching items of clothing. 'You're an absolute midden. Three pairs of dirty socks, an unwashed rugby kit and two pairs of grubby pants, none of it in your wash basket.' She waved the pants in his face.

'Mum!' His face red, 'Thought I'd put everything in the wash. Well, I meant to anyway.'

'You thought! You thought! Never mind your *memory,* did the stinky sweaty smells not somehow alert you to the pigsty condition of your room. No! I'm insulting pigs. They're nothing like as bad. In fact, the skunks at the park would have a collective sense of inferiority against you.'

'Mum! It's not that bad. Anyway, it must have been Josh who's mingin'.'

'Don't blame Josh. I opened your windows, something you might like to do occasionally, and two distressed

243

blackbirds overcome by the smell, fell from the tree. Then a cat, seizing the opportunity went to grab them, then she caught a whiff' of teen spirit and took off in the opposite direction.'

'You really are exaggerating now. Anyway, why are you home now? You're early.'

'To take you shopping for new clothes for the holidays. I'm having to work over the weekend and I don't want to leave things till the last minute. We'll go after tea. The shops are open till eight.'

'Mum! We're not going on holiday for a couple of weeks yet and I'm off school now. And anyway, why can't you just shop online like everybody else?' Ollie snorted in disdain.

'Because I'm not everybody else. I'm your mother. Lucky for you.'

'I'm supposed to be meeting the guys at seven.'

'You'll just have to let them know you won't be there.'

'Mum!' Ollie groaned as he stomped up the stairs. In his room he called Josh, but before he updated him, he asked how things were at home.

'Well, Eddie still hasn't appeared. Nicola's glad he's not there but my mum's like an agitated monkey, screeching at the least thing. Don't know if she's missing him or is just desperate for a fix. Probably more the fix. She's a wreck.'

'Well hopefully we'll get somethin' on him this weekend. Then we'll see you get proper help for your mum. But I'm calling 'cause my mum wants to take me shopping for clothes for the holidays.'

'Lucky you.' Josh could not mask a touch of sadness in his response.

Ollie immediately regretted making his friend feel bad, 'Listen, Josh, I know things at home are real crap right now, but if we can get Eddie out the picture, then get your mum some help, I'm sure things will get better for you all.'

'But what if Nicola an' me get put into care?'

'Josh! No danger! You know we'll take care of you both.'

'But you're goin' off on holiday.'

'Yes, but Grandad's not.' Ollie laughed.

'Yeah, well, I like your grandad. You're lucky you've got one.'

'Play your cards right and you can have him.' Ollie had a thought, 'Hang on,' he said, then still holding his phone shouted over the stair, 'Mum, Josh has a real problem at home, he needs to see me. He wants me to talk to Nicola and tell her she might be able to come stay here for a while.'

'For goodness sake! Right, if we go into town now – what time is it?' Then, 'Right we could be back half-six, but you'll need your tea.'

'No, I'm okay. I can get a carry-out or a burger and chips later if you give me my pocket money tonight.'

'Oh, for goodness sake, okay.' Ollie heard her ask Grandad if he could wait for tea or make his own, then shouted up again, 'Right, get a move on.'

'You catch all that, Josh?'

'Yep, so when will I see you?'

'Hopefully seven at the marina. Cheer up, Josh. If things work out the way we hope they will this weekend, it'll be bye Eddie, and to all the pain he's brought into your lives.'

'Hope so,' came Josh's pensive reply, 'Sooner the better. Okay, see you at seven. Oh, and be nice to Hannah or I might steal her from you.'

'You wish. See ya.'

Having been dragged round the mall and an outlet centre, Ollie was frazzled with the arguments about choices of clothes.

'I'm not a child, Mother!'

'Pity, children's clothes are cheaper *and* VAT free. And

children are not nearly so difficult to please, *and* – are usually more *grateful* for what they get.'

Ollie rolled his eyes and huffed.

After a fraught couple of hours choosing clothes, which included his mother, on a number of occasions, spotting something she just had to try on for herself, and arguing about her taste in clothes for himself, they arrived back home by six thirty. Negotiating ten pounds from his mum, part of which was an advance on his allowance, and part of it for food, he headed to the marina.

Josh and Hannah were at the railings where Josh was giving Hannah some impromptu ballet instruction on the use of the barre. Hannah looked like she was enjoying it standing sideways from the railings with one hand on the top rail, her other arcing above her head. Ollie felt a twinge of jealousy seeing Josh stand in front of her with both hands on her waist.

'Hey you! Hands of my girl!'

Josh turned, smiled, and with a superior expression, said, 'Hannah was asking about ballet again, so we were just setting her up with a barre sequence which begins with positioning exercises. I think she could be a natural. Very graceful and very supple.'

Hannah grinned, obviously pleased with the assessment, then, taking both Josh's hands said, 'Like I said Joshie, think I could enjoy ballet. Thanks for encouraging me.' Sensing Ollie's resentment, she moved over to him and gave him a hug.

Ollie's heart beat faster, 'Have to say you've got the look,' he admitted.

She smiled coyly then, with her head dipped to one side, looked up at Ollie. '*So...* I'm *your* girl, Ollie?'

Ollie felt his face go red and was fortunately relieved that Rav chose that minute to arrive.

'Sorry I'm a bit late, guys. You been making plans?'

246

'No, Rav, not yet. We were waiting for you while Josh was makin' a move on Hannah,' Ollie sniffed.

'Really?'

'Yep.'

'By gad sir, pistols at dawn?'

Hannah laughed. 'Please, no fighting boys. I'll settle for Ollie... for now!'

'Settle! Settle!' Ollie grumped. 'Okay, why don't we chain our bikes here and take a wander along the beach and talk about tomorrow.'

As they made their way to the beach, Hannah and Ollie now holding hands, the boys filled her in the events at McIntosh's place.

'How were the bombs?' she wanted to know.

Rav answered, 'Brilliant. Just perfect. He saw us making our way back up the hill and shouted all kinds of threats, but we just gave him the two fingered salute. But, Josh,' turning to look at him, 'I don't think you needed to keep shouting, "roast pigeon for sale". That got him even more mad.'

Josh laughed. 'Yeah! He definitely wasn't happy when I fired a couple of shots, caused the pigeons a bit of trauma I think.'

Hannah asked if Ollie had managed to get the phone into position?

He described in detail what had taken place and how he had managed to escape.

Wide-eyed, Hannah blurted, 'My hero!' She threw her arms around him and squeezed him tight.

Ollie unintentionally smirked as he accepted the accolade. And the hug.

Concerned, Rav asked if they thought McIntosh might call the police about them.

'Doubt it,' Josh replied. 'Not if he's up to the stuff we think he is.'

'So where did you plant it?' Hannah went on.

'Plant it?'

'The phone, dummy!'

'Oh, yeah.' Ollie told them he'd hidden the phone down behind the cushions on the couch and hid the earpiece where it should remain unseen behind a pleat in the material, but still hopefully pick up conversations.

They were all impressed. Josh patted him on the shoulder, 'Sounds good Ollie. You think he'd notice it?'

'I hope not, but where I had to put it in the couch, I just have to hope it won't be too muffled.'

Hannah, still holding Ollie's hand, gave it a squeeze, 'Why don't we try now?'

'Yeah, of course. Let's do it.' Rav nodded in agreement.

They found a sheltered place in the dunes. Ollie signalled for quiet, then taking a deep breath, asked, 'Okay, guys. Ready?'

When they affirmed, he thumbed the number then held the phone to his ear. Almost instantly it connected. Ollie held his breathe, then smiled and nodded, switched the phone off again and confirmed, 'Good to go.'

Josh was quick to ask, 'You sure? How d'you know? What could you hear?'

'His television, loud and clear.' Ollie smiled and visibly relaxed. There was a joint sigh of relief.

'Great. So good,' a relieved smile on Josh's face.

Ollie put his arm round his friend's shoulder and pulled him into himself. 'We'll do it, Josh. Get rid of that evil bandit once and for all.'

'Yeah, great. But we need to get some real evidence, so I hope McIntosh points us in the right direction tomorrow. A rifle with Eddie's fingerprints would be perfect.' Josh ventured.

Ollie stood still; his mind somewhere else. 'Actually,' he said, 'there might be more goin' on than shooting birds of prey.'

Looking puzzled, Hannah asked him to explain.

'I think we may find out more than we're expecting.'

'What?'

'Well, where did Eddie get the drugs he was selling?'

Josh said, 'I thought he was maybe gettin' them when he went to France with the birds.'

'What about Customs?' Rav wanted to know.

'Says they always just wave him through.'

The four stood in silence digesting the information. Rav was first to speak, 'Listen, tomorrow Ollie, you put your phone speaker-phone on and Josh an' me can tape the stuff we hear in McIntosh's house, and if it's incriminating, pass it on to the police. By the way, all make sure our phones are fully charged, we don't know how long they'll talk.'

Ollie nodded in approval, 'Yeah, Rav, and we'd have some hard evidence.'

Josh looked relieved about that, then asked, 'But what time does that Brunswick guy turn up? And what if he doesn't show at all?'

Ollie chewed on his bottom lip for a minute then answered, 'Well I guess if we call every ten minutes from about two, if they're in the living room we should pick up on them. You said, according to Eddie he turns up at about two every Saturday. But he might be delayed or doing somethin' else, I guess. While we're listening in, we better make sure no one can overhear us. So how about meeting at my place then I can say that, in line with her instructions, I'm encouraging us all to get out among the trees and the countryside and the fresh air, then we can head up the old quarry. In fact, that's probably a good place to not be disturbed'

'Okay,' Josh said, 'but I'll have to go to the studio to rehearse. And I can't get out of it, Danielle's putting me under a lot of pressure.'

Ollie said that he'd maybe get some brownie points if he tidied his room in the morning. That it would keep him in his mum's good books for the upcoming holiday. 'Josh stayed for a couple of nights last weekend. Left it a tip. Minger!'

This time the punch on the arm came from Josh.

'Will you all just get off with all this arm punching. It's sore.' Ollie grouched

'Poor baby!' Hannah pouted, followed by another hit on Ollie's arm. 'Man up woos! But, yeah, I'll be there. What? The quarry at one?' Rav said he was up for it as they headed back towards the marina, a shared tension building between them.

Chapter 33

Day 9 – Saturday

Ollie woke with a start. He had been dreaming about that old film his grandad watched on his antiquated vcr, 'The Birds'. The best horror film Hitchcock ever made, according to Grandad. Except, in his dreams, Ollie was being attacked by a flock of manic pigeons trying to peck his eyes out. Thankful it had only been a dream, he yawned, stretched and would have turned over for a while longer, but for the call of nature. 'Rats bums,' he muttered as he threw back his duvet and headed for the bathroom.

'Oh! You're up then,' Grandad's voice came from below.

'Not much slips passed you, eh Grandad?'

A harrumph from below.

Back in his room, Ollie sat on his bed again. Another yawn. Longer this time. It had taken him ages to get to sleep last night. Maybe they were being crazy because, no matter how capable they imagined they were, they were still only in their teens. But anyway, what action they took next would depend on what they found out today. They would soon know.

He headed down for breakfast. The kitchen was empty. Through the window he saw Grandad pottering in the shed. Peace! He toasted some bread, made a mug of tea and flicked on the wall mounted television. Saturday rubbish! How many cooking programmes were there on telly these days? Yet for some reason his mum's total offering covered about eight dishes in total, including fish fingers and chips, sausage and mash and mac cheese. Finishing his toast, he took his tea upstairs, switched on his laptop, fired up Fortnite and, checking the time, thought he'd play for an hour before showering. Perhaps getting immersed in the game would allow him to ignore the knot that had formed in his gut. His phone pinged. Josh.

'How you feeling about today, Oll? You ready?'

He glanced at the time. Eleven forty. Shoot! He'd have to get a move on. He fired back, "Bring it on," accompanied by a thumbs up emoji. He showered, dressed, pulled up his duvet, kicked an empty crisp packet under the bed and dumped his dirty laundry in the clothes basket, one sock caught by the lid left hanging out. Halfway down the stairs he turned and, hurrying back to his room, sprayed himself with deodorant. At twelve-fifteen he got his bike from the garage and was just mounting when Grandad appeared from round the corner.

'Where are you off to now? You had something to eat?'

'Had a late breakfast, Grandad. Just meetin' the guys.'

'Not enough info, laddie. You know your mother 'll grill me like a rasher of best back bacon about your whereabouts and whatabouts and howabouts if she's back before you.'

'We're just goin' up the quarry. Hannah's got a new camera and she wants to take some photos. Anyway, you heard Mum tell me she wanted me out in the fresh air these holidays. So I think I could mount a sound defence if she objects.'

'Laddie, laddie, laddie,' Grandad scratched his head, 'You know your mother's always right — even when she's wrong! But I suppose it's better outside than sittin' up in yon room glued to a computer screen.'

'Don't worry, Grandad, I've been wary since you told me if I spent too much time online my eyes would shrink and roll out their sockets, probably to be snatched up by passing seagulls.'

'Aye well, be warned, laddie, eyeballs are a real delicacy to them.'

Ollie pushed down on a pedal, 'I'm off.'

'Okay. Have fun. And behave y'self.'

Ollie rolled his eyes, 'I always do, Grandad. With both.'

Hannah was already sitting on the closed gate at the entrance to the abandoned quarry when Ollie arrived. He parked his bike and climbed up to join her, 'Heard from Rav?'

'Yep, he's on his way,' she smiled.

He inadvertently blushed – she's so cute, he thought before gruffly affirming with, 'Good.'

Hannah sidled a bit closer to him and slid her arm round his waist. He put his arm round her shoulder. She snuggled closer. Ollie, his heart pounding, put a finger beneath her chin and tilted it towards him then, tentatively, leaned in and gave her a kiss. She broke away and looked at him her eyes wide open. He thought he must have misjudged the situation till she sighed, then put both arms round him, and they recommenced kissing.

'Oi! That's disgusting. Did you both miss your lunch did you?'

They nearly fell off the gate. 'Rav! Stop sneaking up on people.' Hannah wiped her mouth with the back of her hand.

'Wasn't sneaking, but you two seemed otherwise... engrossed! Looks like things are getting serious.'

'Shut up, you.' Ollie jumped down.

When Rav got off his bike he had, as usual, not a hair out of place. Not a mark or a crease in his clothing.

Hannah laughed, 'Rav, how come you *always* look like a TV advert for a dry-cleaning company?'

'And you two look pathetic sittin' there all smoochie. It's disgusting. What's got into you, Ollie Saunders?'

Hannah stuck out her tongue, jumped from the gate and grabbed Ollie's hand, drawing him close. 'Jealous, Rav?'

'Got other thing on my mind, Hannah.'

253

'Let's get up the top above the quarry. Less likely to be disturbed,' Ollie said.

Securing their bikes to the gate, they skirted up the outside of the quarry till they found a good spot at the top between a couple of rocks, both making convenient backrests. Settling there, Rav took his phone and put it on speaker phone. 'It should all get recorded, then Josh can listen later.' A rising anticipation among them as they moved closer together.

Checking his phone, Ollie said it was only one forty so they had a while. Rav drew a couple of bottles of water from his backpack, 'You two 'll just have to share one,' he said handing it to Hannah.

Rav called the burner phone three or four times over the next half hour before they heard the sound of conversation. All three tensed, glanced at each other and smiled. Ollie gave Rav a thumbs up, 'Can we get a bit more volume?'

Rav fiddled a bit till the conversation became clearer, then he switched on the mini recorder and passed it to Hannah to hold as close to the phone as possible.

It was obvious the first speaker was McIntosh, 'Maybe a good job he's not turned up today. Those brats got the birds so spooked yesterday. I tell you, if I get my hands on 'em...'

'You think they suspect anything?' Concern in the ocean deep voice of the one they guessed was Joe Brunswick.

'Don't think so, think they were just bein' a bunch of smart arsed kids makin' mischief. Bloody school holidays.'

'How many?'

'Think three. One of them banged on my door saying there was a fire at the loft. I shot out the house. There was a lot of smoke — but no fire. They'd set off a series of smoke bombs, home-made I think, but very effective. But there

254

was no actual damage but they had also been letting of what I think must have been a starting pistol. 'Course, the birds got really upset, so I had to try 'n' clear the smoke and get them settled, so I shot back to the house to get my loft keys. The phone rang just as I went through the front door – one of these blasted telemarketing calls. I was just telling them where to stuff their pension plans when I heard a clatter from the hall. It was the kid who'd knocked on the door. Guess he wasn't expecting me back so quick and had to hide in the hall cupboard. He was trying to sneak out while I answered the phone but he tripped over a walking stick makin' a real clatter. I chased him into the kitchen and thought I had him, but he was a wiry little toad, strong for his age. Rammed the big table at me. I went after him but he was a slippery wee sod, sprayed fly killer into my face and managed to get out the front door. Ran away to join his two mates up the top of the hill. The three of 'em up there were takin' the piss.'

There was a silence, then Brunswick spoke again, 'I don't like it. Why would he be in your house?'

'I don't know why, a thief maybe.'

There was the sound of one of them sighing before McIntosh spoke again, 'I don't like it. I don't like anyone messing me about. Specially where my birds are concerned. And I don't want my cover blown.'

'Yeah, I know.' Brunswick agreed.

The three friends looked at one another, wide eyed and with raised eyebrows. Hannah whispered, 'Cover! For what?'

Ollie and Rav hushed her.

Brunswick's voice came on, 'That perfect cover cost me a lot of money. All the state-of-the art technology, and the transporter. Plus the money to take your breeding programme to new levels. None of that came cheap... and it's goin' to take some time to pay back.'

255

McIntosh's voice again. 'Just a minute... when I think about it... when you were here last week, remember there were four kids on bikes had stopped because one had a puncture. Then one of the boys with a girl headed up by the trees. When I checked out back it looked like they were up for a snogging session.' There was silence for a moment, then, 'It was *him*!'

'Him! Who?'

'The boy who'd been snogging the girl with the pink afro... maybe... nah! ... Maybe they were sussing the place out.'

'Why would they do that? They're just kids.'

'Maybe just troublemakers, or maybe looking to nick some of my trophies to flog or maybe thought I'd have cash.'

'I don't like this.' Brunswick's tone was forceful.

There was a silence, then McIntosh said, 'And there's something else,' he hesitated, 'Had a visit from the cops this week.'

'What! When?' Concern in Brunswick's voice.

'Someone had reported finding the carcase of a peregrine falcon a couple of miles away.'

There was a sigh, 'Eddie Swinton's work?'

'Yeah, he told me he'd buried it.'

Brunswick groaned, then let out a string of profanities, 'But why did they come here?'

'Why do you think? Raptors kill pigeons. I've got pigeons. Wanted to know if I had a hunting rifle. Of course, I said no. But don't worry, it's not licensed so there's no records. They had a casual poke about the loft and asked to have a quick look in the house.'

'Did they have a warrant?'

'No.'

'And you *let* them?'

'I thought that they'd think I'd something to hide if I'd

said no. They'd have a job finding it anyway. It's well hidden. They were okay with me.'

'Good. The pistol?'

'Still buried at the bottom of the big feed tub, but they weren't being thorough, just a cursory check, though you do need to get it out of here, an unlicensed rifle's bad enough but a loaded Glock's certain jail time. Ten years. They did ask about the electronic scales but I told them it was for weighing the birds.'

'So, where's the rifle and the drugs?'

'The rifle's well hidden.'

'Where?'

'In the loft.' McIntosh sounded guarded, 'The drugs are where they always are till you move them. I only agreed to this on condition you moved the stuff out quickly. So when the canisters are emptied and the stuff's bagged up and stashed, then I make sure the place is sanitised.'

The eavesdropping friends were wide eyed, smiling. Ollie raised his fist and with a look of delight mouthed, 'The hall! Yes, yes, yes! I knew there was something goin' on.'

Brunswick continued, 'Okay. My guy 'll be here to pick up tomorrow, as per.'

'It won't be ready till Monday.'

'Why?' Brunswick sounded incredulous.

'Swinton never turned up last night to prepare for the run. I've messaged him and left a message on his voicemail, but nothing. I needed him earlier in the week to help me with the waste disposal too, but he never turned up.'

'Waste disposal?'

'Yeah, all the technology is great, sure it collects the birds' droppings — but doesn't dispose of them, and that's his job.'

Ollie and Josh looked at each other, a silent question mark between them.

'But that's not all. I think he could be dealing himself.'

257

Brunswick swore angrily, 'Oh really? So, where's he's getting the stuff?'

'I don't know. It's definitely not ours, but he's getting it somewhere and he drives for me, so if he's fingered, he could bring the cops to my door.'

'Leave that with me.' Brunswick's voice quietly menacing. 'We could be needing another driver, but until then you'll have to do it yourself.'

'I know. I already let Edouard know I'd becoming myself tomorrow. I'll get the birds ready when you leave.'

There was silence for a minute, then Brunswick said, 'Good. I'll get my guy to come round on Tuesday for the stuff. And by the way... I think we need to look at increasing the volume now. Pigeons have got two legs, why not put a canister on each leg?'

McIntosh sighed before saying, 'No! Two would be too much weight for them. I mostly use my tiplers, they're the smallest breed of pigeon, but by far the strongest. Even for them, two could be too much. Anyway − right now, one bird can carry fifty-seven grams of 'H', right? At what? Sixty to eighty quid a *gram* at street value. So, three thousand four hundred pounds per bird... per run. Minimum! And... able to fly below the radar, literally and figuratively. So, let's not get too greedy.'

Brunswick's tone was less affable, 'Listen, you knew what you were getting yourself into. It would be worth trialling a double load on − at least half a dozen birds. Then *one* bird could bring in *over* seven grand a run. Multiply that by four runs a month. What? Forty-eight grand a month – per bird! You only use a hundred of the birds you send out at a time to bring in the stuff, which means we could be doing nearly five million a month... from a hundred birds! Sweet. And that's before it gets cut. Then we'd be over seven mil a month, but it could be so much more. You've got hundreds of birds and the trailer will hold over a thousand. We need to double, even treble up. Or even more!'

Shocked, Ollie gasped and put his hand over his mouth. Hannah and Rav looked equally shocked. 'Five million?' Hannah whispered. 'Five million! O-M-G!'

McIntosh responded, 'Listen, I know I couldn't have the successes I've had at this level without the money you put in and it's important that front's maintained. A good proportion of the birds are here because of my reputation with the training and racing school where costs and winnings can be shared. So, the other owners take an active interest in what's going on — and I don't want them asking awkward questions.'

'Like what?'

'One of them spotted the box with the little canisters and asked what they were for. I showed him the tub with the little lead balls and told him we sometimes put them in the canisters as a weight training exercise. Helps to make the birds stronger. And you know we always put the lead weights in the carrier with the canisters in case we ever get checked at entry to France. Better they see nothing suspicious. But anyway, the average pigeon only weighs around sixteen ounces so no matter how much you want it, the quantities have to be what they are.'

'Well, we'll use more of the birds then. You've got enough. And that's why I brought in the carrier from the States.'

'Yeah okay, we'll give it a try. I'll tell Edouard I'll send three hundred birds next week so he'll have to have more stuff ready. But bear in mind not all the birds are guaranteed to make it back all the time. I can lose a couple on a bad month.'

The phone connection disappeared. 'Blast, the battery must have packed in. Thought it might.' Rav looked disappointed. 'But, I guess, at least now we know.'

Looking excited, Hannah said, 'What now, the police?'

'You get that all taped, Rav?' Ollie asked.

'Yep, hopefully should have most of it.'

'Well, we should take it to the police. Given the evidence, they can have them and Eddie Swinton sent to jail, hopefully for a very long time.' Ollie rose to his feet then put his hand out to give Hannah a hand up.

Rav stood, picking bits of grass from his jeans. 'What now then?'

Hannah suggested the Mall. 'We could look at all the cute girlie clothes.'

The boys said she could, but they would just hang out and check out the eye candy. 'Ouch, ouch! Hannah! Will you stop that.' Ollie rubbed at his arm.

Rav tutted, 'Will you stop it, you two.' Rav bounced the phone in his hand, 'Great news for Josh though.'

'Yeah,' Ollie nodded and said, 'Can't wait till he hears the recording.'

'Me too,' Rav added, 'So good.'

'Where we meeting up?' Hannah asked.

'Guess we'll need to go to the dunes.' Ollie gave a gentle shrug. 'We have to be able to listen to the recording without being overheard.'

Rav and Hannah agreed so Ollie messaged Josh to meet at the marina at seven.

'Can't wait.' Hannah grinned. 'You think Josh 'll be happy?'

Ollie nodded and smiled, 'Yeah, he's gonna love it.'

Chapter 34

Oh no! Oh no! Sod it!... Rav!' Ollie, with a look of incredulity, gave Rav's phone a shake, then tried again, 'You've must not have pressed record, you bozo! There's nothing on it!' He groaned and flung the phone into the scrub covered dunes.

'What? No! There must be.' Rav rose and scrambled into the scrub to retrieve his phone.

Ollie made no attempt to hide his agitation, 'I don't believe it, Rav. I thought you knew what you were doing.' He threw himself down beside Hannah.

Rav straightened up and, shaking his phone and blowing sand from it, said, 'I do. I did. Don't know what's gone wrong. I mustn't have pressed record properly in all the hassle.' He looked at the group defiantly.

'So, what now?' A deflated Josh wanted to know. 'We can't risk going back into McIntosh's house again.'

Hannah got to her feet, 'What now then? We gonna get the phone back from McIntosh's place or leave it and maybe get a chance to listen in again?

'No.' Ollie shook his head, 'Now we know what's going on up there, especially the drugs, we should probably just go to the police.'

Hannah was about to agree, then instead said, 'Yeah... but just a minute. We could get ourselves into trouble. We did break into McIntosh's house after all.'

'But surely we could argue we had 'just cause'.' Rav suggested, 'And with what we now know, the police would have to do a more thorough search... and... after all... it was *only* Ollie who broke into the house.'

'Gee, thanks for your support, Rav!' Ollie's dry retort, 'Well, I think we're gonna have to get into the loft ourselves. See if we can find something the police search missed.

From what McIntosh said it wasn't particularly thorough...
and now we *know* the rifle's there, and it could have Eddie's
prints all over it, and don't forget, the pistol might still be
in the food bin, unless it's moved today, and all that that
could mean a healthy jail sentence regardless of the rifle. I
guess there won't be any drugs in the loft, it sounded like
McIntosh gets them moved to the hall pretty quickly. So
there must be a window of opportunity for the police to
catch them red handed.'

They all looked at him without making any comment.

'Give me a minute.' He went on and, taking his phone
out, he checked something online. After a couple of
minutes his cheeks puffed out and he slowly expelled air,
'Listen — from what we know now, McIntosh thinks he's
got a sweet operation going smuggling in drugs, as he says,
under the radar. And he's been gettin' away with it because
he's got a genuine business in his breeding and racing
programme. I just had a quick look online and it looks like
anyone shooting raptors would get away with a hefty fine.'
Looking to Josh, he went on, 'But, if we can find the drugs,
we can bring the whole operation down and see the lot of
'em go to jail for a long time, including Eddie Swinton. And
you, your mum and Nicola can start a new life.'

Unconvinced, Rav said, 'Yeah, but from what we
heard, somehow they manage to, what did he say,
"sanitise" the hall, though from what we know about
forensic science today, it should just about be impossible
not to leave traces. They must just unclip the canisters and
take them down to the hall and empty them there. I suspect
they'll keep the canisters there too, probably in the same
place they hide the drugs, but I'd think there'd still be
traces.'

'Yes, but he keeps the rifle in the loft.' Josh stressed,
'And if we could find it and make and anonymous phone
call and tell the cops where to find it and say we know

there's drugs bein' smuggled in too *and* that they need to check the hall, they'd have to do something.'

Ollie said, 'So... we're gonna have to get into the loft and find the rifle. But we have to be careful we don't wipe of the existing prints. And having found it, they'd have to take the drug stuff seriously. Even if they're well concealed somewhere at the hall, police sniffer dogs would almost certainly find them. So, we've got to get in and find the rifle first because they could just say they've already searched it and found nothing. But we could also suggest they search the feeding bin for a Glock pistol. They'd have to ask themselves why a respected pigeon breeder and racer would have all that firepower.'

A worried-looking Rav said, 'Not me, count me out. I'm not breaking and entering for anybody!'

'Listen Rav, we know McIntosh is going to have to do the run to France tomorrow, so... we get into the loft and look for ourselves while he's away.'

'Yeah, but who feeds the birds left in the loft and gives them fresh water? He's maybe arranged with someone to come in and do that. And what about timing the birds when they come back?'

'There's an automated system in place to do that stuff,' Josh said.

Ollie stood up and stretched his arms over his head, 'Don't worry, if anyone does come in, I told you, I've got the ostrich egg and the French pigeon recipes.' He smiled.

Hannah squinted and said, 'Yeah. And?'

'So... like I said we, that is, whoever goes in, takes it with them, then − if someone catches us in there, we say we were just playing a practical joke.'

'Yeah, that could work. Kinda thing daft teenagers *would* do.' Hannah said, 'But who's going to do it?'

Ollie said it was his egg so he would do it, but Josh argued that it was his and his family's problem so he should be the one to go in.

'You should probably both go,' Hannah said, 'But the place is securely locked and bolted so how you gonna get over a nearly two-and-a-half metre fence? Pogo sticks? How far would one of your ballet leaps take you, Josh? And you're sure the CCTV cameras are dummy's?'

Josh gave a little laugh. 'Not that height, for sure. And yes 'cause there'd be no reason for Eddie to say so if they weren't. But remember I have my practice in the afternoon and if I don't turn up Danielle won't be happy, so we have to do this in the morning.'

Hannah told them she had church in the morning and her dad would insist on her going. 'So that just leaves you two.' She addressed Ollie and Josh, 'But Ollie, what if you make a hand stirrup and lifted Josh up so far like you did when we heard Eddie laying into the druggie girl. You could lift him up and Josh could pull himself over the fence 'cause he's strong enough.' She moved closer to Josh and squeezed his upper arm, which he obligingly flexed. 'Yep, thought so,' she winked at him.

Ollie considered the proposition, then said, 'Yeah, I guess, but how would I get in?'

'Rav could lift you.'

'Hey! Remember I won't be there. Told you I can't risk it.' Rav was adamant.

Hannah, with a hint of doubt said, 'Well... maybe I could try to bunk of church and I could stirrup Ollie up the fence.'

Ollie laughed, 'Don't think so Hannah. You wouldn't be able to lift me high enough and I'd probably topple on top of you.'

'Hey, I've got an idea.' They all looked to Rav, 'After Ollie's given Josh a leg up, he could put his bike against the fence and, if Hannah's there, she can steady it so then he can get onto the crossbar, and you,' looking at Ollie, 'just

264

pull yourself over the fence. Josh might be in a position to help you too. But you'll need to do it at the back, away from the road.'

They all agreed that could be a workable solution. But Ollie said he would have to pass Josh the ostrich egg while he was balancing on the crossbar. Their only problem was they did not know what was on the other side of the fence or if there would be anything there to break their fall. But then they realised the roofs of the lofts couldn't be too far beneath the fence line. The hope would be that they were strong enough to hold their weight. They then remembered the pigeons would be returning from France, so McIntosh could have someone coming to clock the returning birds in. Josh said that the automated systems in the loft provided landing boards with automatic timers so it wouldn't be absolutely necessary.

'Anyway, he's had to reorganise pretty quickly with Eddie not turning up, but he probably wouldn't want anyone to see the pigeons coming back with the canisters attached to their legs, 'So I think we can risk it. McIntosh is heading out very early in the morning and we've no idea when he'll be back, but it won't be until night at least, but more like the next day.'

Nodding agreement, Rav added, 'Well we're in striking distance to Dover from here and you can more or less drive straight through the Tunnel and, once in France, it's not quite so busy and better roads than here. If he's on main roads or motorways he'll make good time. A lot might depend on whether or not he's involved in filling the canisters with drugs where he releases the birds, or if they're filled already and he just clips them on. But we went to Brittany for a holiday a couple of years ago and it must be a six-hour drive from Dover depending on his destination.

'That's for sure,' Josh nodded, 'Eddie would often get

265

back late the next afternoon, so McIntosh should be away till tomorrow afternoon. We should have plenty time to search the loft. With any luck, we will find the rifle.'

Ollie clapped his hands, 'Okay guys, let's head back to the marina.'

'Ooh Ollie! You're so masterful.' Hannah laughed as she rose and grabbed his arm. The sound of Josh and Rav simulated projectile vomiting followed them.

At the marina they grabbed an empty bench overlooking the moorings. Hannah, Ollie and Rav settled on the bench while Josh perched at the top of the railings looking down on them. 'Listen, guys,' he hesitated, 'I'm really grateful to have such great friends as you, even our newbie, Hannah.' He smiled at her. 'But Ollie, I really don't want any of you to be getting into trouble with the law because of my position. I could just take the egg and try the bike crossbar thing myself.'

'Forget it, Josh!' Ollie's firm response. 'I'll be there, not just for you but for young Nicola too. After all that's why we got into this. Get rid of Swinton and get a new life for you and your family. I'm in all the way.'

'You sure?'

'You know it, Josh.'

Hannah slipped her hand into Ollie's and gave a squeeze. 'I feel bad I can't be there, but I'll see if I can find an excuse to get out of church.'

'Just you go, Hannah. I don't want you getting into trouble, just leave it to me 'n' Josh.'

They sat about sharing a couple of bags of chips and arguing about the merits of the football teams they supported, the latest Netflix offerings and Ollie's addiction to computer games. 'Not had any time this past few days,' he protested. Eventually they broke up, though Hannah and Ollie remained sitting on the bench a while longer talking about families, school, dreams, ambitions and their concerns for Josh and his family, especially young Nicola.

'Their lives have changed so much since his mum got involved with Eddie and got hooked on the drugs he supplies. I don't think that Josh has really thought through though, that if push comes to shove, his mum might choose Eddie instead of him and Nicola.'

Aghast, Hannah responded, 'Oh, wow, surely not.'

'I sure hope not. Anyway, we better head.' Ollie glanced around before sliding his arm round Hannah's shoulder and leaning in for a kiss. Or two. They left the Marina, Hannah with her arm round Ollie's waste and Ollie still with his arm round her shoulder.

Chapter 35

Day 10 – Sunday

Having had a disturbed night, his dreams turning to nightmares in which pigeons, pain and death played prominent roles, Ollie entered the kitchen yawning loudly and scratching his backside. His mother stared at him, and, cradling a mug of coffee in both hands, her elbows on the table, she asked, 'You've not been up playing on that computer half the night, have you?'

'Nah, just couldn't sleep.'

'Mmm.'

'No, I'm telling you, I couldn't get to sleep is all.'

She frowned, 'You're not worried about anything are you?'

'Well, apart from climate change stuff, pollution, the population explosion, lunatic world leaders, the state of the pound and the fear of losing my hair by the age of thirty, not a lot. Where's Grandad?'

'He's out in the shed. What you up to today?'

'Well, in line with your ridiculous draconian rules, Josh and me ...'

'Josh and I!'

Ollie sighed, 'Josh and *I* are going out to the countryside to seek adventure.' He gave sarcastic smirk. At least he wasn't lying about that, 'Then he's got his dance practice this afternoon.'

'No Hannah?' a trace of teasing in his mum's voice.

'She goes to church on a Sunday morning, but I might see her later.'

His mother cocked her head and said, 'My, my, my, this is getting serious. Been asked to meet her parents yet?'

'We're just *friends,* Mother!' Ollie snapped, his face

becoming flushed.

His mother nodded gently, 'Just friends, eh? So ... if Josh and Hannah fell overboard on an ocean-going liner and you only had the means to save one of them, who would you save?'

'What is this? The Spanish inquisition? That's never gonna happen. Stupid question anyway.'

His mother laughed, 'You want some breakfast?'

'Nah, not hungry.' Ollie moved to put the kettle on.

'You have to eat something!'

'Not hungry.'

'Sweet music that.' Grandads voice from the back door.

Ollie asked what sweet music as his grandad was entered the kitchen.

'The sound of the kettle going on laddie,' he responded as he hung his hat on a coat hook. Rubbing his hands together he asked if Ollie was making him a cup too.

Ollie glance at the wall clock, 'Yep, but I'll take mine upstairs, gotta get a move on.'

'On a Sunday?'

'Yep. Only following instructions. Here, stir your own tea.' He handed Grandad the mug, grabbed his own and headed back upstairs. He drank his tea between showering and getting dressed, then sat on his bed, his head in his hands, his stomach churning, thinking about the day ahead. They were being incredibly reckless, stupid even. Maybe they should just have phoned the police. Perhaps not. But at least they could be pretty sure there'd be no one about at the loft and, and if they did find the rifle with Eddie's prints on it, they could point the police in the right direction. Anonymously of course. He rubbed his temples trying to quiet the teeth gnashing, all-consuming gremlins of doubt and fear. Though feeling physically sick, he knew he had to stay strong for Josh. For them both. He let out a deep sigh, stood and scooped some change into his pockets.

His phone beeped. A message from Hannah – 'Take care you. I'll be praying for you both xxx', followed by an emoji of praying hands and a smiley face. He smiled, checked the time and headed down the stairs.

His mum and Grandad were still in the kitchen, grandad watching a cooking programme on TV. 'Eee Sheila, don't know why you can't whack out some dishes like that lass.'

'I'll be whacking something alright, your head with my frying pan, you ungrateful old man!' His mum banged the door of the cupboard under the sink.

'Careful grandad, she means it.' Ollie added as there came a rap on the back door.

'Hi! It's only me.' Josh came through to the kitchen knowing he didn't have to wait for an invitation. After saying 'hi' to the oldies, he asked Ollie if he was ready to hit the road.

'Yep. Let's go. Should be back for lunch,' he informed the room as he headed to get his bike.

'Kids today Sheila, I don't know.' Came the fade-out mutterings from behind as the boys left the kitchen.

Ollie lifted a backpack from behind an old sideboard in the garage, 'Ready to go. One large egg for delivery and two recipes, just in case.'

The boys cycled most of the way to Dalton's Mount in silence, stopping opposite the riding stable to finalise their strategy.

Ollie said, 'Okay, so, we'll put the bikes at the back of the loft so they won't be seen from the road. I hope Hannah's suggestion works and we're able to use them to get over the fence. If not, it looks like maybe only one of us will be able to get in.'

'I'll go, it's my problem anyway, and...' he patted his jeans pocket, 'I've brought a pair of gloves 'cause I wouldn't want my prints to mess up Eddie's.'

'Good thinkin'.' Ollie hesitated, grimacing and shaking his head before saying, 'But remember, there's the two solid looking padlocks that I took photos of when we were scouting the place. They're the same as were at the hall too. Checked 'em online. They're actually called, closed shackle combination padlocks with about a hundred thousand combinations. Expensive and high security. So we wouldn't be able to open it from the outside or inside. We'd have to try and get out the way we got in.'

'There must be something we could get to stand on.' Josh said.

'Yeah, you're probably right. Anyway, we only have a window of opportunity today. We may never get the same chance again. And, if the worst comes to the worse, we do have the ostrich egg as a reason for bein' there.'

Josh looked a little less stressed at that reminder, 'Just make sure you don't break it.' he smiled.

'How are things at home?' Ollie remembered to ask as they mounted their bikes, 'How's Nicola?'

'Better with Eddie having disappeared but my mum's worse. She wails for him all the time. I'm really sorry for her but I'm gonna speak to our doctor 'cause she has to treat things confidentially and she could maybe help, or get her the help and support she needs.'

'Good Josh, but what if he comes back?'

'I'm still going to see if I can get help for her and especially for Nicola, but I don't want us to be separated so I'm wary of getting' Social Services involved.'

They headed up the road passing the old cottages, then the old hall. Ollie was leading and looked over his shoulder to say, 'We need to go past the loft and the house to check there's no one hangin' about, no cars or anything.' They drew side by side as they approached McIntosh's place, their anxiety levels rising.

'You can back out now Ollie, I don't want you gettin''

into trouble. It's not really your problem and I shouldn't be dragging you into it.'

'Hey! Remember the gang hut we made when we were kids and the time we pricked our thumbs to let our bloods mingle and swear to each other we were blood brothers for ever? Well, nothing's changed.'

'But we *were* just kids then and I really don't want you getting a criminal record for my sake.'

'To late Joshie, I'm in. And anyway, you couldn't get over the fence without me.' Ollie pulled ahead then slowed as they approached the loft.

They saw no movement. The house looked closed up. The transit van and the big truck were parked in their usual places but McIntosh's Range Rover and the trailer were missing. Ollie was right, the padlocks were secured, but ever the optimist he said, 'Well we'll just have to find a way of getting out, but it's hopefully easier to break out than to break in. Okay, so we'll go to where Hannah looked after our bikes last time and come up the back of the loft from that side. We'll be hidden from the road that way.'

Ollie was less confident than he tried to appear. There was tightness in his gut and his eyes felt like they were gripped by lemon squeezers. 'Think the coast's clear,' he said, looking back at Josh who now looked like Ollie felt. 'Let's get this done.'

They went on till they came to the track leading to where Hannah had stood guard over the getaway bikes last time.

'Ready?' Ollie said.

Josh nodded and they headed up to the rear of the loft where they came to a stop. 'Think it's clear.' Ollie said. They dismounted and pushed and carried the bikes down behind the loft. 'If anything goes wrong though, we head out down that side, or, we split and run.'

'Won't come to that. Remember, we should be able to

talk our way out of anything with having the ostrich egg. Just a pair of bratty kids.'

Hannah had been right. As they leaned their bikes against the wooden structure, they estimated that by standing on the crossbar Ollie would be able to heave his way over the top of the fence.

'Right,' as usual Ollie took the lead. 'I'll give you a lift up, 'cause as your goin' up I can give you that extra push then I should be able to get up standing on the bike. I'll pass you the egg first.'

They looked at one another then Josh moved to Ollie and gave him a hug saying, 'Thanks Ollie, whatever happens I'll always be grateful to you.'

'Gerrof you! Watch the egg you soft twit.' They fist pumped then Ollie laid the egg beside the fence before lowering himself as though preparing to go into a rugby scrum, then cupping his hands as a stirrup for Josh, he started to raise him. Fortunately, just as his hands were reaching level with the top of his rib cage Josh took grip of the top of the fence easing the strain, then Ollie was able to give him the added boost from below. Josh looking down said, 'Phew, the roof of one of the lofts is just below me, if it holds my weight, it should be alright.' A couple of minutes later he shouted, 'It's fine. Creaking a bit but it's fine apart from the birds inside flapping' about. Hope they don't injure themselves. Can you pass me up the egg?'

'Go for it! I'll get up there in a minute.' Standing on one pedal, he climbed onto the crossbar and finding his balance, passed the backpack up to Josh. 'Right Josh, take the egg out and throw the backpack down beside our bikes,' He pushed the bike a little way away from the fence, and reaching up, and moving one foot onto the handlebars, with a final push he managed to clamber up and over to the roof of the loft, as the bike fell to the ground.

Josh was standing looking up to him, 'Great, you did

it. Good news.' He pointed to a brick box like structure with a slightly sloped lid covered in a rough black waterproof material. 'I think we'll be able to stand on that thing to get us out of here, it looks strong enough to hold us. We'll have to hold onto the top before letting ourselves drop to the ground.'

When Ollie joined him, they started searching the area, checking the space between the loft floors and the ground. The spaces in between the different sections of the lofts were also clear. They opened the lid of the brick structure to see three bins with what looked likely to be pigeon food. The spaces between the bins were clear. There were two brick-built stores near the entrance to the loft area. Ollie checked and found the door unlocked on the first one. 'Everything in here seems tidy. Some tools and lots of pigeon paraphernalia.'

On checking the other shed, Josh discovered it housed the machinery and equipment to service the lofts. He came out looking despondent and suggested they just go, adding 'Looks like we're wrong.'

'Just a minute,' Ollie said, standing, hands on hips scanning the tops of the lofts. He started to walk around looking up to the point where the slanted roofs met the rear walls of the individual lofts, before saying, 'Okay, so the police did a search, but we know they didn't find any weapons. Look, you can see that in the *inside* of the lofts the ceilings are flat, but the roof slants up and ends up with a triangular space... looks like the base is about... what? Eighty centimetres long and the uprights about fifty, so room enough to hold a rifle I'd think.' He walked around checking each of them before saying, 'But there's no obvious finger grips or holes or handles.'

'Well, that's that then. Game over,' Josh could not hide his disappointment.

'Maybe not just yet, Josh,' Ollie said as he continued to

scan the boarded triangular areas.

'Remember, my Grandad sometimes does some DIY and when he made cupboards for the shed, he used spring clips on them. So, if you gently push then remove your finger on the door, it releases the clip and the wooden panel should spring open. If McIntosh has hidden the rifle up there, if he used spring clips, we might be able to find it.'

Josh nodded, a look of hope returning to his face, 'Worth a try Ollie.'

'Okay. I'll give you a leg up, and if you think there's something there, use your phone torch to see inside... and maybe take a couple of pics too.'

'Okay, then I could bring the rifle out and take another photo for proof.'

'Just be careful.'

Josh grinned nervously, 'Don't worry, I'm not gonna shoot you.'

Standing on Ollie's cupped hands again, Josh tried pushing the triangular section in the first loft, it held fast. 'Let's try the one the other side.' Again nothing. There were ten individual lofts within the compound. After number six the boys were beginning to give up hope of finding the rifle. But on the second side of the seventh loft Josh thought he was on to something. 'Hey Ollie, I think there's a couple of hinges embedded in the upright here.'

'You sure?'

'Yep.' He gave the wood panel a push. Nothing happened.

Ollie, anxiously watching the proceedings said, 'Just use one finger and stab where you think the clips could be. Push the hypotenuse and don't hold it, take your finger away quick and if there's a spring clip it should open.'

'Okay.' Josh gave the panel another push on the hypotenuse just using his index finger, it sprung open and he could see a something wrapped in what looked like sacking. He fiddled and tugged with a piece of the material closest to him before being able to peal some back. What he saw looked like the ribbed shoulder panel at the rear of a rifle.

'Yep, it's here.' Josh yelled excitedly, 'I'm gonna bring it out.'

'Don't shout! We don't want to draw attention, and be careful you don't shoot yourself.'

'Okay, but you're goin' to have to lower me slowly. Don't want to shoot you.'

'Probably not loaded.'

When Josh got both feet on the ground, they both untied the string holding the sackcloth round the rifle. Josh tried holding it as far along the barrel as possible while balancing the stock on the flat of his hand. The rifle was mounted with a telescopic sight, and a magazine positioned in front of the finger-guard, all finished in the shade of a spent match, 'Okay, take a couple of pics.'

'Well, I guess that would take out a bird of prey or two.' Ollie said as he photographed the rifle. 'I think you're going to be saying goodbye to Eddie and the drug smuggling.' He grinned, 'Right Josh, let's put it back and get out of here. An anonymous phone call to the cops to follow.'

As Josh closed the wood cover over the roof cavity, they heard the sound of a car coming up the drive. They looked at one another, panic on both their faces.

'Who's that? Can't be McIntosh back already.' Josh asked in a low voice.

'Don't know, but if it's not McIntosh, they won't be able to get in here anyway.' Ollie's spoke in a whisper.

'What about the bikes?'

'Don't think they'll go lookin' round the back.'

'They might. But there's nowhere we can hide in here.' Josh said anxiously.

They heard a padlock being rattled. Ollie froze for a

second or two till self-preservation cut in and he gave Josh a shove, saying, 'There's a bit of space behind the third loft I think, quick.'

Josh had to move a bucket with a long shovel in it from the side of the loft to lean it against the perimeter wall and managed to squeeze himself in behind the loft. Ollie followed holding the ostrich egg above his head. They were willing the pigeons to quieten themselves. They heard the sound of the gate padlocks being removed and door opening. They looked at each other, their mouths dry, fear pounding in both their chests. If they were caught, things were not going to end well!

Chapter 36

'Quick, get that door shut.'

Josh tensed. There was no mistaking Eddie's voice.

Then, 'Right, help me. There's a sheet of tarpaulin folded inside that box. We need to get that out first.'

'Listen Eddie, I think you just maybe need to let it go, an' lie low for a wee while.' A slight Scottish accent.

'Let it go! You've seen what these London goons did to me. Just a warning they said, well they're goin' to get a warning from me that they won't forget. They're on my patch and it'll be *their* last warning. Very last!'

'Eddie man, you're too small time compared to them. These county line guys are no for playin' wi', they've got heavy muscle behind them and you're gonna come oot worst. Let it go, man. The way things work wi' them is, they move in, you move oot.'

Eddie, in a menacing tone, spat, 'Why d'you think you're here?' Without waiting for an answer, he went on, 'Only 'cause I need your help to get that gun, not to give me your crappy advice or opinions.'

'Easy laddie,' spoken softly but with an unmistakable hard edge. 'Right, let's get the lid lifted. The sooner we get oot o' here the better.'

Ollie and Josh managed to turn their heads to look at each other. Ollie mouthed, 'A gun! Not the rifle. Must be the pistol McIntosh was on about.'

Josh nodded slightly. With two bodies cramped behind the loft and a near noonday sun blazing down, the space was becoming airless and if they moved, they were being scratched by the rough-hewn wood of the loft in front and the fence behind them. Still holding the ostrich egg above his head, Ollie's arms were beginning to ache even though he was part resting it against the loft wall and the top of his head.

Josh moved his head closer to Ollie and whispered, 'What we gonna do?'

'Just wait. Is your phone on silent?'

'Yeah. But I need to pee!' Josh's urgent whisper.

'Not now!' Ollie hissed.

They heard scraping noises of the tarpaulin being pulled out the box with accompanying grunts. Then Eddie's voice again, 'We'll spread it out here right, then we've got to lift the first feed barrel out and get it emptied. Hope it's in there, I don't want to have to empty all three, but that's why *you're* here McFadden, 'cause we'll have to get the feed *back* into the barrels and get the barrel back in the box. Then we need to get swept up. Don't want big Mac noticing the gun's gone. When the job's done I'll try and put it back. Don't think the cop's 'll think to come lookin' here. They don't know nothin' about the pigeon run, but if they do, my prints won't be on it.'

His accomplice, sounding wary, asked if the gun was loaded. Eddie answered that they'd see in a minute if he got his finger out and helped to get the feed barrel tipped out onto the ground. Then he added that, if not, he'd probably be able to get some bullets in London. 'I've got some contacts.' There followed sounds of wood scrapping across concrete accompanied by sounds of wheezing and grunting as they manoeuvred the thing to the ground.

'Ouch! Ma taes!'

'Keep your voice down!' Eddie hissed.

There were groaning sounds of them straining with something weighty, followed by a sound like heavy rain on a tin roof as the food pellets were poured on to the tarpaulin.

'Slower! Slower, ya idiot! It's gonna spill off the tarp. Pull it back up a bit,' Eddie's agitation apparent.

Josh turned to Ollie, a pained expression on his face,

279

whispered, 'I *really* need to pee!'

Ollie made a face. 'You need to hold it in – anyway, we're jammed in pretty tight here.'

Josh let out a small moan.

'Quiet, Josh.' Ollie hissed.

They heard Eddie cry out triumphantly, 'Ya beauty, I feel something. It's wrapped tight though. Just a minute.'

There was silence for a couple of minutes, followed by a sharp intake of breath, 'I think it's the gun.' A minute later, 'Yes! Yes! Right let me see.' After a minute, 'Ya beauty! Look, a Glock automatic.' A minute's silence, 'Damn! No magazine.' There followed what sounded like rustling in amongst the bird feed again, 'Yep, there's something... feels like a canvas bag.' There followed a soft clinking sound, 'Ah! I think it's the magazine and spare ammo... Yes! There must be a couple of dozen rounds in here.'

Ollie and Josh looked at each other, worried expressions on their faces.

'Right,' Eddie's voice again, 'I'll load the magazine then we'll get this lot tidied up. Go and get the bucket and shovel from up between these two lofts. McIntosh will never know we were here.'

Both boys held their breath, their hearts in their mouths. The bucket and shovel were just to their left. They heard soft footsteps coming up the side of the loft. A shadow fell across the bucket and shovel. A hand reached out and grabbed the top of the shovel, lifting it from the bucket. The boys held their breath. The same hand reached down for the bucket handle. The side of a man's head came into view. He hesitated, turned his head in their direction and let out a yell. 'Eddie! Eddie quick there's a couple of brats cowering back here. C'm' 'ere ya wee cockroaches.'

Josh squeezed himself towards the opposite end of the loft while Ollie sidled towards the man, the egg still above his head. McFadden stepped closer and grabbed Ollie's T shirt. As Ollie was dragged out from behind the loft, he smashed the egg down over McFadden's head. It cracked and stinking slime oozed down his adversary's face and into his eyes. The man stumbled then fell to his knees trying to get the gooey mess out his eyes, and gagging as he ingested bits of shell and foul-smelling slime. Then Ollie executed a perfect drop kick under McFadden's chin, hearing his neck crack as he was catapulted backwards before slumping sideways to the ground.

Ollie was leaning forward, his hands on his knees, waiting for his heart to stop hammering into his rib cage when Eddie appeared between the lofts. A look of disbelief crossed his face at the sight of his henchman lying groaning and wounded. Cursing, he launched himself at Ollie landing a heavy blow to the side of his face, momentarily stunning him. Eddie grabbed the hair on top of Ollie's head and drew his arm back, his fist clenched, when the crack of a gunshot rang out. The pigeons went crazy, flapping and fluttering and crashing into each other.

'What the...?' Eddie let go Ollie's T-shirt, swung round and rushed out to see Josh standing, Glock in hand pointing directly at him. Coming to a dead stop, a look of uncertainty crossed his face before he sneered, 'You wouldn't use that y' soft little poofter.' He turned his head slightly and spat onto the ground.

Josh stood, mimicking a stance he'd seen many times in movies, holding the gun in both hands, his arms straight out, legs apart. All the anger and fear he had been living with welled up an acid bile inside him. All the hatred. His body felt icy cold but his heart was a burning rage. Images flashed through his mind. His mother becoming a needy pathetic junkie. His sister living in constant fear, having lost any sense of joy and fun as she shrivelled up inside. Her childhood being cruelly taken from her. Josh would not have believed he could ever have hated anyone like he hated the man in front of him. His finger tightened on the trigger. It would be so easy. His arms wavered. Sweat was running down his face and into his eyes. Trying to blink it away and still aiming at Eddie, he loosened his grip on the pistol, and said, 'No. You're right.' Then moving both hands, swiftly turned the gun so as to hold it by the stubby barrel.

A look of incredulity crossed Eddie's face as Josh swung his right arm back then launched the gun out into the scrubland behind the loft. With a howl of rage, he launched himself at Josh who turned slightly to his left and delivered an oblique kick directly above Eddie's right knee. He was stopped in his tracks, a look of surprise and pain on his face. He started to move forward again only to be met with another oblique kick. He tried to ignore the hurt and hobbled forward. Josh hit out again, this time twice in rapid succession. Eddie wobbled, and with a look of indignant surprise took a few steps backwards. Again, he lunged at Josh, but Josh leapt to the side. Eddie went sailing past, clutching at the air and cursing. He swung round to go after Josh once more. Josh had moved back quickly to put space between them and, as Eddie gathered himself, Josh ran forward and launched his *pas de brise,* rising even higher than at the studio practice, and came crashing down into Eddies chest, sending him sprawling and winded in front of the food bin.

Josh stood back to allow Eddie to get to his feet again. As Eddie rose, unsteadily, one hand on the food bin, Josh went side on to him, then bending his torso to the left, and keeping his left foot firmly on the ground, he stretched his left arm out behind him and brought his right foot up planting the flat of his foot full in Eddie's face. He heard the crunching sound of something breaking. Blood poured from Eddie's nose. Stunned and confused by the onslaught,

Eddie staggered back, whimpering like a wounded animal. Josh, blinded with a savage rage, closed in again and pummelled him with both fists.

Still recovering from Eddie's punch, Ollie appeared from between the lofts, shocked to see the violence being inflicted by Josh.

Now Ollie screamed in pain as a punch ripped into his kidneys. A hand on his shoulder spun him round, 'Ya wee minger, I'll have yer guts.' Eddie's accomplice shoved him against the front of a loft and landed a solid blow to his stomach. Ollie gasped, bent double, sank to his knees and started to puke. His turn to get a kick on the chin. He lifted his head trying to guess which way he should counter the blow. His attacker's foot was drawn back when, through the pain and confusion, a pink blur appeared above McFadden's head. A pair of honey-coloured legs wrapped themselves around his waist, an arm wrapped tightly around his throat and two fingers were stuck savagely up his nostrils causing his head to be jerked back and make him lose his balance.

Hannah!

McFadden raged like a wounded animal and hurled himself backwards against a loft making the birds scatter from their perches and flap about, feathers flying.

Hannah, now crushed between him and the loft, let out an 'oof' and yanked back his nose again.

'Am gonna kill ya, ya wee toerag!' he spluttered, sounding like he had a bad cold.

Ollie managed to get to his feet, roared, and ran at McFadden, his drop kick booted firmly into McFadden's groin area. He went down like a lead weight dropped into a jelly. Wobbly and messy.

Ollie grabbed Hannah's arm and shouted, 'Let's go.'

She gave McFadden another kick before Ollie dragged her away.

The sound of sirens could be heard approaching. Ollie shouted to Josh, 'C'mon! Let's go!'

Eddie was staggering to his feet again. Josh ran at him and smashed a flying kick to his face knocking him flat on his back.

Ollie grabbed the padlocks lying beside the bin and pushed Hannah roughly through the door, Josh followed, then Ollie pulled it shut behind him. Sliding the padlocks into the hasps he leaned back against the gate and let out a huge sigh of relief. The three looked at each other, wild eyed and breathless.

'I still need to pee.'

'For goodness sake, just go against the fence. Hannah, look the other way.'

The siren noises were coming closer. A police car screeched to a stop and two police officers jumped out, both wearing Kevlar helmets, body armour, a pistol strapped to each right leg. Both approached holding Heckler & Koch carbines tight into their shoulders. A wave of relief mixed with apprehension washed over Ollie. The officers, putting some space between each other, approached at different angles, moving quickly but cautiously.

One shouted, 'Move apart with hands above your heads, legs spread!' Indicating with his weapon. 'Now!' he barked.

As they put some space between each other, Ollie shouted, 'It's not us officer, the guys you want are in there.'

Still holding his snub-nosed carbine in one hand one of the officers did a quick pat down on all three of them then shouted, 'They're clear.'

'So, who's in there?' the other officer demanded.

'Two of them. One's called Eddie Swinton and someone called McFadden'

'How many weapons?'

'A pistol. But I managed to chuck it over the fence, and

we've got them locked in,' and nodding towards the gate added, 'That's the only way out for them. Oh, but there's a rifle in the roof space of loft seven too.'

'Any of you hurt?'

Though bruised and bleeding, Ollie shook his head, 'We'll survive.'

Addressing the other officer, he instructed him to get the three to the back of the house and keep them out of harm's way. 'Stay with them. I'll cover the loft till backup arrives.'

When they were secured behind the house the officer asked which one of them had called the police.

Josh looked at Hannah, 'Was it you?'

'Nope.'

The officer frowned, 'Well, someone called. Said there was a gun.'

'Wasn't us officer,' Ollie said. 'There's a guy in there knew about the gun hidden in a feed barrel and he came to get it because he's been hassled by a county line gang who beat the crap out of him. We thought the place was goin' to be empty today. We came 'cause we heard there was a rifle hidden here somewhere that we thought was probably bein' used to kill birds of prey to protect the guy's pigeons. One that a police search missed. But we found it. And Josh,' he gestured in Josh's direction, 'managed to get hold of the pistol and chuck it over the fence.'

The officer shook his head with incredulity. 'Where'd you throw the gun?'

'Over to the left side of the loft area where we'd left our bikes.' He pointed up to the tree line and his jaw dropped. Rav was approaching, stripped to the waist and carrying in the flat of both hands what looked like a green t-shirt wrapped round something.

Frighteningly, the officer shouldered his carbine again, directing it at Rav.

'It's the gun,' Rav shouted moving his hands further away from his body. 'I called the cops when I saw Josh throw it over the fence, then came down to get it right out the way. I took off my t-shirt and used it to pick it up so's my prints wouldn't be on it.'

With the carbine still shouldered, the officer commanded, 'Right. Keep your hands in that position, come to the end of the building and place it on the ground, step back three paces then circle and join your mates against the wall. No nonsense, no heroics.' He moved to the corner of the wall and, carbine raised. 'Now!'

Shaking, Rav did as he was told. The officer told him to place his hands above his head and walk towards him. He checked Rav's pockets. 'Right, stand there against the wall beside your mates, and all of you, keep your heads down.

'Thought you weren't comin',' Ollie whispered.

'It was obvious you would need the assistance of someone with a higher intellect, skilled in strategic planning and diversionary tactics.' Rav sniffed, 'Good job I came, eh?'

Ollie shook his head and managed a smile.

The officer put a finger over his earpiece and spoke into his throat mike confirming the friends were contained and that another one had turned up. He listened to the response then asked the estimated time of arrival of a backup team. He was told less than five minutes. He was no sooner informed when, sirens blaring, another two-armed response vehicle arrived, followed by an ambulance.

The vehicles drew up and four armed officers, in full Kevlar protection, jumped out. One officer opened the boot of the car, taking out a large shield, about one and a half metres high and three quarters of a metre deep. An officer from the second vehicle did likewise. They would already have stab proof vests, but these would be a poor protection against bullets.

Another car screeched to a halt and four unarmed officers alighted. Ollie and the others were informed that one of them was the PIO – the Police Incident Officer to co-ordinate the scene, except for the armed officers who took their instructions from their own commander working from a control room.

A police Transit van drew up, from which a further six armed officers alighted. The PIO called one of the new arrivals by name, instructing him to set up a four-hundred-metre cordon round the loft, and to keep any press well away. Another ambulance arrived. The PIO told the ambulance crews to stay where they were and they would be kept updated on the situation.

The PIO ordered that the young friends would have to stay where they were as it would be too dangerous to move them across a possible field of fire.

The police were now in position. The armed response officers placed themselves strategically awaiting orders to proceed.

The PIO asked the original two responders if they knew who was in the loft.

'One of the kids said one's called Swinton, does some driving, taking pigeons to France for the owner, Ronnie McIntosh. I've checked – he's not on our radar. But there's someone else in there, someone called McFadden. We ran a check. He's got form. Mostly assault charges. If they don't come out peacefully, we're going in.'

The PIO called to one of his officers to bring the megaphone. Then, before doing anything else, he spoke into his throat mike alerting the team about what was going to happen. He raised the megaphone, 'Swinton and McFadden, you are surrounded by armed police officers. There is no escape. We are going to open the gate. You will lay down any weapons you have and move to the gate with your arms above your head. Do you understand?'

287

Eddie Swinton's curses came over the fence.

The leading armed officer ordered one of the other officers to get into position to lift the padlocks out the hasps. Meanwhile, the officers with the shield lifted it in front of them. The first officer crouching slightly to allow the other officer to put one hand on his shoulder with his carbine above the shield. The other four armed officers were deployed, one at the rear of the loft and one each on either side, the fourth standing behind the right front corner.

With one last quick assessment of the situation the PIO used the megaphone again, 'The gate's unlocked, come out one at a time, with your hands above your heads. '

A voice from the other side of the fence shouted, 'I'm comin' out. I'm unarmed.'

'It's McFadden,' Ollie said to the officer looking after them.

'You know him?'

'No. He's come to help the other guy. Eddie Swinton.'

'He's in there too?'

'Yeah. He's possibly got a loaded rifle, but I don't think McFadden will be armed.'

'Right, keep your heads down,' the officer said as he moved to the end of the building.

The gate opened slowly, 'I'm not armed, I'm not armed.' McFadden, looking bloodied and bruised, stood shaking in the doorway, hands above his head.

'Which one are you?'

'McFadden.'

'Right, McFadden, move forwards slowly. Keep your hands on your head. Where's Swinton?'

'He's...'

The crack of a shot. A looked of shocked bewilderment crossed McFadden's face. Another shot in quick succession, causing him to be thrown forward, landing flat on his face, blood soaking the back of his shirt.

No further instructions were given. The two armed officers with the Kevlar shield moved towards the gate, manoeuvring their way round McFadden's body. Two shots smacked against the shield. The second officer rose quickly from behind the shield, the red marker in his sites highlighting the target point. He squeezed the trigger. The bullet slammed into Eddie's chin taking out bits of gum and teeth and ripping through his cerebral cortex. Thrown back against the loft, with blood pouring from his face, he was dead before he hit the ground. Pigeon feathers floated down settling on him like drifting grey snowflakes.

The two armed officers moved into the area, both with carbines raised. Before moving to the body, they visually swept the area. Then checked for a pulse amongst the mess of Eddie's neck before shouting, 'Clear!' In all the lofts, alarmed pigeons fluttered about crashing into each other, desperate to escape to the skies.

Chapter 37

4 days later

A tremulous voice behind her asked, 'Am I grounded too?'

Turning round, Ollie's mum's heart went out to the impossibly skinny young girl, whose big brown eyes were filled with tears. She crouched down in front of her, and drawing her to herself, kissed the top of her head. Nicola began to sob.

'Hey, come on, you've not to worry, everything's going to be alright. Your mum's away to get all better, then you and Josh will go back to live with her.'

'In the flat?' A look of apprehension crossed Nicola's face.

'No, no, no. I think you'll be moving to a nice new house where you'll even have your own bedroom.'

'Really?'

'I promise.'

Almost in a whisper, Nicola asked if Eddie would be there. A tear trickled down her face.

Using her thumb to dry the tear, Ollie's mum promised her she would never see Eddie again and neither would her mum or Josh. Nicola gave an involuntary shiver and cuddled in close to her. After a couple of minutes, she lifted her head, 'So... am I grounded too?'

Ollie's mum laughed gently. 'No! Not at all. It's just those two silly boys getting into all kinds of nonsense.'

'How long will they be grounded for?'

After a moment's consideration, she answered, 'At least ten years, I'd think.'

'Mother!' Ollie came into the kitchen. 'Don't listen to her, Nicola. It was only for a couple of days, so now Josh and I have served our sentence.'

'You wish, boy! Your dad was on Face Time again first thing. He was going to come home, but I told him everything is alright now. Where's Josh?'

'He's just been doin' some warmup stuff. He'll be down in a minute. Grandad outside?'

'He's just out checking on the marrows he's growing for the show. Remember you've got the police coming to see you today.

'What for? We told them everything we knew on Sunday night *and* Monday – for *hours!*'

'To go over your statements and ask some more questions.'

Ollie sighed, 'We've told them everything.'

'One thirty, they said. Is Hannah going to be here?'

'She said she'd be here after lunch.'

'Rav?'

'No. He seemingly went to the police station with his dad yesterday.'

'And when are you all seeing your counsellors again?'

'Next Wednesday. Don't really see the point though, we're fine and, most important, Josh and his family can have a fresh start.'

The back door banged and Grandad came into the kitchen, one hand cupped in front of him holding three freshly picked strawberries. Nodding in Ollie's direction, he plonked himself down in his usual chair and called Nicola over. Her eyes lit up when she saw the fruit in his hand, 'For me Mr Caldwell?'

'Aye, lass, just for you.'

Instead of taking them, she climbed onto his knees, flung her arms round him giving him a big hug. Grandad felt a lump in his throat as she clung to him.

'Ee, lass, you're squashing the strawberries,' his voice gruff. 'Oh... and you can call me Grandad too, if you like.'

Nicola's face lit up. 'Thank you for the strawberries...

Grandad.' She took one strawberry then offered Ollie's mum one but was told Grandad had picked them especially for her. 'And I can tell you, Grandad doesn't give his strawberries to just anybody. You must be a special girl.'

'She sure is,' Josh agreed as he entered the kitchen

Nicola jumped from Grandad's knee and rushed over to him. Josh picked her up and held her tight, her arms wrapped tightly round his neck. 'How's my little Squidgle this morning?'

'Josh!'

Josh laughed, 'Okay, right. How's Nicola today?'

'Can we stay here forever, Josh? I'll give you a strawberry.'

'Well, looks like we don't have a choice. Mrs Saunders has grounded Ollie and me... for life, I think.'

'And don't forget it! Morning, Josh. What would you like for breakfast?'

'I'm not too hungry thanks, Mrs Saunders.'

'You have to eat, Josh.'

'I'll just have a slice of toast then. I'll have to break the grounded rule this afternoon though. I've got my ballet practice after the police are done. Hope they don't drag on, Danielle asked me to be there about three.'

'What's she going to say about your black eye and the other cuts and bruises?'

'Probably that it makes me look more manly, more dangerous, but it could have been worse. I might have ended up looking like Ollie... even before he got battered! Ouch! Don't you start Hannah's nonsense now.'

'How are you doing though, Josh?' Grandad asked.

'Doin' okay considering, thanks, Mr Caldwell.'

'Josh! It's Grandad, not Mr Caldwell.' Nicola corrected, giving grandad a confirmatory little nod.

Josh screwed up his face peering at Grandad, 'Looks like Mr Caldwell to me,' he laughed.

'Looks like a few things, most I wouldn't like to mention.' Ollie added high-fiving Josh.

'Eee, Sheila lass, you've done a bad job in raising that one.'

'I was doing a fine job thanks, until you came to live here, and taught him all your nonsense.'

Grandad sniffed and muttered under his breath before inviting Nicola to come and help him in the garden.

'I don't know about gardens, Grandad. I've never had one.'

'Eee, don't you worry, my pet. Grandad will soon teach you how little girls can help.'

'Keep her away from anything sharp, Dad.'

'I think we're safe. Ollie's tongue's in the house. Come on then, lass, let's go.' He held out his hand and Nicola took hold of it, her smile a relief for Josh to see.

Hannah arrived just as a car drew up outside the house. Two men alighted and came through the gate as she rang the doorbell. Ollie answered, his left eye bruised, his bottom lip split and a graze running down the left of his face. She reached out and touched his face, 'Poor Ollie.'

The taller of the two men held out a police identity card, 'This the Saunders home?'

'Yep.' Ollie nodded. 'You better come in.'

His mum's head appeared round the kitchen door, 'Take them into the sitting room, Ollie. I'll get Josh. Oh! Hi Hannah, you okay? I'll see Nicola's okay and be with you in a minute or two.'

When Ollie, his mum, Josh and Hannah were all seated, the plain-clothed officers brought them up to date on the current situation. 'They were clever. Very clever! McIntosh had earned a reputation as a good breeder and had brought on some prize-winning birds, birds that have won thousands of pounds. As well as running a breeding programme, he could command big sums of money selling to other breeders and racers, so he was doing very well for himself. Though some other fanciers had started to ask questions about the whole operation. Where he got the money to do it on the scale he did. Though he had a reputation for having an eye for a good bird and some impressive wins, he had expanded from a fairly small beginning, but over the past few years a fortune had been spent on the operation. It was rumoured he must have a backer, a silent partner, and he did. Joe Brunswick.'

Josh, Hannah, Ollie and his mum nodded.

'Brunswick invested to take things to a new level. Helped pay for the construction of the 'super loft'. Brought over a state-of-the art trailer from the States and a truck that could transport over ten thousand birds. So, McIntosh became the trusted "go to" man to transport thousands of birds for pigeon federations, especially for the big continental races. And he was good. He had perfected great blood lines that could command tidy sums of money and, with some buyers, especially from China and the Far East, prepared to pay eye-watering amounts for good birds, so he was doing well and didn't need to be bringing in drugs from France. But because he'd let Brunswick get involved at the beginning, he couldn't get off the hook. So, he sent his posh trailer, towed by a beat-up Transit van, over to France weekly, supposedly for training. The pigeons were taken to a place not far from a town called Tregueux in Brittany where the canisters would be loaded with heroin that had been brought in through Marseilles. Swinton would then drive up to the west coast of Britany and release the birds to fly up the Channel. But Brunswick and McIntosh weren't the only people buying from them, they were supplying drugs across Europe. It was a fairly major operation. Interpol's now on the case.'

Josh nodded, 'Yeah well, we knew Eddie Swinton was doing the pigeon run. Got him some pin money, but better, it got him away for a night, sometimes two. Gave us some peace.'

The second officer said, 'More than pin money. He was dealing in a small way for himself. We asked our French counterparts to check the address where Swinton attached the canisters. He would drive to an orchard to the south of Tregueux in a well-hidden location. We've been told, to reach it in the first place, he needed to travel along some fairly minor roads then turn into a well concealed entrance leading down a twisting dirt path with thick high hedges and trees on either side, to an old French smallholding. There, there are scores of fruit bearing trees, mainly apples, all looking pretty as a picture, I'm told, with a small pond, a couple of large barns and a ramshackle house. However, tucked away beyond and behind the house was a substantial new building. Very solid with a reinforced steel door, no windows and a flat roof and well camouflaged. The French police were delighted because it had become a European centre for the distribution of class A drugs into northern France, Belgium, the Netherlands and Germany and, of course, southern England. And this is where McIntosh got his pigeons fitted with the canisters.'

'Wow!' Josh exclaimed, 'We overheard them talking about it but never imagined the scale of this. Still. Wow! A million pounds a month from a hundred birds. And Brunswick was pushing for two hundred.' Josh said.

'Probably more. The stuff they were bringing in through Marseilles was delivered pure, best quality, but there's no reason it couldn't be cut when it got back here.'

Ollie's Mum frowned, 'Cut? What do you mean?'

'Well, some dealers "cut" the pure heroin with caffeine or flour, talc or powdered milk, chalk even. That can add a whole lot more to the money pot. Nobody *ever* gets to buy the pure stuff on the streets. But more, and unbeknown to McIntosh, Eddie Swinton was getting supplied with smaller quantities of drugs himself. Small time dealing in comparison with McIntosh and Brunswick, but still lucrative for him.'

Ollie's mum was really shocked, 'That's it! You're *all* grounded for a year!'

'Actually, Mrs Saunders, they *were* foolish but they did a good job. We had no idea about McIntosh's involvement but now a lot of dangerous drugs are off the street. McIntosh will be a very old man when he gets out of prison. Brunswick was a much bigger fish. From London, and as well as drugs he had his finger in money laundering, protection and casinos, as well as some other disreputable stuff. He had networks and tentacles reaching all along the south coast and into London and the Home Counties. The Met had him in their sites but knew nothing of the pigeon run, and this is what's going to bring his whole operation down. So... even though Ollie's Mum's mad at you all, and I have to agree you were foolish, you've certainly helped to take some very dangerous people of the streets.'

'We did it for Josh and his family, that's all,' Ollie said. 'We'd heard another bird of prey had been found shot dead, and we suspected it was Eddie and only wanted to find the rifle with Eddie's prints on it in the hope of getting him out their lives.'

'Well, he won't be bothering you again for sure.'

Josh asked if Eddie had ever been stopped by Customs.

'Once seemingly, but that was the beauty of it. Especially in the summer there are thousands, and I mean thousands, sometimes up to twenty thousand birds at a time are shipped over the channel to compete in prestigious big money and races and it'd be very rarely that checks were made. Seemingly Eddie was checked once coming back from France and the vehicle was clean though there were questions about a box of small empty canisters. But they were ready for that and he pulled out a container of lead pellets, which, he explained, were put into the canisters to work as a kind of weight training for the birds. Good cover.

The other officer took up the conversation. 'Right, you've given your statements and in due course you will be called to testify in court but until then just try to lead a normal teenage life, eh? You're only young once and things could have turned out very differently for all of you. Stay safe.'

After the officers left, they went back to the kitchen and Josh checked on how Nicola was doing. Hannah gave Ollie a hug, clinging to him for a couple of minutes. 'I'm glad I came to save you,' she whispered.

'So am I.' Ollie gave her a squeeze.

'Right you pair, none of that lovey-dovey nonsense round here... or anywhere else come to think of it,' Grandad said as he, Josh and Nicola, who was carrying a small bunch of flowers, came into the kitchen.

'Grandad! I was only comforting him. Look at his poor battered face and the scrapes on his hands,' Hannah stepped away but still held on to Ollie's arm.

Josh laughed, 'Okay, I'll get my stuff, got to get to my rehearsal. Ballet School waits for me, the stage waits for me, nay – the world waits for me. Nicola, you give Grandad a hand in the garden. I'll see you when I get back.' He slung his bag over his shoulder and, smiling towards Hannah and Ollie, said, 'And you two behave yourselves.' He winked.

'They jolly well better,' Ollie's mum added.

'Aye,' Grandad had lowered himself into his chair, 'Now here's the rules you two. You can hold hands. You can hug... but only short hugs, and... under no circumstances is there to be any kissing until the day you get married, whether to each other or anyone else.' He bent his head and looking over his specs, raised both eyebrows for emphasis.

Hannah moved to sit on the arm of his chair, put her

hand on the back of his and with a coy look said, 'But Grandad, what if we got married... and he wasn't a good kisser?'

Grandad spluttered, then said, 'Well now, I'll tell thee, lass. You go out and get y'self a nice goldfish.' Grandad looked at her as if waiting a confirmatory response.

'A goldfish? What's that got to do with kissing?'

'Well, all I'll say is, make sure you get a nice-looking one.'

Puzzlement on Hannah's face. 'Eh?'

'Yes, then you take it home. Now... have you noticed what goldfish do all day?'

'Swim about opening and closing their mouths.'

'Aye, that's right. So, you've got this good-looking goldfish, and every day you lift it gently out its bowl, and hold it up to your lips for a minute. Then you move your lips in time with the fish. There's your practice at kissing.' Grandad demonstrated a goldfish opening and closing its mouth.

'Yuck! Grandad, disgusting!' Hannah made a face.

'Grandad, you're gross,' Ollie added.

'Aye well, mind on. And I'll tell ee this, Hannah, if you've been kissing a goldfish for a few years and then you kiss Ollie... when you're wed... you'll think he must be the greatest kisser in the history of the world.'

'Yeah, right, Grandad. Come on Hannah. You fancy a walk?'

'Thought you were grounded.'

'Naa. I'll follow the first instructions and not sit about all summer but get out into the fresh air and exercise.'

His mum overheard him as she came into the kitchen and shaking her head said, 'Alright you two. But stay out of trouble.'

As they left, Grandad rose from his chair and leaned against the sink gazing out the window. He burst out laughing, 'Sheila, look at this.'

She joined him and also burst out laughing. Ollie and Hannah were walking down the road hand in hand, their mouths mimicking goldfish, opening and shutting, opening and shutting before bursting into a fit of giggles.

'Ee, Sheila lass, I don't know.'

Acknowledgements

To those who believed and encouraged me in this project from the beginning. Particularly to author and playwright Oliver Eade whose patience, advice and never-ending encouragement have been such an inspiration.

To Iona Carroll for her read-through, formatting and helpful comments. Iona has taught creative writing workshops for a number of years and is a successful author in her own right.

To Helen Kimmet, my sister, who like me is an avid reader. I am grateful for read through, her affirmation and encouragement.

The Author

Robert has written numerous humorous articles for newspapers and has had short stories published in anthologies and literary magazines.

He is a member of the Borders Writers Forum, the Kelso Writers group, The Alliance of Independent Authors and the Federation of Writers (Scotland).

He has appeared on local radio in the UK, Majorca and in Atlanta, Georgia.

In the past he managed his family-owned award-winning hotel and restaurant, recognized by the Hotel & Catering Training Board for its work in training and developing young people in all aspects of the hotel and restaurant trade.

He has been heavily involved in marketing and negotiated extensive gift ware and crystal ware contracts with major UK high street chains, also with Bid Up TV UK and QVC USA.

He has also been in church ministry and was involved with two high schools as chaplain for over twelve years, one with eight hundred and fifty pupils and another with nearly fourteen hundred pupils.

He was heavily involved in both and was always available to students and able to offer a listening ear during his well-attended weekly drop-in centres.

The Pigeon Run characters are based on an amalgam of the best and the worst of the countless teenagers he has known.